I0632951

The Mysterious
Doctor Cornelius
2. The Island of Hanged Men

The Mysterious Doctor Cornelius
2. The Island of Hanged Men

by
Gustave Le Rouge

translated, annotated and introduced by
Brian Stableford

A Black Coat Press Book

English adaptation and introduction Copyright © 2014 by Brian Stableford. Cover illustration Copyright © 2014 by Vincent Laik.

Thanks to Jean-Luc Boutel.

Visit our website at www.blackcoatpress.com

ISBN 978-1-61227-244-3. First Printing. February 2014. Published by Black Coat Press, an imprint of Hollywood Comics.com, LLC, P.O. Box 17270, Enci- no, CA 91416. All rights reserved. Except for review purposes, no part of this book may be reproduced or transmitted in any form or by any means, electronic or mechanical, including photocopying, recording, or by any information storage and retrieval system, without permission in writing from the publisher. The stories and characters depicted in this novel are entirely fictional. Printed in the United States of America.

TABLE OF CONTENTS

The Story So Far

When a series of mysterious murders imperils the future of Jorgell City in the U.S.A., its founder, the billionaire Fred Jorgell, teams up with Harry Dorgan, the son of another billionaire, who is in love with his daughter Isidora, to set a trap for the murderer. The guilty party turns out to be Fred Jorgell's son Baruch, who flees the country when he is found out. Although the role played by his two accomplices, the plastic surgeon Cornelius Kramm and his brother Fritz, an art dealer, remains undiscovered, they also leave the city, relocating to New York.

After being robbed and left for dead in Brittany, Baruch Jorgell is taken in by a Chemist, Gaston de Maubreuil, who lives with his daughter Andrée and another stray he has taken in, the young hunchback Oscar Tournesol. Maubreuil's nearest neighbor is another scientific genius, the naturalist Prosper Bondonnat, who resides in a little artificial Eden with his daughter Fréderique and two laboratoty assistants, Antoine Paganot and Roger Ravenel. When Maubreuil succeeds in realizing his long-held dream of synthesizing diamonds, Baruch cannot resist temptation, and murders him in order to steal the gems, fleeing once again.

Back in New York, Baruch seeks help from his old allies, Cornelius and Fritz Kramm, who conceive a daring plan to make use of him, by remodeling him as a duplicate of Harry Dorgan's brother, Joe. In order to make the substitution, they have Joe kidnapped by a gang led by Slug, a key member the criminal organization they have long been building up, the Red Hand. Cornelius completes the identity exchange by remolding Joe into the physical image of Baruch, and then deliberately inducing brain damage, the effects of which include amnesia. While Baruch takes Joe's place, Joe is arrested as Baruch, tried, but found to be insane, and committed to Greenway Lunatic Asylum.

Cornelius, Fritz and Baruch—now established as the third Lord of the Red Hand—provoke a financial war between Joe's father, William Dorgan, and Fred Jorgell, in spite of Harry's attempts to prevent the conflict. With Isidora's help, Harry prevents Fred Jorgell's complete ruination, but William Dorgan nevertheless ends up with complete control of a Trust monopolizing American production of cotton and corn. In order to improve the yields of the two crops, Baruch attempts to imitate a technology developed by Prosper Bondonnat, and when it fails, the Lords decide to kidnap Bondonnat and force him to work on their behalf.

One of Cornelius Kramm's many secret projects involves the "resurrection" of criminals condemned to death whose executions, thanks to interference by the Red Hand, have been botched. Until they can be provided with new identities and brought back to the U.S.A., the supposed "dead men" are accommodated on an island in the northern Pacific bought from the US government by Fritz Kramm, which becomes the Red Hand's secret base, known to its residents as "The Island of Hanged Men." That is where Bondonnat is imprisoned after his abduction, and also where an eccentric millionaire, Lord Burydan, and an Indian named Kloum, are cast away after a shipwreck, and similarly kept prisoner.

The Lords of the Red Hand are now within sight of obtaining William Dorgan's billions, but, in reaching that position, they have acquired more adversaries than Harry Dorgan. Lord Burydan and Kloum escape from the Island of Hanged Men with Bondonnat's dog Pistolet, although Bondonnat fails to get away with them. After recovering from an injury sustained during Bondonnat's abduction, Oscar Tournesol travels to America, soon followed by Andrée de Maubreuil and Frédérique Bondonnat, with their fiancés Antoine Paganot and Roger Ravenel. Thanks to Oscar, who has made contact with Fred Jorgell, the Red Hand's first attempt to get rid of these new adversaries, using a contingent of the Red Hand known as "the Knights of Chloroform," goes awry, and the contest begins to heat up.

Now read on...

7. A DRAMA AT THE LUNATIC ASYLUM

I. A Terrible Malady

All the talk in New York was of the imminent marriage of the engineer Harry Dorgan and Isidora, the daughter of the billionaire Fred Jorgell, the director of the Lightning Steamship Company. Fred Jorgell was well liked in financial and industrial circles. His Lightning Steamships, constructed with the collaboration of Harry Dorgan, held all the speed records. Thanks to their ultralight nickel-aluminum hulls and their oil-fired engines, they could make the crossing from Le Havre to New York in four days. Thus, the company's shares, issued at a hundred dollars, were now trading at three hundred dollars in all the stock exchanges in the world.

Even though, because of certain family misfortunes, Isidora's marriage was to be celebrated in the strictest intimacy, that did not affect the innumerable and fabulous gifts addressed to the bride from all over America. Among other marvels, there was said to be a exact replica of the famous "queen's necklace" that Marie-Antoinette was to have bought and which was stolen the Comtesse de Lamotte-Valois; a dressing-table set in solid gold with incrustations of opals and aquamarines; a drawing-room suite in molded quartz, which is to say, in rock crystal; and a silver-plated bicycle—not to mention the old master paintings, the jewels, the precious furs and *objets d'art* of every sort.

Every morning, in company with her reader, the excellent Mrs. MacBarlott, and Fred Jorgell's private secretary, Isidora took pleasure in opening the boxes and jewel-cases that were arriving in abundance at the paternal palace personally.

Only just convalescent from a wound he had received during a nocturnal attack, Fred Jorgell's secretary, a Frenchman named Agénor Marmousier, was still very weak and pale, but Isidora's joy had hastened his recovery and he savored a child-like joy in helping to unwrap the wedding gifts.

"What's this?" asked Mrs. MacBarlott curiously, as she cut the string surrounding the silk paper that contained a jewel-case. "Pooh!" she added, scornfully. "An emerald brooch—we already have seven or eight of them."

In the meantime, Agénor was carefully unwrapping a long cedar-wood box. The box contained another, made of mahogany.

"I wonder what can possibly be in there?" said Isidora, devoured by a feverish curiosity.

"We'll soon see," Agénor replied, drawing back the silver bolt that sealed the mahogany box.

The young woman uttered a cry of surprise on perceiving a silver scale model of the latest steamer that Fred Jorgell had launched, which was named *Isadora*. The slightest details of the vessel had been scrupulously mimicked, but all the copper components were reproduced in gold, the red and green beacon lights were represented by rubies and emeralds, and the portholes by little diamonds. The miniature ship was an enormous gem of fabulous value.

At that moment Isidora felt herself gently seized around the waist; two hands were placed over her eyes and hot lips brushed her forehead. The young woman uttered a little squeal, but she was quickly reassured and smiled on recognizing the author of the affectionate jest as Harry Dorgan, who had come into the drawing room on tiptoe.

"I'm furious," Isidora said, with a radiant smile that was in stark contradiction to her words. "Is that any way for a serious man to behave?"

"Forgive me for my childishness."

"All right, but on one condition—which is that next time, you'll embrace me in a less shocking fashion."

"I'm prepared to do that," said the engineer, and again he applied his lips to the young woman's pure forehead, in a long and tender kiss.

"You're not staying with us, Master Harry?" asked Agénor. "You can help with opening all these mysterious boxes."

"Impossible. I only came to wish my dear Isidora good day before going to the office. The launching of three new liners is giving us an awful lot of work."

"I won't keep you any longer," Isidora murmured, shaking her fiancé's hand with a delicious emotion. "Until later, my dear Harry."

Once the engineer had gone, the examination of the gifts continued.

"Who can have given Miss Isidora the beautiful silver ship?" asked Agénor.

"Perhaps it was Mr. Jorgell," Mrs. MacBarlott replied.

"I'm sure that it's him," said Isidora. "The silver ship is surely the surprise that he mentioned to me yesterday at table. The present is doubly dear to me, because it reminds me of both my father and my fiancé. Wasn't it Harry—and I'm justly proud of it—who drew up the plans for the ship, the fastest in the world?"

At that moment, two servants carried in a long sandalwood box ornamented with the young woman's initials. Mrs. MacBarlott opened the box with an impatient hand. "This comes from Paris!" she exclaimed. "Here's the trademark of the great couturier Worth. It's doubtless a dress more beautiful than those you've already received."

"Let's see," said Isidora. And with a slight fever of coquetry she unfolded the numerous layers of silk paper.

"I suspected as much," said the governess. "It's a white satin dress embroidered with pearls."

"It's splendid, What do you think, Monsieur Agénor?"

"It's a pure marvel—a veritable work of art. We need to unfold it so that we can admire it in its entirety."

Aided by Mrs. MacBarlott, Isidora carefully laid out the luxurious virginal dress on one of the drawing room divans.

Suddenly, however, the young woman uttered a cry of fright. On the corsage, over the heart, a bloody hand was embroidered in little rubies, and that frightful imprint stood out clearly against the immaculate whiteness of the cloth, with silver gleams.

"I'm accursed!" cried the young woman, recoiling with a shiver of horror. "My enemies want to make me understand by this insult that the name I'm bringing to Harry is soiled by a bloody stain and that I'm the sister of Baruch the murderer. Oh, I see now that I'll never be happy!"

"Pull yourself together, Mademoiselle," Agénor murmured. "Don't believe that anyone wants to insult you. I rather fear that this gift comes from the association of the Red Hand, of which your father has always been a determined enemy..."

Isidora was no longer listening. The emotion was too much for her. The young woman had just fainted. Agénor and Mrs. MacBarlott only just had time to catch her as she fell.

The care customary in such cases was lavished upon her. She came round, and, by virtue of ingenious reasoning and kind words, her friends succeeded in reassuring her slightly

The fatal dress was hidden from all gazes, and it was agreed that Fred Jorgell would not be told about the incident—but all the bride's joy had been spoiled. It was with a languid indifference that she watched the unwrapping of the other gifts. The Red Hand had extinguished the smile from every face and sown anguish in every heart.

Everyone was thinking about the fatal dress, but no one dared talk about it. The governess was the first one who hazarded to say: "Don't you think, Miss Isidora, that it would be a good idea to tell your fiancé?"

"No," the young woman murmured. "Not that!"

"If you're in danger, though, is that gift isn't just a macabre joke, if it's a real threat on the part of the redoubtable association..."

"What does it matter? It's already sufficient that I'm suffering myself, without my dear Harry's joy and tranquility being troubled by those wretches."

"But Miss, have you really thought about it?"

"Yes. I tell you once and for all, I don't want my fiancé to be told, and I'll be grateful to you, Mrs. MacBarlott, and to you, Monsieur Agenor, never to remind my about that bloody hand."

After this declaration, the young billionaires, leaving the drawing room where the gifts were piled up, went up to her bedroom to think.

The courageous young woman was possessed of enormous self-control, and when she came down again two hours later to sit down beside her father and her fiancé, her face was utterly serene. She seemed calm, happy and cheerful, as she was every day. Perspicacious as he was. Harry Dorgan could not read the slightest trace of any care or preoccupation in her features.

The engineer was in an excellent mood. He had just discovered a mechanism that would permit a saving of twenty per cent on fuel.

"Everything's going very well," he told Fred Jorgell, "and I'm far enough advanced in my work for the leave I'm taking on the occasion of our marriage not to impede the work of the Lightning Steamship Company in any way."

"You can take as much leave as you wish," said Fred Jorgell, laughing out loud. "Can't he, my darling Isidora?"

The young woman only replied with a timid smile, lowering her eyes and blushing.

"This morning," said the engineer, suddenly, "I received a very interesting letter from an unknown inventor. It concerns a new turbine engine."

He took an envelope from his pocket, which contained a square piece of card covered on both sides with microscopic handwriting. Fred Jorgell darted a glance over the missive and handed it back to Harry Dorgan.

"Those letters are too small for my eyesight," he murmured. "It will be simpler if you give me a brief explanation."

Harry put the letter back in his pocket. "In fact, he said, "those fly-specks are almost indecipherable. It took me a good half-hour to read them."

At that moment Isidora noticed that the engineer had two red patches at the tips of his thumb and forefinger, which resembled burns. "What's that?" she asked, taking the young man's hand. "Have you hurt yourself, my dear Harry?"

"No. It's a slight irritation of the skin; I don't know what to attribute it to, but it's causing me a certain discomfort."

"You didn't have that redness this morning, did you?"

"No. It started suddenly while I was reading my mail. Bah! It will go of its own accord, just as it came."

The incident was forgotten, and after a rapid lunch, the engineer went back to his office and plunged himself into absorbing work. By the evening post, he received a further letter from the unknown inventor of the turbine engine.

The text, and even the signature, were as barely legible as those in the first missive, and Harry spent a good deal of time deciphering them. When he had finished reading, he suddenly perceived that his fingers were very swollen, and then felt a strange malaise, a kind of vertigo.

He left his office sooner than usual, convinced that the fresh air would dissipate the headache, which he attributed to his recent overwork. Once in the street, however, the illness, instead of getting better, only increased and got worse. His legs became unsteady beneath him; he saw flashes of light, his eyes were buzzing.

He felt so weak that instead of going home on foot, as he had intended, he was obliged to take a cab.

At dinner, he scarcely touched his food. An ardent thirst was devouring him and he could see myriads of black dots dancing before his eyes, as happens in certain kinds of fever. Finally, he felt weighed down by a terrible fatigue. In order not to worry Isidora, however, he stiffened himself against the pain and succeeded in taking part in the conversation, as usual.

Isidora, however, had not failed to take note of his pallor, and she had observed that the suspect red patched at the tips of the thumb and index finger were surrounded by violet rings and hollowed out in the center like two small wounds. On the young woman's insistence, he promised to attend to what he referred to as an insignificant scratch, and under the pretext of having urgent work to do, went back to the furnished apartment he rented a short distance away from his future father-in-law's house.

Once he was alone in his room, Harry was gripped by tremors and afflicted by stabbing pains in his abdomen. He felt so ill that he was obliged to go to bed, sending is manservant to fetch a doctor.

After examining the invalid, the practitioner declared that his condition was not serious and must be attributable to a fever caused by fatigue. He advised sleep, rest, a warm bath and sedatives.

Soon after the doctor's departure, Harry fell into a leaden sleep. He did not wake up until late the next morning.

"What!" he stammered, darting a glance at the electric clock set beside his bed. "Nine-thirty already! But I should have been at the office an hour ago!"

He made an abrupt movement to get up, but he was unable to do so. His limbs were numb, and he had a dull pain in all his joints. With difficulty, he raised himself up on to his elbow and his gaze went to the large looking-glass opposite the bed, in which his image as reflected. He uttered a cry of surprise.

His face, lividly pale, was dotted with violet spots; his lips were white and his eyelids red and swollen.

"I'm ill," he stammered. "Very ill. What will Isidora say?"

He extended his hand to the electric bell-push situated above his bed-head. A few minutes later, the manservant came into the room. At the sight of Harry Dorgan he stepped back, vaguely fearful.

"What's wrong, Master?" he asked. "Are you ill?"

"Yes," stammered the engineer, in a weak voice. "Will you go inform Mr. Fred Jorgell that I won't be in the office this morning and that I won't be able to come to lunch. But don't exaggerate. Say that I'm slightly indisposed, and that I'll doubtless be better this evening..."

The manservant hastened to carry out this instruction.

13

When he went into Fred Jorgell's study Isidora was with her father. On hearing about her fiancé's illness she was overtaken by a funereal presentiment. Immediately, she thought about the bloody hand embroidered on the bridal gown.

"My God!" she murmured. "Harry is ill! I'm trembling in anticipation of a catastrophe. And I didn't want my father or my fiancé to know about the terrible threat suspended over their heads!"

Isidora felt remorse tormenting her heart. Exaggerating her fault, she regarded herself as the cause of the engineer's illness. "I should have warned him!" she repeated.

She resolver to repair the error and immediately told her father the truth.

The billionaire was deeply affected by what she had told him, but he tried to reassure his daughter. "Evidently," he said, "you were wrong not to warn me, but I'm convinced that there's no correlation between Harry's illness and yesterday's insulting gift."

But Isidora had risen to her feet. "I want to see Harry!" she cried, impetuously. "My place is at my husband's bedside!"

"I'll go with you," said Fred Jorgell, agitatedly, "but before then, I'll give orders to notify the chief of the New York Police and have my house put under special surveillance, guarded if necessary by twenty robust detectives. Anyway, perhaps you're wrong to worry. The servant only talked about a slight indisposition."

"No, Harry is seriously ill. I feel it, I know it, I'm sure of it.

A quarter of an hour later, the billionaire and his daughter went into the invalid's room. On perceiving Harry's disfigured features, Isidora uttered a heart-rending cry.

"My presentiments weren't mistaken," she murmured, dejectedly. "Harry's very ill! Since that's the case, I shan't leave his side; I'll care for him, watch over him and cure him myself!"

Making a supreme effort to summon up all his energy, the engineer had straightened up, smiling—but it was a heart-rending smile. "I'm not as ill as you think," he stammered, in a voice as faint as a breath. "I assure you, my dear Isidora, that I already feel much better..."

"I want to look after you myself. Isn't it as if I'm already your wife—and I won't I be, in a few days?"

The sick man made a swift gesture of negotiation. "No," he articulated, painfully. "I don't want that. The malady from which I'm suffering might be contagious, and it's already an imprudence for you to have come here and shaken my hand."

Fred Jorgell had drawn near. "Harry," he said, "I already consider you to be part of the family. I approve entirely of Isidora and find her devotion quite natural. Anyway, you're not as gravely ill as you think, and I've already taken measures to have the most celebrated physicians in New York brought here. Your malady would have to be very serious indeed not to yield to science."

"Besides," added Isidora, "when one fights disease energetically, it goes away. It's a battle like any other. It's a matter of being victorious."

"Energy I have," the invalid murmured, in a feeble voice.

"And we shall add ours to yours, if necessary. I'm not going to be deprived of a collaborator whose services are so valuable to me, damn it!" And the billionaire, even though he was seriously alarmed, laughed cordially, as if did not believe that the engineer's illness was serious.

Leaving Isidora at her fiancé's bedside, Fred Jorgell left, having observed that Harry was mentally reassured by his visit. The billionaire intended to return soon afterwards, accompanied by the physicians he had summoned by telephone. He had just left the furnished house when a man dressed as a domestic came into it.

"I'd like to see Mr. Harry Dorgan," he said to the doorman.

"Unfortunately," was the reply," Mr. Dorgan is very ill. He's confined to bed, awaiting several physicians who have been called to a consultation. On whose behalf have you come?"

"On behalf of Mr. Fred Jorgell."

"But he's just left," replied the doorman, suspiciously.

"Our paths must have crossed. I'll run to catch him up." And the man went away without asking for further explanations.

A hundred yards away, he went into the back room of a bar that was almost deserted at present, where two men were waiting for him. They were Joe Dorgan, the engineer's brother, and a physician famous in New York, where he was known as the sculptor of human flesh, Dr. Cornelius Kramm. The man gave them a rapid account of his mission and withdrew.

Once they were alone, Cornelius and Joe Dorgan exchanged diabolical smiles. "I believe," said Cornelius, "that Miss Isidora's marriage is not ready to be concluded. The charming young lady might well be widowed before the wedding."

"The detested Harry will finally disappear," murmured Joe, with a hateful contraction of his features.

"As to that, have no fear. With the microbe that I've inoculated him, which is only known to a few rare scientists, Harry Dorgan only has a week to live, at the most."

The two bandits chatted for a little longer, and then went back to the automobile that was waiting for them a short distance away.

The Red Hand had triumphed yet again. Harry Dorgan was about to die.

II. Green Leprosy

The engineer Antoine Paganot and his fiancée, Mademoiselle Andrée de Maubreuil, were taking tea in the company of Oscar Tournesol in a small drawing room at the Preston Hotel. Their friends, Roger Ravenel and Frédérique, had gone out to make some purchases.

All three were plunged in sadness and discouragement.

"We've had nothing but bad luck since our arrival in New York," said the young woman. "First there was the attempted murders by the Knights of Chloroform, to which we almost fell victim. We were counting on Fred Jorgell's aid to find Monsieur Bondonnat, but now the billionaire's future son-in-law has fallen ill, and all our plans have been adjourned, put off until an indefinite date."

The hunchbacked Oscar reflected. "I can't get rid of the idea," he murmured softly, "that the strange malady from which Harry is suffering is due to poisoning. The most famous physicians have been unable to identify the strange infection, and that patient is at the last ditch."

"Have you had news this morning?" Andrée asked.

"The engineer is dying. It's only a matter of days, perhaps hours."

"There's certainly something inexplicable about it," said Antoine Paganot.

"Three days ago," Oscar went on, "Harry was full of life and health. Today, he's almost a cadaver. His face is livid, blotched with violet patches, his eyelids swollen with blood. The patient has a horror of food and is experiencing intolerable pain in his head and abdomen. All his limbs are agitated by a convulsive tremor."

"That's odd," said the engineer. "Those symptoms are strangely similar to those caused by a little-known malady that caused frightful ravages in Russia and Poland during the Middle Ages, when it was known as green leprosy.[1] I'd be very interested to see the invalid at close range."

"Who knows," said Oscar, clutching at the hope, "whether you might not be able to discover the cause of the sickness?"

"Go see Mr. Dorgan," Andrée approved. "I'd be very happy if you could save him. How Miss Isidora must be suffering! I can imagine myself in her shoes. What chagrin I would endure if I saw you attained by a frightful disease!"

"Well then, we'll go."

Oscar Tournesol and the engineer had already risen to their feet.

---

[1] Le Rouge improvised this term for an imaginary disease; he was not to know that it would be recoined for application to a kind of algal blight attacking cave paintings.

Half an hour later, they presented themselves at the billionaire's house, where everyone was plunged in consternation. Oscar went straight to the study occupied by Agénor, Fred Jorgell's private secretary.

Agénor listened to the hunchback's explanations attentively and applauded his initiative. He knew Paganot, who was as renowned as a physician as he was as an inventor.

"That's an excellent idea, my dear compatriot," he said. "Come with me—let's not lose a moment, for in the lamentable state that poor Harry is in, hours, and even minutes are precious."

All three of them jumped into the automobile that was stationed in the courtyard night and day, and arrived at the furnished house in which Harry's apartment was located. After Agénor had said a few words to Fred Jorgell, they were introduced without difficulty into the sick man's room. There, they found themselves in the presence of a heart-rending spectacle. Somber, his face hollowed out by chagrin and aged by ten years, Fred Jorgell was standing in a corner. Nearby, Isidora was weeping silently. Nothing could be heard but the sound of her sobs and the hoarse gasps escaping the throat of the dying man.

"What use are my billions?" murmured the old man, clenching his fists with a dl range. "All these physicians are donkeys, only good for extracting dollars from the naïve. They can't even tell me the name of the disease from which my daughter's fiancé is in the process of dying."

"I don't know whether I'll be any luckier than my colleagues," said Antoine Paganot, modestly, "but I'll try."

Isidora looked up, her beautiful face bathed with tears. "Oh, Monsieur," she stammered, joining her hands together in supplication. "Save my beloved Harry, and my father's entire fortune is yours!"

"Yes, my entire fortune," repeated Fred Jorgell.

"It's not a matter of that," said Paganot. "Let's see the patient."

He approached the bed on which Harry Dorgan was lying, plunged into a kind of coma, his head tilted backwards, his eyes turned up. His lower lip was slack and his nostrils were already pinched like those of a dying man.

Isidora felt her heart beats furiously in her breast while Antoine Paganot, in the midst of a tragic silence, proceeded to examine the invalid.

"I wasn't mistaken!" he exclaimed, suddenly. "It really is green leprosy."

"Is it a curable disease?" asked the young woman, palpitating with anguish.

"Sometimes," replied Antoine Paganot, reflecting anxiously, wondering by what hazard the microbe of green leprosy, only cultivated as a curiosity in a few European and American laboratories, could have infected Harry Dorgan.

Suddenly, Paganot's attention was attracted by the patient's right hand, the thumb and index finger of which bore tumorous swellings forming a hideous wound.

Those, he thought, *are singularly located scratches. Might it not have been by that route that the microbe was introduced into his body?*

His gaze wandered distractedly around the room. Suddenly, it fell upon a card covered with delicate handwriting, at the corner of which there was a clearly-marked imprint of a thumb. He picked it up and looked at the other side. A fingerprint was marked there—doubtless that of the index finger, for the natural way of holding a card white lading it is between those two digits.

Now, it was precisely the invalid's thumb and index finger that bore wounds corresponding to the imprints. That observation gave the young man pause for thought. He remained silent while he felt a strange prickling at the tips of his own thumb and index finger, in which he was holding the card, mechanically. He looked at his fingers; they already bore traces of a slight redness. He could not help going pale and throwing the card away precipitately. Then, perceiving a bottle of Lysol on a shelf, he rapidly made use of it to disinfect his right hand.

Isidora and Fred Jorgell had followed all his actions with poignant curiosity. They understood that the moment was decisive.

"What is it?" demanded Fred Jorgell, feverishly. "What have you discovered?"

"Harry Dorgan has been poisoned," Antoine Paganot declared, gravely.

"The Red Hand's threat!" murmured Isidora, shivering.

Silence and consternation reigned for a few more moments, while Antoine Paganot searched the corners of the room nervously. Suddenly, he spotted a second card covered in the same tiny and illegible handwriting. Like the first, it bore two imprints disposed in the same fashion, but of a different color.

"When did Harry receive these cards?" he demanded, curtly.

"The day before he fell ill."

"That's it—I can explain everything. Those two cards must have reached him at an interval of a few hours."

"Which means," said Isidora, "that one of them arrived in the morning post and the other in the evening post."

"I know enough now," said Antoine, "to be sure of the method the criminals employed. I'll explain that later; the most urgent thing is to combat the disease."

Rapidly, he scribbled a prescription and handed it to the hunchback, who ran out in order to get it filled.

"Now," the young man continued, "You can have the explanation. The first card was impregnated with a vesicant substance, something akin to cantharides, contact with which, even for a short time, produces excoriations and blisters. I've just provided an example myself." He showed them the tips of his fingers. "It's in order the person to whom the letter was addressed would be obliged to hold it for a long time that the handwriting is so tiny, so dense and so difficult to read."

18

"Yes," Fred Jorgell reflected. "Harry told us that it took him more than half an hour to decipher it."

"The second card had been dipped in a culture of the microbe of green leprosy, which found in a ready-prepared terrain the slight wounds in the thumb and index finger—a comfortable entrance that allowed it to intrude into the body."

"I'll punish the poisoners!" exclaimed Fred Jorgell, clenching his fists with a menacing expression.

"I think you'll have great difficulty discovering them. The means they've employed shows that they're highly intelligent individuals—and the address on the card must be false, of course, just as the signature is illegible.

At that moment, Oscar came back carrying an assortment of bottles and a Pravaz syringe.

"I hope that I've arrived while there's still time," said Antoine Paganot. "I'm going to try hypodermic injections to combat the blood poisoning, but I need to be alone to carry out that operation. In half an hour, I'll be able to tell you whether you can still conserve any hope."

Everyone left the room.

Isidora was the last to leave; she turned round to dart a glance charged with mute supplication at Paganot. "You'll save him, won't you?" she murmured.

"I'll do everything possible, Miss, but it doesn't depend on me, alas. If only I'd been called a day earlier."

The half hour wait went by, for Fred Jorgell and his daughter, and for their friends, in all the horrors of anguish. Taking refuge in a small drawing room in the furnished house, they watched the march of the hands on the dial of a pendulum clock anxiously, the minutes seeming as long as years.

"It's ten minutes since the half hour passed!" Isidora exclaimed, getting to her feet impatiently. "Let's go and see."

"No," said Fred Jorgell." Let's wait a little longer.

At that moment, however, Paganot came into the room abruptly. The young man's features were radiant. "My friends," he said, in voice tremulous with emotion, "A salutary reaction has taken place in the patient's condition, and I now believe that I can answer for his life. There's nothing more to do than to continue the treatment I've begun. In two days' time, the improvement will be manifest. I'll watch over him myself, to see that my prescriptions are followed in every detail."

Too emotional to thank the engineer in any other manner, Fred Jorgell crushed his hand with an energetic handshake. Isidora stammered vague words of thanks, but the pallor had disappeared from her face and a gleam of hope was alight again in her beautiful eyes.

The energetic treatment applied by Paganot was, indeed, a complete success. That evening, the invalid came out of the coma in which he had been plunged. The blue-tinted patches on his face improved, and he spent a tranquil night.

The next day, his general condition was further improved, and two days after that, Harry Dorgan could be considered conclusively out of danger.

In the meantime, the billionaire's house and the furnished house where the engineer was being cared for were visibly guarded by elite detectives. The cards were analyzed by an expert chemist and Antoine Paganot's assertions were completely verified. The first card had been dipped into a vesicant mixture of extraordinary activity, and the other, examined under a microscope, allowed the bacilli of green leprosy with which it was impregnated to be clearly discerned.

Needless to say, the police searched in vain for the sender of the poisoned missives. The only things that seemed certain was that they emanated from affiliates of the Red Hand. As Fred Jorgell said to his daughter, however, there was nothing to be done, for the moment, against the ungraspable bandits. The best thing to do was to be very wary, and wait for the police finally to get their hands on the leaders of the association—which could not be long delayed, because a group of capitalists, headed by Fred Jorgell, had offered considerable rewards that ought to stimulate the zeal of the detectives.

Meanwhile, Harry Dorgan's recovery made rapid progress. He was entering into convalescence. Isidora resolved to take advantage of the fact that Harry no longer had any immediate need for her presence to pay a visit of thanks to Antoine Paganot. She therefore went to the Preston Hotel, accompanied by Agénor, who was old enough and serious enough to serve as her chaperon.

As she went up in the elevator that was to deposit her on the landing of the floor on which the French guests were staying, Isidora could not suppress a strange emotion. Was she not, perhaps, about to find herself in the presence of the woman whose father had been murdered by Baruch? In her haste to thank Antoine Paganot, she had not thought about that eventuality, but it was too late to turn back. Already, a bellboy was introducing her and Agénor into a small drawing room in which Mademoiselle de Maubreuil and the engineer were sitting.

On seeing the American woman come in, Andrée rose to her feet. Without ever having seen her before, she recognized Isidora from the description she had been given. In spite of all her self-control, she went pale, all her blood flowing back to her heart. She was in the presence of the sister of the father's murderer.

Isidora had divined what was passing through her mind, and, advancing toward her, she murmured in a voice tremulous with emotion: "Mademoiselle, I know that I ought not to be here, and that my presence must reawaken cruel memories in your heart, but I had to thank Monsieur Paganot, to whom I owe my fiancé's life. It's necessary that I express all my gratitude to him, and also that I ask him, on my father's behalf, what recompense he desires for the inestimable service that he has rendered to us. Mademoiselle, can you not forgive me for having come?"

"Miss Isidora," Andrée de Maubreuil replied, effortfully, "I know that you are honest and generous. I cannot hold you responsible for someone else's crime. Let there never again be any mention between us of that bloody past..." While speaking, Andrée held out her hand to Isidora.

The young woman took it and shook it, but they were both so emotional that they had tears in their eyes. There was a moment of sad silence.

Agénor was the first to resume the conversation. "Don't forget, Miss Isidora," he said, "that we've come to ask Monsieur Paganot what honorarium he desires for the miraculous cure he has just achieved."

"There can't be any question between us of any recompense whatsoever," he engineer declared. "I'm only too glad to have been able to help the protector of our friend Oscar."

"Do you know," said Andrée suddenly, "what would give Monsieur Paganot the greatest pleasure?"

"Tell me," said Isidora. "It's granted in advance."

"Well," said the young woman, "find the father of my friend Frédérique Monsieur Bondonnat, and we'll be handsomely recompensed for the service that my fiancé has rendered you."

"We'll find him," said Isidora, gravely, her hand extended as if she were swearing an oath. "We'll find him, if my father has to spend his entire fortune to do it."

At that moment, Frédérique came into the room, not knowing that there were visitors. Paganot made the introductions, and the billionaire's daughter and the newcomer took an instant liking to one another.

"Excuse me for having come in like that without warning," she said, "but I've brought good news."

"What is it?"

"I've just received a letter from my father. Here it is—I'll read it to you." She took a crumpled envelope out of her corsage. Everyone came closer as Frédérique read.

My dear child,

I am, fortunately, alive and well. I am, it's true, sequestered and closely guarded in a place about which it's impossible for me to give you any information, but I'm not in any danger. I'm in the hands of rich capitalists who are forcing me—somewhat reluctantly, I admit—to work on certain discoveries, but they ought to compensate me and, which is much more important to me, eventually set me free.

My jailers have forbidden me to give you any more details, but don't worry about me; I shall soon return.

Give my other daughter Andrée a big hug on my behalf, and be patient.

A thousand kisses from your old father.

Prosper Bondonnat

P. S. My compliments to my excellent collaborators, Roger Ravenel and Antoine Paganot.

"A strange letter!" exclaimed Agénor, when Frédérique had finished reading.

"Oh," the young woman replied, "it's definitely my father's handwriting. He has a particular way of crossing his *t*s, forming his *f*s and adding a flourish to his signature that are typical of him. I'd recognize it among a thousand.

"Let's see the envelope," said the engineer. "This letter has been addressed to Brittany, and then forwarded to New York."

"But where did it come from—that's what we need to know."

"America," said Paganot, examining the postmarks attentively. "That proves one thing, which is that Monsieur Bondonnat really is in America and that we were right to come to search for him here. The letter was posted in New Orleans."

"Well then," declared Andrée and Frédérique, with one voice, "we'll go to New Orleans. We'll leave as soon as possible."

"My father has numerous correspondents in New Orleans," Isidora said, "who will put themselves at your disposal for any information imaginable. Tomorrow, I'll give Oscar a dozen letters of introduction, which will, I'm sure, be very useful to you."

Andrée and Frédérique thanked Isidora, who took her leave of them, renewing the promise she had made to aid them, with all the power of her father's billions, in the search that they were undertaking.

That day was happy for everyone. The little clan of French travelers was glad finally to have news of Monsieur Bondonnat, and Isidora and her father saw with indescribable satisfaction that Harry Dorgan was convalescing well.

As for the threats of the Red Hand, no one wanted, or dared, to think about them.

III. Cabin 29

After a fatiguing railway journey, Andrée, Frédérique and the two young women's fiancés had arrived in St. Louis, on the Mississippi. Saying at an excellent hotel situated on the river bank, the Louisiana Hotel, attracted by the name's French associations, they got up rather late in the morning. They had a summary breakfast and were getting ready to take a walk into the city when their attention was caught by a gigantic gaudily-colored poster in the hotel's interior courtyard.

Precious advertisement
for ladies and gentlemen loving tourism
OXYGEN—CELERITY—MUSIC
Vivifying atmosphere of the Mississippi forests
Extra-rapid voyage on the luxury yacht
ARKANSAS
Orchestra of 30 musicians.
French and English cuisine.
First-rate comfort.
Innumerable on-board attractions.
Fishing. Hunting. Sports of every kind.

The Arkansas *makes the journey from St. Louis*
to New Orleans in thirty hours.

Ticket prices: First class $120. Second class $80.

The four French travelers were busy reading this poster, worthy of Barnum, when one of the hotel employees approached them and, after having bowed respectfully, said in excellent French: "Mesdames et Messieurs, I noticed in the hotel register that you're traveling to New Orleans. If you'll permit me to give you some advice, I urge you to book passage on the *Arkansas*. It's a little more expensive than ordinary steamboats, but that inconvenience is amply compensated by other advantages.

"What?" asked Paganot.

"The poster lists the majority of them. In addition, the Arkansas only being able to carry a hundred passengers, all people of the highest society, you'll be able to avoid he disagreeable promiscuity of ordinary steamboats. All those who go down the superb river in those conditions have nothing but praise for the journey." Forestalling an objection that he read in the engineer's expression, the employee added: "I can assure you that I have no personal interest in your taking one boat rather than another."

"The proposition is attractive," said Andrée de Maubreuil, not having noticed the employee's suspicious persistence.

"We'll think about it," added Frédérique.

"You'll need to give me an answer within six hours," the man said, doggedly. "The *Arkansas* raises anchor in the morning."

"That's enough," said Roger Ravenel, impatiently. "You'll have your answer in good time."

The four left the hotel, without noticing that the obsequious employee was following them at a distance, with an expression that was both ironic and full of hatred. "They seem to be almost decided," he muttered, between his teeth. "I believe they'll embark."

He was not mistaken. After having seen the *Arkansas*, an elegant steel steamer of recent construction, the young travelers decided to adopt that mode of transport, which everyone recommended to them as the quickest, least tiring and most practical.

They had their baggage sent to the yacht, and he next day, at nine o'clock, they took possession of their cabins while the *Arkansas* raised anchor to the sound of a feverish orchestra playing, with typical American fury, *Yankee Doodle*, the *Marseillaise* and the *Blue Danube*.

The stars and stripes was run up the mizzen mast, and they set off.

The passengers, who were covering the deck, were dressed with a certain elegance, which would have seemed a trifle garish in France. They were wearing brightly-colored check suits, improbable cravats and red waistcoats. Almost all of them were wearing traveling caps ornamented with little flags or the emblems of the sporting clubs to which they belonged. Many were equipped with binoculars, collapsible telescopes and Kodaks, which they aimed alternately at the two banks of the river.

At that point, the Mississippi is almost as wide as a lake. It's yellow and muddy waters roll between two marshy shores covered with a tangle of aquatic plants that continued further away in immense acreages of cotton and corn, interrupted at intervals by clumps of trees. Here and there, towns and villages appear, gathered in the depths of little bays, with their factories and tall black chimneys, and their breakwaters of wooden stakes advancing into the muddy waters of the river.

The heat was overwhelming; black servants hastened to set up large twill awnings on the deck, under which the majority of the passengers installed themselves on rattan seats, while waiters circulated with trays laden with incendiary cocktails.

At eleven o'clock the lunch bell rang. The menu was little different from those at the hotels where the four travelers had already stayed; there was the inevitable oyster soup, Canadian salmon and giant steaks surrounded by an arsenal of corrosive sauces in little bottles with multicolored labels. The stout and pale ale were excellent, but the wines, described as French wines and priced accordingly, were execrable. In sum, the fare did not belie the promises of the prospectus to an excessive extent.

It was during that first lunch that Andrée and Frédérique noticed two middle-aged guests whose physiognomy and manners inspired an instinctive repulsion in them. One of them had one of those faces that remain engraved in the memory after they have been seen once. His enormous skull was completely bald, his lashless eyes like those of a bird of prey were shielded by large gold-rimmed spectacles and the expression of his gaze had something hypnotic and disquieting about it. His lips were taut, his face thin and clean-shaven almost skeletal. He expressed himself with a glacial slowness and dryness, and gave the impression at first sight of an intelligence of genius combined with a diabolical malevolence.

His companion, doubtless his brother—for there was a vague resemblance between them—was entirely different in his physiognomy and appearance. Whereas the other was thin, wan and morose, he was corpulent, rubicund and jovial. His benevolent smile and his bright gray eyes full of frankness rendered him likeable at first, but if one observed attentively his over-developed jaw, his vast ears and his enormous hands with stubby fingers and bulbous thumbs, one felt much less reassured.

The two men in question were enigmatic and disturbing. Throughout the meal, they only pronounced a few words, but they did not take their eyes off the French quartet; Frédérique, especially, felt the hypnotic gaze of the man in the gold-rimmed spectacles weighing upon her, and experienced a strange malaise. It was with a veritable relief that she saw the two unknown man get up from the table and go up on deck, where they went to smoke a cigar.

"What strange faces!" the young woman murmured, with a slight shiver. "Veritable characters from Hoffmann or Edgar Poe. They've taken away my appetite.

"One only sees faces like that in America," Roger Ravenel replied. "They might, however, be perfectly honest men."

"I seriously doubt that," said Paganot, shaking his head. "I've heard it said that one of them is a well-known physician; the other must be some kind of businessman."

The conversation gradually changed direction, and when lunch was over, everyone went up on deck to admire the landscape, which was incessantly renewed as they advanced.

They saw numerous alligators, the youngest as alert and nimble as lizards; the largest, the patriarchs, allowed themselves to be drawn lazily along by the current at the surface of the water, their backs covered with a greenish moss that made them resemble old drifting tree-trunks.

The two strangers with the disquieting appearance had disappeared. Soon after lunch they had retired to a cabin, number 29, and had ordered chilled champagne and cigars to be brought to them.

"It's tonight, then," said the man in the gold-rimmed spectacles, lowering his voice.

"Yes, my dear Cornelius; it's high time we were rid of these accursed Frenchies, who have already caused us considerable trouble."

"Baruch doesn't know anything?"

"No, we'll tell him about it when it's finished. That's infinitely preferable. If he's not happy, we'll tell him that we didn't have time to consult him, that the danger was urgent."

"Yes, that's much better—but our man's taking his time."

"Oh, he's not late," said Fritz, taking out his watch. "His name is Dodge; he's already been condemned to death for theft and murder, and he's entirely devoted to the Red Hand. Furthermore, he's spent several months on the Island of Hanged Men and was one of the sentinels watching old Bondonnat. I'd far rather have had Slug, though."

"Yes, but Slug hasn't yet recovered from the bullets Fred Jorgell put into him. I really thought he wouldn't pull through..."

At that moment, someone knocked three times on the cabin door, spacing out the raps. Fritz and Cornelius hastened to put on their rubber masks, and then waited. The knocking was repeated.

"Come in," said Cornelius.

The man who came into the cabin was a robust fellow dressed in blue overalls, his hands and face blackened by coal dust. He was holding his cap in his hand, respectfully.

"Shut the door," said Fritz.

"I've received instructions to come to cabin 29, sirs." He showed a noted bearing, by way of a signature, a hand crudely traced in red ink.

"That's right," said Fritz. "We sent for you. We have orders to give you on behalf of the Lords of the Red Hand. Tonight, when all the passengers are asleep in their cabins, the *Arkansas* has to sink, with no survivors. Nothing's easier than to contrive a leak in the hold; it's sufficient to prize loose a few planks. It shouldn't take more than an hour. You'll have taken care, of course, to ferry us ashore in one of the launches before the accident."

Dodge, one of the stokers of the *Arkansas*, seemed hesitant. Cornelius read a certain reluctance in his gaze.

"Remember," he said, in any icy voice, as trenchant as a December wind, "that you must obey the Lords' orders. Anyway, you're not running any risk, and you're not unaware that without the Red Hand, which covers you with its powerful protection, you wouldn't have forty-eight hours to live."

"Sirs," said Dodge, humbly, "I'll come to look for you in this cabin at half past eleven exactly, to take you to the dinghy."

Fritz handed the stoker a fifty-dollar bill. "Here," he said. "That will permit you to buy a drink for the crew. They need to be drunk enough not to disturb you at your work. You can go now."

26

Dodge went out backwards.

As soon as he had gone, Fritz and Cornelius took off their masks and hastened to leave cabin 29. They went back up on deck just as the ship's bell announced that the Arkansas was about to put in at the wooden quays of a riverside village in order to drop off a few passengers and take others aboard.

The exchange of passengers was rapidly completed. Only ten or so came aboard, most of them rich local planters. Among them was a young man with elegant clothes and manners, the sight of whom made a strange impression on Mademoiselle de Maubreuil. She had a fleeting sensation of having seen those features somewhere before—but where? She could not say.

The unknown man came across the gangplank and his eyes met Andrée's. Beneath his magnetic gaze, the young woman felt a dolorous disturbance. That gaze had, so to speak, physically wounded her, as if she had been stabbed with a dagger. She turned her head away with a kind of instinctive repulsion, while the young man, after having followed her with a long stare, was lost in the crowd of passengers with which the deck of the steamer was cluttered.

By virtue of some strange association of ideas, Andrée de Maubreuil suddenly recalled the nightmare that had haunted all her Saturday nights for a long time, but which now rarely recurred. She could not help shivering, but she dared not confide the strange presentiment that had assailed her to anyone else.

Meanwhile, the unknown man, advancing through the crowd of passengers, did not take long to perceive Fritz and Dr. Cornelius. He exchanged an imperceptible wink with them, and all three of them went down to cabin 29, specially chosen by Cornelius because it was isolated from the others. The two brothers did not try to hide their discontentment at seeing the newcomer.

"Well, my dear Baruch—I mean, my dear Joe—what's happened to make you run after us?" asked Cornelius. "Your arrival is a genuine surprise."

"Very serious things are happening," said Baruch, whose physiognomy expressed anxiety and ill humor. "First of all, I've just received, by telegram, some very unwelcome news. Lord Burydan has escaped from the Island of Hanged Men, in company with the Indian Kloum."

"But at least old Bondonnat hasn't escaped?" asked Fritz, precipitately.

"No, but it was a close run thing. He'd already climbed into the gondola of his airship—of which, parenthetically, Lord Burydan has taken possession—when one of our faithful agents, Sam Porter, grabbed him around the waist and prevented his escape."

Fritz and his brother exchanged furious and spiteful glances.

"I always said," growled Cornelius, "that the old Frenchman was as wily as the Devil and that he's finish up slipping through our fingers one day, like an eel."

"Oh," said Baruch, "I've telegraphed orders to double the surveillance and I don't believe the old man will be able to put together a new escape plan any time soon. But that's not the only bad news I've brought. My brother, Harry

Dorgan, is now completely recovered. The famous green leprosy didn't keep him in bed much longer than a mild cold in the head."

"We know that," Cornelius replied, impatiently, "since its Paganot, a pupil of our prisoner on the Island of Hanged Men, who succeeded in identifying the microbe and applying an appropriate treatment to the patient."

"Yes," replied Baruch, passionately, "but what you don't know is that my pseudo-father, William Dorgan, on learning that his offspring was seriously ill, set aside all his pride and rancor and went to see him. Everything I could do the prevent it proved futile. Now they're reconciled, and William Dorgan has even consented to his son's marriage to Isidora."

"Damn! That spoils things," murmured Fritz, between his teeth.

"Yes," Cornelius added, in the same tone. "It's high time to intervene in an energetic fashion."

"At any rate," Baruch continued, his long-restrained anger breaking free, "it's necessary to avoid certain blunders like those that have been committed without anyone telling me about them."

"What blunders, if you please?" demanded Cornelius whose predatory eyes were flashing behind the lenses of his gold-rimmed spectacles.

"My sister Isidora received a dress embroidered with a blood hand. Why did you do that? It's as ridiculous as it is clumsy?"

"We had our reasons," replied Cornelius, dryly. "That emblematic dispatch, preceding Harry Dorgan's sudden illness by a few hours, was designed to strike Fred Jorgell and his daughter with such terror that..."

"Well," said Baruch, with a sinister snigger, "the result was quite different from the one for which you hoped. Now, Fred Jorgell and the French contingent have joined forces. They'll move Heaven and Earth to find Bondonnat."

Fritz shrugged his shoulders. "The French contingent won't bother us much longer."

"Why is that?"

"Because after tonight, they'll no longer exist. The *Arkansas* will sink with all hands. There are affiliates of the Red Hand on board, and our arrangements have been made."

Baruch had gone white with rage. "That won't happen," he declared, clenching his fists. "I've observed that for some time, you no longer take the trouble to consult me when it's a matter of making important decisions. Our association will soon come to an end if discord breaks out between us."

"It's not a matter of that," Fritz replied, in a conciliatory tone. "It's urgently necessary to get rid of the French group, who are a danger to us. We seized a good opportunity on the wing. We were convinced that you'd agree with us. There's no reason for you to get angry."

"When you left New York," Baruch said, "there was no mention of this plan. The letter sent to Mademoiselle Frédérique was simply to have been a means of separating Fred Jorgell and his allies and drawing the latter to New

Orleans in order to make them waste time in futile investigations, thus giving us time to make a decision in their regard."

"Yes, but on the way we decided that it was much better to get rid of them at a stroke, in a catastrophe that would appear to be natural to everyone, and wouldn't require the law to intervene. When the *Arkansas* is at the bottom of the Mississippi, it'll take a clever man to figure out how the shipwreck happened. If you think about it for a moment, you'll agree with me."

Baruch had had the time to calm down and had gradually recovered his composure. "Well," he said, in a cutting tone, "I've thought about it. The catastrophe mustn't happen. I'm absolutely opposed to it."

"Why?"

"Because I don't want Andrée de Maubreuil to perish. I've just seen her on deck and our eyes met. I love her as much as I did before, when I was in her father's house. She detested me then, and doubtless still detests me, but it will be my triumph to make her love me, voluntarily or otherwise, and that's why I want her alive."

Cornelius and Fritz consulted one another with a glance and remained hesitant and perplexed.

"Understand, moreover," Baruch continued, "that it's a bad time to attract attention to the Red Hand. I know that Harry Dorgan detests me, and he has good reasons to do so; I'm sure he suspects me of having something to do with his illness. It will only require a cleverly-conducted investigation to discover that we're the famous Lords of the Red Hand, whose existence has become legendary in America. Think about it in your turn, and ask yourselves whether it isn't preferable to be prudent."

The argument went on for an entire hour. Very reluctantly, Cornelius and his brother ended up yielding to Baruch's reasoning. They knew that he was right about shields being raised against the Red Hand. Great caution was necessary, at least for the time being.

As soon the three bandits had reached agreement, someone knocked on the door of cabin 29 in the prearranged manner. With a rapid gesture, the three Lords covered their faces with their masks; then Fritz went to open the door. It was Dodge, the stoker.

"Sirs," he said, "my preparations are made. I await your definitive orders. The dinghy that will take you ashore is already hoisted on to its davits.

"Your preparations are unnecessary this time," said Cornelius. "The planned catastrophe won't occur. Go back to work and forget what you've seen and heard."

"What about the fifty dollars?"

"Keep them—they're yours."

The stoker withdrew, very surprised by that unexpected denouement.

A few hours later, as night fell, the three Lords of the Red Hand took advantage of one of the steamboat's ports of call at a riverside town to get off. They had themselves taken to the nearest railway station and caught the express to New York.

IV. The Alligators' Feast

Throughout the time that Baruch had been aboard the *Arkansas*, Andrée de Maubreuil, being subject, without realizing it, to a kind of suggestion, had been prey to a malaise akin to anguish. As soon as the bandit and his two accomplices had left the vessel, she experienced an immediate relief, without being able to identify its cause. She breathed more easily, as if she had just been liberated from a crushing burden, She spent the night in a tranquil fashion in the cabin she was sharing with Frédérique, which, without being luxurious, offered very adequate comfort.

Having risen early, the two young women went up on deck, where their fiancés had already preceded them. All four waxed ecstatic over the panorama, which was splendid. A more luxuriant vegetation, of a different character, advertised the approach of the tropical zone. The banks were bordered by giant bamboo-trees, wooded areas became more frequent and palm-trees, tulip-trees, laurels and cedars were numerous therein. The river had doubled in breadth and was now strewn with marshy and verdant islets, from which the steamer's approach caused flocks of aquatic birds to take flight. Boats of every sort—steamboats, sailboats, barges, canoes and so on—were flocking around the *Arkansas* in considerable numbers. Andrée and Frédérique even saw enormous trains of wood floating downstream. There was evidence of an intensity of traffic that the calm rivers of old Europe cannot give the slightest idea.

The temperature had become intolerable. Yellow-tinted vapors rose from the overheated waters of the river, and the alligators became innumerable. They were frolicking in hundreds or thousands around the steamer. The clicking of their jaws could be heard distinctly, and their ferocious little eyes could be seen, as if illuminated by a bloody gleam.

At first, the passengers amused themselves throwing them morsels of various sorts: bread-crusts, banana-peel, and even rolled up newspapers. Then, the sportsmen aboard took it into their heads to kill a few of the monsters with hunting rifles.

That idea was a great success; all the firearms aboard were requisitioned, and the steamship was soon advancing amid a continuous volley of gunshots, the crackle of an authentic fusillade.

The majority of the improvised hunters' bullets ricocheted off the alligators' thick armor. To kill them, it was necessary to hit them in the eye or the belly, the only two parts of their bodies that were vulnerable. That was not easy to do. Only a few skilled sharpshooters succeeded in that feat, but as soon as an alligator was killed, its fellow fell upon it and tore it apart ferociously, with little cries reminiscent of those of a new-born baby.

The river was tinted with blood over a large area. Andrée and Frédérique, who found the spectacle of that butchery profoundly repugnant, were just about to go down to their cabin when a wholly unexpected incident occurred.

In order to avoid the waves that were rising at that moment in the middle of the stream, the steamer had been obliged to get closer to the shore, where immense fields of cotton appeared, dotted with villages comprised of straw huts and inhabited by black people, mostly former slaves, who are very numerous in the region.

Suddenly, the passengers on the *Arkansas* saw two men in rags burst out of a thicket of banana-trees and prickly palms. They were running as fast as their legs could carry them, doubtless hoping to find refuge in the vast marshes with which the river was edged. They were being hotly pursued by a mob of black men armed with sticks, pitchforks and even rifles and revolvers. The negroes were gaining on them with every passing minutes, and were already uttering howls of triumph and firing their guns in the direction of the fugitives, who seemed to be at the end of their tether.

The captain of the *Arkansas*, who was passionate about sports, like any true Yankee, gave orders to the helmsman to get closer to the shore, in order to allow the passengers to follow the progress of the contest. It was then seen that the fugitives were a white man and an Indian. Bets were already being laid.

"Five dollars on the white man."

"Ten on the Redskin for me. He's got superb hams."

"Done?"

"Done!"

"I'll take the blacks at ten to one."

Suddenly, however, things took a different turn. Everyone knows how much scorn and hatred the white men of America have for negroes. The latter have special places in theaters; they are only permitted to travel in certain carriages on the railway; even in restaurants, it is never advisable for a black man to sit down at a table where a white man is already seated.

The gamblers, initially amused by the pursuit, did not take long to pass from curiosity to indignation.

"It's shameful," shouted a fat grain-merchant from St. Louis, a pure-blooded Yankee. "Now, see, black men are starting to hunt American citizens as if they were wild boar."

"It's vile."

"We have to stop that."

"Let's get the darkies!"

"Shoot the negroes!"

"That's it!"

Their heads had reached a state of intense excitement. A few men, more determined than the others, intimated to the captain that he should take the *Arkansas* as close to the shore as possible and also put out a motor-launch to pick up the fugitives. The Yankee captain, who was fundamentally of the same opinion as the passengers, did not have to have his ears tugged before doing as he was asked. Tacking cautiously between the mud-banks and the reeds, the steamboat drew closer to the shore. In the meantime, the sharpshooters who had just been exercising their skills against the alligators hastened to reload and ran to fetch more ammunition from their cabins.

As soon as they were within range, the blacks were greeted with a general discharge. Three or four fell, more of less grievously wounded, to the joyful cries of the audience.

"Good shot, sir!"

"Superb shot!"

"Hooray for old America!"

"Death to the blacks!"

Seeing their comrades wounded, the negroes had stopped dead, utterly bewildered by the unexpected intervention They refrained from returning fire, knowing how serious it would have been for them to attack an American ship. The least they could expect would be to be strung up like common pirates.

After a brief deliberation, they beat a hasty retreat and had soon disappeared into the immense undulating ocean of cotton and corn plantations. The two fugitives, without anyone trying to stop them, reached the launch comfortably, which brought them aboard the steamship.

Scarcely had they set foot on the deck than they were surrounded by a circle of curious people fully of sympathy for the lamentable state they were in. They offered, it must be said, a pitiful spectacle. Of their torn vestments, burned in places, only tattered shreds remained. They were covered in mud and blood, scored by scratches and bruised by blows.

Exclamations rose up on all sides, growing in volume.

"Rascally blacks! Just look at the state of these poor fellows!"

"We need to give them some clothes."

"Before anything else, give them a drink of whisky—that'll put them right."

"They must be hungry!"

"No—the whisky first; they can eat afterwards."

Five minutes had not gone by before the two fugitives, so miraculously saved from death, were each in possession of a sailor's jacket and trousers in check cloth, holding a pewter goblet fill of excellent bourbon. They absorbed the generous liquor in long draughts.

"That's true velvet in the stomach," said the white man.

The Indian made no comment, but drank a second goblet of the ardent liquor, which an obliging passenger had just poured out for him, as if it were water.

"Now," someone said, "they can explain where they've come from, and tell us about their adventures."

"Gladly," the white man replied. "I certainly owe you..."

He did not finish his sentence. In the crowd of passengers, he had just perceived the stoker Dodge and his physiognomy had taken on an expression of frightful hatred and anger. "Aha! There's one of the scoundrels!" he roared. "I swore I'd strangle the first one who fell into my hands." And he added, in a thunderous voice: "Gentleman, that man is a bandit, a tramp. I know him, and I'll do him justice right away."

In spite of the layer of coal-dust covering his face, Dodge had gone lividly pale. "It's not true! It's a lie!" he stammered, in a strangled voice.

"It's not true, is it? Wait a moment—you'll see what I'm made of!"

Taking advantage of the general surprise, the fugitive had seized Dodge by his cravat and was twisting it to strangle him. A short struggle ensued, but Dodge was by no means as strong as his adversary. In the blink of an eye had had been knocked down, choking, beneath a knee.

The gallery was already preparing to applaud when there was an unexpected turn of events. The victor grabbed the vanquished bodily and, lifting him into the air by the force of his arms, he threw him overboard.

A cry of horror escaped all throats. The passengers leaned over the rail. At the place where the wretch had fallen, nothing remained but a huge bloodstain, in the middle of which a dozen alligators were fighting furiously, snapping their jaws in a sinister manner.

When the first moment of surprise had passed, the passengers of the *Arkansas*, indignant at a bloody deed whose motivation had not been explained to them, fell upon the two fugitives with threatening howls.

"Lynch them! Lynch them!" was the dominant cry.

"Throw them in the water!"

"Both of them!"

"The white and the red!"

"They're as bad as one another!"

"That'll be a feast for the alligators!"

In the presence of all the menacing fists raised against him, the unknown man remained impassive. He and his companion, the Indian, had backed up against the door of a cabin and seemed determined to sell their lives dearly. The first man who approached them received a formidable punch in the pit of his stomach. Another was launched across the deck by a kick. Five adversaries were rendered *hors de combat* in succession.

Someone proposed shooting the redoubtable boxer with a revolver, but that motion was greeted by unanimous protests.

"No—no shooting."

"That's not fair play!"

"We need to see who's the strongest."

The Americans are very appreciative of veritable courage, in whatever form it is manifest. As was evident, the resolute attitude of the two fugitives had already won them a certain sympathy among the passengers.

Antoine Paganot judged that it might perhaps be an opportune moment to intervene in favor of the two men, whose conduct was too extraordinary not to have a serious reason.

"Ladies and gentlemen," said the Frenchman, boldly advancing into the middle of the group, "it seems to me that it would be imprudent to act recklessly. These men have the right to be judged legally. I'm sure, in any case, that there's some mystery behind all this."

"Yes," the unknown man replied. "I acted as I had to; the man I've just thrown to feed the alligators is a member of the Red Hand."

"After all," said a few voices, "he might be right."

An animated discussion began between the partisans of the opposed opinions, but the captain suddenly appeared, flanked by four robust sailors armed with Brownings and cutlasses. "I'm the sole master aboard my ship," he declared. "I know what I have to do." Taking out his chronometer, he added: "I'll give these two vagabonds three minutes to yield to discretion. After that, I'll kill them like dogs."

The four sailors had taken aim at the fugitives, and the captain, his eyes of his chronometer, waited for the last second of the three minutes to give the order to fire.

In those conditions, all resistance was impossible. The fugitives surrendered. They were securely tied up and they were locked in an empty cabin,

The captain's show of force had made a deep impression. A profound silence reigned on deck for some time, and it was only after ten minutes that the conversations and arguments recommenced, as passionate and as noisy as before. Everyone's curiosity was excited to the highest degree. Everyone wanted to know who the two strange passengers were who had just put up such a spirited defense, and how they had got there.

A few of the more important passengers begged the captain to proceed with an interrogation that would satisfy the genera opinion, and the matter was settled without difficulty, because he was intrigued by the adventure himself.

In order to give his actions some kind of legal form, he deputized a constable who was going to spend his vacation in New Orleans, and a suet-merchant who had served on a jury the previous year.

The Indian declared that his name was Kloum. As for his companion, he affirmed that he was the very same Lord Astor Burydan whose death had been announced several months earlier by all the newspapers That affirmation was already implausible, but when the captain asked him where he had come from he told a story so incredible that it became evident to the members of the improvised tribunal that they were in the presence of two madmen—for the Indian Kloum supported all his companion's affirmations energetically.

The pretended Lord Burydan recounted that, having found himself in the company of Kloum on a ship laden with the coffins of Chinamen, he had been shipwrecked, cast away an icy island, the Island of Hanged Men, which belonged to the Red Hand, where he had been charged with watching over fur-seals.

"Your brain is addled, my lad," said the captain. "Where is this island?"

"I don't know."

"And how did you escape?"

"In a marvelous airship that deposited us in the middle of a village of black people. The wretches smashed our machine, and you know the rest of our story."

"And why did you kill my stoker?"

"Because I recognized him as one of the Red Hand bandits who were responsible for guarding me on the Island of Hanged Men."

The captain did not want to hear any more. His opinion and those of his assistants was henceforth irrevocably fixed. He was dealing with two dangerous madmen escaped from some asylum.

And in spite of all their protests, Lord Burydan and Kloum were locked up, watched more closely than ever, and that evening, when the *Arkansas* reached New Orleans, they were taken under escort to the city prison to await a decision as to their fate.

V. The Signature

In spite of the proposition that had been put to him, Oscar Tournesol had refused to accompany his friends in their journey to St. Louis and New Orleans. The hunchback had plans of his own. With the independence of character and stubbornness that were his dominant character traits, he had said to himself that, thus far, they had not employed the best means to pick up Monsieur Bondonnat's trail. In his opinion, he needed to become an affiliate of the Red Hand, and he was convinced that that was the only means of achieving a result. He therefore promised himself that he would explore the underworld of the city of New York, and make the acquaintance of one of the bandits, at any price.

One morning, he went to find Fred Jorgell, who was in an excellent mood, because that day, for the first time, Harry Dorgan had been able to go down to the garden, supported by the arms of Isidora and Agénor Marmousier.

"I've come to ask you for a leave," he said to the billionaire. And he explained his plan clearly.

Fred Jorgell greeted his request with a smile. The initiative and originality of the hunchback were become more and more appealing to him.

"You want a leave my lad," he replied. "Well, so be it. Act as you wish. After the service you've rendered me, I can refuse you nothing. If you need a few hundred dollars as well, ask my friend Agénor, who'll let you have them from the cash-box."

"I accept your offer, but I won't abuse it. So, don't be astonished if I disappear for a week, perhaps more."

"Where are you going?"

"Permit me not to tell you that. In order for my plan to succeed, it has to be carried out in the utmost secrecy."

"As you please," said the billionaire, without insisting. "*Au revoir*, my boy—and good luck!"

A few hours later, Oscar Tournesol, who had put on his dilapidated old shoeshine-boy costume, made his first appearance in a bizarre establishment known as the Gorilla Club, which was situated in the most sordid and disreputable part of the Irish district.

The Gorilla Club was an establishment of a very special kind, whose like would certainly not have been found anywhere else in America. It was a kind of professional school in which, in return for a modest fee of three dollars a week, tightrope-walkers, athletes, human serpents, fire-eaters, snake-charmers—in a word, fairground performers of every sort—came to perfect their art. A former circus director, the honorable Mr. John Sleary, supervised the running of that novel kind of institution, of which he was also the owner.

The name "Gorilla Club" came from a troupe of clowns who, dressed in monkey-skins, performed feats that were both dangerous and comical, which had been applauded in various cities in the Old and New Worlds. A modicum of glory had been reflected on the school in which they had made their modest debut.

After traversing the muddy streets where semi-naked children were playing, occasionally stepping over drunkards lying on the sidewalk, peacefully sleeping off their whisky, Oscar stopped in front of a coaching door with broken hinges. Above it could be read, in golden letters partly washed away by the rain: *Sleary Professional Academy*, and beside it, in larger letters which seemed to have been drawn in crayon: *Gorilla Club*.

Once inside the building, Oscar went into an entrance hall, where he perceived a bushy-haired man of about forty sitting at an old-fashioned desk covered with ink-blots. He was round-faced and plump, and he was writing in a dirty ledger. A glass and a bottle of gin were within arm's reach. It was the director himself, John Sleary.

Everything about his person testified to his former profession, from the enormous ring that he wore on his finger to the heavy gold chain from which the claws of a tiger were suspended, displayed over a scarlet waistcoat.

On seeing the hunchback come in, he got up and came toward him with an affable smile.

"Greetings, young sir," he said, in a voice that gin and asthma rendered both hoarse and breathless. "I have a slight cough—don't pay any attention to it. *Heu heu!* Fatigues of the trade, you know..."

"Monsieur..." Oscar put in.

"Yes, I can guess what brought you here. You want to become a celebrated artiste. You can say that you've been inspired in coming here. Without boasting, you won't find another establishment like John Sleary's in New York, not so say the whole of America. How many companions, after having completed their artistic education under my supervision, are earning wage-packets of twenty-five dollars a night!"

"I don't have such great pretentions," said Oscar, modestly.

"You're wrong, young man! *Heu heu!* It's necessary to be ambitious. *Heu heu!* You have a slightly round back—that's an excellent trump card in your game. All the hunchbacks I've known...*heu heu!*...have achieved superb situations. Would you like to take a glass of gin with me? *Heu heu!*"

"Thank you."

"But what are your intentions? *Heu heu!*"

"I'd particularly like to take lessons in gymnastics."

"Excellent idea! That's...*heu heu!*...one of the specialties of the establishment. You seem to me to be cut out to make a first-rate clown. At any rate, my lad, get one thing into your head, which is that our epoch...*heu heu!*...is the epoch of muscle. A man who doesn't have solid muscles can be as intelligent as he likes, but he'll certainly…*heu heu!*…be trampled underfoot in the struggle for existence."

"That's exactly my opinion. So, what are the conditions?"

"Three dollars a week for the lessons…*heu heu!*…but if you want to lodge in the establishment, that'll be another three dollars or a comfortable room…*heu heu!*…and another twelve dollars if you take your meals in the artistes' residence. I believe that's…*heu heu!*…very reasonable."

Oscar did not make the slightest objection, and he paid for a fortnight in advance, which immediately put him in the illustrious John Sleary's good graces.

"Now that little formality's out of the way," he said, pompously, "I'll take you to the exercise hall right away."

He opened a door, and Oscar followed the director into a vast space in which, beneath a thick fog caused by tobacco smoke, a host of fantastic individuals was agitating. The "exercise hall" consisted of a large square courtyard, around which stood four semi-ruined buildings. It was in those buildings that the Gorilla Club's boarders resided. The courtyard was covered by a glass roof, but a number of the panes had been broken by stones, and cobwebs cast a discreet shadow over the hall.

As his eyes became accustomed to the smoke, the hunchback made out sixty acrobats, presently hard at work, so absorbed in what they were doing that they had not noticed him come in. High above, seemingly floating above the fog of smoke, tightrope-walkers and trapeze artists in cherry-red leotards were passing back and forth. Lower down, clowns were whirling like meteors around fixed bars and jumpers were bounding across a series of trampolines with the agility of squirrels, while on the ground, human serpents were squirming, along with legless women and other cripples—which did not prevent a young bareback rider, Miss Regina Bombridge in person, mounted on an old white horse, from jumping through blazing hoops and coming down neatly in the saddle.

In one corner, Canadian sharpshooters were firing expertly at a human target, and an old man of respectable appearance, armed with a whip, was teaching two gorillas, sadly sitting at a zinc-topped table, to read a newspaper and smoke a cigar like gentlemen of the highest society.

Fraying a passage between a thin young man who was practicing walking on his head and a Japanese busily occupied in jugging blazing torches, he stopped in front of a corpulent individual wearing boxing gloves on his hands, who was in the middle of a bout with a kangaroo.

At the sight of Mr. Sleary he interrupted that violent exercise. "Come on, Mr. Tony," he said to the animal, "that's enough for the moment. Let's have a little rest, if you please." At the same time, he brandished his whip. The kangaroo understood the injunction, and remained quiet with a remarkable docility. Mr. Sleary was able to proceed with the formal introductions.

"Young man," he said, "may I introduce Mr. Bombridge, the famous clown, well-known in the States of the Union and even in the Old World. He's the man whom, on my recommendation and as a special favor, will take charge of your artistic education. You're in good hands, and with such a master, you'll go far."

Mr. Bombridge, whose voice was almost as hoarse as that of his employer, thanked the latter for the honor that had been granted to him, and after having exchanged various compliments, they both went out to drink to the health of the novice, whom they left in the hall in order that he could "drink in the atmosphere of the house."

An hour later, a drum roll summoned the boarders to the "dining room"—a long whitewashed room decorated with musical instruments and the fur of a bear that had been Mr. Sleary's devoted collaborator for a long time. There, Oscar ate a mediocre meal of cod and potatoes, washed down with bitter beer. The director, who, according to patriarchal custom, presided at their feasts and occupied the high end of the table, declared with remarkable pertinence that sobriety was one of the necessary conditions of success in the acrobatic arts—which did not prevent him from taking a big swig from the bottle of gin that was his inseparable companion, during dessert.

After having spent the rest of the day in tiring flexibility-enhancing exercises under the direction of Mr. Bombridge, who really was a good teacher, Oscar went to the garret that had been assigned to him as a residence. The eccentric and slovenly environment in which he found himself did not astonish him, and he went to sleep thinking that he would be very unlucky if he did not make the acquaintance, in this heterogeneous and shady society, of some member of the Red Hand.

After a week Oscar wrote a long letter to Agénor in which he described the curious individuals with whom he found himself in daily contact and made him party to his hopes.

Fred Jorgell, to whom Agénor showed the letter, read it with great interest and had a further fifty dollars sent to the future clown by way of encouragement.

After the frightful anxieties that he had just gone through, the billionaire found a period of calm, and good fortune. His troubles seemed to have come to an end. The Lightning Steamship Company was returning magnificent dividends and, which was much more important to Fred Jorgell, Harry Dorgan was completing his convalescence. The day came when the doctors declared that he could go out in an automobile in the company of Isidora and the indispensable Mrs. MacBarlott.

It was a warm spring day. Harry Dorgan, still slightly pale, breathed in the pure air of the great avenues on the bank of the Hudson joyfully. Isidora smiled as she silently contemplated her fiancé, who had so miraculously escaped death, and gazed at him fondly, as if he were a treasure.

The two young people passed lightly over several topics of conversation, and then, Mrs. MacBarlott having pronounced Baruch's name, they began to talk about the wretch detained in Greenaway Lunatic Asylum in a suburb of New York.

Isidora was not entirely convinced of her brother's guilt. Long reflection had led her to think that a profound mystery hung over the entire affair, and that Baruch might not be as culpable as it appeared. She was the only person who still paid any attention to him and continued to provide him with a small pension in order that he should be well treated and kept apart from the rabble of demented paupers.

"It's been a long time since I went to visit the poor fellow," she murmured, not without emotion.

"Would you like me to go to Greenaway with you today?" Harry offered, striving as ever to satisfy his fiancée's slightest caprice.

"I daren't ask you that—but I don't want to inflict such a painful confrontation on you. We'll go to Greenaway, but you can wait for me while I go to see the poor fellow."

"No, I'll come with you."

In fact, the engineer was not sorry to have the opportunity to see for himself what transformations that time, malady and captivity might have made in the material and moral physiognomy of the murderer. An order was therefore shouted to the chauffeur, and the automobile soon stopped at the solid date with the gilded spears that gave access to the grounds of the Lunatic Asylum.

Mrs. MacBarlott, having declared that the sight of the insane was always disagreeable to her, asked to remain in the auto. Harry and Isidora went in alone, and the concierge handed them over to an athletic individual dressed in a yellow uniform with metal buttons and a soft leather cap, who was the chief warder.

As soon as she went in, the young woman was struck by the state of disorder that seemed to reign in the establishment. The sandy pathways had been invaded by weeds, the corridors had not been swept, they were wandering around carelessly smoking pipes, and from the wooden barracks where the poor inmates were locked up a popular song rose up, howled in chorus by hundreds of exasperated voices.

Isidora could not help manifesting her astonishment at such a state of affairs.

The chief warder smiled, in a fashion that said a great deal. "You see, Miss," he explained, "since the arrest of Mr. Johnson, the former director—a worthy man, although he committed a few abuses of power—everything here has changed. The new director, Mr. Palmer, is a former jockey. We never see him; he spends all his time at the racecourses. So everyone does as he likes, and if it weren't for a few serious warders like me, I don't know what would happen."

"While speaking, he had opened a small iron door fitted with a judas-hole. He introduced the visitors into an enclosure whose meager grass was shaded by a few stunted trees. That, no doubt, was the magnificent garden for fresh air treatments pompously advertised by the prospectus. Some thirty inmates were there, some gesticulating and talking to themselves, others prey to a bleak depression.

Isidora had drawn closer to Harry Dorgan. She felt a construction in her heart. "My dear Harry," she murmured, "these visits to my brother, so guilty but so terribly punished, are so painful to me that I'm glad you're with me to help me support my dolorous emotion."

"Must I not share unhappiness with you as well as happiness?" the young man replied, squeezing the young woman's hand tenderly.

"There's my brother," she said, pointing along one of the sad garden's sandy pathways at a pale man dressed in black, whose attitude and physiognomy reflected a poignant sadness rather than madness.

Harry Dorgan felt a strange emotion, but, as he examined the inmate, a strange surprise took possession of him. Was that seemingly frail and timid individual really the audacious Baruch? It seemed impossible? "How he's changed!" he could not help saying to Isidora, as she took the invalid's hand gently and smiled at him.

The madman seemed very preoccupied by the presence of the engineer, who was invaded by a kind of anguish himself. Their gazes met, and one might have thought that a flash of lucidity passed through Baruch's vague gaze. He seemed to be making an extraordinary effort to remember where he had seen the visitor before and what his name was.

"How are you?" Isidora asked, solicitously

To Harry's great surprise, Baruch replied in a very rational manner: "I'm very poorly, Mademoiselle. I thought for a moment that I was going to get better, but then had a relapse. I no longer have my memory...I can no longer remember..."

"My dear Isidora," said the engineer, "let's no prolong our visit excessively. Aren't you worried that you might tire the patient?"

"No," she replied. "Today he seems to be better. He replied sensibly to my question. Who knows whether time and rest might not reignite the flame of reason? But how he's changed!"

"That's what I said just now."

There was a pause. Baruch picked up Isidora's umbrella and amused himself mechanically, like a child, writing in the sand of the pathway.

Suddenly, Harry uttered an exclamation of amazement. "Look, Isidora, at what he's just written!"

Surprised, the young woman read the clearly-traced words: *Joe Dorgan.*

"Perhaps he's mistaken me for my brother," the engineer murmured. "But I've got an idea." Taking a notebook and pencil from his pocket, he handed them to the patient. The latter did not have to be asked to write the words *Joe Dorgan* again, which he underlined with a complicated flourish.

"Why" exclaimed the engineer, almost snatching the notebook from the madman's hands, "that's astounding! Look, Isidora: he's just produced my brother's signature. It's incomprehensible. That's Joe's own writing, and his flourish."

"What does it signify?" murmured the young woman, utterly astonished. "Give the notebook and pencil back to him. We'll see."

Baruch did not hesitate to write again when he was invited to do so, but one might have thought that he did not know anything but the signature *Joe Dorgan*, He reproduced it several times, and then traced inconsequential words: *memory...dead...doctor...*

"You know Joe Dorgan, then?" Isidora asked him.

"Yes...Joe Dorgan..." He repeated, dazedly.

"Write *Baruch Jorgell*."

He obeyed meekly, but to Harry's increasing surprise, the words "Baruch Jorgell" were written in the handwriting of Joe Dorgan.

"There's a strange mystery in this!" the engineer exclaimed. "I need to clear it up. I daren't take my thought to its conclusion..."

"Let's not try to explain the inexplicable," said Isidora, profoundly troubled. "I've always said myself that there's a mystery here."

"It's time to go. I need to think hard about what I've just seen."

"Yes, you're right—let's go."

They took their leave of the inmate, who had now fallen back into bleak depression. The fugitive spark of lucidity that had shone momentarily was extinct. He scarcely seemed to perceive the departure of his visitors.

Obsequiously, doubtless scenting a tip, the chief warder was waiting for Harry and Isidora at the door to the garden. While he was escorting them through the unkempt pathways to the main entrance, the engineer abruptly said: "I'm convinced that if the madman were in the hands of skilled specialists, removed from the promiscuity of the lunatics, he'd eventually be cured, and then we'd have the key to the enigma."

"I'll do my best to get him out of here," the young woman stammered, agitatedly. "I'm sure, too, that my brother is curable."

"There's one problem with that," the chief warder put in, "Which is that Mr. Baruch Jorgell, having been condemned to death, can't leave here."

"But the director will be compensated," the young woman objected.

"It's impossible. It's not a question of compensation. The law's the law. The director is responsible for his prisoner, and if we applied the rules strictly, he'd be locked up in a cell equipped with iron bars. It's only as a favor that he's permitted to remain with the placid inmates."

Isidora made no reply to that statement, which brought back cruel memories and reminded her that, so far as society was concerned, Baruch was still a criminal.

A few minutes later, she got back into the automobile, where Mrs. MacBarlott was waiting for her impatiently.

The return to New York was silent. The engineer could not help wondering, anxiously, whether it really was the murderer Baruch that he had just visited.

VI. A Jovial Reception

As it was every morning, the exercise hall of the Gorilla Club was in full animation. Jugglers, athletes, riders and trained animals were ardently plunged into their work under the benevolent surveillance of the illustrious John Sleary and his no less illustrious friend, the clown Bombridge.

Oscar Tournesol, who had made rapid progress since his arrival at the club and for whom his teachers had high hopes, was occupied in executing out a series of perilous somersaults clad in a fur adapted to his figure, which gave him the appearance of a great ape, when John Sleary, his face very animated, came to tell him that a gentleman of rare distinction was asking for him in the office.

"He's...*heu heu*...certainly someone belonging...*heu heu*...to the Old World aristocracy," he said. "He's wearing an embroidered shirt, a made-to-measure suit and arrived in a very luxurious...*heu heu*...auto."

Without taking off his picturesque disguise, Oscar hastened to follow the director to the office situated near the entrance, and there found himself unexpectedly face to face with his compatriot and friend Agénor Marmousier. They shook hands effusively, and their first concern was to get rid of Mr. Sleary, who was obstinate in wanting to have his visitor take a glass of gin.

"That old drunk is tiresome," said Oscar. "He's so steeped in alcohol that I'm sure he'd catch fire like a punch if one touched him with a lighted match."

Agénor seemed so preoccupied that he paid no heed to the strange costume that his friend was wearing, which was completed by a cardboard head with a hideous mask, tipped back like a hood for the time being.

"My dear Oscar, I've come to confide my embarrassment to you. I find myself in a singular situation. And to complete the difficulty, Mr. Jorgell, Harry Dorgan and Miss Isidora have set off by auto to meet your friends Andrée and Frédérique and their fiancés, who are coming back from New Orleans without have obtained any result from their research."

"I expected that," Oscar murmured. "But what's the matter?"

"I'll tell you. I've talked to you many times about my benefactor, Lord Astor Burydan, who possesses the imagination of a poet and the generosity of a prince, in whose company I spent the happiest three years of my life."

"But you told me that he was dead—that he's perished in the wreck of the *City of Frisco*."

"Fortunately, he isn't—but Lord Burydan, which only astonishes me slightly in his respect, is presently in the strangest of situations. Here, read this, and you'll be more rapidly informed."

Agénor handed the hunchback a copy of the *New York Sun*, in which there was an article headlined:

DRAMA ON THE MISSISSIPPI
PRETENDED LORD THROWS STOKER OF YACHT TO FEED ALLIGATORS
TWO DANGEROUS LUNATICS

The beginning of the sensational article contained a slightly exaggerated account of the events we have seen unfold aboard the *Arkansas*. It recounted the arrest of Lord Burydan and the Indian Kloum. The two fugitives had initially been locked up in the prison in New Orleans, but Lord Burydan had demanded to see the English ambassador from New York and had made a great fuss. The English consul in New Orleans having supported his affirmations on principle, the lord and his companion had been sent under escort to New York. The eccentric lord, who had highly-placed and powerful connections in the diplomatic community had not doubted that once he had arrived in the capital of the Union, justice would be done.

Unfortunately, the ambassador had shown an extraordinary ill will, and, as Lord Burydan had no papers to prove his identity, he had been locked up with his so-called accomplice in Greenaway Lunatic Asylum while waiting for a deportation order to be drawn up.

What the newspaper did not say was that one of the English ambassador's attachés was the son of a distant relative of Lord Burydan, who, on the news of his decease, had been provisionally put in possession of his immense fortune. In those conditions, the eccentric had a good chance of a long stay in the padded cells of the Asylum, where, on express instructions, he had been immediately straitjacketed as a dangerous madman.

"You know," said Agénor, when the hunchback had finished reading the article, "that during the shipwreck I succeeded in saving Lord Burydan's papers, which I was carrying. As anyone would have done in my place, I hastened to take those papers to the English ambassador, but I was given a poor welcome and virtually thrown out, with the advice not to get mixed up in matters that don't concern me. Very surprised, I went to the Lunatic Asylum. They wouldn't even let me in, and I was very insolently told that I must be an accomplice of the two internees if I wanted to see them. It's absolutely necessary that I help my friend and enable him to escape from that asylum. For them not to take account of my claims, he must have powerful enemies. If I don't make haste setting him free, he might be taken to some provincial hospice where it will be impossible for me to find him."

"Wait for Fred Jorgell to get back."

"I can't wait. I'd never forgive myself if any delay on my part caused my benefactor to come to harm."

"I understand. But how can I help?"

For a few moments, Agénor studied Oscar's ape costume attentively. "Well," he said, "by means of your disguise."

"I don't understand."

46

"Here's my plan: I'll get you locked up in the Lunatic Asylum."

"What!" Oscar exclaimed, his hump quivering.

"Don't be astonished, and hear me out. You're agile; it must be child's play for you to scale a wall or get over a gate?"

"Of course."

"Well, it's a matter of getting Lord Burydan and the Indian out. I'll give you a file, a revolver and half a dozen hundred-dollar bills. If you don't succeed with all that, you're unworthy of the high opinion I have of you."

"I'm a Parisian," said Oscar, swelling up. "Although it doesn't look very easy, I'll try it. But I'll have to make my excuses to Mr. Sleary and tell him that you're taking me on holiday."

After half an hour of conversation, Oscar, slightly hesitant at first, had become enthusiastic about the highly original plan, which could only have been hatched in the brain of a poetic fantasist like Agénor Marmousier.

After various preparations, the two friends got into an automobile and had themselves taken to Greenaway Lunatic Asylum. Oscar was still in his ape costume, and the hideous cardboard mask that he had pulled down over his face completed the disguise miraculously.

As they were about to get out in front of the establishment's gilded gate, Oscar said to his companion: "I hope to bring you news soon, but I recommend, above all, that you not breathe a word of this adventure to Mademoiselles Frédérique and Andrée or their fiancés. I've promised them not to do anything that doesn't have the objective of finding Monsieur Bondonnat, and I'm breaking my word in order to help you out by letting myself get locked up in that asylum.

Agénor made the promise that his friend demanded of him; they both went gravely to the concierge's lodge and then headed for the director's study. In his amazement, the concierge had not recognized Agénor as the gentleman who had wanted to talk to Lord Burydan a few hours earlier.

They rang, and it was Mr. Palmer himself who came to open up to them, very annoyed at having been disturbed in the work of studying the form in the sporting newspapers, to which he devoted himself before going to the racecourse, as was his praiseworthy habit.

At the sight of the quadrumane accompanying Agénor, he frowned. "What's the meaning of this practical joke?" he growled.

"It's not a joke," said Agénor, gravely. "I've brought you a client—a paying client."

Mr. Palmer smiled benevolently.

"Yes," said Agénor, "my unfortunate nephew, whom you see clad in this ridiculous disguise, has the awkward but inoffensive mania of believing himself to be an ape. He spends his time climbing trees, cracking nuts and making hideous grimaces. I don't doubt, though, that a few weeks of treatment will bring him back to complete rationality."

"You can be sure of it," said Mr. Palmer, whose quick imagination was already working on a new series of bets. "But it's customary, you know, to pay three months in advance, at a hundred dollars a month."

Without the slightest objection, Agénor handed over three banknotes. Mr. Palmer caused them to disappear into the depths of his waistcoat with the skill of a professional conjuror; then, forgetting the presence of his visitors he darted a radiant eye over the sporting journals, annotated in blue pencil, and murmured between his teeth; "I'll definitely bet on the favorite; that's sufficient."

"If it's not sufficient..." Agenor said, having great difficulty maintaining his seriousness.

"No, a thousand thanks—I was thinking about something else. You say that the madman is inoffensive?"

"Absolutely."

"That's good. I'll proceed with his installation personally, and I guarantee that he'll be better in no time." And he bid farewell to Agénor, who suppressed a strong desire to laugh.

During this dialogue Oscar had remained in a corner, pretending not to hear the conversation, but as soon as Agenor had gone he began to dance around, leaping over the furniture and ripping up the newspapers that chanced to come to hand.

Mr. Palmer, vaguely anxious, took refuge as far away from the ape as possible and rang for one of the warders. One of those functionaries, clad in the yellow uniform of the establishment, put his head around the door. It was the chief warder, who had served Isidora and her fiancé as a guide during their last visit to the Lunatic Asylum.

"Rugby," said the director, with a disgusted expression. "Take this gorilla to some padded cell or other and begin by putting him on bread and water to teach him to live. Oh, my lad, I'll teach you to play the monkey—just you wait."

"Is he dangerous?"

"Harmless, completely harmless—and what's more, he's a paying client."

"Very well, sir—but I need to tell you something..."

"What is it now?" asked Mr. Palmer, furiously.

"The inmates are refusing to eat the black pudding."

"Then give them salted herring. We still have half the stock that I bought at auction last month."

"They don't want salted herring either. They say that it gives them a terrible thirst, and there isn't any more beer in the cellar. The brewer refuses to make any more deliveries on credit."

"Oh, damn all these crackpots! They really are very difficult. For now, try to get them to settle for black pudding and salted herring, and give them water with a little whisky in it to drink. I'm going racing. I have some hot tips. If I win, the lunatics will have a nice horsemeat roast this evening, with potatoes, and beer if they want it."

"But sir..."

"Enough! I don't have time to listen to your nonsense. Take your gorilla and get out."

The hunchback, who found that scene infinitely amusing, followed the warder meekly, but before leaving the room he took care to tip over a bottle of ink, the contents of which inundated all Mr. Palmer's papers.

While the latter was cursing and swearing, Oscar followed the warder, who was secretly laughing, and allowed himself to be taken to an inner courtyard almost entirely surrounded by barred cells. The warder opened one of them and shoved him inside brutally, not without gratifying him with a kick.

"There!" he said. "Stay here! You can play the ape at your ease."

Oscar looked around and saw a narrow room furnished with a camp-bed, a stool and a water-jug, on top of which was placed a ration of bread.

"This is nice!" he exclaimed. "I wonder how they treat the inmates who can't pay and aren't inoffensive?"

He spent the rest of the day very sadly, and was quite surprised when, that evening, he was brought a slice of roast meat surrounded by potatoes and accompanied by a pint of beer. He assumed that Mr. Palmer must have won.

After his meal, which the warder watched, the latter, who seemed to be in a better mood than in the morning, designed to wish him goodnight and left him to meditate on his bizarre situation without a candle. Soon, a bell announced that everyone in the establishment ought to go to sleep. Oscar was only waiting for that moment to get to work.

First, he took from the inside pockets of his ape costume a minuscule electric torch, flat in shape, a screwdriver and a file. In the blink of an eye, he had unscrewed the lock of his cell with the screwdriver. Once in the courtyard, he reflected. It was obvious that Lord Burydan had to be in one of the neighboring cells. Putting out his light he knocked on one of the doors; he obtained no reply. He knocked on another, then another, and then a fourth. He was beginning to despair and wonder whether the man he sought might be in another part of the establishment, and it was without any great expectation that he shook his fist at the fifth door—but to his great joy, a cultured voice replied from within: "Who's there? What varlet is permitting himself to disturb my noble sleep?"

"Shh!" said Oscar. "Are you Lord Burydan?"

"Why, yes, but…"

"Shh, I tell you. "I've come on behalf of Monsieur Agénor Marmousier."

The eccentric lord could hardly retain a cry of joy. "Dear Agénor!" he exclaimed. "He's alive! How glad I am that he escaped the shipwreck!"

"Don't shout so loudly. I've been sent by your friend to set you free, but be prudent, and don't be surprised by the bizarre costume in which you'll see me dressed."

"Good—I'm all ears."

"Put your hand between two of the bars of the opening at the bottom of the door. I'll give you three objects: a file, a screwdriver and an electric torch. With that you can be free in ten minutes."

The noble lord did not need the invitation to be repeated. Oscar heard the screwdriver scraping; soon the lock came away and the door opened.

The two new friends exchanged a cordial handshake, and then started searching for Kloum's cell; he was liberated in the same manner.

"Now," said Oscar, "we just have to get over the wall or through the gate."

"But the wall is eighteen feet high," said Lord Burydan, and I'm still suffering from an injury to my leg. It seems to me to be preferable to get hold of the keys that the warder always carries attached to his belt. I already know that the garden door lets out into a deserted side-street. We need the key to that door."

"We need to get the warder to come here."

"How?"

"By uttering ferocious howls and lighting your electric torch."

This stratagem was a complete success. After ten minutes of howls accompanied by flashes of light, the fugitives heard a key grating in the lock of the courtyard door. Immediately, they switched off their torch and hid in a dark corner. A warder—but not the chief warder—went past them without seeing them. As soon as he had gone by, the impassive and silent Kloum grabbed him around the throat, gagged him with his handkerchief and tied him up securely. The man was then thrown in the cell that Oscar had occupied. The electric torch was lit again and the vociferations recommenced. The trick was an excellent one, for a second warder was captured in the same fashion, and then a third who came to look for the first two. Finally, it was the turn of the chief warden, who, after a brief struggle, went to join his colleagues in the cell.

Kloum took the keys that were attached to the functionary's belt, while Oscar exclaimed, joyfully: "The affair's in the bag. Now, it only remains to get out."

"One moment," said Lord Burydan. "I don't want the passage through this establishment of the man they call the 'eccentric lord' to end without some noble deed. I'm not leaving without giving my colleagues, the lunatics, a good meal."

Oscar attempted to raise a few timid objections, but Lord Burydan cut him off and demonstrated to him clearly that such a meal was all the more indispensable because the inmates were almost dying of hunger, reduced as they had been, for several weeks to a diet of scraps and spoiled tinned food.

The methodical takeover of the establishment by the three companions continued, and to begin with, they took possession of the concierge's lodge. The latter, surprised in his sleep beside his wife, was promptly rendered harmless

The threat of the revolver that Oscar was carrying and Lord Burydan's solid fists rapidly reckoned with the other warders, surrounded in the lodgings they occupied, and Kloum, calmly going out of the main gate, jumped into a cab, giving the driver the address of a restaurant that was open all night. He returned half an hour later with the elements of a Pantagruelesque supper: hams as pink as the modest cheeks of young maidens, phenomenal sausages, tasty steaks and truffled poultry, not to mention several baskets of wines of various vintages, including champagne.

While the Indian fulfilled the functions of head waiter, Lord Burydan and Oscar opened the doors of the dormitories one by one and announced that, unusually, the honorable Mr. Palmer, having had a big win, was offering all his boarders a celebratory feast.

That news excited a real enthusiasm. In the blink of an eye, everyone was out of bed; the electric lights were switched on throughout the building; them Mr. Palmer's private domicile was invaded and it was from there that the napkins, embroidered tablecloths, crystal glasses and porcelain crockery deemed indispensable to the feast were obtained The lunatics laid the table, and then each one took his place there.

The party soon presented the most lively and animated of spectacles. To the great surprise of Lord Burydan, who threw himself into it wholeheartedly, the guests, apart from a few bursts of piercing laughter and a few excessively sharp replies, maintained a perfect decorum. The men offered drinks to their neighbors and passed them plates with an exquisite politeness. One might have thought that they were in an ordinary restaurant.

As the wine went to those disequilibrated heads, however, a change took place in the attitude of the guests. They had not reached the dessert when the cat-man leapt on to the table, arched his back and began executing an entire scale of the most joyful mewling in the world. The automobile-man, who went around all day swathed in pneumatic tires, loudly demanded gasoline; he was given a siphon of soda water from which to drink and declared that he had a full tank and would soon be setting off. A fat lady that thought she was a mutton-chop offered a knife and fork to let neighbors in order that they could sample a piece of her plump shoulder. A few charitable lunatics, thinking that they had been wounded in the Balkan wars, transformed Mr. Palmer's embroidered napkins and tablecloth into slings. A few of them sang hymns, and others drinking songs.

The bacchanal had become indescribable. Crockery was smashed for amusement, and bottles thrown out of the windows. Someone had just proposed organizing a dance when the honorable Mr. Palmer, who had come in quietly through the small door in the gate, to which he had a key, and who had been filled with astonishment to find his establishment lit up at such a hour, appeared at the door of the room where the feast was being held. In the presence of that astonishing spectacle, his eyes widened and his face expressed the most complete stupor, but soon, recognizing the shreds of his ripped-up table linen and the debris of his plates and glassware, the uttered a cry of rage and his face turned scarlet.

"Long live Mr. Palmer!" shouted the guests, enthusiastically.

"Rogues! Thieves! Bandits!" he howled, drawing his Browning. "You'll pay for this!" And, threatening the lunatics with his revolver, he tried to retreat in the direction of the door.

That was no longer a possibility. At a signal from Lord Burydan, Kloum had grabbed his wrist and disarmed him. He continued to utter terrible threats, but the inmates surrounded him, howling, and executing a crazy saraband around him.

"This is the wretch who made us eat salted herring and black pudding!"

"Hang him!"

"Roast him with potatoes!"

"Tar and feather him!"

"Yes, that's it!" cried a dozen voices, supportively.

And immediately, someone went down to the cellar for a barrel of tar and all the feather pillows and mattresses that could be found were brought from the dormitory.

Mr. Palmer, undressed in spite of his supplications, was carefully tarred and feathered. One might have thought him a chicken miraculous escaped from a kitchen while in the process of being plucked. He was such a pitifully comical sight that all the lunatics burst into frightful laughter.

"We ought to feather the warders," someone suggested.

This proposal was warmly applauded, and everyone headed precipitately for the cells.

No one remained in the hall but Lord Burydan, the Indian, Oscar and one sad, timid inmate dressed in black, who was hiding behind the curtains at the window.

"That's enough, now," said Lord Burydan. "Let's go."

"Yes," said Oscar. "It's a good time."

All three headed toward the garden alongside the wall. They did not notice that the black-clad inmate was following them slowly, thirty paces behind.

The day after the evening on which these memorable events unfolded, Agénor was slightly surprised not to receive news from Oscar, but he was not unduly worried. He thought that the hunchback must have found it impossible to write, and that he would doubtless receive a letter the following day. In any case, the poet's attention was reclaimed by Fred Jorgell and Isidora, who had returned sooner than expected in company with the French quartet.

That morning, too, Isidora found a letter in the post that had arrived two days earlier and whose tenor caused her some anxiety. It was signed by Rugby, the chief warder of the Lunatic Asylum. It said, in substance, that the establishment had gone from bad to worse since the young woman's last visit. There was no longer any organization or discipline; furthermore, the director, Mr. Palmer, betting all the money he could get his hands on at the racecourse, was no longer paying the suppliers. The inmates and warders were severely malnourished, when they were fed at al. The Lunatic Asylum had become a true powder-keg, and Rugby foresaw a catastrophe. He considered it his duty to warn the honorable Miss Jorgell of the state of affairs, in order that she might take suitable measures, and he declared by way of conclusion that the young woman would be grateful for his vigilance and devotion.

That letter alarmed Isidora so much that immediately after lunch she went to Greenaway in the company of Frédérique, who had kindly agreed to accompany her.

They were unable to get into the establishment, however. The gates were locked and barricaded internally. There were no warders to be seen. From the top of the walls, on which they were perched, the lunatics were making threatening gestures.

They fled, fearfully, to the nearest police station, where they recounted what they had just seen. The senior officer, knowing that he was dealing with Fred Jorgell's daughter, hastened to respond to her request and sent a dozen men, accompanied by a locksmith.

The gate was forced and the policemen penetrated into the establishment. First of all, they saw Mr. Palmer and the warders, who, clad in nothing but their improvised plumage, had sought refuge in the trees of the driveway. The unfortunates were collected in order to procure them the cares necessitated by their condition.

It required several hours to take control of the buildings where the inmates were retrenched, and it was only with great difficulty that they could be returned to their cells. In spite of diligent searches, however, no trace could be found of Lord Burydan, Kloum the Indian, or Baruch Jorgell, any more than of the ape-man whose name was unknown and who must surely have been one of the principal instigators of the revolt.

8. THE PHANTOM AUTOMOBILE

I. Mr. Steffel is Unhappy

Mr. Steffel, the chief of the New York Police, was in a very bad mood. He was striding back and forth in his luxurious office, brandishing a report that he had just received from the officer in charge of the station at Greenaway.

"Truly," he shouted, "it's enough to make one lose one's head! I'm overwhelmed. I need twice as many men. Not a day goes by when the newspapers aren't poking fun at me with regard to the famous association of the Red Hand." Nervously, he crumpled the report he was clutching in his hand, and added: "How the hell can I destroy the bandits of the Red Hand? They're better organized than the police. There are times, in truth, when I'm tempted to believe it! Not to mention that there are not a few functionaries in my organization, major and minor, who are in the pay of the bandits! Truly, it's depressing. There are days when I'm tempted to hand in my resignation."

Mr. Steffel deposited the report, the reading of which had irritated him, among the piles of paper cluttering his desk, but he had not finished letting out his ill humor. It had only required the revolt of the Lunatic Asylum's inmates to complete the series.

The police chief ran for one of his aides.

"Fetch Agent Grogmann, he said to the office boy who responded.

A minute later, a red-faced individual with a long russet moustache and a pot belly came into the director's office. There was a naïve smile on his affable features.

"So," said Mr. Steffel, impatiently, "You were present at the siege at the Lunatic Asylum. You can give me precise details?"

"Yes, sir. It was necessary to display genuine bravery to get into each wing of the building. The inmates threw all kinds of objects at us: bits of wood, rotten apples, even cooking-pots, chamber-pots and old shoes."

"That's not what I'm asking!" exclaimed Mr. Steffel, shrugging his shoulders. "You seem very proud of having been bombarded with old boots and chamber pots, but it's nothing to brag about. Tell me the exact number of escapers and their descriptions."

"There are only four."

"Doubtless you think that's not enough. Go on..."

"Firstly there's the pretended Lord Burydan and Kloum, his Indian domestic. Then there's an unknown man who was admitted dressed as an ape..."

"An unknown man? So Mr. Palmer didn't take down his name and age, as the regulations require?"

"No, sir."

"That's good! Palmer will be called the account. Send him to my office as soon as he's been sufficiently soaped and rid of the tar and feathers with which he was coated. Who's the fourth escaper?"

"The famous Baruch Jorgell, the billionaire murderer."

Mr. Steffel's face was a picture of consternation. "That's very annoying," he murmured. "The papers will kick up a fuss; if I can't recapture the scoundrel within twenty-four hours they're bound to say that I've been bribed to let him escape."

"It might not be as easy as that to catch him," said Grogmann, tranquilly.

"It's all the same to you, of course!" exclaimed M. Steffel, exasperated. "It's not you who's responsible. I want all four of them caught today, you hear? You're the one I'm ordering to make the quadruple arrest, and I'm holding you responsible for it."

"But sir..."

"Shut up. Do you at least have a description of the escapers?"

"It's just that..." Grogmann stammered, hesitantly.

"What?"

"The description of Baruch Jorgell is bound to be in the old file. As for the madman disguised as an ape, I don't have one, nor of the other two. All I know is that Kloum is an Indian and that the fake Lord Burydan is a white man..."

"We're off to a fine start!" cried Mr. Steffel, thumping the table angrily. "You might as well have said straight out that you've nothing to go on. All the more so as even Baruch is said to have changed a great deal, and to have aged considerably, since his internment..."

Mr. Steffel was interrupted by the arrival of the office boy, who had brought him half a dozen letters and telegrams.

"Hand them over," he said, nervously.

Immediately, he opened a large envelope with red seal, but the contents of the letter must have been satisfactory, for as he read it his face cleared. When he finished the missive, which bore no date or signature and was written on a typewriter, he uttered a sigh of satisfaction.

"Well," he said, "fortunately, here's an anonymous denunciation that might save us a few futile steps." And he re-read, aloud: "The four lunatics who escaped from Greenaway have found refuge in a tavern in a suburb of New York mostly frequented by Indians and half-breeds: the Grand Wigwam at Tampton. The Redskin Kloum took his companions in flight there. If the police take appropriate measures, especially if they act without delay, they can lay their hands on them without any resistance."

Mr. Steffel rubbed his hands. "I certainly won't waste any time," he said. "Grogmann, take two squads of men and leave immediately. In the meantime,

I'll telephone the Tampton station to tell them to send out two or three squads to surround the Grand Wigwam—with which I'm quite familiar. It's notorious as a lair of vagabond Indians, drunks and bad lots of every sort."

Mr. Steffel did not have a moment's doubt about the accuracy of the information that had reached him in such a timely fashion in the anonymous note. He was so accustomed to denunciations of that sort that he was able to tell at a glance that this one was telling the truth.

The chief of police would, of course, have been quite astonished had he known that it was the Lords of the Red Hand themselves who were informing him so obligingly. It was, in fact, Cornelius who had sent the note. The diabolical doctor had thought that the best means having the four individuals whose revelations he feared so much under his control was to have them sent back to the Lunatic Asylum, where they would be at his mercy.

As soon as Grogmann had left to carry out the order he had just received, Mr. Steffel seized the receiver of the telephone set on the table and demanded to speak to the senior officer at the Tampton police station. At that moment, however, the office buy handed him a visiting card bearing the inscription: *Agénor Marmousier, Private Secretary to Mr. Fred Jorgell.*

"Send him in," said Mr. Steffel, immediately—and, assuming an expression that was both dignified and cheerful, he greeted the billionaire's representative and courteously offered him a chair.

"Monsieur," said Agénor, "I've come with regard to last night's revolt at Greenaway Lunatic Asylum..."

"And you're doubtless aware that Mr. Jorgell's son is one of the four fugitives who succeeded in getting over the establishment's wall..."

"That's precisely why I've come, but first of all, I should tell you that it's not the inmate's father who sent me. He has cursed his unworthy son once and for all and does not want to hear any mention of him under any pretext whatsoever."

"On whose behalf have you come, then?" asked the police chief, astonished.

"On behalf of Miss Isidora, Baruch's sister. Having more pity than the billionaire for the insane murderer, she is fearful that the poor fellow, lost in New York and not being in possession of his reason, might fall victim to some accident, and she begs you urgently to search for him and take him back, without any violence, to the establishment where he is receiving the care necessary to his condition." The poet deposited a small wallet on the desk. "Here," he added, "are a few hundred-dollar banknotes to stimulate the zeal of your agents."

Mr. Steffel threw the wallet carelessly into one of his desk drawers. "Thank the charming young lady on behalf of my men," he said, "but the reward isn't necessary..."

The police chief was interrupted by the sonorous ringing of his telephone.

"A moment, my dear Monsieur, if you'll permit?" he said to Agénor. Taking hold of the receiver he had put down when his visitor entered he said "Hello?.... You're the senior officer at Tampton... Excellent! It's a matter of having your men surround, without losing a moment, a den of Indians and half-breeds you've already been given orders to watch: the Grand Wigwam tavern... Yes, I know. That's where the all four of them are. Two squads have already set off, and will arrive from the south. Arrange your squads to the north, and don't let anyone pass! You can make the arrest at nightfall... Right, I'm counting on you. The arrests, especially those of Baruch Jorgell and Lord Burydan, are very important!"

Mr. Steffel hung up the receiver, and, turning with his most amiable smile to Agénor, who had gone pale on hearing those shreds of conversation, of which he had not missed a word, he said: "As I was saying, my dear sir, there's no need at all for Miss Isadora to offer a reward to my agents. We already know where the refugees from the Lunatic Asylum are. I've sent men to make the arrest. All our measures are in place. You can reassure Miss Isadora and tell her that her unfortunate brother will be treated with all possible care and taken back to the sanitarium where he is being treated without any violence."

Agénor hastened to take his leave of the public servant and as soon as he was outside police headquarters he leapt into a cab. He promised the driver five dollars and gave him the address of the Grand Wigwam tavern in Tampton.

"As long as I get there in time," he muttered, darting impatient glances at his watch as the minutes went by.

For half an hour, the cab, harness to a vigorous horse from the Far West, galloped through the dismal brick-and-concrete landscape of the New York suburbs. As they came over the top of a hill Agénor saw half a dozen policemen five hundred meters ahead of him, advancing at a steady pace under the leadership of a sergeant, who was none other than Mr. Grogmann.

The poet reflected momentarily. He could see an accumulation of sordid huts in the distance that looked more like a gipsy encampment than a dwelling of Yankee city-dwellers.

"Stop!" he shouted to the driver. "How far away from Tampton are we?"

"We've been in it for several minutes."

"And those buildings over there—is that the Grand Wigwam tavern?"

"Yes, we're just about to arrive there."

"That's all right—I don't need your services any longer."

Agénor got down, paid the driver and stated walking with long strides along the deserted road. He had to difficulty overtaking the small group of policemen, who were continuing to advance with typical British phlegm, like men confident, no matter what might happen, of drawing their pay at the end of the month.

Agénor's presence did not appear suspect to Grogmann, for he had seen him as he left Police Headquarters; the honest sergeant assumed that such a well-dressed gentleman following the same road as himself was doubtless a superior agent charged by Mr. Steffel with making the arrest of the four escaped lunatics personally.

II. The Grand Wigwam Tavern

When one had got to the other side of a worm-eaten door made of planks torn off packing-crates, for which strips of leather served as hinges, one found oneself in a long, low and smoky room in which the senses of sight and smell were equally disagreeably affected; a vile odor of smoked fish permeated the air, mingled with the odors of cheap alcohol and rancid grease. The smoke of pipes combined with that of the hearth, which escaped through a hole made in the roof after having saturated the atmosphere of the room, forming a fog so thick that one could not see further than three yards.

When the gaze became accustomed to the gloom, one distinguished barbaric panoplies hanging on the walls, which must once have belonged to some redoubtable chief. There were crowns of eagle feathers, necklaces made from the teeth of pumas or the claws of grizzly bears, bows, arrows and tomahawks, mingled with deerskin moccasins, and bracelets of seeds or glass beads. One also saw scalping knives, a few old-fashioned rifles, stone pistols, the antlers of elks and reindeer, a whole arsenal of little embroidered bags for carrying tobacco, and calumets, some of which—the oldest—were formed of hollow stones fitted with reed steam.

In addition to these panoplies, which covered the walls completely, the furniture consisted of a few rickety stools, straw mats and a set of shelves that supported a dozen bottles of whisky.

Such was the strange lair known in the locality as the Grand Wigwam Tavern. It was there that the Indians from two leagues around met to converse about matters concerning their race and, especially, to drink "firewater" until they fell down dead drunk.

The owner of the establishment in question, the only one of its kind, was an old squaw as desiccated, withered and black as a mummy. She was generally huddled by the fire, relentlessly smoking an old clay pipe that she had used for many years. The regulars of the establishment claimed that she owed her great longevity to the fuliginous atmosphere, and affirmed that she would never die, conserved as she was by the smoke, like kippered herrings and smoked hams.

The venerable matron's two daughters, two tall red-skinned creatures with blue-tinted hair, flat noses and long teeth, served the drinkers and, it was said, had much to do with the prosperity of the establishment.

The manageress of the Grand Wigwam being a distant cousin of Kloum's; the latter had had the idea of taking his friend to that lair, where they had a good chance of not being found. On leaving the Lunatic Asylum, therefore, they had headed straight for Tampton. They had arrived at daybreak, all four of them greatly fatigued by their sleepless night and all the excitement they had had.

I was not after leaving the Lunatic Asylum that Lord Burydan had perceived that a fourth inmate of the establishment had taken it into his head to follow them.

"What are we going to do with him?" Oscar had asked, who did not recognize the newcomer as the Baruch he had known in Monsieur de Maubreuil's house, so much had captivity and nature altered the work of the sculptor of human flesh.

"My word, I don't know." Lord Burydan had said.

Kloum, more categorical, had declared that it was necessary to get rid of the inconvenience at all costs, and, with a brief and imperious gesture, he had ordered the lunatic to get away as fast as possible.

It was then that the pseudo-Baruch had thrown himself to his knees before Lord Burydan and put his hands together in such a supplicant manner that the eccentric had been moved to profound pity.

"The poor devil seems harmless," he had said. "Let's keep him for now; later, we'll see."

Like a lost dog that attaches itself to the heels of the first friendly passer-by, the lunatic had marched meekly behind his companions.

A short distance from the Lunatic Asylum, the fugitives had been lucky enough to find a cab. The cabbie had imagined, on seeing Oscar's ape disguise, that he was dealing with people returning from some masquerade, and had let them climb into his vehicle without protest. It was in that fashion that they had reached Tampton, but they had been prudent enough to get down some distance away from the Grand Wigwam in order that no one would know where they were going.

Kloum and his friends had been warmly welcomed by the old squaw and her daughters, and Oscar had been able to take off his ape costume, which he had hung on the wall, where it did not seem out of place among the grizzly skins and the barbaric panoplies. The hunchback had put on some blue overalls that the Indian women had given him, which had been left there by Indians working in a nearby quarry.

"The first thing we have to do," declared Lord Burydan, "is rest. We can stay here all day; I don't think that anyone will come to look for us here. After dark, we'll leave."

The old Indian woman, informed of his decision by Kloum, let the four friends into an obscure closet annexed to the main room, from which it was only separated by a curtain made of a brightly-colored blanket. The fugitives threw themselves down on the mats with which the room was furnished and did not take long to fall profoundly asleep.

It was Kloum who woke up first. He was still snoring when a singular prickling sensation at the back of his head extracted him from his dreams. It was one of the Indian women, who, using a trick of her people, had tickled him gently over the ear. Kloum opened his eyes, without having made the slightest sound or pronouncing a single word. He saw one of the two sisters in front of him, who, putting a finger over her lips, signaled to him to look cautiously into the main room.

The Indian gently moved aside the blanket that served as a door and, a few yards away from a party of Indian quarrymen occupied in quaffing firewater in large gulps, he perceived Agénor in the course of negotiation, not without loud cries and gesticulations, with the old squaw, still impassive, her pipe in her teeth, beside the hearth.

Immediately, he uttered a cry of joy and woke Lord Burydan and the other sleepers. A moment later, the eccentric lord and his friend threw themselves, weeping, into one another's arms.

"My dear Agénor! How glad I am to see you again!"

"And me, who mourned our death!"

"Me too—I imagined that you'd perished in the shipwreck of the *City of Frisco!* But now, I hope, our troubles are over!"

"Alas, no!" Agénor replied, abruptly becoming grave. "Let's not lose any time in needless effusions, because you're seriously threatened, and that's why I'm here."

"What is it now?" Oscar asked.

"The house is surrounded by policemen, who found out where you're hiding—I don't know how. They'll be here in a quarter of an hour."

"Damn!" murmured Lord Burydan, discontentedly. "I have no intention of going back to prison or the madhouse!"

"We need to make a plan, and quickly," murmured Agénor, "but first, I'll give you back your papers, which I was able to save from the shipwreck. They're in this wallet, into which I've also slipped a few banknotes, in case of need."

In the meantime, Kloum was holding a discussion with the whisky-drinking Indians. After a few minutes, one of them hoisted himself up by his wrists through the hole that took the place of a chimney and climbed on to the roof. He did not take long to come back down, his expression anxious.

"Four troops of police," he explained, counting on his fingers. They're occupying all the roads leading away from the Grand Wigwam."

"Damn!" said Oscar. "What are we going to do?"

"My word, I don't have any idea," replied Lord Burydan. "We're not numerous enough, and not well enough armed, to fight our way out.

There were a few minutes of real anguish. Whichever way they went, flight was impossible, and the policemen, more easily distinguishable by the minute, where approaching with the implacable slowness of Destiny.

Suddenly, Kloum laughed silently, and point at a number of small hand-carts that the quarrymen had left there while they slaked their thirst.

Everyone understood. It was simply a matter of hiding inside the little vehicles and thus passing under the noses and beards of the policemen. They did not have a moment to lose, however, and it was first necessary to persuade the quarrymen to lend their assistance to the escape. Kloum's eloquence, supported by a few dollars, obtained that result without difficulty.

Agénor shook his friends' hands hastily.

"Above all," he advised Lord Burydan, "don't neglect to write to me and tell me where you are."

"I won't fail—all the more so as I have revelations to make to you."

"Yes," said Oscar. "We know where Monsieur Bondonnat is—Lord Burydan has been his companion in captivity."

"Where is he?"

"The Island of Hanged Men."

"And where's that?"

"I don't have time to explain it to you. My next letter will tell you everything in the greatest detail."

One last handshake as exchanged, and then the eccentric aristocrat and Oscar lay down in the bottom of the first handcart, while Kloum and their companion, who was still mute and docile, took their places in the second.

The two Indian women covered the fugitives' bodies with old blankets, over which the quarrymen scattered a few spadefuls of sand, in large enough quantity to sustain the illusion without preventing air from penetrating.

When those preparations were terminated, the Indians started pushing the handcarts along the rails with their habitual nonchalance, walking toward the squad of which the honest Grogmann was in command. The phlegmatic attitude of the Indians convinced the policeman completely. He did not have the slightest suspicion. He continued marching in the same majestic manner at the head of his men, in the direction of the Grand Wigwam tavern.

He arrived just as Agénor emerged and, still convinced that he was a senior policeman, he asked: "Have you seen them?"

"No," Agénor replied, shaking his head. "The birds have flown."

"Damn! Too bad! But I'll search anyway. These Redskins have diabolical ruses and our madmen might be hiding in some cellar or ventilation shaft."

"Yes, that's right—conduct a thorough search," said the poet, at hazard, taking the road back to New York without anyone raising any objection.

The policemen moved all the sordid rags that composed the drinking-den's furniture without discovering anything.

In the meantime, the four fugitives had arrived without difficulty in the granite quarry where the Indians worked, which was five hundred meters away. They hastened to emerge from their uncomfortable vehicles, and thanked their saviors warmly.

Night was falling rapidly. Henceforth, all danger had disappeared. It was, therefore unhurriedly, albeit by means of a path that permitted them to avoid the main road, that Oscar Tournesol and his friends arrived at Tampton railway station. There, Lord Burydan, who had already made a plan, bought four second-class tickets to Montreal, for he knew Canada well, where he possessed immense properties.

Before the train had even left the station, the four fugitives had taken their places around a table in the restaurant car and were in the middle of ordering a substantial meal when Oscar suddenly uttered a cry of amazement and sat there wide-eyed and open-mouthed, his hands trembling, as if he had just had a vision.

"What's the matter?" Lord Burydan asked, anxiously.

With his finger, Oscar pointed to the road, which was only separated from the railway track by a wooden barrier, at which an enormous red and black automobile had just stopped. At the steering-wheel, as if haloed by the dazzling light of the headlights, was a man with harsh and energetic features; and inside, there was an old man with a clean-shaven face and the profile of bird of prey, whose hypnotic eyes seemed to be scintillating behind the lenses of gold-rimmed spectacles.

"Look," said the hunchback, with indescribable emotion. "The young man driving that automobile is the same one, I'm sure of it, who took part in the kidnapping of Monsieur Bondonnat and who knocked me out with the butt of his gun."

At that moment, however, the train pulled away, and a few minutes later, the mysterious automobile—"the phantom automobile," as Oscar was already calling it, mentally—had disappeared, hidden by a bend in the track.

III. For a Woman

The billionaire Fred Jorgell firmly believed that, if one wanted to be served well, it was necessary to pay one's servants well. Thus, all those close to him, from the engineers of the Lightning Steamship Company to the humblest domestics, were paid magnificent wages. Even the concierge of his palace was an important individual, and the annual salary he received, including benefits of various sorts, equaled the salary of a general or a senior civil servant in Old Europe.

The concierge in question was named Edward Edmond, and he was Irish by birth. He had been in Fred Jorgell's service for nearly ten years; the latter had never had the slightest cause for complaint about him and held him in high esteem. It was to Edward Edmond that the important function devolved of receiving the billionaire's voluminous correspondence and sorting out the letters, and he carried it out to general satisfaction.

Physically, Edward Edmond was a man of commanding appearance and a jovial expression. His symmetrical features were framed by blond side-whiskers and the ensemble of his physiognomy gave an impression of frankness, good health and good humor that made him seem instantly likeable to everyone.

Edward Edmond declared himself that he was the happiest of men. He had no worries; his work was not very onerous; and he was able to put by considerable sums every year. He was waiting patiently for his savings to reach a certain figure that he had fixed in order to retire to his homeland and lead the peaceful existence of a man with a private income.

Abruptly, the character of that model servant changed completely. Edward Edmond became melancholy and distracted. He only carried out his functions in a mechanical fashion and ceased to talk about his plan to go and live in Ireland, which had once been the bedrock of his conversation. One almost insignificant event had sufficed to trouble the bliss of that serene existence.

One evening, prompted by having nothing to do, Edward Edmond had gone into a music hall almost exclusively frequented by sailors of all nations. He was extraordinarily amused by the grimaces of Irish comedians dressed in naval uniforms and grotesquely coifed in straw top hats. Then there was a choir of black musicians in red and green coats who played the banjo and performed eccentric dances. There was also a human serpent who, by dint of making himself thin by degrees, succeeded in getting inside an enormous crystal carafe, in which his made-up face appeared as hideous as that of a pickled fetus in a jar. There was a Canadian sharpshooter with an infallible aim, who shattered the clay pipe that his associate was placidly smoking with a single bullet, at a range of third meters.

The audience, however, gave the most tumultuous acclaim to the celebrated Dorypha, the Spanish dancer, whose name was displayed in enormous capital letters on the poster. When she appeared, a thunder of bravos greeted her entrance, and then everyone fell silent. Even Edward Edmond, at the sight of the creature in question, was agitated by a strange frisson.

Dorypha was no older than twenty. She was a blond gypsy with huge dark devouring eyes beneath the velvet of long lashes. With her neckline cut to the pink tips of her small breasts, she wore a long bodice that hugged her wasp-like waist and emphasized the roundness of her buttocks, almost tangible to the gaze beneath a short black silk skirt with gold spangles.

She danced the tango, accompanied by two guitars and a mandolin, which seemed to be moaning amorously when the young woman, voluptuously tilted backwards, made her hips roll, suggesting, with a series of passionate mimes, all the tortures and delights of voluptuous embraces. Sometimes she pretended to fall, like a woman abandoning herself to her lover's arms, and then stiffened completely, her flesh vibrant, half-swooning.

Edward Edmond had never experienced such an overwhelming sensation. He never took his eyes off the large rose pinned in her blonde hair, reddened as if by the fires of hell. His tongue stuck to his palate; his eyes glittered with lust. He thought that a single kiss from that woman would be capable of rejuvenating old men and waking the dead asleep in their tombs.

Throughout the hall, moreover, the breathless spectators were delirious, their hearts pounding and their heads reeling at the sight of the blonde witch, who seemed to embody within herself all the sugary spice of femininity, all the sweetness and all the impetuous brutality of caresses.

The dance finished amid the din of ovations, and Señora[2] Dorypha, her breasts moist with the fatigue of the dance, descended from the stage, rosy and smiling, to make her collection. She slid through the groups like a snake, and her body exhaled a heady perfume of carnation, pepper and praline. Sous, piastres and dollars rained down like hail into the Basque drum that she held out with an ingenuous smile, and she thanked people graciously, almost timidly, her long black lashes modestly lowered, while the corners of her red, greasy and arched lips were raised in an expression of deceptive roguishness that belied the false candor of her gaze.

For his part, Edward Edmond gave her a gold eagle, and was thanked with the most seductive flutter of her eyes. He sensed at that moment that the woman could do whatever she wanted with him, that he was entirely hers, and that nothing could extract from his heart the passion that had grown there with lightning rapidity and had taken root forever.

---

[2] Here and elsewhere I have retained Le Rouge's invariable practice of referring to unmarried women of Spanish descent as "Señora" rather than "Señorita."

From then on he never quit the music hall. He overwhelmed the beautiful Dorypha with gifts, bouquets and jewels; ever provocative, however, she refused herself—but not without a certain enticing smile, which, more eloquent than any words, promised that her resistance might not be eternal.

After a month, Edward Edmond's savings had been profoundly eaten away, but he had triumphed. Dorypha was his, and when, one morning, he emerged from the dancer's bedroom, his back aching from a fatigue that was simultaneously dolorous and voluptuous, he regarded himself as the luckiest of men.

A few weeks passed thus. The Irishman led an ardent, feverish existence, which left him no time to think or to reflect, and he was utterly surprised when, at the bank where he had deposited his money, he was told one day that nothing remained but an insignificant sum. He went to tell Dorypha about that misfortune, but the dancer greeted him with a burst of mocking laughter.

"I'm very sorry for you," she said, "but if you're poor, you can't continue to be my lover. I have all sorts of desires and all sorts of needs. I need money—a lot of money. Have I not been faithful thus far? Find money, and I'll continue to be for you what I have been in the past...but a man who doesn't have the power to satisfy my caprices isn't worthy to have me for a mistress."

"That's all right," murmured the Irishman, somberly. "I'll get some of that accursed money!"

That day, he borrowed a hundred dollars from one of his friends, went to a gambling-den he knew, played and won—but that resource was precarious. A week had not gone by when the "sharks," who had let him win at first in order to get him hooked, had plundered everything he had left.

Dorypha took no count of his sacrifices. The money that cost him so dear she spent on whims, on useless objects she often threw into a corner without even having looked at them. She said to him, in a tranquil tone: "What do you expect? It isn't my fault; it's the way I'm made. If you can't do it, leave; there's no lack of idolaters eager to take your place."

Literally bewitched, Edward Edmond had arrived at the worst expedients. One day, having occasion to be in Isidora's apartment, he stole a diamond ring the young woman had accidentally left in a cup. A few hours later he sold the trinket to a fence for five hundred dollars, a quarter of its value. Furnished with that money, he went to the gambling-den, convinced that he could win a large sum and buy back the ring.

As he crossed the threshold of the long room where the sharpers of all nations were playing baccarat, bridge and écarté in a tumult of vociferations, outbursts of laughter and insults, however, he was assailed by a baleful premonition. He sat down nevertheless at a card table and immediately, the sharks circled around his banknotes. Two hours had not gone by before he had not only lost the five hundred dollars but was a further hundred dollars in debt. He was desperate.

66

I'm finished! he thought. *There's nothing left for me to do but blow my brains out.*

He took a photograph of Dorypha from his pocket in order to look at it one last time, furtively, in a corner. Then, making sure that his Browning was in his overcoat pocket, he sidled into a corridor that led to a dismal little garden behind the gambling-den. He was as calm now as a man whose resolution has been made. The icy night air refreshed his burning forehead delightfully, and he listened as if in a dream to the distant voices of the gamblers, which seemed to be coming from the other world.

"Come on!" he murmured, effortfully. "It's all settled; it's necessary to get it over with! Adieu, Dorypha!"

He took his weapon from his pocket and made sure that it was functioning as it should.

At that moment, however, a shadow leapt out of the bushes. Edward Edmond felt his wrist crushed by an iron hand. He dropped the Browning without even trying to resist, so unexpectedly had he been gripped.

Letting him go almost as abruptly as he had seized him, his attacker picked up the revolver, which had fallen in the grass. He put it in his pocket and said, in a very calm tone: "I need to talk to you, and I forbid you to kill yourself before having heard what I have to say."

"What do you want with me?" murmured Edward Edmond, in a strangled voice. "Nothing can interest me now."

"Well, that depends," the unknown man sniggered. "Know that I'm aware of your situation, Master Edward Edmond. You've got into debt because of a woman. You've stolen a ring from your mistress, Miss Isadora."

"What does that have to do with you? Anyway, it's not true..."

"It's perfectly true."

"Mind your own business. I don't know you, and I haven't asked you for anything."

"Well, I know you and I have something to offer you. What would you say if, right now, I put a thousand-dollar bill in your hand?"

As Edward Edmond remained silent, the unknown man continued in a more urgent tone: "What would you say if I enabled you to earn a similar sum every month? Would you still want to commit suicide like an imbecile? The beautiful Dorypha would laugh at you, and she'd certainly have good reason."

"Don't mock my misfortune. If you have a serious proposition to make, make it quickly."

The unknown man had taken a banknote from his wallet, which he rubbed between his fingers, teasingly.

"The proof that my proposition is quite serious," he said, "is that it only depends on a word from you whether or not you get hold of this thousand dollars immediately."

"What do I have to do?"

"Not much," said the unknown man, lowering his voice. "You're in Fred Jorgell's service. It's simply a matter of permitting me to examine the letters he receives and giving some of them to me."

"That's impossible!" Edward Edmond exclaimed, in a last revolt of half-vanquished probity. "Ask for something else, but I can't betray my master. Fred Jorgell has been very good to me..."

"It's not as serious as you imagine," said the tempter, continuing to fondle the banknote with a seductive rustle of silk. "You won't cause any harm to Fred Jorgell. I'm simply a private detective working for an agency. I need certain information. If you don't want to procure it for me, I'll get it some other way, that's all."

Edward Edmond was more than half-persuaded. "If I thought," he murmured, "that it wouldn't cause any prejudice..."

"None. Your conscience really is too timorous. Everyone does it. Fred Jorgell knows full well that his every step is watched, that al his letters are read by agents in the service of his financial rivals, but he doesn't care; no one can do any serious harm to a man like him..."

That argument was decisive. The Irishman had often heard Fred Jorgell reasoning in a similar fashion in his presence.

"Well, all right," Dorypha's loved exclaimed, abruptly. "I accept, on the conditions you've proposed. A thousand dollars now and as much every month."

"Agreed. Here's your first banknote. From now on, I'll visit you regularly when the post comes, and if anyone happens to notice my assiduity, you'll say that I'm a cousin or brother-in-law from Ireland who's looking for work. Oh— one more instruction: from the moment you enter my plan, I forbid you to set foot in this gambling-den. They're nothing but thieves. Within a week you'd be back in the same situation, and that's what I don't want!"

The Irishman made no objection. In response to the unknown man's invitation, he left the gambling-den; to seal their agreement, the two men only parted after having drunk a glass of whisky at a nearby bar.

"What's your name?" asked Edward Edmond, as they were about to part. "I need to know that in order to receive you when you come to ask for me."

"Slug," replied the other, briefly—and he drew away at a rapid pace.

From the next day onwards, Fred Jorgell's concierge received regular visits, when the post arrived, from the mysterious Mr. Slug, who did not stay in his lodge for long. He examined the postmarks of each of the missives that were handed to him meticulously, but he only took away a few of them, preferentially those sent from Canada, which were generally addressed to Agénor Marmousier.

Thus, the poet, who was waiting impatiently for news of Lord Burydan and Oscar experienced a keen surprise, which soon turned to anxiety, on seeing that they gave no sign of life. He informed Andrée de Maubreuil and Frédérique of the situation. The two young women were seriously alarmed; for the hunchback not to send them his news, he must have fallen victim to some catastrophe.

Without daring to admit it, they feared that the bandits of the Red Hand might have got rid of the courageous street-urchin.

Their dread was, moreover, not without foundation, for all the letters stolen by Slug were immediately transmitted to Dr. Cornelius, who thus found himself admirable well-informed of the actions and intentions of his adversaries.

These precautions, however, were soon thwarted. One day, when Slug was in the concierge's lodge, the telephone rang. It was Agénor for whom the caller was asking.

Edward Edmond was about to put the Frenchman in communication with the unknown caller when Slug seized the receiver brutally and put it to his ear.

"Monsieur Agénor Marmousier?" repeated a distant voice.

"Who's calling?" said Slug.

"His friends Oscar Tournesol and Lord Burydan."

"Monsieur Agénor isn't here. He left America several days ago and returned to France."

"That's singular," the voice replied, discontentedly. "Since that's so, put me in communication with Fred Jorgell himself. Tell him that it's his former protégé Oscar Tournesol who's asking for him."

Slug let a certain time go by in order to give the impression that he had contacted the billionaire, and then resumed the conversation into the apparatus.

"Mr. Jorgell is very angry. He doesn't want to have any further communication with you henceforth. He's very annoyed with you for leaving without telling him. Write to him or come to see him if you want more ample information."

Then, in order to cut off further questions, Slug hung up the receiver. Turning to Edward Edmond, whom he now commanded as a master, he said: "Pay attention to this. On the day when either of those two individuals, Oscar Tournesol or Lord Burydan, succeeds in entering into telephonic communication with Fred Jorgell or his secretary Agénor, your pension of a thousand dollars a month will be stopped. You've been warned—and the same applies, of course, if you let any of the letters I've identified pass without giving them to me."

The beautiful Dorypha's lover bowed obsequiously. He understood, a trifle belatedly, that in the person of Slug he had acquire an imperious and tyrannical master, who had him entirely under his thumb.

Slug left after issuing that warning, leaving Edward Edmond to his reflections.

The affiliate of the Red Hand had scarcely turned on his heels than Agénor came into the lodge. "Nothing for me today, Monsieur Edward?" he asked.

"Nothing, Monsieur," replied Edward Edmond bleakly.

"Too bad. If a letter comes for me, send it up immediately."

Agénor went back to his room, very anxious. The poet was remorseful. During his visit to the Grand Wigwam he had only thought about the salvation of his friends, tracked by the police, and had completely forgotten the mission with which Miss Isidora had charged him relative to her brother Baruch. He had quickly reflected, however, that, placed under the protection of Lord Burydan, the madman could not have fallen into better hands—and as he had expected a letter from Oscar imminently, he had contented himself with telling Isidora that he did not know what had become of her brother, putting off telling the young woman the truth until he could give her definite information.

The absence of letters and news of Oscar and Lord Burydan put him into a cruel dilemma. He reproached himself for perhaps having caused the madman's death by his negligence, and, when Isidora asked him to organize a search for him, he did not know what to say, and lowered his head in shame.

Since the drama at the Lunatic Asylum, Agénor could no longer sleep and had completely lost his appetite.

IV. The Blue House

Monsieur Denis Pasquier, a French Canadian, had an exceptional position in Winnipeg. Highly esteemed for his probity, and elected to municipal functions by his fellow citizens on several occasions, he was the busiest business lawyer in the city. He was the person charged with all delicate transactions and all important land-sales. He had also succeeded, thanks to that very probity, in amassing a considerable fortune.

Denis Pasquier was a stout and placid man whose bright green eyes, pink cheeks and russet beard trimmed to a French point were a sufficient revelation of his Norman origin. Very slow and very reflective, he never hurried business matters, and the employment of his time was distributed with a mathematical regularity from which he never departed. He would never have brought forward or put back his meal times, even if it was a matter of making a substantial profit.

In sum, he was one of those upright, good-natured and fanatical men of law, of a type that still existed in France sixty years ago, but which has almost completely disappeared.

Seated in his study next to the large faience stove on which a large gleaming copper kettle stood, installed in his old leather winged armchair, Denis Pasquier was busy examining a file with his habitual methodical slowness when his clerk handed him an envelope containing a visiting card.

The businessman immediately opened the envelope with his paper-knife, but as soon as he had cast an eye over the card, he shivered, and promptly rose to his feet.

"Show in the person who is waiting," he said to his employee.

"There are two of them," said the clerk.

"Well then, show them both in."

The reason for Denis Pasquier's emotion is easily understandable, once one knows that the card that had just been handed to him was that of Lord Astor Burydan, whose death had been announced in all the newspapers several months before.

If he's not a ghost, he thought, *he can only be a swindler.*

He was interrupted in his reflections by the arrival of their object. Lord Burydan came into the room, accompanied by Oscar Tournesol. Kloum and the madman had remained in the hotel where the fugitives were staying.

"My God—it's not a swindler; it really is a ghost!" murmured Denis Pasquier, at the sight of the noble lord, who came toward him holding out his hand.

"My dear Denis," said Lord Burydan, with a joyful burst of laughter. "You seem utterly nonplussed."

"Um...with good reason, my lord."

71

"Pull yourself together. I'm not a phantom. You'll soon know how it came about that I was thought to be dead. I only ask you to lend me all your attention."

And Lord Burydan recounted, in detail, the story of his shipwreck, his captivity on the Island of Hanged Men, his escape in an airship, his internment in the Lunatic Asylum and his flight.

As the eccentric's story progressed, Denis Pasquier began to shake his head anxiously. "What a story!" he repeated. "What a story!" He added, swiftly: "You know that your cousin, the old miser Matthew Fless, your nearest relative, has taken possession of your house and al your properties in Winnipeg? At this moment he's taking the steps necessary to obtain full title to all your other property, situated in Scotland and England."

"I know that," the lord replied, "And that's why, as soon as I escaped from the lunatic asylum, I took the train to Montreal, and then to Winnipeg."

"What are your intentions, my lord?"

"They're not difficult to guess, damn it, my dear Denis. Firstly, to recover possession of my wealth, and, as soon as that's done, to equip a fleet to go and destroy the bandits of the Red Hand in their lair on the Island of Hanged Men. That's a pleasure I've promised myself."

"Do you know," said the lawyer, "that it won't be very easy to recover possession of what belongs to you? It'll be a long and thorny process. Don't be under any illusion, my lord. In the eyes of the law, and the whole world, you're well and truly dead. I even have a copy of your death certificate here, drawn up by the consul in San Francisco in due legal form."

"That's too much! It seems to me that someone's in great haste to bury me!"

"There's a reason for that, as you'll understand. You know your cousin, Baronet Matthew Fless?"

"Hardly at all. I've never met him. All that I know is that he's a miser who'd shave an egg and cut a farthing into four. I also know that people hereabouts call him 'Baron Skinflint.'[3] That's the full extent of my knowledge."

"The baronet is fully worthy of that gracious appellation, but it's important that I inform you more fully on his account. Matthew Fless is legendary throughout Canada for his avarice. His costume, comprising a bonnet made of

---

[3] The appellation given in the original is "Fesse-Mathieu"—a French term meaning miser or usurer—which is a weak pun on the character's name, slightly strengthened by the fact that the author spells his forename in the French fashion even though his title and kinship to Lord Burydan suggest English rather than French descent. Le Rouge was apparently insufficiently familiar with the English peerage to refer to the individual in question as "Sir Matthew Fless, Bart," as a more punctilious writer might have done, or to specify exactly what Lord Burydan's title is supposed to be.

the skins of hares that he killed himself, and a fur coat of the same manufacture, makes him resemble both the Wandering Jew and Robinson Crusoe. When he comes to town, he delights the street-urchins, who form a procession behind him and sing, in spite of all the efforts of the police."

"What a jolly chap!" cried Lord Burydan, laughing. "I won't be sorry to make his acquaintance."

"He's not as jolly as all that, my lord, for he's pitiless toward the poor. He's had a widow and her five children thrown out of a house that belongs to him for a miserable debt of five or six dollars. He's detested throughout the region. He has great difficulty finding servants; he overwhelms them with work and feeds them so badly that no one had ever remained with him for longer than a fortnight. They flee half-dead of starvation, preferring to lose their wages than remain in the house of such a vile creature. He lives more meagerly than a Trappist, scarcely eating anything but the game he kills and the eggs laid by his chickens, and drinks nothing but water."

"I certainly won't allow that old rogue to install himself permanently in my house," said Lord Burydan. "I'd rather cut off his ears. But that doesn't explain why my death certificate was drawn up so quickly and why my heir's acquisition of possession was so rapid."

"I know why," said the business agent, lowering his voice. "The baronet's older son is an attaché in the English consulate in New York. He must have used his influence with the consul in San Francisco."

"You're right. That also explains which Agénor's claims on my behalf weren't heeded. This Matthew Fless and his son are definitely two scoundrels. According to what you've told me, they knew perfectly well what they were doing in locking me up in the Lunatic Asylum, where I'd certainly still be without brave Oscar, whom you see here."

"You know, the Canadian went on, after having reflected for several minutes, "that I'm entirely devoted to you, my lord—but be prudent. You've been able to take account of the fact that you're dealing with a man devoid of scruples, devoured by his passion for money, who won't stop at any means to suppress you legally and remain in possession of your estates. You ought to leave the hotel where you're staying today. Then, in my opinion, this is the best thing for you to do. I own a small house four leagues from Winnipeg, situated in the woods, which I used in the days when I went hunting. Anyway, it's comfortable furnished and equipped with all the necessities."

"Well, rent it to me."

"No, I'll lend it to you. And my advice is to go to ground in that retreat like a hare in its den, and avoid showing yourself in town as much as possible. If anyone asks me for information about you I'll say that you're emigrants from Northern Canada to whom I'm selling some land. That will seem sufficiently plausible."

"I accept, gratefully."

"Now, give me your papers. I'll telegraph England to obtain those you lack, and gather a body of evidence that will permit me to demand, with a good chance of success, the retraction of your death certificate and the expulsion of that old rogue of a baronet—to whom, in parentheses, I won't be sorry to do a bad turn. It's necessary, on your part, to write to the peers you know in House of Lords, in order that they can use their influence in the affair."

Changing his one abruptly, Pasquier went on: "It's five minutes to noon. We've been talking about serious matters; now I hope you'll give me the pleasure of sharing my modest lunch. The cuisine won't be anything complicated—simply a good salmon from Lake Winnipeg and a leg of Scottish mutton. Madame Pasquier and my sons will be delighted to make your acquaintance. The clerk will go to your hotel to tell your friends not to expect you."

Lord Burydan accepted the layer's invitation wholeheartedly, and admired the patriarchal simplicity of the family of worthy individuals. He thought he had gone back in time a hundred years.

After the meal, which was very cheerful and washed down with a few bottles of old French wine that Denis Pasquier kept in his cellar for special occasions, Lord Burydan and Oscar took their leave of their hosts, who had put a trap and two horses as their disposal, and a domestic, to guide them to their new residence.

While it was being hitched up, Pasquier renewed his recommendations. "Above all, be prudent Avoid the town as much as possible. I know the baronet well enough to know that he wouldn't hesitate for a moment to denounce you and hand you over to the American authorities.

"You can be tranquil; we'll follow your advice to the letter."

"Oh, one more item of information that I forgot. The miser has a second son, a worthy fellow, whom he kicked out because of some amorous affair..."

The trap was hitched up, and the horses between the shafts pawing the ground. A final handshake was exchanged and the two fugitives took their places on one of the benches of the rustic vehicle, while Laurent, the domestic, took the reins.

They stopped at the hotel just long enough to settle the bill and pick up Kloum and the madman, and then set off again.

As soon as they were outside the city and on a beautiful road, solidly made and bordered by firs and poplars, the two horses adopted a brisk trot, which they did not abandon until they reached their destination.

The landscape was magnificent. The travelers could see verdant forests of firs, beeches and chestnut-trees, interrupted at intervals by flourishing fields of wheat, oats, hemp and buckwheat. Everything exhaled tranquility, serenity and abundance. The countryside was utterly deserted; from time to time, they encountered a peasant leading a herd of cattle, a flock of sheep or a forage-cart, who greeted the travelers amicably on perceiving the lawyer's servant, Pasquier being well-known throughout the region.

As they went further, however, the country became more uneven and more heavily wooded, and cultivated fields became rarer. Soon, they were in a forest whose vast tree-branches seemed to want to join up above the road. In the distance, the noise of a torrent was audible—the Roaring Stream, which, the Canadian servant explained, served as the boundary between Denis Pasquier's property and that of Baronet Matthew Fless, before eventually flowing into Lake Winnipeg.

The trap had left the main road to take a side-road carpeted with grass, which zigzagged between the thickets. Soon, the elegant mass of a wooden house with balconies and an overhanging roof appeared between the trees.

They had arrived.

"This is the Blue House," said the Canadian. "I'll give you the key, and you'll be installed within a quarter of an hour. There's crockery and glassware in the dressers, linen in the cupboards, beer and whisky in the cellar. Nothing's lacking.

Laurent had leapt down from the trap. He opened the door, and Lord Burydan and his companions were able to observe that the house lost in the woods was provided with all the necessities. It even had hams and sausages hanging from the beams of the kitchen.

The Canadian opened a small cabinet that contained several well-maintained rifles and an assortment of nets, traps and fishing-lines. "With that," he said, laughing, "you won't risk dying of hunger, and can easily wage war on the game in the forest, the salmon in the lake and the trout in the stream. Besides which, as Monsieur Denis said, one of you can go into Winnipeg every week to pick up supplies."

After having allowed his horses to rest for an hour and shown the guests the cellar, the pantry and the bedrooms, Pasquier's domestic climbed back into the trap was soon lost in the distance. The fugitives were alone in the midst of nature, in a deserted region.

"Finally!" said Lord Burydan, uttering a long sigh, "We'll be able to rest, far from liners, railways, madhouses, the bandits of the Red Hand and hotels provided with all modern comforts."

"It won't be too soon," the hunchback approved, although he seemed very preoccupied. "We'll be able to talk here, and make the necessary decisions."

The rest of the day was employed in settling in, and the fugitives saw immediately that the Blue House would be a very comfortable refuge.

On the ground floor there was a kitchen, a dining room, a parlor and a drawing room. Four bedrooms, to which a broad staircase gave access, comprised the first floor. Everything was bright, cheerful and very neat. One might have thought that the owner of the house had only left the day before. It was a true gift that Denis Pasquier had made to his friends.

V. Two Model Servants

Slug had just left Edward Edmond, Fred Jorgell's concierge, after having watched the opening of the latest post, and he was strolling philosophically, smoking a cigar, back to the furnished hotel in the Irish district in which he was staying. From time to time he went into a bar, drank a whisky and soda, and then set off again placidly. He was very serious in his intent, for he only made three stops of that kind during the evening. Indeed, although he regarded it as legitimate conduct to refresh himself in that manner, he had a horror of drunkenness, which he regarded as the most repugnant of vices—except that if anyone else but him had refreshed themselves with as many glasses of whisky per day, that man would have been dead drunk before sundown.

Slug had just made his third and last stop, and was crossing a deserted side-street devoid of gas-lamps when an individual wearing a broad-brimmed hat and a silk cravat that hid his features almost completely came up to him, shook his hand in a particular manner and whispered a few cabalistic words in his ear.

Slug started. "On behalf of the Lords?" he murmured. "I'm all yours."

"Good," said the mysterious stranger. "But I need to cover your eyes first."

Meekly, Slug allowed himself to be blindfolded. "Are we going far?" he asked.

"Don't worry about that. Anyway, you won't get tired—we're going by car."

Guided by the stranger, who had taken his hand, Slug took twenty paces, and was then helped to climb into a vehicle and take his place on a soft seat.

Immediately afterwards, the automobile departed at top speed. It traveled thus for half an hour; then the unknown man, who had not said a word thus far, shouted an order to the driver to stop immediately. Slug got out, assisted by his guide, who, taking him by the arm, led him across a large empty space that must have been a courtyard, went up a staircase and went along a corridor, at the end of which was a door. Slug then felt the other let go of his arm, and he was shoved into a room whose floor was covered by a thick carpet.

"Take off your blindfold," said a curt and hoarse voice, which was not that of the guide.

Slug obeyed, and his eyes, dazzled by the bright light in the room, looked around. He was in a high-ceilinged room whose walls were covered from floor to ceiling with paintings in ornate gilded frames. There were also statues in white marble and bronze; display-cases crammed with precious gold jewelry, with scintillating gems; furniture encrusted with lapis and nacre; weapons damascened with gold; and antique tapestries in which legendary characters agitated in fantastic landscapes.

In the center of the room, three men whose faces were covered by rubber masks were sitting around a table made of Sèvres porcelain cluttered with piles of papers, among which Slug recognized the majority of the letters that he had removed personally from Fred Jorgell's mail.

The three men were looking at Slug curiously, and seemed amused by his bewilderment.

"Sit down, Slug," said one of them, eventually, "and answer my questions sincerely. You've belonged to the association of the Red Hand for a long time?"

"Yes, Milord—five years.

"You've never had any desire to leave the organization?"

"No, Milord. I'm utterly devoted to the Red Hand."

"Has anyone ever offered you money to betray our secrets?"

"Several times, Milord, but I've always refused and immediately identified the people making the offers."

"I think we can count on him," said the masked man, in a low voice, to his companions. "He has an excellent service record. He was in command of the tramps who kidnapped Joe Dorgan in the Sierra. He's fulfilled the role of captain-governor of the Island of Hanged Men zealously, and was recently seriously wounded while attacking Fred Jorgell. Finally, he's taken charge, very intelligently, of examining the American's correspondence."

The three Lords examined Slug silently for some time. The latter could not help feeling a certain embarrassment under the crossfire of the three pairs of inquisitive eyes, but the examination was favorable.

"You know," the masked man continued, "that the moment is facing a veritable crisis at present. A syndicate of billionaires, headed by Fred Jorgell, has offered considerable rewards to anyone who succeeds in destroying us. You're a trusted man, to whom we can speak frankly."

"Yes, Milord," said Slug, swelling with pride.

"Well, bad news is arriving from all directions. Fifty of our men in New Jersey are in prison awaiting trial. In Illinois, a dozen tramps have been lynched in a single week. Finally, very recently, one of the bankers with whom the Red Hand's capital was deposited has been denounced, and more than three hundred million dollars in bonds belonging to the association have been seized from the bank."

Slug's consternation was visible.

"Don't worry," his interlocutor continued. "The Red Hand is richer and more powerful than people suppose, and will emerge triumphant. No one suspects the power of its formidable organization. But if we've summoned you, it's because the Council of the Lords has decided to charge you with a delicate mission that isn't without danger. It's a matter of stealing from an old miser who lives in an isolated manor house a sum of more than three million dollars in gold and banknotes."

"I'm ready!" said Slug, with a noble enthusiasm.

"Silence—and don't permit yourself to interrupt me again."

Slug lowered his head humbly and stammered vague apologies.

"But it isn't in New York that the sum is located," the masked man continued. "It's a long way away in Canada, near Winnipeg. The miser's name is Matthew Fless, and it will be easy to enter his service as a domestic."

"Shall I be undertaking the expedition alone?"

"No; at any rate, it's preferable that there are two of you. We'll give you a reliable man as a companion—Sam Porter, for example. Do you think, in those conditions, that you'll be capable of success?"

"I believe so, Milord. An isolated house, an old man—it seems quite easy to me."

"That's also the opinion of the Lords, but that's only half of what you have to do. A short distance from the miser's house, four redouble enemies of the Red Hand are residing. It's necessary for you to get rid of them. Two of them are already known to you: Lord Burydan and the Indian Kloum have, in fact, been confided to your guard on the Island of Hanged Men. The other two are a lunatic escaped from the Asylum and a Frenchman, a cunning little hunchback named Oscar Tournesol. The suppression of these four individuals is as important as the other affair—and above all, it's essential that the Red Hand, which is virtually unknown in Canada, doesn't come under suspicion."

Slug received a host of further instructions, minutely detailed, and it was agreed that an exceptionally robust and ultra-rapid automobile would be placed at his disposal, thanks to which, once the double crime had been accomplished, he would be able to take rapid flight with the proceeds of the theft.

A few days later, as night was falling, an enormous red and black automobile entered the city of Winnipeg and came to a halt in front of the establishment of a Yankee mechanic who had arrived in Canada a few months earlier. The Yankee in question, whom no one suspected, was an affiliate of the Red Hand who had been obliged to leave the country in the wake of a robbery. He gave a fine welcome to Slug and Sam Porter, locked their automobile in a special garage, and gave them all the information they needed. Finally, he provided them with means of disguising themselves.

The next day, two men wearing brown hats, shod in gross hobnailed boots and dressed in dirty overalls, came out of the mechanic's workshop before daybreak. Each of them had a canvas bag slung around his neck and a set of agricultural implements over his shoulder. Everyone would have taken them for the kind of nomadic day-laborers who go from farm to farm, offering their services to anyone until they have amassed enough money to buy a ploy of land-who are very numerous in Canada, where they attract no attention.

Slug and Sam Porter, for it was them, left Winnipeg without having excited any curiosity, and after walking for two hours they reached the bank of the Roaring Stream, whose course they followed upstream for some time.

Having arrived at a wooden bridge that the Yankee had indicated to them, they went over the torrent and found themselves in a vast and majestic avenue of firs, at the extremity of which they glimpsed the steeply-pitched roofs and sculpted turrets of a manor house. As they approached that aristocratic but far-from-luxurious dwelling, however, they saw increasing indications of the most profound dilapidation and neglect.

The courtyard had been invaded by weeds and the roofs were covered with moss and lichen. The uncurtained windows had numerous broken panes, which had been replaced by pieces of wood or bundles of straw. A few emaciated chickens were pecking here and there, and a cow was lying down nonchalantly on the front steps.

The two bandits had scarcely had time to take in this spectacle with a glance than two dogs of Apocalyptic thinness, which must have been fasting for several days, leap at their legs, barking furiously. Slug and his companion were having great difficulty holding off the attacks of the hungry animals when an old man emerged from a side door.

"Down, Fanor! Down, Tom!" he shouted, in a peevish tone.

The two newcomers were amazed by the sight of this individual, who was none other than Baronet Matthew Fless, more commonly known as Baron Skin-flint. As, for reasons of economy, he never made use of scissors or a razor, his long white beard came down to his navel and his hair, which dangled over his shoulders, was crowned by the strange hare-fur bonnet that he had made himself. He did indeed resemble the Wandering Jew of the old *Image d'Épinal*. He had two little dark eyes, as keen as those of a merlin, accompanied by a long hooked nose, and his hands, with talon-like nails, were clutching a large-caliber revolver.

As for his costume, it was simultaneously reminiscent of a dressing-gown, a fur coat and a soutane. It must originally have been tailored in olive-green cloth, but its owner, doubtless to make it warmer, had lined it with the skins of rabbits and other animals, and had studiously patched it up with pieces of fabric of different colors. The decrepit old man's footwear consisted of a pair of gross clogs.

The bandits had all the trouble in the world suppressing a violent desire to laugh. Never, in the course of their various adventures, had they ever found themselves in the presence of such a grotesque individual.

Sam Porter wondered, incredulously, how it was possible that this old beggar possessed so many millions of dollars. As for Slug, he studied Baron Skin-flint with the satisfaction of a true connoisseur.

Meanwhile, the old man, troubled by the silence of his two visitors, advanced toward them, taking aim with his revolver in a threatening manner. "What do you want?" he cried. "And who gave you permission to come into my home?"

"Sir," Slug replied, humble, "we're honest laborers in search of work, and on seeing your beautiful manor house, we thought that you might perhaps have some to give us."

"Hmm!" retorted the baronet, with a hoarse chuckle. "There's no lack of work, but people of the present epoch have become so idle…they want high pay and to stuff themselves without doing anything…"

"We don't belong to that category," Slug replied, with modest assurance. "You could travel all over Canada without finding two workmen as industrious, as sober and as docile."

The miser was evidently tempted by that accumulation of laudatory epithets—all the more so as his three domestics had abruptly quite two days before, heaping the worst insults upon him. "Hmm!" he said "Those who work as well as you say want to be paid very dear. If I hire you, I'll wager you'll demand the eyes out of my head."

"We're the least demanding people in the world," said Slug, with an expression of goodwill that was entirely accommodating.

"You'd agree, for example, um…to three dollars a week?"

Slug and Sam Porter exchanged glances, as if they were hesitating.

The miser thought that they were about to refuse his derisory offer. "Wait!" he exclaimed, swiftly. "You'd be fed. Good soup in the morning, good soup at midday and good soup in the evening; game and fish every time I go hunting or fishing." And he added, with an irony that only he understood: "I give you my word of honor as a gentleman that you'll be as well-nourished as I am."

"And what does one drink in your house?" asked Slug, who wanted to be persuaded.

"Hmm!" said the old man, slightly embarrassed. "Water—good spring water, with a little vinegar in heat-waves, to slake the thirst."

The two bandits pulled frightful faces. With one accord, they shook their heads negatively.

"Listen," Baron Skinflint persisted, not wanting to let them leave. "We can reach an understanding. I'll send for some beer! Yes, truly, small beer! But not until next week, because I haven't notified my brewer…"

"Oh, to that I won't say no," said Slug, stifling a desire to laugh. "If you give us beer, we can come to an understanding. And I guarantee that you won't regret the expense. My comrade and I do as much work as four ordinary men."

After a discussion that went on for more than an hour, the honest Slug and his friend Sam Porter consented to enter definitively into the baronet's service, at a rate of three dollars a week, but with the brilliant prospect of eating every day at the table of the lord of the manor, and being nourished in exactly the same fashion as him.

VI. Madame Sibylla

It was the beginning of autumn. The Canadian forest, so melancholy in winter under its mantle of snow and ice, then offered magnificent views of its clearings and its avenues bordered with giant trees, where the first rays of morning sunlight set thousands of birds singing.

The foliage was beginning to take of beautiful tints of copper and dark orange, the pale bark of the birch trees was gleaming softly in the distance, like silver columns.

Every morning, the four residents of the Blue House went out on an expedition, either to hunt or to fish. The banks of the lake and the torrent were swarming with aquatic game. Wild mallards, pintails, teal, Canada geese, lapwings and bustards were abundant there. In the woods, the hunters encountered fieldfares, woodcock, Arctic hares and snow-partridges, or ptarmigans. The fishing provided superb salmon, rainbow trout, eels, gigantic pikes and crayfish that tasted particularly exquisite.

Thanks to the skill of the Indian and Lord Burydan, who were both excellent shots, the larder of the Blue House was always abundantly supplied with game. As for Oscar, he had discovered a fortunate talent for angling, and had become a first-rate master of that contemplative sport in a short time. The fourth member of the party, ever taciturn, sometimes spent entire days without saying a word, but he obeyed all the orders that were given to him and showed himself to be biddable, mild and obliging in all circumstances.

"That boy isn't mad," said Lord Burydan one day, having observed him carefully. "I think he's simply suffering from amnesia, and that it wouldn't be impossible to cure him."

"At any rate," said Oscar, "he's completely inoffensive. Let's leave him tranquil and he'll get better. One might think that his condition has improved sensibly since he's been in our company."

"I'm convinced that he must have been the butt of all kind of ill-treatment at the Lunatic Asylum. When my affairs are sorted out, I'll endeavor to discover the poor devil's name and his antecedents."

Several times, they had asked the invalid what his name was, but he had never given any reply other than a dolorous sigh, and every time they questioned him on the subject he fled into the woods and stayed there for half a day before returning. They ended up by letting him alone.

In any case, as we have already had occasion to remark, time, sequestration and stress had so altered the work of Dr. Cornelius that the resemblance to Baruch that had once been striking was considerable attenuated. Oscar, who had been perfectly familiar with the murderer in Monsieur de Marbreuil's home, and who knew that Baruch had been locked up in the Asylum, had never thought for a moment that it was Monsieur de Marbreuil's murderer that he had helped to escape.

In sum, while waiting for the measures undertaken by Denis Pasquier to succeed, as they surely would, the inhabitants of the Blue House would have been perfectly happy had it not been for the disappointment they suffered in not having had any response to the letters they had addressed to Fred Jorgell and Agénor. That obstinate silence worried them, and they could not help thinking that some maneuver of their enemies, the Red Hand, might be behind it.

One evening, the four fugitives were sitting under the mental of the vast fireplace of the Blue House, where a cheerful fire of resinous wood and pine cones was blazing, chatting about all sorts of things while savoring a hot toddy. Each sitting at a corner of the fireplace, Kloum and the invalid, as taciturn as one another, were only contributing rare syllables to the conversation. Oscar Tournesol and Lord Burydan, who had quickly become fast friends, were discussing the situation.

"I know Agénor, who is loyalty personified," said Lord Burydan, "too well to believe that he has returned to Europe, utterly uninterested in what has become of me."

"Who knows?" said Oscar. "Perhaps our friend was recalled to Europe by some family tragedy."

"He no longer has any relatives. I believe that our letters must have been intercepted."

"That's impossible. A perfect order reigns in Fred Jorgell's house. All the people close to him are trusted servants, and he gives large tips every year to the postal service, in order that his mail should be delivered to him with perfect exactitude."

"I don't know what to think. It is, I suppose, necessary to believe what was said to us when we telephoned."

"It's vital that I clarify the situation," said the little hunchback, rising to his feet with a decisive gesture. We're going to Winnipeg tomorrow. If I don't find any letters from our friends at the *poste restante* address I gave then, I'm going to leave for New York."

"Perhaps you're right, in truth."

"I don't have the right to stay here any longer, especially when I'm in a position to bring Mademoiselle Frédérique and her friends news of Monsieur Bondonnat for which they're waiting impatiently. I've written six letters giving them a detailed account of everything you saw on the Island of Hanged Men, and not had a word in reply. You must admit that it's very strange."

At that moment, Kloum suddenly stood up, cocking an ear. "It seems to me," he said, "that I heard a cry for help."

Oscar and Lord Burydan listened, but all they could hear was the noise of the rain that was falling in torrents, mingled with the roar of the wind in the forest and the rumble of thunder.

"You must have been mistaken, my dear Kloum," said the hunchback.

"I was saying," said Lord Burydan, "that there might be a means of explaining that. Suppose, for example, that Monsieur Bondonnat has succeeded in escaping, and has gone back to France with his daughters, and that, for one reason or another, their mail hadn't been sent on from Europe."

"But that doesn't explain Fred Jorgell's silence," said the hunchback.

"Perhaps he's fallen out with the French party."

In reality, if Andrée and Frédérique had not replied to Oscar Tournesol's urgent messages, it was, as our readers know, because there was an agent of the Red Hand at the Preston Hotel, who, in the same fashion as Slug at Fred Jorgell's house, was carefully combing through the Frenchwomen's mail and stealing all the letters coming from Canada. Cornelius and his affiliates, who understood how important Lord Burydan's revelation would have been for Frédérique, had left no stone unturned to make sure that the existence of the Island of Hanged Men remained secret. The day when that inaccessible retreat was located, it would be the end of the Red Hand. It was necessary to avoid that, and to get rid of those who possessed the secret; that was why Slug's journey had been decided.

Lord Burydan and the hunchback fell silent, becoming pensive, thinking about the extraordinary complication of the circumstances in which hazard had placed them—but they were abruptly snatched from their reflections.

Kloum had risen to his feet again, his face anxious, "This time, I'm sure," he said. "Someone's about to knock on the door."

He had hardly finished speaking when Lord Burydan and the hunchback heard three distinct raps rudely struck on the exterior door.

"Go and open it," said Lord Burydan to the Indian, "but don't let go of your revolver. I wonder who could possibly be paying us a visit at this hour, in this deserted spot?"

Kloum drew the bolts, and as soon as he had opened the door a tall young man of respectable appearance came in precipitately, supporting—or, rather, carrying in his arms—a semi-conscious young woman. They were both soaking wet and covered in mud, and their clothes had been ripped in various places by thorn-bushes.

"Apologies, sirs," said the stranger, with such an expression of honesty and candor that he gained all sympathies, "but my fiancée, Miss Ophelia, and I were caught in the storm. We had gone astray, and almost drowned in the Roaring Stream, which has overflowed, when we saw a light between the trees. Without knowing who you were, I thought that you wouldn't refuse us hospitality for a few hours."

"You're very welcome, sir," replied Lord Burydan, with an aristocratic gesture. "You're at home here—but I think the first thing to do is to take care of this charming young lady, who requires immediate care."

Immediately, everyone got busy. New logs were thrown on the fire, and a toddy was warmed up and given to the lovely Ophelia to drink. Her pale face immediately resumed its color. Oscar Tournesol dug out some women's underclothes from a cupboard and a dressing-gown that belonged to Madame Pasquier, and the young woman, who had been soaked to the skin, was able to change her clothes and repair the disorder of her apparel.

Ophelia was a blonde with a delightfully pink complexion. Her limpid blue eyes expressed softness and tenderness, and her smile had the charm of a caress. Her figure was slim, in spite of the solidity of her hips and the opulent bosom that is one of the particular beauties of Canadian women. Ophelia had the beauty of a Diana the Huntress who would not have renounced marriage. Lord Burydan contemplated her with admiration. Kloum was literally ecstatic, and even the poor amnesiac could not look at that ravishing individual without a charmed smile.

Only Oscar, entirely given over to his preoccupations, merely gave the young woman a distracted glance. Suddenly, he turned to the young man, who was occupied in emptying a cup of toddy with small sips. "Would it be indiscreet, my dear sir, to ask to whom we have the honor of speaking?"

"Not at all," replied the young man, whose open and honest features clouded over. "I'm well known in the vicinity. My name is Noel Fless."

"Are you related to Baronet Matthew Fless?" asked Lord Burydan.

"I'm his son," the young man relied, with a bitter smile.

As we have said, Denis Pasquier had made the most urgent recommendations to Lord Burydan with regard to the discretion he ought to maintain until his identity was recognized, but it was not in the eccentric's character to impose any restraint whatsoever on himself, the moment he discovered an amusement. The idea that he was facing the miser's son amused him greatly.

"Mr. Fless," he said, "I'm all the more delighted to meet you because you and I are cousins."

"Is that possible?"

"Yes, cousin. I'm the same Lord Burydan of whose follies you might perhaps have heard tell."

Noel was prey to the profound amazement. "But Lord Burydan is dead," he protested, "and my father has taken possession of his vast estates."

"Lord Burydan is as far from dead as it is possible to be," the eccentric replied, giving himself a solid thump on the chest. And it will not be long before the proof is given to your honored father, along with a request to restore the house and lands of which he has taken possession a trifle too hastily."

Lord Burydan, who was the innate enemy of all dissimulation, recounted his adventures to his cousin and explained his present situation clearly. He concluded, however, by asking Noel and Ophelia to keep his secret.

"Unfortunately," said Noel, "I've often had occasion to blush at the actions of my father and my brother, and I ought to tell you that I quarreled mortally with Sir Matthew because I would not give in to his mania for avarice and thought it shameful to live like a beggar when he possesses millions."

"In that case," said the eccentric, excitedly, "I can almost look upon you as an ally?"

"Assuredly. I disapprove with all my heart of the unworthy fashion in which he has acted in your regard, and, on reflection, I perceive that it must have been my brother, the embassy attaché, who has contrived this scheme. Know, my lord, that I have no worse enemy than my brother. We were born of two different mothers, and from our earliest childhood there has been nothing between us but animosity and hatred. My brother is the most hypocritical of men..."

"I've been told," Lord Burydan put in, "that your brother is very prodigal, that he likes to live well and is known to have several mistresses. It's rather strange that, in those conditions he remains on good terms with the baronet, whose...let's say economy...is proverbial."

"What you say is true. My brother leads a very dissipated life, but you have no suspicion of the play-acting to which he lowers himself in order to make my father believe that he is as miserly as him. When he comes to the locality he stays at an inn about a league away from the house. There, he enjoys a good meal; then he changes his gentlemanly attire for a threadbare old suit that the innkeeper keeps in storage for him. It's in that accoutrement that he comes to see my father, to whom he speaks of nothing but privations, sobriety and economies. They both partake of a meal of bread-crusts and water, and then my brother goes to his room. As soon as everyone in the house is asleep, however, he leaps out of the window and runs to the inn to compensate himself for the meager fare he has had with a substantial supper. Everyone in the vicinity knows the story and is amused by it."

"I confess," said the eccentric, "that the adventure is passably humorous—but how do things stand between you and your father?"

"As badly as they could be. I've shown a great deal of patience, but a rupture between us was inevitable. When I told him that I had the firm intention of marrying Ophelia, who has no fortune, he became furious and threw me out. I live frugally in a small house that I inherited from my mother, two leagues from here. The produce of the garden, which I cultivate myself, along with my hunting and fishing, are largely sufficient to my needs. My happiness only lacks one thing, and that's the ability to marry my beloved Ophelia."

"Why can't you do that?"

"My fiancée is an orphan. She had been taken in by one of her aunts, an old woman of exaggerated devotion, and the aunt won't consent to our marriage until my father has given his consent—which he will never do, I'm sure, for he detests me."

"Oh, yes," murmured Ophelia, sadly, "he detests us."

"Mademoiselle," said Lord Burydan, gallantly, "I bless this hour, without which I would probably not have had the pleasure of making your acquaintance."

"The rain and the tempest," Ophelia replied, "have certainly played a part in this introduction. My aunt, Miss Judith, has gone to Montreal, in consequence of a pilgrimage that ought to procure her a hundred days of indulgences. I took advantage of the opportunity to spend the afternoon in my dear Noel's cottage. I was returning to Winnipeg, where I wanted to arrive before nightfall, when we were surprised by the tempest."

"It will therefore be necessary, my dear future cousin, for you to accept our hospitality until tomorrow morning. My friend Denis Pasquier is sending his trap to pick us up at an early hour, and you can take advantage of it."

This arrangement satisfied everyone. Ophelia was given the best room and a bed was made up for Noel in the dining room.

They stayed up so late that everyone slept deeply, and the inhabitants of the Blue House were only woken up the next morning by the cheerful cracking of the whip wielded by the lawyer's domestic, who had arrived with his vehicle.

In the blink of a eye everyone was up and about, and they drank the coffee prepared in haste by Kloum and his friend the amnesiac. Then Noel Fless said farewell to his cousin, for whom he felt the keenest sympathy, and they arranged to meet the following day in order to have a longer chat about their affairs.

As had been agreed the previous evening, Kloum and the amnesiac remained at the Blue House while Lord Burydan and Oscar took their places in the trap alongside Ophelia.

During the journey through the countryside refreshed by the storm and bathed in sunlight, which was charming, Ophelia was more loquacious than the previous day, and completed gaining Lord Burydan's good graces, definitively. She recounted, with a delightful naivety, how she had made Noel's acquaintance in the house of one of her friends, how they had sworn eternal love to one another and had promised to marry when they could.

"Unfortunately," she said, with a sigh, "we've already been engaged for more than a year, and the situation does not seem any nearer to changing. That's because of the stubbornness of the old miser. Oh, if I possessed a fine dowry, Baron Skinflint would be the first to give his consent..."

The poor girl almost had tears in her eyes.

"Don't despair," said Lord Burydan. "Everything will work out before long, I promise you. But I can't tell you yet how long it will take for me to triumph over the old miser."

Comforted by this promise, vague as it was, Ophelia lost her contrite expression and, until they came to a halt outside the lawyer's door, she delighted her companions with her merry chatter.

Because Lord Burydan had to confer with Denis Pasquier for a long time, regarding important communications he had received from London, Oscar took responsibility for escorting Ophelia back to the cottage where she lived with her aunt, which was situated in an outlying district of Winnipeg.

As they were going through a deserted quarter, the young woman suddenly drew the hunchback's attention to a small house with green shutters, on the door of which there was a copper plaque bearing the inscription: MADAME SIBYLLA, and stopped abruptly.

"Mr. Tournesol," she said, lowering hr voice, "I have to confess something to you. I have the weakness of being superstitious. For a long time I've been dying to consult Madame Sibylla. She might perhaps tell me whether my marriage will soon take place—but I dare not go into the witch's house alone...for Madame Sibylla is a genuine witch, credited with all sorts of prodigies."

The hunchback, skeptical by nature and education in his capacity as a Parisian, could not help smiling. "Would you like me to accompany you?" he asked.

"I didn't dare ask you, but that would give me a great deal of pleasure. I know that it's a ridiculous caprice I have, but it's stronger than I am."

"Well then, let's go in."

With a hand slightly agitated by emotion, Ophelia pulled the bell-cord, after having checked with a rapid glance that no one would see her going into the devil's house. A moment later, an aged black man introduced the visitors into a comfortably furnished waiting room. Very modern, Madame Sibylla had a horror of stuffed owls, toads and all the paraphernalia by means of which certain seeresses attempt to impress their clients. The only frightening object that could be seen in her consulting-room was a death's-head, which a large white cat appeared to be contemplating with the most complete indifference. The furniture was American, and the whole room was scrupulously tidy.

Madame Sibylla did not take long to appear. She was a woman of about thirty-five or forty, who must once have been very beautiful. With her nose like an eagle's beak, her piercing eyes and her coppery complexion, she seemed to belong to the race of Spanish gypsies, who have handed down witchcraft from mother to daughter for generations.

Without saying a word, she invited hr visitors to sit down and taking the hand of the tongue-tied Ophelia, she contemplated its lines attentively.

"Mademoiselle," she said eventually, "you are in love and you are beloved. You've come to find out when you'll be united with your fiancé.

"That's true," Ophelia stammered, surprised by the witch's perspicacity,

Madame Sibylla had an enigmatic smile. "Be happy," she said. "You won't have long to wait. Several people of distinguished rank are doubtless working for your happiness—but beware; I can see murderers and traitors becoming involved in your affairs. Your wishes will be granted, but there will be fire and blood...the skeleton in the black shroud will blunt his scythe against the fiery sword of the white angel in the silver armor."

"Will I have a son?" asked Ophelia, timidly.

"Beware," replied the witch, with a profound stare, "of becoming a mother before you are a wife."

Ophelia, blushing and confused, dared not ask the seeress for any explanation. The latter turned to Oscar, who, like a true Parisian street-arab, was smiling in a slightly mocking fashion.

"And you," she said. "Have you nothing to ask?"

"No," said the hunchback, "I don't believe in all these tricks."

"You're wrong," said Madame Sibylla, resting her sharp eyes upon him. "I see a great danger suspended over your head. Beware of an automobile—that's all I can tell you."

"That's all right," said Oscar, impressed in spite of himself. "I'll try to pay attention to not being run over. Thanks very much for the information. How much do we owe you, Madame?"

"Whatever you wish," said the gypsy, indifferently. She held out her hand to the hunchback, who deposited two dollars in it.

Once they had left he abode of the pythoness, Oscar took his leave of the young woman, who was only a few steps from home, and hastened to run to the Post Office, where, as he feared, he did not find any letter addressed to him.

There and then, his resolution was made. He would take the train to New York the next day.

After having lunch with Denis Pasquier, Oscar and Lord Burydan spent part of the afternoon making various purchases, and it as almost dark when they took the road back to the Blue House on foot. Lord Burydan told Oscar that he was very satisfied because, thanks to various documents sent from London, the lawyer had told him that his case would soon be settled.

Carried away by the vivacity of their conversation, the two friends had covered three-quarters of the distance without being aware of it. Darkness had fallen completely, and the obscurity was further augmented by the shade of the tall black fir-trees bordering the road.

Suddenly, Oscar and his companion heard the roar of an automobile engine behind them. They turned round.

The vehicle, which was a gigantic red and black automobile, was coming toward them with its headlights blazing at a vertiginous seed. They only just had time to leap on to the roadside.

"The phantom automobile!" Oscar exclaimed. "The one from New York!"

He did not say any more. Two gunshots had rung out. The hunchback fell to the ground uttering a cry of pain, and Lord Burydan heard a bullet whistle past his ear.

The automobile, which had slowed momentarily in order to permit those inside it to aim more accurately, had resumed its hectic course, and was already melting into the darkness like a nightmarish apparition.

VII. Baron Skinflint's Misadventure

That morning, Slug and Sam Porter had been collecting firewood in a wood on the estate and had finished unloading it in order to pile it up in the courtyard of the manor when an adolescent dressed in black, who was none other than Denis Pasquier's clerk, appeared at the entrance to the courtyard. He handed a large yellow envelope to Slug and then disappeared, running as fast as if the Devil were carrying him away.

"What's this now?" muttered the baronet, taking off his hare-fur bonnet in order to put on an ancient pair of horn-rimmed spectacles, which must have dated from the era of the death of General Montcalm.[4]

As soon as he had cast an eye over the piece of paper that the envelope enclosed however, he made an angry gesture and started pacing back and forth in the large courtyard.

Slug and Sam Porter were amused by the miser's antics, and from time to time one or other of them would retreat behind the wood-cart in order to chuckle at is ease. Half an hour went by in that fashion, but suddenly, Tom and Fanor began barking furiously, and Slug had great difficulty preventing them from hurling themselves upon a young woman of simple and modest appearance but striking beauty, who was emerging from the avenue of fir-trees and heading for the manor.

"It's annoying," grumbled the miser. "Disturbances all the time—in truth, one is no longer at peace in one's own home." That reflection might have seemed all the more humorous to an impartial witness because the baronet, whom everyone in the vicinity avoided like the plague, often went an entire month without receiving any visits whatsoever.

The miser advanced towards the visitor. "What do you want?" he said, sharply. "I don't have time to waste chatting.

The young woman blushed at such a discourteous welcome, but she undoubtedly had courage, for she replied, without showing any emotion: "It's absolutely necessary that I speak to you, Baron." And she added, with a noble simplicity: "I'm Ophelia, your son Noel's fiancée."

The miser made an angry gesture, and shook his fist under the young woman's nose. "Our conversation will soon be over, then," he cried. "You know my intentions. I haven't changed my opinion in your regard, and I never will.

---

[4] Louis-Joseph de Montcalm-Gozon, Marquis de Saint-Veran (1712-1759) was the commander of the French forces in America during the first phase of the conflict known there as the French and Indian War, a part of the more general Seven Years' War (1756-63). His early successes against the British were undone by counterattacks that culminated in his death in the Battle of Quebec.

It's rather brazen for you to come to badger me at home." He turned on his heel, making as if to mount the steps of the dilapidated perron.

Ophelia had stored up an extraordinary measure of intrepidity. "I know that your decision is immutable, Baron," she murmured, "but the situation is no longer the same now."

The old Wandering Jew spun round with the agility of a squirrel, and a kind of smile was designed on his face, emaciated by fasting. "Have you come into some money, my dear child?" he asked, graciously.

"No, Baron," Ophelia replied, her face covered with a blush of shame, "but your son has rendered me a mother, and it's now a duty for you no longer to oppose our union."

This revelation had the same effect on the old man as if he had suddenly set his hand on an electric pile. He jumped, at the risk of ripping the trousers that he had been wearing for decades. He tugged at the tufts on his long white beard as if he wanted to rip out handfuls of it, like the Hebrew prophets when some public calamity occurred. Then he raised his arms to the heavens and, pointing a finger as fleshless as that of a skeleton at the avenue, he howled: "Get out, whore It's not enough to have debauched my son Noel, and to have made him quarrel with me—now you want him to recognize the bastard to which you're going to give birth!"

Ophelia, frightened by this coarseness, fled in tears.

Slug and Sam Porter, who had witnessed the scene from a distance, remained prey to the sharpest surprise.

The baronet was in such a state of exasperation that, breaking with his usual habits of discretion and egotism, he advanced toward his two domestics in order to make them party to his indignation.

"What bad luck!" he wailed. "I really am very unfortunate! My son's behaving unworthily; he's dishonoring me. And if that weren't all"—he brandished the letter that he had just received—"now some swindler, some bandit, who's taken on the name of my relative Lord Burydan, a malefactor sought by the New York Police, a madman, a scoundrel of the worst species, wants to expel me from my house and steal my estates!"

Slug and Sam Porter had exchanged a singular glance.

With an expression of almost tender compunction, Slug said: "It's necessary to hope that this bandit doesn't succeed."

"But I don't know anything. Everyone in England, it seems, has taken his side. He's defended by Denis Pasquier, who is one of my personal enemies. What can a poor old man like me do against so many enemies. Oh, if I only knew where he is, the rogue!"

"Baron," said Slug, with hypocritical compassion, "you know that I'm profoundly devoted to you. I regard you as my benefactor."

"I know you're both good fellows," the miser murmured, tenderly.

"Well, Baron, "Would you permit me to give you, at the same time as some useful information, some excellent advice? When I went to Winnipeg yesterday, where you had sent me, I was able to learn many things."

"Speak, quickly."

"Well, do you know where this pseudo-Lord Burydan, who is causing you so much trouble, is living? Half an hour from here, on the other side of the torrent, in the cottage called the Blue House, which has been rented—or rather lent—to him by the lawyer Pasquier."

"Damn!" murmured the miser, scowling. "The enemy's at the door!"

"That is precisely the circumstance from which you might obtain a great advantage. The swindler is on the run from the American police. He's committed murder and pillaged a sanitarium."

"So what?"

"It would be sufficient for you to denounce him for him to be put in prison and extradited—and that would change the face of things considerably."

The miser's face blossomed into a broad smile. He was radiant. "Slug," he stammered, "you're the most devoted and intelligent of servants, and you have my word as a gentleman that I'll mention you in my will. I'll run to Winnipeg right away."

When the meager silhouette of the old man had disappeared between the trees of the avenue, Slug and Sam Porter burst into loud laughter. They held their sides and slapped their thighs as if the hilarity would never end.

"He's a hoot, the old man!" said Slug. "I'll always remember the time we've spent here. It's one of the joys of my life."

"Possibly," said Sam Porter. "But if we hadn't had our provisions with us, it wouldn't have been long before we starved to death." In a more serious tone he added: "But what's your plan, with this denunciation business?"

"It's quite simple. Lord Burydan, the hunchback—who, in parentheses, you were maladroit enough to miss the other day—the Redskin and the other one will be arrested, and naturally, we'll help in that arrest. They'll put up resistance, it's certain. We'll be very unlucky not to be able to kill all four of them in the skirmish."

"Ah! I understand..."

"We might perhaps be reproached for showing too much zeal, but in sum, we'll be congratulated. We'll have had policemen as collaborators in the affair, and the Red Hand won't be in any way compromised, or even suspected. Then we'll devote our attention to the strong-room."

"That doesn't seem to be all that easy. The old miser is as wary as a fox. He's never apart from his revolver. Every evening, he locks himself in his iron-reinforced room, the door of which we've tried to force in vain. And you said it would be easy!"

While discussing the best means of getting their hands on the miser's treasure, the two bandits took advantage of his absence to go to their secret larder and have a substantial lunch, copiously washed down by Canadian whisky.

When the baronet returned, three hours later, he found his two model servants working feverishly, but scarcely paid any attention to them. He seemed dejected.

"All is lost," he murmured. "The swindler has had himself recognized as the true Lord Burydan, and I'm going to be issued with an expulsion order tomorrow. I'll be obliged to quit this beautiful manor, where I counted on ending my days, and these vast estates that I counted on leaving to my children."

The fellow had tears in his eyes.

Slug seemed deeply touched by his grief. "Baron," he said, full of indignation, "what's happening is truly shameful. You're the victim of an abominable conspiracy, and if I were in your place, I wouldn't hesitate! After all, it's legitimate self-defense!"

"What do you mean?"

"Me, I'm as frank as gold, I don't beat around the bush. If you say the word, I'll take responsibility for getting rid of Lord Burydan for you."

"What's your plan?" asked the old man, beginning to hope again.

"Oh, it's quite simple. I go to the Blue House to ask Lord Burydan to come and talk to you, under the pretext of settling things. There's only one route by which to get here. It's necessary to cross the torrent of the Roaring Stream over the wooden bridge. The bridge is passably worm-eaten, and, well, an accident could easily happen..."

"I understand!" cried the miser, whose face lit up. "You have an idea of genius there, my dear Slug."

"All the more so," Slug continued, "as it will be dark in an hour. In the dark, it's easy to make a false step."

Without giving the baronet time to repent of his decision, Slug and Sam Porter armed themselves with an ax and a pick, and disappeared in the direction of the Blue House.

Left alone, the old man went into the kitchen of the manor and sat down under the vast mantel of the chimney next to the fire of dead wood, prudently covered with ashes.

The baronet was agitate and perplexed. He passed his thin fingers through his long white beard with a gesture full of anxiety and got to his feet every five minutes to go to the door, on order to see whether his emissaries were coming back. A thousand contradictory sentiments were colliding within him. At times, he regretted having confided in Slug and Sam Porter—who were, after all, strangers and vagabonds—but at others he applauded his decision.

Finally, the two bandits appeared on the threshold of the vast kitchen, seemingly as calm as honest woodcutters returning from their work.

"Well?" the miser asked, anxiously.

"It's done," Slug replied. "Now you have nothing to fear from Lord Burydan."

"And you can have masses said for the repose of his soul," added Sam Porter, in a slightly mocking tone.

"Tell me about it," said the baronet, avidly.

"Oh, it went without the slightest hitch.," Slug replied. "I arrived at the Blue House; I saw the so-called Lord Burydan, and I explained politely that you would be happy to see him in order to conclude the difference separating you amiably. He replied, insolently, that he didn't want to come to any arrangement with you, but that he wouldn't be sorry, even so, to see an eccentric of your sort at close range. While I was making that visit, Sam was giving a few good blows of the pick to the base of the stakes holding up the bridge, and a few strokes of the ax to the worm-eaten beams. Then, when I'd rejoined him, we both hid in a ditch to see what would happen."

"And then?" demanded the miser, who, entirely engrossed in Slug's story, had not noticed Sam Porter slyly moving behind the armchair in which he was sitting.

"Everything happened as I had foreseen. Lord Burydan and a Redskin who habitually serves as his bodyguard went on to the bridge. They took three steps…I was beginning to think that Sam hadn't done his work well when, all of a sudden, there was a mighty crash, a loud scream, and then nothing more. And as you know, a man who falls into the Roaring Stream can be considered doomed."

The miser uttered a sigh of relief. "*Oof!*" he exclaimed. "That removes a nasty thorn from my foot…"

The rest of the sentence stuck in his throat, because Sam Porter, obeying a significant wink from Slug, had grabbed him unexpectedly and was in the process of strangling him.

"Don't squeeze so hard!" Slug exclaimed. "That's stupid. If you start by wringing his neck, who's going to open the door of the strong-room for us?"

Sam Porter understood the wisdom of this advice and allowed the baronet, who was already half-suffocated, to breathe a little. Slug had taken a long piece of cord out of his pocket, and he tied the old man up with a thoroughly professional dexterity. The latter was so terrified that he could not pronounce a word.

"Old man," said Slug, brutally, "it's now a matter of giving us the key to the strong-room. You'll understand that it's not for your pleasure that we've remained in your house, dying of hunger and working like beasts of burden."

"The key? Never!" murmured the miser, in a hoarse voice.

"We'll do without your permission," said Slug, briskly exploring the pockets of the fur coat, from which he removed a host of miscellaneous objects: bread-crusts, bits of string, rusty nails and even pieces of charcoal. Finally, triumphantly, he brandished a bunch of keys of all dimensions.

"That won't do you any good, bandit!" roared the miser. "Only I know the means of opening the strong-room. I won't tell you—you'll kill me first!"

"We aren't going to kill you," said Slug, with frightful self-composure. "I know a radical means of making the obstinate talk."

Sam Porter had knelt in front of the hearth and was blowing with all the force of his lungs on the firebrands covered in white ash. Soon, the flames were crackling cheerfully. In the meantime, Slug had taken off the miser's clogs and his grey woolen socks; two fleshless feet appeared, equipped with toenails as curved and trenchant as those of Goya's devils.

The miser, who had understood what kind of torture was intended for him, trembled in all his limbs, and his teeth chattered.

"Would you like to tell us the secret of the strong-room?" asked Slug, one last time, in a menacing tone.

"No, no, a thousand times no!"

"That's all right. Sam, move the Baron a little closer to the fire."

Seizing the miser's clawed feet, Slug placed them on the ardent embers. The old man uttered a savage howl. "Help! Help! Mercy! Pity! Let go of me!"

"Open the strong-room for us," Slug repeated, insistently.

"No, no! It's impossible! I beg you!"

"So much the worse for you, then." And the bandit applied Matthew Fless's feet to the embers again. He uttered a second howl of agony.

At that moment, however, the door burst open and a troop of men, revolvers in hand, irrupted into the miser's kitchen.

Half a dozen gunshots rang out.

Sam Porter, hit by a bullet in the middle of his forehead, was killed outright.

Slug, slightly wounded, charged the assailants like a wild boar, cleaved a passage through to the door and disappeared.

The newcomers—Lord Burydan, Kloum, Noel Fless, Ophelia, Oscar Tournesol and the amnesiac—gave no thought to pursuing the bandit. They hastened to render assistance to the old man, who seemed to be about to lose consciousness.

Lord Burydan and Kloum, both excellent swimmers, had succeeded in escaping the waves of the Roaring Stream. They had had no difficulty deducing the nature of the trap to which they had just fallen. Returning in haste to the Blue House to change their clothes, they had encountered Noel and Ophelia on the way, and informed them of their adventure. It was then that they had decided to go to the miser's house to reproach him for his treason.

When they had bandaged the baronet's wounds, Lord Burydan said to him, severely: "You're going to leave the manor. You would have deserved finding other lodgings in Winnipeg Prison, but I think you've been punished enough. I won't make any complaint against you—but on the express condition that you immediately give your consent in writing to the marriage of Noel and Ophelia, for whom I shall provide a dowry."

Ashamed and confused, the miser signed everything they wished without saying a word. In gratitude for his good will, Kloum was left with him as a nurse to care for his burns.

Before returning, Lord Burydan was able to observe that his manor house had been literally pillaged. The old master paintings, the precious tapestries and the stylish furniture had all been sold by the miser and converted into cash. He postponed the matter of the damages and compensation that Baron Skinflint could not fail to be sentenced to pay until later, however.

Everyone returned to the Blue House, where Lord Burydan wanted to offer his friends a joyful supper to celebrate his triumph over his dishonest heir. As they were crossing the main road to Winnipeg, however, an automobile traveling at a furious speed brushed past them, almost knocking them down. It was a red and black vehicle. There was only one man in it, whom Ophelia thought she recognized as Slug.

"The phantom automobile," murmured Oscar, whose injured arm was still in a sling.

"What do the bandits matter to us?" cried Lord Burydan. "Now that I've recovered possession of my name and my fortune, I'm going to wage a war to the death on the Red Hand. I swear a solemn oath, here and now, that I'm going to exterminate the tramps in their lair on the Island of Hanged Men!"

9. THE HAUNTED COTTAGE

I. The Old Grille Bodega

The bodega known as the Old Grille,[5] miraculously preserved during the last earthquake, is situated in the Queen City district of San Francisco. It is one of the oldest establishments in the city and its construction dates back to the heroic and already-legendary era of the invasion of California by gold prospectors.

The old grille that gives the place its name is composed of iron bars as thick as a man's wrist entirely separating the room in which the drinkers sit from the counter containing bottles of alcohol of every provenance.

In the times when gold fever was rife, when women brought by slave-traders from Chile and Mexico were commonly sold by auction, all the bars were provided by similar grilles. It was not rare, in fact, for a man to be murdered for a slice of ham or a glass of whisky; if one includes the summary execution of thieves and pickpockets there was an average of two or three hundred murders a day. In those days, barmen only served their clients with revolvers in their belts and only handed over the drinks that had been ordered after pockets the handfuls of gold dust that represented their price.

Over time, those ferocious mores had been modified, and San Francisco, rebuilt several times after fires and earthquakes, had become a luxurious city, but the bodega, preciously conserved had survived all the changes.

The grille, it is true, was now merely a picturesque feature, and the present proprietor of the establishment had supplemented the narrow counter of old with a long room provided with a stage for music hall performances, crowded every evening with a disparate clientele in which one would have been able to find specimens of all the human races. There were Chinese, Japanese, Germans, Mexicans and a few Papuans, Maoris and individuals of other Oceanian races, who had come to America on boats laden with nacre, copra and tortoiseshell, recognizable by their gilded brown skins and their mild and pensive facial expressions.

Atrociously made-up songstresses displayed themselves by turns on the stage at the back of the room, but they were hardly visible through the thick cloud of cigar-smoke, and hardly audible in the midst of songs, laughter and

---

[5] The French *grillage* has a straightforward double meaning that refers both to the kind of latticework grille described in the next paragraph and to the process of grilling or toasting; translation just about preserves the weak pun.

vociferations that the band, composed of Mexican guitarists, could not succeed in drowning out.

That evening, the vast hall, whose low ceiling was decorated with the flags of all nations, was so full that the negro waiters had difficulty circulating through the narrow alleyways between the tables.

In one corner, three men sitting at a table around a punch-bowl were talking animatedly while smoking Manila cigars.

One of them was not contributing much to the conversation; he was a sailor with stupid but honest features and enormous hands, who answered to the name of Hardy.

His companions formed a complete contrast with one another. One, dressed almost with luxury, had the placid appearance of a bank clerk or a domestic in a wealthy house; his blond side-whiskers were carefully trimmed and his attire was perfectly correct. The other looked like a veritable bandit. His tanned face was framed by graying hair and a beard and his yellow eyes had the particular mobility of those of malefactors, expressing cunning, cupidity and anxiety. His garments, made of coarse fabric, contrasted with the numerous rings with which his fingers were charged and the bunch of trinkets that clinked on his watch-chain.

The latter's name was Christian Knox, and even in the underworld of San Francisco, where people are very accommodating with regard to questions of morality, he possessed the most deplorable reputation. Already twice accused of murder, but acquitted for lack of evidence, he was reputed to be a pirate.

"Mr. Edmond," said the captain to his companion, "I was in the shipyard today where the famous yacht is under construction, and was able to see that you have not exaggerated in the least."

"That's because, I can assure you, the banknotes haven't been spared," replied the man with the side-whiskers. "Everything is top quality, from the steel hull to the engines, which are fitted with the latest improvements."

"From what I've seen, it's a boat that could easily make her thirty knots," said the captain, and added: "But I can't help wondering what purpose such a vessel might serve."

"That's true," Hardy put in. "One might think that it were a warship."

"On that subject," said Edward Edmond, "I don't know any more than you."

"But what crossing will it make?"

"I don't know."

"You must know who's having it built, damn it?"

"That's as may be…but I don't have the right to tell you anything."

"As you please," muttered Captain Knox, in a sullen tone. "But all these secrets don't suggest anything good. I've been told that the boat's intended to race, or to sink Chinese junks and English sailing ships in Polynesia—which wouldn't surprise me."

"What can possibly make you think that?"

The mariner shook his head suspiciously. "You see," he said, "I'm an old hand who can't be persuaded that black is white. Your damned boat doesn't look like a pleasure yacht or a commercial steamer."

"Then it wouldn't do you any good to get you aboard in the capacity of first lieutenant? Everyone knows that you're an energetic man and an excellent mariner."

"Possibly—but when I go to sea, it's for my own account, and in my own ship. I don't like taking orders from anyone."

"As you please," said Edward Edmond, whose features expressed disappointment.

At that moment, the conversation was interrupted by the applause of the spectators, who were giving an ovation to some Javanese dancing girls, as thin, brown and agile as crickets. When the racket had calmed down, Edward Edmond turned to the sailor.

"What about you, Hardy?" he asked. "What do you think? What would you say to a three-month engagement at double pay, first-rate nourishment and not too much fatigue?"

The ma laughed thickly. "My God," he said, "I'm in. One doesn't find such an opportunity every day. Then again, no one will ever convince me that such a beautiful ship is destined for piracy."

"It's understood, then—you'll come to my office tomorrow to sign on. Even though the yacht isn't taking to sea for six weeks, I'll give you a month in advance..."

As Edward Edmond was pronouncing these words, a hand fell upon his shoulder. He turned round abruptly, but at the sight of the newcomer he went pale and his face expressed a certain anxiety. "You here, Mr. Slug?" he said, nervously.

Slug, who was a man of athletic build whose gray beard came down to his belt, smiled maliciously. "As you see," he replied. "Delighted to see you. I need to have a word with you. Do you have a moment?" Without waiting for his interlocutor's response, he took him by the arm in a familiar manner and took him to an empty table a few yards away.

"So," said Slug, without and preamble, "you're no longer fulfilling the functions of chief concierge in Fred Jorgell's home? You've become a recruiter of sailors."

"Who told you that, Mr. Slug?" asked the Irishman, embarrassed.

"It doesn't matter. The main thing is that I'm well-informed. I'll continue: you haven't left the billionaire's service, but as he has great confidence in you— a confidence, that, just between us, is misplaced—it's you he's commissioned to recruit solid and honest fellows for a mysterious expedition whose goal is still completely unknown to you."

"Exactly."

"Well, my dear Mr. Edmond, I've taken it into my head to help you in your task and I have reason to believe that you'll follow my advice point by point. Thus, for instance, this Hardy you've just hired—I don't want him."

"Why not?" asked Fred Jorgell's representative, astonished.

"Simply because I don't like him."

"But…"

"That's the way it is."

Edward Edmond remained silent. A violent conflict was taking place within him. Eventually, he said: "It doesn't seem possible for me to do as you wish. This Hardy, for example…"

"You'll send him away and compensate him," said Slug. "Anyway, you must realize that you won't lose anything by this arrangement. You received a thousand dollars a month for letting me examine Fred Jorgell's mail; you'll get two thousand, on condition that you only hire the sailors I indicate to you."

Edward Edmond seemed hesitant. "It's just," he stammered, "that I can't do exactly what I want in this matter; I'm not the master. I'd like nothing better than to be agreeable to you, but…"

"As you please," said Slug, with glacial coldness. And he fixed the Irishman with a stare that made him shiver.

There was a long pause.

"I'll do all that's within my power to be agreeable to you," stammered Edward Edmond, profoundly troubled.

"I don't want a half-promise of that sort," Slug replied, brutally. "You'll do exactly what I say, or you'll do nothing at all, and it will be so much the worse for you."

There was another silence between the two men.

Suddenly, the Mexican guitarists struck up the furious rhythm of a habanera; the electric lighting blazed more brightly, and in a hurricane of applause and hurrahs, Dorypha appeared, a scornful smile on her lips, sure of her power over the crowd.

"The tango!" cried some.

"No, no!" others shouted. "The mexicana."

"No! The habanera!"

Dorypha continued smiling enigmatically, slowly rolling her hips in a harmonious movement, and her indecision brought the enthusiasm and desires of the spectators to a peak.

While putting on a semblance of indifference, however, the dancer was searching the crowd with her keen gaze, and she immediately picked out Edward Edmond. Their eyes met, and the Irishman shivered as if he had put his finger on a red hot iron.

That mute scene had not escaped Slug. "Well?" he demanded. "What's your decision?"

"I'll do anything you want," replied Fred Jorgell's employee, with a feverish urgency. "You have only to command; I'm your man."

The gypsy's presence had sufficed to triumph over all Edward Edmond's hesitations. He had been her lover for several months. In Dorypha's presence, the Irishman was no longer himself. A single glance from her beautiful languid eyes was sufficient to annihilate his firmest resolutions.

"I'm glad to see that you're being reasonable," said Slug, who did not seem at all surprised by that change of attitude. "The men I'll introduce to you are solid fellows in whom one can have full confidence. Anyway, you'll get a thousand dollars on account whenever you wish—tomorrow, if you like."

Meanwhile, Dorypha, who had had time to exchange an imperceptible signal with Slug, had begun to dance the habanera, which was her great showpiece, and in the silence that suddenly fell upon the hall, nothing could be heard but the sound of respirations painting with desire, and the beating of all those racing hearts.

Slug rapidly took his leave of Edward Edmond, and he later went to sit down again with Captain Christian Knox and Seaman Hardy. Neither could help thinking that he had some grave preoccupation, because he had suddenly become taciturn and melancholy, and his gaze no longer quit the dancer, who, her body arched and, breasts thrust forward, her rump vibrant, now seemed to be offering herself to all that multitude, gasping with lust.

Slug had slipped away, and, reaching the far side of the room, had gone into a small "parlor," the door of which opened almost directly opposite the famous grille. There were two men sitting at a table inside, in front of sherry gobblers. They were not wearing masks, but motoring goggles, broad-brimmed hats and ample silk handkerchiefs hid their faces completely. On going in, Slug took off his hat and sat down respectfully in front of the two gentlemen.

"Well, Slug," asked one of them, in a muffled voice, "did you succeed?"

"Yes, Milord. The Irishman will be the most faithful of the Red Hand's slaves from now on."

"It wasn't necessary to tug his ear, then?"

"Hmm! He didn't seem firmly decided, but it only took one glance from Dorypha to render him docile. He's mad about the girl. She'll eat him up to the last dollar and send him to the gallows."

"That's good Slug—you can go. You'll receive new instructions tomorrow."

The bandit bowed obsequiously and disappeared.

As soon as the door had closed behind him, the taller of the drinkers said to the other: "You know, my dear Cornelius, that just now, when I cast a glance into the room, I saw the dancer. What Slug says about her is no exaggeration. She's veritably maddening."

"You think she's beautiful?"

"Marvelous."

"Watch yourself Baruch. With the preoccupations we have, the woman question needs to be firmly set aside, and least for now."

"Oh, don't worry, Doctor. If I mentioned the girl, it's in an entirely disinterested fashion."

Dr. Cornelius made no reply. His attention had just been abruptly attracted by an object placed on the mantelpiece of the parlor. It was a simple bottle of green glass, but by virtue of a long sojourn on the sea-bed, it was covered with stony concretions, seashells and coral, which gave it the bizarre elegance of some vase wrought by the caprice of a Chinese or Japanese artist.

"That's very curious," said Baruch.

"It's more than curious," Cornelius replied.

"From a scientific point of view?"

"Not at all. But that bauble might be useful to our plans..."

Cornelius had pressed an electric bell-push. A waiter appeared.

"Ask the publican how much he wants for that bottle," said Cornelius.

"I know that he's very fond of it," the man replied.

"That's all right. Let him name his price; I won't haggle."

The waiter came back five minutes later. The owner wanted five dollars.

"That's not too dear," the doctor said. "Here's the money—but try to find me a little cardboard box so that I don't damage the item in taking it away."

Five minutes later, Dr. Cornelius and his companion left the Old Grille bodega as mysteriously as they had entered, taking advantage, in order not to be observed, of the moment when the walls of the music hall seemed ready to crumble under the frantic cheers of the spectators applauding Dorypha.

101

II. A Reassuring Letter

The builder of the yacht whose construction was setting the heads of all the seamen in San Francisco abuzz was the billionaire Fred Jorgell. No one had any doubt that the speculator, famous throughout America for his audacious enterprises, was preparing an expedition of an original and grandiose genre. No one, however, was able to furnish the slightest information about it. The billionaire and his entourage were observing the most complete reserve with everyone. The curious were reduced to conjectures.

Some said that Fred Jorgell was going to exploit a gold-mine situated on some unknown island, without bothering with any legal formalities. Others talked about a bed of pearl-bearing oysters discovered near some Oceanian reef. For others, it was a matter of a deposit of guano richer than those in the Chincha Islands.

The rich Yankee did not contradict any of these rumors, but he maintained an absolute silence, and after several weeks, the indiscreet were no further forward than on the first day.

Required by his multiple business affairs to shuttle back and forth between San Francisco and New York, the billionaire was continually in transit between the two cities, and the luxury carriage that he owned was, so to speak, permanently attached to one of the express trains on the Central Pacific Railroad, which cuts straight across the American continent.

Ten leagues from San Francisco, in an enchanting location, Fred Jorgell had installed his daughter Isidora in a vast and luxurious cottage, where several of the billionaire's friends had also found hospitality. Golden Cottage was a veritably unique residence. Built in a verdant valley at the foot of a wooded hill, where a few of the giant sequoias that sometimes reach a hundred meters in height could still be seen, the dwelling was constructed on the exact plan of one of the elegant and simple villas that are found in the region of Rome.

With its galleries of white marble columns, its balustrades and its terraces furnished with precious faience vases containing rare trees, Golden Cottage fitted in perfectly with the beautiful blue Californian sky, and stood out poetically against the dark background of cedars, maples and gigantic pines whose branches fused into a natural dome higher and more magnificent than that of the Panthéon.

The villa's garden designed in the Renaissance style, was populated with statues, fountains and rocky grottoes, surrounded by large clumps of lemon-trees and orange-trees.

The superb cottage had been uninhabited for a long time, its previous owner having died, the victim of a murder whose perpetrators had never been discovered. The inhabitants of the nearby hacienda claimed that Golden Cottage was haunted, that sinister noises could be heard there at night, and that it had brought misfortune to everyone who had lived in it, but in America, an exceedingly pragmatic land, superstitions of that sort are not admitted for long. Fred Jorgell had found a magnificent property at a moderate price in an isolated situation in the middle of the countryside—precisely what he wanted—and he had not hesitated for a moment before acquiring it.

Among the villa's guests was Harry Dorgan, Isidora's fiancé, whose marriage to her, announced long ago in the Union's newspapers, had been delayed by various circumstances. The engineer spent his days in San Francisco, where he was supervising the construction of the yacht *Revenge*, and only came back to Golden Cottage in the evening.

Harry was assisted in his work by two first-rate French scientists, the engineer Antoine Paganot and the naturalist Roger Ravenel. They too returned to the cottage every evening, where they found their fiancées, Andrée de Maubreuil and Frédérique Bondonnat, two intimate friends of Isidora.

The billionaire's other guests included the eccentric Lord Astor Burydan, once famous in Paris under the name of Milord Bamboche, and his friend and secretary Agénor Marmousier. Finally, there was an Indian named Kloum, in the lord's service, and an intelligent young hunchback, Oscar Tournesol, a former protégé of Monsieur de Maubreuil, who was now everyone's intimate friend.

The day after the scene in the Old Grille bodega, the three young women were alone in the cottage, as they were almost every day. Fred Jorgell, Harry Dorgan and his collaborators were in San Francisco Lord Burydan had gone on an excursion into the forest; Agénor, the Indian and Oscar had gone with him. Isidora, Andrée and Frédérique were sheltering from the heat of the day in a arbor furnished with marble benches, refreshed by the moist spray of a fountain.

Except for Mademoiselle de Maubreuil, who was still a trifle melancholy, the young women were radiant.

"Do you know, my dear friends," said Isidora, "that Harry received a letter from his father this morning. What is astonishing about it is that William Dorgan also thinks that my marriage ought to be delayed."

"For what reason?"

"Since my future father-in-law has been reconciled with his son, he's decided to give him a sum at least equal to my own dowry, and is waiting for the settlement of the quarterly accounts to fix the amount; he doesn't want the marriage to take place until the question's completely settled."

"Harry must be glad to be back in his father's good graces."

Isidora smiled sadly. "It's strange," she said. "One might think that a kind of fatality is opposing my marriage to Harry. Every time we think it's about to happen, some reason comes up to delay it—as when, the date having been fixed, my fiancé fell gravely ill, poisoned by the bandits of the Red Hand and afflicted with an almost-unknown malady."

"Green leprosy," said Andrée de Maubreuil.

103

"But for Monsieur Paganot, it would have been the end of him."

"But since Harry's entirely recovered," said Andrée, "you could have got married weeks ago."

Isidora took the hands of the two young women and squeezed them affectionately. "I know that," she said, "and I could have done, but it was me who didn't want to—and my fiancé and my father approved completely of my decision. After the immense service that you've rendered us, I've decided that I'll only marry Harry when Monsieur Bondonnat has been set free."

"You're the most generous and best of friends, Isidora," murmured Frédérique, emotionally. "We'll never forget the devotion you've shown to us— and it's almost egotism on our part to accept such a sacrifice." Sadly, she added: "Who knows whether we might not have to wait a long time for my father's deliverance?"

"No," Isidora replied, warmly. "All the more so as, since the return of Lord Burydan, who was a prisoner on the Island of Hanged Men himself, we possess definite information. The world isn't so vast that, with the means of action at our disposal, an island situated in a glacial region can escape discovery by us!"

"How long do you think it will take to find my father?" Frédérique asked.

"Be sure that the result will be rapidly achieved. Personally, I think six weeks, give or take a little."

"That will mean," Andrée said, "that our three marriages can take place on the same day."

"My father and father-in-law," said Isidora, "have promised to put on a superb celebration that day. You'll see, my dear friends, that the series of misfortunes will finally come to an end and that the future will compensate us abundantly for the past."

"I no longer have the courage to believe in happiness," Andrée murmured. "We've had so many cruel disappointments! Don't you fear that the bandits of the Red Hand...?"

"Don't think about that," Isidora interjected. "You know very well that since the mass arrests have been carried out, no more mention has been heard of them. They're a gang of wretches who don't have the strength to contend with my father's billions and my fiancé's science. If they try anything, they'll be defeated in advance."

At that moment, the Scottish governess, Mrs. MacBarlott, came into the arbor. She announced that Lord Burydan and his friends had returned. They did not take long to present themselves in the arbor to show the three young women the game they had killed.

With rifle slung over their shoulders and Bowie knife in their belts, the eccentric Lord and Agénor were dressed in superb hunting costumes and wore large Mexican straw hats. The hunchback and the Indian, more simply dressed in khaki, were bowed down under the weight of game. They displayed to the gazes of the young women chaplets of wood-pigeon and red grouse, wild peacocks, turkeys, and even a large red vulture, which Lord Burydan's infallible bullet had sought out almost in the clouds.

The hunters received the congratulations to which they were entitled. The cynegetic exhibition had not concluded when a domestic came to tell Lord Burydan that a stranger was asking to speak to him about an urgent matter.

"Well, send him out here," said the eccentric. "I wonder what he wants—I don't know anyone around here."

The domestic soon returned, followed by an individual with a bronzed face and an oblique and fugitive gaze, who had the disquieting appearance of one of those adventurers, half-merchants and half-pirates, who are numerous in San Francisco. He was carrying a rather large cardboard box under his arm.

Leaving his friends a little to one side, Lord Burydan advanced to meet the visitor, who did not see at all intimidated by the numerous company into whose midst he had just been introduced.

"Why are you?" asked the eccentric, scarcely disposed in favor of the newcomer by his appearance and expression.

"I'm Captain Christian Knox, well-known in San Francisco, the former commandant of the schooner *Rocket*, which unfortunately went down with all hands a month ago on a coral reef near Easter Island. Are you Lord Burydan?"

"Yes."

"Then I have something to put into your own hands."

The captain had opened the cardboard box. He took out a bottle that a long sojourn on the sea bed had covered with seashells and calcareous deposits—the same one that Cornelius had bought from the "publican" of the Old Grille. It had been subjected to clever trickery, however, and an inscription that appeared to have been engraved with the aid of hydrofluoric acid, like the labels on bottles of Seltz water, was now clearly visible on one side of it.

"What's that?" asked Lord Astor, surprised.

"I don't know, in truth," the adventurer replied, "but what's certain is that it's addressed to you. Read it."

Lord Burydan took the bottle and deciphered the words engraved in the glass, not without difficulty. They were traced in a cursive script in compact characters, as if they had been traced with a brush dipped in the acid.

Aloud, Lord Burydan read: "A hundred dollars reward to whomever hands this bottle to Lord Burydan."

The two young women had drawn nearer and were examining the singular bottle carefully. Frédérique suddenly uttered a cry of surprise. "That's my father's handwriting!" she exclaimed.

"Where did you find this bottle?" asked Lord Burydan,

"At sea off the coast of Chile, while fishing over a reef. One of my men discovered it in the midst of a mass of marine plants filling our net."

"Is the sailor still alive? Can you bring him here?"

"Alas, no, Milord. The poor devil died with his comrades in the wreck of the *Rocket*, and it was by pure chance that I saved this bottle, which was found in my chest with other effects."

"That's all right—thank you. The sender of the bottle promised a hundred dollars—here's two hundred."

Captain Christian Knox pocketed the sum with a satisfied smile, bowed deeply and withdrew, after having taken care to hand Lord Astor a greasy piece of paper bearing the address of the Old Grille, where the pirate had taken up residence.

The impatience of all the witnesses of the scene had reached its height. In accordance with what Mademoiselle Bondonnat had said, they were convinced that the bottle contained a message from the old scientist. It is well-known that that hazardous means of correspondence has been employed by sailors in peril for centuries, and, extraordinarily enough, it is much more frequent than one might imagine for such missives to reach their destination.

In the midst of a solemn silence, Lord Burydan scraped away the seashells covering the cork and neck of the bottle with his hunting-knife.

Beneath the seashells there was a lead capsule, which he extracted, and which had protected the cork so well that it had suffered hardly any damage from the corrosive action of the sea-water. When it was removed, Lord Astor perceived a long round object that he extracted from the bottle and examined carefully.

"It's a tube of glass sealed at both ends and covered in leather," Lord Burydan declared, in the midst of a pregnant silence.

"That's where the letter must be," said Frédérique, her heart palpitating with anguish.

The glass tube had been sealed with a blow-lamp and had to be broken. It contained a piece of paper, tightly rolled up. In her impatience Frédérique almost snatched it from Lord Burydan's hands and unfolded it precipitately.

"My father! My father!" she stammered. "It's from my father! It's his handwriting! I can't be mistaken! Oh, how happy I am! But I'll read it aloud to you."

And she read it, in a tremulous voice.

Milord,

I don't know whether this letter will reach you; however, given the direction of the currents, which I've studied carefully, it appears to me to be quite possible. I've made twenty copies of it, enclosed in as many bottles thrown into the sea at intervals. I've taken the most scrupulous precautions to make sure that the water can't affect the paper or the writing. Thanks to the products that I have in my laboratory, I've even been able to engrave your name in the glass, promising a reward to anyone who gives you the bottle.

If I'm writing to you, it's because I'm sure, given the perfection of my air-ship, which the brave Kloum knows how to maneuver, that your escape has succeeded.

I hope and desire with all my heart that you're safe, with Kloum and my dog Pistolet, and I'm certain, if that is so, that you'll do the impossible to get me out of the hands of my torturers. Left alone in their hands after the failure of my escape attempt, I feared that they might take their revenge by subjecting me to all kinds of vexations. Fortunately, nothing of the sort has happened. They've contented themselves with watching me more closely, and to help me in my research they no longer give me anyone but bandits with sinister faces, with respect to whom any attempt at corruption is futile. My health is still good, in spite of the ennui and anxiety by which I'm tormented.

But let's get to the point. The objective of this letter, my dear lord, is to give you some information without which you will have the greatest difficulty discovering my place of exile You don't know the latitude and the longitude of the Island of Hanged Men, which I have succeeded in discovering, and which are 110° east longitude, Paris meridian, and 50° south latitude—which is to say, in approximate region of the Antarctic Circle, between Cape Horn and the Land of Desolation...

Lord Burydan interrupted the reading to say: "Kloum, did Monsieur Bondonnat ever mention these figures to you?"

"I don't believe so," the Indian replied, searching his memory. "It seems to me that he did mention the words latitude and longitude, but he doubtless regarded me as too ignorant to comprehend something like that."

"I'll resume reading," said Frédérique.

I assume that with this precise indication it will be easy for you to discover he bandits' lair. You are my only hope, for I fear that, in spite of all their promises, the rogues detaining me will never set me free unless they are forced to do so.

I beg you also to communicate this news to my daughter and to keep her informed of any attempt you make to save me

Believe in the gratitude of your companion in jail.

Prosper Bondonnat

"It goes without saying," said Lord Burydan, "that this letter presents all the characteristics of authenticity."[6]

---

[6] A truly remarkable observation, from a man who has twice made the journey between the vicinity of the Aleutians and North America without passing through the tropics, and who spent almost all of his imprisonment on the Island

"It's certainly from my father!" declared Frédérique.

"I think so too," said Andrée.

"And me," said the poet Agénor.

Only the hunchback and the Indian said nothing. Both of them, without being able to explain it, scented a trap. They examined the letter and the bottle in vain, however, unable to find any serious objection to offer to their friends.[7] They were obliged to agree that the arrival of the message was, after all, no more extraordinary than many other events that they had been privileged to witness.

Isidora did not hide her enthusiasm. "Now," she exclaimed, "we can fix the exact date on which the three marriages can be celebrated. Harry will be so glad!"

Andrée de Maubreuil reflected. "I can explain now," she said, "why the first letter we received from my dear guardian was sent from New Orleans. It evidently came from the south, via Chile or Peru, and was put into the post by one of the Red Hand's correspondents."

"Poor Pistolet," said the little hunchback, suddenly. "Monsieur Bondonnat will be desolate when he learns that his faithful companion has disappeared."

"It wasn't my fault," said Lord Burydan, "or Kloum's. When our airship came down near the negro village and we were attacked by them, Pistolet was hit by stones and perhaps, I fear, revolver bullets. He fled in panic, and must have hidden in a cotton-field. We were being chased ourselves, and weren't able to go to his aid."

"We'll find Pistolet," said Isidora, cheerfully, who was envisaging the future in the brightest colors. "If necessary, my father will send skillful detectives to look for the dog, since he's your friend."

They smiled at this joke. Everyone shared the young woman's optimism. Now that they knew exactly where Monsieur Bondonnat was, they regarded his rescue almost as a *fait accompli*.

Everyone waited impatiently for Fred Jorgell and the three fiancés to return, in order to show them the famous bottle and read them the illustrious prisoner's letter.

---

of Hanged Men in the company of Eskimos, presumably aware of a local fauna including reindeer, elk and Arctic foxes (but no penguins).

[7] Not even the small point that if the bottle had floated, it would not be covered in debris from the sea bed (which, incidentally, must have taken far more years to accumulate than the duration of Bondonnat's imprisonment), whereas if it had not, it could not possibly have reached the vicinity of the Chilean coast unless it was actually dropped into the water there. Given that a scientific genius like Dr. Cornelius had failed to think of those details, however, what can one expect of his intellectually-disadvantaged adversaries?

The residents of Golden Cottage would have experienced the most bitter disappointment had they been able to suspect that the letter that caused them such satisfaction had been written by one of the Red Hands most skillful forgers, and that the recipient enclosing it had been addressed to them by their cruelest enemy.

The yacht *Revenge* was about to head for the South Pole, whereas the Island of Hanged Men was in the vicinity of the North Pole. Who could tell what might become of Fred Jorgell and his friends, led astray by false clues into the deserted Southern Seas, far from any hospitable coast or civilized people?

III. A Manager's Misfortunes

Installed on the terrace of Golden Cottage, from which one could see one of the most beautiful landscapes in the world, Fred Jorgell's guests were savoring the freshness of the breeze, embalmed by the scents of the forest, and listening to the thousand mysterious sounds rising from the dormant countryside. Overhead, the sky was a velvet blue, spangled with dazzling stars, of whose glorious gleam nothing in our moist and crepuscular climate can evoke any idea.

Isidora was sitting beside Harry Dorgan, Frédérique next to Roger Ravenel, Andrée de Maubreuil next to Antoine Paganot. Each couple had struck an identical pose. Staring into one another's eyes, their hands tightly enlaced, the fiancés abandoned themselves to the charm of the beautiful evening. The great silence was only occasionally troubled by the imperceptible sound of a sigh or a furtive kiss.

Suddenly, Lord Burydan stood up. "They're so happy!" he murmured. "What a pity that I don't have a charming young lady for a fiancée! In the meantime though, I think it's urgently necessary that I find some distraction. It's a long time since I've been to San Francisco."

"Nothing simpler, my lord," said Fred Jorgell. "I've made sure that I always have an auto or two ready to depart."

"Well, my word, that's an idea. It's only nine o'clock. I'll get to Frisco just in time to take a turn around the taverns in the harbor."

"It's well known," said the billionaire, "that you're a lover of the picturesque. I regret being unable to accompany you, but I'm rather tired."

"Who will accompany me, then?"

"Me, Milord!" cried the hunchback, enthusiastically.

"Me too," said Agénor. "But where the devil is Kloum?"

"The honest Indian has already gone to bed," Oscar replied. "Anyway, we can do without him."

"Well then, it's agreed!" exclaimed the eccentric, rejoicing in the idea of the escapade. Give me time to get a gun from my room and I'm all yours!"

Ten minutes later, Lord Burydan, Agénor and the hunchback were heading at top speed along a white road bordered with magnificent trees, at the extremity of which a kind of halo of light was visible, which revealed the proximity of the city of San Francisco.

The capital of the Pacific does not have any of the dreariness of the puritan cities of the East and Center. It is a city in which people stay up late, enjoying themselves. When Lord Burydan and his friends arrived there, the main arteries—Market Street, California, Kearny and Montgomery Streets—were still thronged by an active and joyful crowd.

The auto was left in the garage of the gigantic Palace Hotel, which has no less than five hundred rooms and is an entire city in itself. The three friends made use of the Cable Car—a kind of funicular—which took them to the Queen City district for a few cents.

They had scarcely had time to take a few steps when they were accosted by a grave and formally-dressed individual. He was a detective who, for forty dollars, offered to take them on a tour of the most dangerous dens of vice: sailors' taverns, opium dens and brothels.

Lord Burydan refused the police officer's services. "I'm only interested in visiting low dives," he said, "when I find them for myself and I can run some danger there. Besides which, I don't have anything to fear; I'm Lord Burydan."

"That's different," muttered the stranger, drawing away discontentedly. "I know that Milord Bamboche is well-regarded by all the rabble."

The nickname of Milord Bamboche, which the populace of Paris had given the eccentric, had—God only knows how—made him well-known in San Francisco, where it had immediately won him favor. A few nocturnal strolls had sufficed for Milord Bamboche to become as popular with Californian adventurers as he had once been with the apaches of Paris.

The three nocturnal strollers, relying solely on their own inspiration to discover picturesque lairs, entered at random into two or three sordid establishments, but found nothing there except uninteresting drunkards. They had better luck on going into a long corridor at the entrance to which a negro clad in a sort of robe demanded a entry fee of a shilling.

They thought they were going into a music hall, and did not change their opinion on emerging into a square hall where a large number of negroes of both sexes were agitating. Accompanied on the banjo, a large black man in a white chemise was howling the words of a song in a bizarre unknown language, with forceful gesticulations.

The black man was like a man possessed. Milord Bamboche enjoyed his grimaces greatly, and when he had finished he applauded loudly, while calling energetically for champagne. That demonstration was poorly received; it was not a music hall but a chapel of howling Methodists that the eccentric lord had found. All the negroes making up the audience put down their banjoes and threw the intruders out with forceful complaints.

"That was interesting," said Oscar. "Let's continue our wandering. Look, let's go this way—here's a back street that might be curious."

The hunchback pointed to a narrow alleyway in which, at intervals, swinging lanterns advertising furnished hotels or taverns of the meanest category.

They had taken a few steps along an uneven pavement cluttered with barrels, crates and all manner of abandoned objects when a bizarrely-clad drunkard wearing a top hat and long boots tottered toward them. His equilibrium was so poor that in passing close to Agénor he lurched into him and almost knocked him down

As often happens, the drunkard imagined that it was him who had been jostled. "Imbecile!" he shouted at the poet.

"Imbecile yourself," retorted Lord Burydan, who not very patient by nature.

"Idiot!"

"Cretin!"

"Brute!"

"Wine-sack!"

These epithets, and others even less gracious, were being exchanged between the eccentric lord and the drunkard, but the latter suddenly became furious. "Me, a wine-sack!" he bellowed, in a hoarse voice. "*Heu heu!* Me, who never drinks anything but gin and...even...with water..."

Fists forward, he charged Lord Burydan. The latter, as we know, was an expert boxer. Nonchalantly, he gave his adversary two or three straight lefts and as many right hooks, which had the result of sending the awkward sot sprawling on the ground a few yards away.

He got up in an extremely pitiful state. The back of his overcoat was covered in mud and his top hat, on which he had sat when he fell, now resemble an accordion. That observation redoubled the drunkard's fury.

"And with what, now, *heu heu!*" he said, tearfully, "can I introduce myself in society. A true gentleman is recognized...*heu heu!*...by his impeccable dress..."

He was so exasperated that, doubtless thinking that he was dealing with one of the cut-throats who pullulate in San Francisco, he pointed the barrel of an enormous Browning at Agénor.

It was then that Oscar, who was a past master in the art of kick-boxing, sent the weapon spinning away with a thrust of his foot, while Lord Burydan, exasperated in his turn, grabbed the drunkard by the collar and dragged him all the way to a drinking-fountain situated at the end of the street.

"You've drunk too much, my lad," he said, "but I'll apply the hydrotherapeutic treatment, which will certainly do you a great deal of good."

Methodically, he placed the drunkard's head under the tap of the fountain and began to refreshing him with a copious douche; then, perceiving a pewter cup on the end of a chain, he filled it and, holding his patient's nose, forced him to drink a copious draught.

"What do you think of the treatment?" mocked Lord Burydan.

"Mercy! Mercy, Milord!"

"No, that's not sufficient. Here, have another cupful...and another...and another...."

Between two cupfuls, the drunkard uttered a lamentable sigh. "Sir," he said, humbly, "you've sworn my death! It's ten years since I drank as much pure water, *heu heu!* I'm choking...*heu heu!*"

Oscar Tournesol, who was watching the scene laughing wholeheartedly, suddenly uttered a cry of surprise. "But it's old Sleary!" he exclaimed. "I'm not mistaken! Let him go, my lord—he's harmless. What the devil can he be doing in San Francisco?"

"If he's a friend of yours, that's different," said the eccentric, who rendered the unfortunate director of the Gorilla Club his freedom of movement, while the hunchback returned his top hat and his Browning, which he had taken care to pick up.

"Who are you, then...*heu heu*?" demanded Mr. Sleary, in astonishment, somewhat sobered up by the cold water.

"What?" the hunchback replied. "You don't recognize Oscar Tournesol, one of the most brilliant boarders of the Gorilla Club, the favorite pupil of the illustrious clown Bombridge?"

A feminine silhouette had just appeared in the middle of the alleyway, and an irritated voice shouted: "Hey, Mr. Sleary! Where are you? Hurry up and come back in. You've drunk enough."

"Here comes, in fact," said the manager, "Miss Regina Bombridge, who's looking for me everywhere. But I recognize you perfectly, Master Tournesol...*heu heu!* Delighted to see you...*heu heu!* And me, who took your friends for veritable bandits!"

"Mr. Sleary!" shouted the young woman, again.

"She's impatient, you see...*heu heu!*...let's go join her! All the more so as I wouldn't be sorry to have a hot toddy...*heu heu!* I absorbed so much water just now, as much externally as internally, that I might get fluxions in my chest...*heu heu!*"

Everyone approached the young woman, to whom Oscar reintroduced himself and reassured her as to the consequences of the singular combat in which Mr. Sleary had taken part. Then they went into a bar a few paces away. Lord Burydan, who was curious to hear about the drunkard's adventures, ordered a bottle of champagne.

While it was being uncorked, the honorable director of the Gorilla Club tidied up his clothing, restored the shape of his top hat with a blow of his fist, and finally resumed the respectable allure for which he was known.

As for Miss Regina Bombridge, a short, thin and pallid blonde with pretty blue eyes full of candor, she could not get over the surprise of her director's encounter with such well-dressed gentlemen, who seemed to have pockets full of banknotes.

Gravely, Oscar Tournesol made the introductions, which seemed to cause Mr. Sleary, who was always very respectful of propriety, great pleasure. Then the hunchback enquired about the adventure that had brought the director of the Gorilla Club to San Francisco.

At first, the latter only replied with a shake of the head and a sigh; then, on the reiterated insistences of Lord Burydan, he decided to tell the tale of his misfortunes. "My establishment, the Gorilla Club, has been sold, *heu heu!*" he murmured, dejectedly. "I owed my landlord three months rent...my boarders were all behind in their payments...finally, I confess, *heu heu*...that I was not always very wise in my administration. I'm an artiste, myself, what do you expect? I'm not a number-cruncher...*heu heu!* But let's not dwell on that catastrophe..."

"All right," said Oscar, filling the manager's cup. "Let's not dwell on that—but tell us how it is that I find you in San Francisco."

"Quite naturally, I tried to get back on my feet...*heu heu!*...and with the aid of those of my boarders who were without employment—which was almost all of them—I put together a troupe that, without boasting, was first-rate. We gave some rather brilliant performances in Chicago, but, as you know, when bad luck has it in for someone, everything he attempts goes awry. In San Francisco, there was a disaster! Our cashier ran off with the takings...they refused to let us hire halls...*heu heu!*...."

"And where are you now?" asked Lord Burydan, very interested.

"At the ultimate degree of poverty and misery," Mr. Sleary replied, in a cavernous tone. "There are moments when I think about suicide—so, don't be surprised, my lord, to have encountered me in a state of inebriation ill-befitting a true gentleman. I only drink to forget my chagrin!"

This declaration had the effect of raising, even on the part of the blonde Miss Bombridge, a gale of laughter that was only suppressed with difficulty. Very vexed, Mr. Sleary emptied his champagne-glass with an expression of disgust and pursed his lips like a man determined not to lavish his confidences on people who were unworthy to hear them.

"The truth," he explained, "is that our entire troupe is the prisoner of a publican who has taken possession of our costumes and baggage. He heaps bitter reproaches on us every day and only grants us a derisory quantity of nourishment for every meal. He claims that it's a mean of stimulating our genius in order to make us find brilliant engagements that will permit us to pay him."

"Let's go see the publican!" cried Lord Burydan, with the rapidity of decision typical of him.

Everyone got up, even the ceremonious Mr. Sleary, and they went to the wretched furnished hotel—fortunately, it was only a few steps away—where the lamentable wreckage of the Gorilla Club had washed up.

The publican, a fat apoplectic man with a bald skull, russet side-whiskers and a glowering, mistrustful gaze, was standing on the threshold of his establishment, watching out for Mr. Sleary's return, but when he saw him with a numerous company his wrath knew no bounds.

"Drunken vagabond!" she shouted, with a strong German accent. "Not content with stuffing yourself to my expense, you doubtless want to introduce more starvelings into my house! That shan't be, *der Teufel!* No one will come in here unless they have ready cash!"

On hearing that tone of voice, Lord Burydan felt the mustard rising to his nose.. He needed all his strength of will not to inflict an exemplary correction on the miscreant immediately.

"How much does Mr. Sleary owe you?" he asked.

"A hundred dollars!"

"That's all right—I'll give them to you. Except, I warn you that if you don't show my friends and me the most exquisite politeness, nothing will prevent you from administering the most magisterial clip round the ear that you've ever received."

At a sign from his friend, Agénor held out a banknote to the astounded publican, who was already exclaiming in a honeyed tone: "Will your honor please excuse me; I was only talking about these villainous acrobats. Will your honor please take the trouble to come in."

"Try to be more respectful toward my friends the acrobats," replied the eccentric. "You're the one who's nothing but a rogue—or, as they say in France, an infamous *taulier*."[8]

And without waiting for the man's response, he went inside the hotel and followed Mr. Sleary to a low room where the members of the Gorilla Club were sadly finishing their evening, playing poker for beans for want of any more substantial stakes. A single gas-lamp, whose flame had been lowered by the publican for reasons of economy, illuminated that scene of desolation, leaving the strange and melancholy faces of the performers in a kind of penumbra.

"Hey, fellow!" shouted Lord Burydan. "Light! Champagne! And supper for all these worthy people, whom you appear to be allowing to die of starvation. And make sure that the food and drink is top quality, or you'll have to answer to me!"

That order was carried out with surprising celerity. In the blink of an eye, floods of light inundated the room, mirrored cheerfully in the gilded necks of bottles, the engaging whiteness of plates and the metal of cutlery. The acrobats, even the less agile, had leapt up in surprise, and a cheer soon went up from every throat.

"Milord Bamboche! Long live Milord Bamboche! Three cheers for Milord Bamboche!"

When that cheerful din had died away, the eccentric was able to admire the bizarre figures surrounding him at his leisure.

They included Goliath, the chain-breaker, the athlete who, suspended by his legs from a trapeze, could lift a horse and its rider with his teeth, the strongest man in the world, whose biceps were a meter round; Fulguras the salamander, the human torch, as comfortable in fire as if it were his natural element; Bob Horwett, the expert swimmer nicknamed "the modern triton"; Romulus, the human cannonball who had himself loaded into a cannon and, projected by the

---

[8] A slang and uncomplimentary contraction of "hotelier."

explosion toward he vault of the hall, seized a trapeze in mid-flight, on which he executed the most perilous exercises; the brothers Macoco and Cambo, incomparable in their imitations of the simian tribe; the prestidigitator Matalobos; the Chinese juggler Yan Kai; and finally, the Robertsons, two thin clowns, first-rate artistes. And let us not forget the honorable Mr. Bombridge, the master and example of the entire lineage of clowns.

With regard to the ladies, we shall cite the beautiful Nudita, admirable in plastic poses and luminous dances; the equilibrist Winny, an Englishwoman who, like the Frenchman Blondin, had traversed Niagara Falls on a tightrope; and the trick-riders Isabella, Olga and the blonde Regina Bombridge.

Mr. Sleary, whose ill humor had dissipated as if by magic, gravely introduced all the members of his company to Lord Burydan, and took advantage of the opportunity to offer a complete and detailed eulogy to the talents of each and every one. That ceremony of introduction lasted a good half hour, but the artists and the ladies did not wait for it to be concluded before launching a very serious attack upon a vast dish of ham and sauerkraut with Frankfurter sausages that the publican had deposited in the center of the table.

The sauerkraut disappeared as rapidly as if the prestidigitator Matabolos himself had spirited it away into one of his sleeves. It was replaced by an enormous joint of cold roast beef, which suffered the same fate.

Lord Burydan contemplated the appetite of the worthy folk admiringly. One might have thought that they had not eaten for weeks. The publican, trotting incessantly between the dining room and the kitchen, his arms laden with victuals and bottles, had the greatest difficult keeping up with his role.

Finally, the frenzied feast gradually began to calm down. Only Goliath continued to attack the collapsed ruins of a vast pâté, while his comrades engaged in a general conversation.

Everyone was making a fuss of the little hunchback, to whom, in sum, they owed the blowout, but Oscar hardly seemed to hear them. He was sitting beside the blonde Regina, and they were both engrossed in a hushed conversation so interesting that they seemed to have forgotten the rest of the world. However, he could not prevent himself feeling a certain emotion when the two clowns Macoco and Cambo, who had absented themselves briefly, reappeared dressed in their ape costumes. Slightly inebriated by the champagne they had drunk, they delivered themselves to a thousand capers, of which the one best appreciated by the audience consisted of leaping on to the publican's shoulders and forcing him to take part in a game of leap-frog, in spite of his energetic protests.

"Say, my dear Oscar," said Macoco, "to show us that you're not proud, you ought to put on your old costume."

"Yes," Regina approved, "that's right."

"It'll remind us of the Lunatic Asylum."

"You don't have to beg me," said the hunchback. "You'll see that I haven't forgotten the Gorilla Club's lessons!"

A few moments later he reappeared in the gorilla suit and, to the enthusiastic cheers of the audience, he executed a series of perilous somersaults over the table, with complete success.

The joy was at its peak. Goliath had already wrenched the leg off a table to demonstrate his strength. The beautiful Nudita had leapt on to the table and, arming herself with two fragments of a plate by way of castanets, began to perform a characteristic dance. Fulgura, the incombustible man, shouted for punch in order to show off his talents. The clowns balanced items implausibly on the ends of their noses. The Chinaman had disappeared and was only found the next day rolled up in a carpet, where he was sound asleep. As for the prestidigitator Matabolos, he made everything that came to hand disappear into his double-bottomed pockets: cutlery, bottles and food alike.

The publican, white with consternation, thought he was dealing with a troop of unchained devils. He dared not raise the slightest protest. Lord Burydan was plunged into veritable ecstasy. Far from opposing the acrobats' japes, he suggested a thousand baroque ideas to them, which they hasted to put into execution.

Mr. Sleary, who was drunk again, had ended up falling asleep under his chair, his top hat tilted over his ear and an empty bottle in his arms, but he retained a dignified appearance nevertheless.

The animation finally died down, however. The poet Agénor was the first to notice that the clowns were beginning to yawn mightily and that the young bareback-riders were rubbing their eyes like people who would not be sorry to go to bed.

Lord Burydan summoned the publican and demanded the bill along with a final round of extra-dry. The most torpid guests woke up then to drink the health of the honorably Amphitryon, but the eccentric imposed silence on them with a gesture.

"My friends," he said, "I've just spent a very agreeable evening in your company, but let's talk a little more seriously now, if you please. I have a proposition to make to you."

There was a profound sensation in the audience, and it was in the midst of the most perfect attention that Lord Burydan continued.

"I know that you're devoid of an engagement at the moment, that you even have debts—that you are, in sum, in a bad way. Well, it's nothing less than a matter of getting you out of that unfortunate situation in the most brilliant fashion."

"How's that, my lord?" several voices asked, impatiently.

"I've had the whim to become an impresario. If you consent, therefore, I'll hire you all, on conditions that none of you will have cause to regret. It's not in my character to haggle. You can fix the level of your wages yourselves."

A frantic acclamation drowned him out. The poor devils had never dared to hope for such a windfall. They would assuredly accept!

Amid these delirious acclamations, "Long live Milord Bamboche!" was repeated a thousand times.

"One moment, if you please," said the eccentric. "I haven't told you everything. It might be that I'll take you a long way from here, that we'll be obliged to make a long voyage..."

"That's okay with us," the clowns interjected, impetuously. "We all accept. When do we leave?"

"I don't know that myself. It might be in three weeks, perhaps a month, perhaps later, but from tomorrow on you'll receive your wages as if you were already performing. That's all I can tell you. The rest is a secret that only concerns me."

Lord Burydan and his friends were not long delayed in taking their leave of the acrobats, after the most enthusiastic demonstrations of sympathy on the one hand and gratitude on the other.

Carried away, the little hunchback thought it amusing to return to Golden Cottage wearing his gorilla costume, and it was in that accoutrement that he climbed back into the automobile with Agénor and Lord Burydan.

When the three night birds came back into the cottage the most profound silence reigned there; all the inhabitants were plunged into sleep—which was not at all surprising, given that it was four o'clock in the morning.

It was not until he was in his room that Oscar began to feel the full fatigue of the sleepless night he had spent. Suddenly, he experienced such lassitude that, without taking the trouble to get undressed, he threw himself on his bed, where he did not take long to fall soundly asleep.

He was woken up two hours later by a ray of sunlight that slid through the gap in the shutters, which he had left ajar. He rubbed his eyes, shook himself, yawned, stretched his limbs, and was profoundly surprised at first to find himself so bizarrely dressed.

"Have I been changed into an ape?" he muttered, "or am I back in the Gorilla Club?"

That idea drew a frank burst of laugher from him, and he suddenly recalled the incidents of the previous night. His head felt heavy and he had a sour taste in his mouth, and it was with a veritable enjoyment that he breathed in the fresh and pure air of the garden, deserted and silent at that moment, its clumps of bushes and trees still covered with moist pearls of dew.

That's an idea! he thought. *I'll take a turn around the garden paths. No one else is up yet. Then, when I've had a breath of air, I'll take a bath, and I'll feel much better.*

By virtue of a mischievous impulse perfectly excusable at his age, the little hunchback did not forget to don the hideous cardboard mask pierced with two eye-holes that completed his disguise. Then he went quietly downstairs and wandered through the arbors of orange-trees, where the birds were waking up, with a joyful twittering that mingled with the sobbing of the fountains.

He went into one of the rocky grottoes at the far end of the garden, where rustic seats had been carved in the rock. He was about to sit down on one when Isidora, emerging from a covert in the grotto, suddenly came into view.

The young woman had had the same idea as Oscar. She had come downstairs before anyone else was up, to take an early morning stroll. At the sight of the hideous animal she uttered a scream of terror and fled. Oscar ran after her in order to reassure her, but Isidora, even more frightened, seemed to have winged heels. She leaps nimbly over the flower-beds, the little streams and the ponds.

"Don't be afraid, Miss!" shouted the little hunchback, breathlessly. "It's me, Oscar Tournesol!"

Finally, the mistake was explained, and the young woman started laughing wholeheartedly at the fright the young man had given her.

They both went back into the grotto, and Oscar, with his habitual verve, brought the young billionairess up to date with his adventures of the previous night. The description of the supper given by Lord Burydan to Mr. Sleary's troop amused her greatly.

"Of course," she said, "I'm wondering what your eccentric friend is going to do with all these clowns and acrobats. Doubtless he's planning some new folly."

"On the contrary; he has a very serious plan, and he confided it to me when we were coming back in the auto last night. He's going to utilize all these individuals, whose strength, skill and agility is extraordinary, to lay siege to the Island of Hanged Men. He thinks, with reason, that the swimmers and the strong man will be the most precious of collaborators in such an enterprise."

"It's possible—but it seems to me that the acrobatic troop will take up a great deal of room on our yacht."

"That's why Lord Burydan has decided to charter another vessel, which will travel in convoy with the yacht. His immense fortune permits him to make that sacrifice, and he expects the best results from his plan."

The conversation between the little hunchback and Isidora was interrupted by the arrival of Lord Burydan himself. He had just found a letter with a Canadian postmark in his mail. It was from Mr. and Mrs. Noel Fless, who were living in the Blue House, of which they were now the owners, and who had kept the amnesiac with them in the hope that fresh air, physical exercise and care might bring about an improvement in his condition.

Isidora had the satisfaction of learning that although Baruch's condition remained unchanged, her brother's health was now as good as one could wish.

IV. A Fantastic Tenant

Thanks to its exceptional situation, Golden Cottage had no immediate neighbors. It was necessary to go nearly ten miles to reach the pigeon-farm that was the nearest habitation.

The people of the locality had experienced a true satisfaction in learning that the property that had been so long abandoned had been bought by a billionaire from New York. They had said to one another that the country was finally about to be rid of the tramps, Redskins and vagabonds of all kinds who had made Golden Cottage their favorite meeting place for some while.

Their joy did not last long. After staying there for a few weeks, the billionaire and his friends deserted Golden Cottage as suddenly as they had installed themselves there.

This is why: Fred Jorgell had been obliged to return to New York in the company of Harry Dorgan, their presence rendered indispensable by the distribution of dividends in the Lightning Steamship Company. Antoine Paganot and Roger Ravenel did not leave San Francisco, closely supervising the fitting of the engines to the yacht Revenge. It was then that the eccentric had the idea of a long excursion by automobile to the Mexican frontier. After some hesitation, Isidora and the two Frenchwomen decided to accompany him, and naturally, Agénor, Kloum and the hunchback were invited along on the excursion, which promised to be very picturesque.

Acting in a fashion quite different from Fred Jorgell, the eccentric had entrusted the construction of his yacht to an industrial company with whom he had made a contract stipulating the delivery of the vessel on a fixed date. That way, he did not put himself to any trouble and avoided the cares and the responsibilities that Harry Dorgan and his two friends had assumed.

Golden Cottage, therefore, reverted to silence and abandonment.

The people of the locality, who knew nothing about Fred Jorgell's plans, did not fail to speculate that if the billionaire had abandoned such a comfortable and well-situated habitation, it must be because he had been pursued by apparitions and had heard strange noises in the night, and that the reputation that luxurious cottage and the estate surrounding had of being haunted by evil spirits was further augmented.

Thanks to the bizarre telegraphy of which vagabonds and malefactors make use for rapid communication of interesting news over long distances, the rumor did not take long to spread among the tramps that Golden Cottage was undefended again and, furthermore, furnished with a sumptuousness that permitted an opulent booty to be attained without risk.

Tramps are little inclined to superstition; they only shrugged their shoulders on hearing that he cottage was haunted. The property's bad reputation appeared to them to be a further guarantee of security for their operations.

Only a few days had gone by since Fred Jorgell's departure when two of the knights of the highway scaled the garden walls and, armed with skeleton keys and lock-picks, gained entry to the cottage. Just as they were about to break down a door, however, they were assailed by a large animal, whose species they could not discern in the obscurity, which bit them cruelly in the legs and on the face.

The two thieves fled as fast as they could, abandoning their burglary tools and not knowing what to think. One of them was convinced that the animal that had bitten them was none other than a puma, an American carnivore that was once very numerous in the region, where it had almost been exterminated. The second tramp thought, more plausibly, that their enemy was simply a guard dog, which proved that the villa was not abandoned, as they had thought.

What remained unarguable were the terrible bites that the two vagabonds had received, whose scars they were to bear for a long time.

Other tramps, duly informed, also attempted the adventure, but were no more fortunate. They too came back without any kind of booty, after having received dangerous bites. The animal that had inflicted them could not have been a dog, because they had not heard any barking; furthermore, they were convinced, after asking around that the billionaire had not left any caretaker in his country house. There was something incomprehensible about it, and the legend of the haunted cottage was thus enriched by a further episode. There was talk of a diabolical animal, in which the soul of the former proprietor who had been murdered was doubtless reincarnated.

The phantom in question would not allow anyone into Golden Cottage. It was invulnerable. The steel bullets of the most advanced revolvers passed through its body without doing it the slightest harm. It must have chased away Fred Jorgell, and it chased away everyone who set foot in the accursed house in the same fashion.

Colonists sometimes had occasion to spend the night on the road that passed alongside the grounds of Golden Cottage. They had heard groans that had nothing human about them, and the sound of footsteps, as if someone were running precipitately up or down the stairways. It was concluded that the murdered man was returning to the house to search for some object that had incurred him a penalty in the other world, and that he had to find it in order to have the right to eternal rest. For some, the object in question was a dagger, for others, a treasure, and for others still, a box full of mysterious papers.

Imaginations were working overtime. A short time sufficed to make Golden Cottage a place of repulsion and fear, near to which people did not like to pass, and where no one would have dared to set foot after sunset.

There was, in fact, an element of truth in these legends, but there was nothing fantastic about the animal that gave rise to them. It was a simple barbet dog with a curly black coat, of the intelligent, faithful but ferocious race that is credited by stories with an almost human sagacity. It was the very same Pistolet that had been abducted in an airplane with Monsieur Bondonnat and which, after having spent time on the Island of Hanged Men, had been brought away by Kloum and Lord Burydan.

When the latter, after having landed safely near a negro village situated not far from the Mississippi, had been obliged to take flight, Pistolet, separated from his friends by a howling mob and chased away from them by stones and revolver shots, had only escaped death by taking refuge in a cotton field, where he had stayed until nightfall, dying of hunger and thirst.

At the dead of night, he had decided to emerge from his hiding place and, making prudent detours, he had picked up the trail of Lord Burydan and Kloum, and had followed it as far as the river. There, however, the poor animal had not known which direction to take. He had started wandering at random.

What had been happening then in the dog's mind? What reasoning had he employed? At any rate, after two days of vain searching, he had become convinced that his protectors were definitively lost. Courageously, he had set out marching northwards. His instinct doubtless indicated to him that it was in that direction that he would escape the heat, the mosquitoes and the black men, three enemies that gave him no respite. Every time he encountered negroes, in fact, they tried to capture him, and that was understandable, because he was wearing a leather purse attached to his collar by a string, which Monsieur Bondonnat himself had fastened there. That was what made the negroes believe that the stray dog might be carrying a treasure.

Pistolet avenged himself in his own fashion on his enemies. He rarely passed a night without stealing a chicken, a rabbit or some other animal of a similar sort. Once, he killed a piglet, which he took into a cornfield to eat. Hotly pursued by the animal's owner, he lost an ear to a rifle bullet.

The Island of Hanged Men was located in a cold latitude, so Pistolet, still inconvenienced by his thick coat, nearly succumbed to the heat. The ardent tropical sun left him devoid of strength and courage, devoured by an inextinguishable thirst, but after a few days, Pistolet found a remedy for his discomforts. Doubtless he said to himself: *Since it's too hot during the day, I'll sleep during the day and travel by night.*

And he did as he had resolved.

The savant meteorologist Prosper Bondonnat could not have reasoned more logically.

As for the mosquitoes, Pistolet found a means of deterring their attacks. He rolled in the river mud, which, when it dried out mingled with his coat, provided him with a suit of armor proof against the sharpest stings. He was, of course, hideous. With his missing ear and his savage attitude, showing his teeth to anyone who approached him, he would have resembled a wild beast but for the leather purse still hanging from his collar.

After a short while, the intelligent animal had adapted to that vagabond existence.

As we said, his instinct caused him to turn his back on the hot country and head northwards, but he was arrested by an insurmountable obstacle. He had left the Mississippi to his right, but soon found himself confronted by one of its major tributaries, the Republican, a river almost three times as wide as the Seine. Pistolet might perhaps have succeeded in crossing that extent of water, immense to him, but he quickly perceived that it was infested by alligators.

One day, when he was placidly slaking his thirst, he was nearly devoured by one of those reptiles, whose jaws he heard snapping shut a few inches from his ear. That adventure caused Pistolet to reflect profoundly. From then on, when he was thirsty, he took the greatest precautions, and almost began to drink on the run, like the Nile dogs of which Herodotus speaks in the chapter on crocodiles in his description of Egypt.

Limited to the east by the Mississippi and to the north by the Republican, and feeling the heat, Pistolet was thus obliged to head westwards. For several weeks he followed the bank of a watercourse descending from the Rocky Mountains that eventually flowed into the bosom of the Father-of-Waters.[9]

This itinerary, let us say, did not displease Oscar Tournesol's pupil overmuch. As he climbed p toward the heights from which the sources of the river flowed, in fact, he found a cooler atmosphere more appropriate to the lungs of a French barbet, whose ancestors for many generations had only known a temperate climate.

He found another reason for satisfaction in the complete disappearance of his enemies the negroes. In fact, the slopes of the Rocky Mountains in that part of America are primarily colonized by white men and Spanish half-breeds. The farms, far distant from one another, are a long way from railways and cities. Pistolet was, therefore, now traveling almost as a tourist. At any rate, he found abundant food supplies by surreptitiously taking possession of unwary lambs, for the country through which he was traveling was pastureland, and not a day went by without him encountering immense untended flocks grazing the lush

---

[9] The author inserts a footnote here to derive *"Père-des-Eaux"* [Father-of-Waters] from *"Meschacébé,"* which he claims to be the Indian name for the Mississippi. The word is, indeed, a corruption of an Ojibwe term, whose phonetic rendering is open to negotiation, but modern anthropologists tend to translate it simply as "big river." The Republican River as now identified does not flow into the Mississippi but into the Kansas River, which does subsequently flow into the Mississippi, but that makes no difference to the story of Pistolet's journey, which must be assumed to take him through what are now the states of Missouri, Kansas and Colorado.

grass carpeting the valleys. Pistolet was definitely something of an apache dog, now living entirely by murder and pillage.

Meanwhile, he continued to move straight ahead for, by virtue of instinct as much as reason, he knew that the road was closed to him in a southward direction In addition, he was doubtless conscious of the fact that it would be unwise for him to retrace his steps through the theater of the murders with which his passage was strewn.

Soon, however, the landscape changed: no more farms, no more flocks, no more beaten tracks; even water became scarce.

Pistolet now found himself in the heart of the mountains. He was surrounded by wild heathlands, ravines, precipices and sheer slopes. Sometimes, his route was barred by gigantic masses of granite or impetuous torrents that he was obliged to go around, and in those desolate solitudes he suffered from hunger more than once.

Under the spur of necessity, however, his hunting instincts reawakened; his brain recovered the confused memory of ancestral cunning employed in the pursuit of prey in primitive epochs. He learned once again to drive hares from their lairs, to catch partridges, and to seize aquatic marsh-birds on their nests.

In the same way that he had survived by pillage he survived by hunting. It was thus that in the Middle Ages, for want of miscreants and heretics to treat violently, noble knights had contented themselves during periods of leisure and peace with chasing stags and forcing wild boar.

It was during one of these hunts that, without even noticing it, Pistolet went through one of the passes situated on one of the highest summits on the chain. On the high plateaux of the Rockies, the poor animal had been very cold; it was, therefore, with a veritable satisfaction that he descended again into the more cheerful regions extended on the western slopes.

The same logic—or, if you wish, the same necessity—that had driven him to head toward the sources of the Mississippi's tributaries led him to skirt the banks of the rivers that flowed into the Colorado River, and eventually the Colorado itself. He might perhaps have followed the river all the day to the place where it flows into the Gulf of California if the presence of his ancient enemies, alligators, and the increasing heat had not caused him to turn northwards. It was in that fashion that he was led to cross the Sierra Nevada, even wilder and colder than the Rockies.

As soon as he had come back down into the valleys, however, Pistolet had found himself in the heart of a civilized region, The cities and villages were almost connected. Roads and railways lines were abundant. Game was much scarcer, and our hero was thus forced to resume his existence of pillage, sleeping by day and traveling by night, taking advantage of the well-traced roads that furrowed the state of California, converging toward its capital, San Francisco.

It was thus, without a doubt, that Pistolet got closer from day to day to his friends, obedient to the fatality of the force of events that is exerted on the humblest of creatures as well as the noblest of intelligences.

One night, when Pistolet was trotting briskly along the dusty road, occasionally barking gruffly at the resplendent moon, he suddenly came to a stop, uttering a growl of amazement and pleasure that attested to the profound emotion he had just felt. He remained motionless, his nostrils quivering, his eyes half-closed, agitated by a solemn disquiet.

That was because, in the imperceptible corpuscles that the breeze brought to his olfactory papillae, he had just recognized familiar emanations. All those to whom the poor animal was attached, and who had been good to him, had passed through this place not long ago, and in his canine reasoning he listed Lord Burydan, Kloum, the little hunchback, Andrée, Frédérique, Roger Ravenel and Antoine Paganot. He bayed triumphantly at the heavens, and then started turning round, bounding and gamboling as a sign of satisfaction, his tail wagging and his one ear pricked.

That moment of exaltation did not last long. As a practical dog, he had reflected that it was necessary to find his friends as quickly as possible, and, his nose in the dust, he patiently followed their tracks. The ones he discerned most clearly were those of Kloum and Lord Burydan. They led him to a little wood where the eccentric lord and his servant had been hunting a few days earlier. The wood was bordered by a spiny cactus hedge, which Pistolet managed to get through, not without a few scratches, and found himself in a magnificent garden, which was that of Golden Cottage.

Pistolet spent that entire night, better than a professional detective could have done, in disentangling and following the tracks he had discovered. Unfortunately, all the villa's inhabitants had arrived there and left by automobile, and there inevitably came a moment when each track stopped dead, at which point Pistolet, growling with disappointment, was obliged to retrace his steps.

By daybreak, the faithful animal was worn out with fatigue. He had been going round in circles all night, as if in an invisible labyrinth. He went to sleep in one of the rocky grottoes that ornamented the garden, and resumed his investigations the following night, with no more success than the one before.

On the third night, hunger forced Pistolet to go to a nearby village, where he contented himself with a few bones gleaned from a rubbish-heap, but after that improvised meal he hastened to return to Golden Cottage. There, henceforth, he found himself a prisoner, like the knights of legend who cannot get out of a enchanted circle. All night long he traversed the gardens like a soul in torment, incessantly retracing is steps, thus condemning himself to a torture that a Dante of the canine race would certainly have placed in the cynegetic inferno.

Up to that point, Pistolet had not been able to get inside Golden Cottage, although he had scratched at the doors many a time while barking and whining plaintively. The first burglars that he had put to flight after having bitten them had provided him with the means of getting into the building through the door they had broken.

Pistolet went through all the rooms in the cottage with as little result, evidently, as his exploration of the garden. Disappointed, but not discouraged, he had established his base in a kind of attic where he found a stock of straw, and from then on his life became routinely ordered. After a siesta that lasted all day he went out hunting at sunset, and as soon as he had found some food he came back to devote himself to his patient but futile searches.

Having become almost wild, Pistolet waged an incessant war, as we have seen, on the marauders that he recognized from afar by the suspect odor that he had already scented on the Island of Hanged Men. He flattened himself on the ground as soon as anyone made the gesture of taking aim at him, so he was never wounded, which accredited the legend of his invulnerability.

Pistolet was in the third week of his sojourn at Golden Cottage when an incident occurred that led to a certain modification in his habits and way of life. One day, as he was passing through the spiny hedge, the string attaching to his collar the leather purse that had excited the curiosity of the black men so greatly broke, and the bag fell to the ground.

Pistolet, who had doubtless understood that the object had a certain importance, seized it between his teeth and carried it to his lair. There he stated playing with it, tossing it into the air and catching it, as a professional footballer might have done.

That violent exercise resulted in the thread tied around the neck of the leather bag coming loose. The bag eventually opened, and the twenty-four letters of the alphabet cut out in pieces of wood by Monsieur Bondonnat on the Island of Hanged Men fell out noisily and scattered on the floor.

Pistolet stood still. An entire laborious process took place in his brain. He remembered the patient lessons that he had been given, first by Oscar Tournesol and then by Monsieur Bondonnat himself.

Suddenly, obedient to the secret impulsion of habit, he started forming words, which he immediately erased with his paw in order to form others, while barking joyfully.

V. The Trap

In spite of the zeal of Harry Dorgan and the two Frenchmen who were assisting him, the work of constructing and fitting out the Revenge had initially proceeded with extreme slowness. In spite of the money lavishly distributed by Fred Jorgell, nothing went as the engineer wanted. Not a day went by without some hitch or accident occurring. Sometimes it was the pitch of a screw that was wrong and had to be changed, sometimes steel plates that presented a crack or some other defect.

"I'm not unaware," said Harry Dorgan, "that these difficulties must be caused by the Red Hand. In spite of all the precautions we've taken, the bandits have been able to deduce the goal of our enterprise and they're seeking to cause delays by every possible means."

Many times, before Lord Burydan's departure on his excursion, the engineer had had to respond to the eccentric's gibes and jokes. "You see," the latter said, "that's it's me whose chosen the best method. My yacht, the *Ariel*, whose construction I confided to private industry without breathing a word of my intentions to anyone, was started in the shipyard a long time after yours, and yet it's just as advanced and will be ready at the same time."

"There's a good reason for that, of course," Harry replied. "The *Ariel* is considerably smaller than the *Revenge*, which has a tonnage of no less than two thousand."

"The *Revenge* will be our first-class ironclad, our dreadnought, while the Ariel will be our cruiser. Two units aren't too many to lay siege to the Island of Hanged Men, which, as I've been able to see for myself, is admirably fortified."

"Fred Jorgell intended to ask the American Navy to put an ironclad at his disposal," said the engineer, "but the directors of the ministry have so far refused to grant his request. They're convinced that the Island of Hanged Men doesn't exist, or doesn't have the importance that we want to attribute to it."

"I wouldn't be surprised if the Red Hand didn't have a few affiliates among the senior functionaries of the Navy, just as it has in all the major administrations."

"So far as I'm concerned, there's no doubt about it."

"Well, too bad. We'll do without the State's ironclads, that's all. If everyone showed the same initiative as us, the bandits of the Red Hand would have been exterminated a long time ago."

It was almost always on this conclusion that conversations between Lord Burydan and Harry terminated. Thanks to the energy of the latter, however, who expelled workmen suspected of the slightest sabotage from the shipyard and stimulated the zeal of serious workers with large bonuses, the work was now proceeding with much greater rapidity. Harry Dorgan, who had expected at first that the yacht would be ready in January, now reckoned with satisfaction that the *Revenge* would be ready to put to sea by the end of December.

He immediately wrote to Lord Burydan to tell him the good news, and the eccentric, who was then traveling along the border between Arizona and Mexico, hastened to cut his voyage short and set off for New York, where he had other business to attend to.

Andrée and Frédérique, whom Isidora was piloting around the shops, took an entire week to make all the purchases necessary for the long sea journey that they were about to undertake, for, from the very beginning, Mademoiselle de Maubreuil and her friend had affirmed insistently that they had no intention of being separated from their fiancés and that they would make their own contribution to the liberation of Monsieur Bondonnat, no matter how much danger they had to run.

In New York, they met up with Fred Jorgell, loaded down with work for the moment because of the expansion of the Lightning Steamship Company—which now had no less than fifty ships in the Atlantic—that he was currently organizing.

The departure of the expedition had been fixed for the second half of January. It was agreed that the two Frenchwomen, as well as Lord Burydan and his friends, would spend a fortnight resting at Golden Cottage, in order to be in a better condition to tolerate the fatigues of a long voyage.

Isidora, Frédérique and André, as well as Lord Burydan, Oscar, Kloum and Agénor, were due to travel in the private saloon car owned by Fred Jorgell, which, because of the billionaire's frequent journeys, was shuttling back and forth continually between New York and San Francisco. Fred Jorgell, whose business affairs were almost concluded, would join them two days later.

On the eve of the young women's departure, however, Mademoiselle de Maubreuil received a summons to the French consulate, where she was required to attend to certain family documents. In fact, in consequence of the disappearance of Monsieur Bondonnat, her legal guardian, she had asked to be emancipated and to administrate her fortune herself—a request that had been granted without any difficulty.

Andrée showed the summons she had received to Isidora and Frédérique. "We'll be obliged to wait for a day or two," said the latter.

"Why wait for me?" Mademoiselle de Maubreuil asked. "There's a simpler way of arranging things."

"How?"

"Leave today, as arranged, and I'll come with Mr. Jorgell when my affairs are sorted out."

"That's right," Isidora approved. "That way, we won't cause any inconvenience to our fiancés, who are expecting us."

Things were thus arranged. Andrée de Maubreuil said goodbye to her friends, whom she accompanied to the station of the Central Pacific Railroad.

She was to rejoin them at Golden Cottage as soon as she had fulfilled the necessary obligations at the consulate.

However, Fred Jorgell found that he was delayed for longer than he had expected by his own business affairs. He advised the young woman to wait for him, unless she preferred to leave on her own.

It was the latter course on which she decided, Mademoiselle de Maubreuil had already become accustomed to American mores, and it is well-known that in the United States, young women, and sometimes even children, undertake long voyages without being accompanied by anyone, defended solely by the respect with which women are universally surrounded in America.

The billionaire wanted to install the young woman in a Pullman car reserved in advance for her and Mrs. MacBarlott, Isidora's Scottish governess, who was to serve as André's chaperone and keep her company during the long journey. The two women were to get off at Juwilly station, situated an hour's journey from San Francisco, which was the station closest to Golden Cottage.

Once they had arrived in San Francisco, however, Isidora and Frédérique did not hurry back to the villa. On the urging of Harry Dorgan and Roger Ravenel, supported by Lord Burydan, the two young women decided to stay for a week at the Palace Hotel, in order to visit the city and its surroundings, in which picturesque sites are abundant, in detail.

Andrée de Maubreuil was informed of this decision by a telegram from Antoine Paganot, which told her not to get off at Juwilly as previously agreed but at San Francisco itself, where her friends would meet her at the station.

Unfortunately, that telegram did not reach its destination. The agents of the Red Hand, always on the alert, had intercepted it and transmitted it to Baruch, who, under the features and appearance of Joe Dorgan, was one of the lords and directors of the redoubtable association.

The train on which Paganot expected Mademoiselle de Maubreuil to arrive reached San Francisco at eleven o'clock in the evening. Isidora and Frédérique had accompanied the young man to meet their friend, but the crowd of travelers passed through the turnstiles and dissipated in the vast hall of the station without any glimpse of Mademoiselle de Maubreuil.

At first astonished not to see Andrée, the three young people did not take long to become profoundly anxious about her absence.

"How is it that she hasn't come?" murmured the engineer. "Her last letter told me that everything she had to do at the consulate had been concluded, and asked me to meet her when she arrived."

"She must have received our telegram," said Isidora

"In any case," said Frédérique, "if she had missed the train for some reason, she would have warned us telegraphically."

"Provided," murmured Paganot, who scarcely dared complete his thought, "that the Red Hand..."

"Don't say that!" said Frédérique, fearfully. "I don't want to think for a single instant that my poor Andrée might have fallen into the hands of those bandits."

"Let's seek information," said the engineer, forcing himself to control the anxiety that was invading him.

"Yes," Isidora approved, "let's talk to the train conductor; perhaps he can give us some useful information."

Like all the functionaries of that kind on American railway lines, the train conductor was a colored man, whom the name of Fred Jorgell and a large tip immediately rendered docile and obsequious. When he was asked whether he had noticed a young woman dressed in black, with blonde hair and blue eyes, in the Pullman car, accompanied by a lady of about forty with slightly masculine features and a large hat decorated with poppies, he immediately remembered that two individuals matching that description had boarded the train in New York.

"I noticed them all the more," he said, "because I had occasion to carry out a few little services during the journey, for which they rewarded me with generous tips."

"Where did they get off?" asked the engineer, anxiously.

"A little way before arriving in San Francisco, at a little station named Juwilly."

"There's no longer any doubt," said Frédérique. "Andrée didn't receive the telegram. She must think we're still at Golden Cottage, where she won't find anyone."

"Perhaps it's a perfectly natural accident," said Isidora, privately less reassured than she wanted to appear. "Telegrams go astray every day."

"No," said the engineer, shaking his head. "I fear that there's something more serious at the bottom of this."

"In any case," said Frédérique, "even if it's just a simple misunderstanding, we need to go to Golden Cottage."

"And without losing a minute," said Isidora. "When she didn't find anyone at Juwilly station to meet her, our friend will have found herself in an awkward situation."

"Perhaps," said Frédérique, "She'll take refuge in a hotel until the next train comes through."

"But that train was the last."

Mortally anxious, all three got into an automobile had had themselves taken o the Palace Hotel to warn Lord Burydan and Roger Ravenel—who, without hesitation, declared that they too would go to Juwilly. Oscar insisted on going with them, and everyone piled as best they could into the automobile, which departed in third gear in the direction of the little suburban station.

When they arrived, they found the station deserted; the employees had gone home. Only the stationmaster had not yet gone to bed. That functionary was plied with questions, and he too remembered perfectly that two female travelers, whose descriptions corresponded to those of Andrée and Mrs. MacBarlott, had got off the New York express.

"They seemed to be in a very good mood," he said, "and they climbed into a luxurious automobile that was parked outside the station, whose driver seemed to be waiting for them."

"My God!" cried Paganot, in anguish. "That car can only have belonged to the Red Hand, Andrée is doomed!"

They all looked at one another in consternation, having the presentiment of some catastrophe. They knew full well that the villa was deserted, that there was no automobile there and that no driver could have received an instruction to pick up the young woman. What brought their perplexity to a peak was finding out that Andrée had got into the unknown vehicle without hesitation.

"It's only too obvious," murmured the eccentric, "that Mademoiselle de Maubreuil has fallen into a trap."

"Let's got to Golden Cottage right away!" said Isidora,

"Why knows whether we might find Andrée there!" murmured Frédérique, anxiously.

"I fear that we might have arrived too late," added Paganot, in a scarcely perceptible voice.

They climbed back into the automobile, which, driven by Lord Burydan, was launched at top speed along the road that led to Golden Cottage.

The information furnished by the conductor and the stationmaster was perfectly accurate. Andrée de Maubreuil and Mrs. MacBarlott had got off the train at Juwilly station, having spotted Fred Jorgell's large green automobile, which usually made the trip between the station and the cottage. The driver obsequiously opened the door for them and they got in without raising the slightest objection.

"I'm slightly surprised," said Andrée, "that Frédérique or Monsieur Paganot haven't come to meet me."

"There's nothing astonishing about that," said Mrs. MacBarlott, as the accelerating vehicle left the lights of the village surrounding the station behind. "Mademoiselle Frédérique and Miss Isidora might have been retained at the cottage by the arrival of visitors. As for Monsieur Paganot, you know that he's almost always in San Francisco."

"It still astonishes me that he didn't come," Andrée murmured.

The journey continued in silence. Golden Cottage was not far from the station. After a quarter of an hour they perceived the lights of a dwelling, and the automobile son went through a large iron gate that had been left open, doubtless intentionally, and stopped in front of a perron.

The chauffeur opened the car door; the two women got out and went up the steps, while the car, after a skillful turn, headed back to the gate, which closed as soon as it had gone out.

There was a spacious garage at Golden Cottage. In any other circumstances that two women might perhaps have been surprised to see the vehicle that had brought leaving again in the middle of the night, but they did not pay any attention to that detail, which ought to have seemed suspicious. They were in haste to see their friends again.

The Scotswoman, who was walking a few paces ahead of Andrée, opened the door to the vestibule. To her great surprise, it was not illuminated. She had scarcely gone in when something cold, which might have been mistaken for a handful of snow, was pressed over her face, and at the same time, two robust arms took hold of her.

She fell, inanimate, into the arms of her attacker, who had been waiting for her in the darkness and had applied a mask to her face filled with chloronal, the terrible odorless chloroform invented by Dr. Cornelius.

The man threw her body, as lifeless as a cadaver, under a velvet curtain and advanced toward Mademoiselle de Marbreuil. The entire scene had happened so rapidly, Mrs. MacBarlott having been subjected to a kind of vanishing trick, that the young woman, having come up the steps, had only just had time to reach the vestibule. She too was very surprised to find herself suddenly in darkness.

"Where are you, Mrs. MacBarlott!" she exclaimed. "Why isn't there any light? Why isn't Frédérique here?"

Nervously, Andrée opened one of the door in front of her, which gave access to a drawing room.

The room was empty. By the light of electric lamps, however, which inundated it with a harsh glare, Andrée saw a man in front of her whose face was covered with a strange rubber mask.

The young woman uttered a terrible scream and stepped back precipitately, but the man had seized her wrists.

"Mademoiselle," he said, rudely, in a voice whose tone made her shiver—a voice that she seemed to have heard before—"neither Mrs. MacBarlott nor your friend Fréderique can hear you. We're alone in this house."

"Help!" shouted Andrée, who, after almost fainting in fear, drew energy from the very excess of her terror.

"There's no point in shouting," said the man, continuing to maintain an inflexible grip. "No one can hear you. There's no one here, I tell you. You need to listen to me."

"No, never! Help! Help!"

Andrée suddenly realized that she was in the presence of a bandit. As she had come into possession of a considerable sum of money a few days before in

New York she thought that she might have a means at her disposal to rid herself of the audacious malefactor.

"Do you want money?" she stammered, in a strangled voice. "I've got ten thousand dollars in banknotes in a wallet. Take them, but let me go, I beg you."

"I don't need your dollars," the man replied, resting his harsh, imperious and hypnotic gaze upon her for a long time. What I want is for you to listen to me. I'm not what I seem to be. I love you madly. You have to come with me, and you will come, willingly or not, for you're in my power."

"Never! I'd rather die!"

The young woman launched a heart-rending cry for help toward the deserted countryside—and his time, it seemed to her that a distant cry replied to her voice.

"Spare yourself those futile cries," said the bandit, impatiently. "No one will come. No one can come to your aid. You have to come with me. It's the only means of escaping a terrible danger that threatens all your friends."

He tried to drag the young woman toward the door, but she struggled, with a desperate energy. In the fact of that unexpected resistance, the masked man lost his composure, stammering inconsequential phrases, while brutally pulling his victim along.

She continued to shout for help with all her might.

"I should have taken you away first," he growled, "and explained my plans afterwards. Listen to me, I beg you."

Mad with terror, Mademoiselle de Maubreuil did not pay any attention to his words. She continued to shout for help, in a shrill and plaintive voice that resonated strangely in the silence of the sleeping countryside. But this time, she was sure, she had distinctly heard a voice that responded to her own. It seemed to her that someone had shouted: "Courage!" or "Hold on!" She could not be precise, but she was certain that someone was coming to her rescue. Reanimated by that hope, she struggled even more furiously against the bandit's grip.

"Shut up!" he cried, angrily. "You *will* shut up!" And letting go of one of the young woman's wrists, he placed a large palm over her mouth, crushing her lips, thus reducing her, bruised and breathless, to silence. "You'll come now!" he roared.

He dragged her violently toward the entrance to the vestibule—but there, a dull growl caused him to recoil.

Before he had time to assume a defensive stance, some kind of wild beast launched itself out of the darkness and, biting his hand, forced him to let go of Mademoiselle de Maubreuil. Then, renewing the attack, it leapt at the bandit's throat and sank its teeth into his flesh.

Obedient to an instinctive impulsion, Andrée had taken flight, but after taking a few steps she stopped.

In the hideous animal armored in mud, missing an ear, that had just come so strangely to her defense, she thought she had recognized the dog taken away by the bandits at the same time as Monsieur Bondonnat.

A glance darted at the brass collar now vividly lit by the electric light left her in no doubt.

"Pistolet!" she cried.

The dog responded with a joyful bark, which gave his adversary a moment's respite—but on hearing the name *Pistolet*, the masked bandit seemed to have been struck by amazement and an unspeakable fear. With a desperate effort, he tore himself away from his enemy's teeth, bounded to the door and ran out into the darkness.

Pistolet barked furiously, and was already launching himself in pursuit of the rogue, but Andrée called him back.

"Here, Pistolet!" she stammered, in a faint voice. "Don't leave me, my good dog. Stay here to defend me!"

The faithful animal obeyed, and came to lick his mistress's hands tenderly.

Although exhausted by the struggle she had just put up, Andrée still had the strength to drag herself, tottering, to the door of the vestibule, the heavy bolts of which she rammed home.

She felt safe then from a further attack by her aggressor.

At that moment, the strident sound of an automobile horn was heard; the entrance gate grated on its hinges, and Andrée soon saw, with immense happiness, her friends getting out of the car that had brought them. Joy restored her strength. She reopened the door to the vestibule, which she had just locked, and threw her arms around Frédérique, who was the first to run to her.

The succession of violent emotions she had just experienced was too much for the young woman, though; she lost consciousness in her friend's arms. She would have fallen if Frédérique had not supported her, seizing her round the waist in order to deposit her gently on a sofa.

Antoine Paganot immediately made her breathe from a bottle of lavender salts, with which he had taken care to equip himself.

Andrée opened her eyes, and her pale face brightened with a weak smile. Everyone waited impatiently for her to recover sufficiently to give them an explanation.

Already, Pistolet and the little hunchback were renewing their acquaintance, and there was a concert of barking and affectionate exclamations on either side.

"Poor Pistolet! How dirty he is! He only has one ear! It's certainly him who's just saved Mademoiselle Andrée's life!"

The brave dog was stroked, pampered and congratulated by all the people present, in turn.

It was in the midst of these emotional scenes that Lord Burydan thought he heard a deep sigh behind one of the luxurious Venetian velvet curtains. He went to see where the noise had come from and found the inanimate body of Mrs. MacBarlott lying on the ground. In all the turmoil, she had been completely forgotten.

Fortunately, Paganot was there. He had no difficulty in recognizing that the Scotswoman had been the victim of the same kind of poisoning of which Andrée and Frédérique had nearly perished at the Preston Hotel, at the hands of the Knights of Chloroform. Thanks to the cottage pharmacy, which was well-stocked, he was able to apply energetic medication to the unfortunate governess.

After two hours of treatment, the Scotswoman had almost recovered from the stupefying effects of the chloronal.

Fortunately, Andrée had not taken nearly as long to come to her senses; no trace of the struggle she had sustained against the bandit remained except for blue rings around her wrists and a large rip in her sleeve.

She gave a detailed account of the fashion in which she had fallen into the trap and how, thanks to Pistolet, she had contrived miraculously to escape it safe and sound.

Lord Burydan, who had followed the story with extreme attention, had no difficulty in persuading his friends that once again they were in the presence of a plot hatched by the mysterious bandits of the Red Hand. The skill with which it had been organized showed how redoubtable and well-informed they were, and it was unanimously decided to take precautionary measures even more severe than in the past, in order to avoid any surprise.

This conversation was prolonged far into the night. It was too late to go back to San Francisco, so they camped in the apartments of Golden Cottage, under the guard of Pistolet, to whom the role of sentinel as officially granted.

Everyone slept peacefully that night, except for Oscar, who did not close an eye. That was because, on the way to the cottage that evening, the little hunchback had seen a red and black vehicle heading in the opposite direction to the vehicle in which he was riding: the vehicle that he called the phantom automobile, the appearance of which in New York, Tampton and Canada had always followed or preceded some catastrophe.

VI. A Canine Detective

In one of their recent meetings, the three Lords of the Red Hand—Dr. Cornelius, Fritz Kramm and Baruch—had decided that all the members of the expedition organized against the Island of Hanged Men would be pitilessly annihilated.

They were unaware, it is true, that Lord Burydan was having a yacht constructed for his own use, but that would not prevent the eccentric lord and his friends from inevitably falling victim to the sectarians of the Red Hand.

So, certain of exterminating their enemies at a stroke, the three Lords had left them alone for a while.

"On their yacht," said Cornelius, they'll be at our mercy, and without our having to run any risk. Once they're in the southern seas, where the fake letter from Bondonnat found in a bottle will draw them, they'll no longer be able to count on anyone for aid. The Ocean surrounding the Antarctic Circle is absolutely deserted. There, we'll be the masters of the situation.

And meticulously, the doctor had explained at length the infallible plan that he had made that would lead to the irredeemable doom of Lord Burydan and his friends.

Baruch, in spite of his hidden agenda, had ended up agreeing with the opinion of his partners, but—and this was the reason for his secret discontentment—he did not want Andrée de Maubreuil to be condemned to death. If he had dared, he would have come to the young woman's defense, as he had once before on the *Arkansas*.

At first Baruch's love for Andrée had only been a kind of caprice, but it had become a veritable passion, a strange passion in which there was as much hatred as affection. He wanted to have at his discretion the proud beauty who had once shown him nothing but scorn, when he was an assistant in Monsieur de Marbreuil's chemistry laboratory at the Manor of Diamonds.

He would have liked to see Andrée, vanquished and supplicant, on her bended knees, imploring him for pity, and he would have paid a great deal for that triumph of his self-esteem and rancor.

Kept scrupulous up to date by his spies with what Fred Jorgell and his friends were doing, he had read the telegram in which Andrée had been asked to go directly to San Francisco, and it was on reading it that a plan had germinated in his head. He was the one who, by means of his agents, had contrived difficulties capable of retaining Fred Jorgell in New York, in order that Mademoiselle de Marbreuil would be traveling alone.

Very mistrustful on this occasion, Baruch had not taken anyone in to his confidence regarding his plan. The chauffeur he had needed to bring the two women from the station at Juwilly to Golden Cottage knew nothing, and, habituated to passive obedience, like all the members of the Red Hand, he had not even asked why her services were required. He had been ordered to procure a green automobile of a particular make and model—which is to say, exactly similar to one of Fred Jorgell's—and had obeyed without seeking to know any more.

As we have seen, Baruch had almost succeeded. If he had had a little more self-control, and had not lost his head in the face of Andrée's resistance—or if, in fact, he had been content to chloroform her as he had done with Mrs. MacBarlott—he would certainly have captured her. The intervention of Pistolet, the accursed dog who appeared to him even in his nightmares, and which he had never succeeded in killing, had ended up causing him to lose his presence of mind completely. He had run to his automobile and fled without daring to look back.

In any case, that had been lucky for Baruch, for if Lord Burydan and his friends had found him at the cottage, struggling with Mademoiselle de Maubreuil, they would certainly have lynched him without any kind of trial.

Baruch had also been lucky that he had not been attacked by the dog while he was alone in the house waiting for the two women. Having arrived at night, he had got through the main gate using a skeleton key and then, finding the door that the tramps had broken down—which had also let Pistolet into the cottage— still open, he had gone in. Thinking that André might perhaps be surprised if she did not see any lights, had switched on the electricity in two or three rooms.

During that time, Pistolet was out raiding a distant farm, and it was only after having dined substantially on a duckling he had taken by surprise that he had arrived back at the cottage, just at the moment when Andrée, her strength exhausted, was on the point of being abducted by the bandit. There is no doubt that had Pistolet been there when Baruch had come through the gate, he would have satisfied his old grudge against Monsieur de Marbreuil's murderer.

Andrée and her friends had, on thinking about it, fully realized the immense debt of gratitude they owed to the courageous animal. Thus, he was spoiled by all kinds of pampering; first of all he was bathed, combed and perfumed, resuming the appearance of a civilized dog.

With his habitual sagacity, Pistolet understood very rapidly that there would be no further need for him to go out hunting and marauding, and that he had acquired the right to idleness and wellbeing, but he nevertheless testified his surprise when he was brought delicious soups and succulent roast fowls.

At a stroke, Pistolet had renewed all his old acquaintances, from the little hunchback to the Indian Kloum, not forgetting Lord Burydan, for whom he had a particular esteem. In addition, Pistolet had promptly familiarized himself with Isidora, Agénor and Harry Dorgan. At Golden Cottage, he was not considered as a simple barbet. He had the right of entrance to every room, and, gravely sitting on his backside, he listened to all the discussions, in which one might have thought he was taking part, so pensive and reflective was his manner.

It was thus that one day, the question of the latitude and longitude of the Island of Hanged Men came up.

The words "latitude" and "longitude" undoubtedly awoke a precise memory in the dog' mind, for he suddenly uttered here curt barks and, tugging the little hunchback imperiously by the sleeve of his jacket he made him understand, in his own fashion, that he wanted to show him something.

Oscar did not fail to respond to that invitation. He followed Pistolet, who, after having run nimbly up the stairs of the cottage, led him to a closet into which the hunchback had never gone.

There, there was a bale of straw and, on the ground, the twenty-four letters of the alphabet cut out by Monsieur Bondonnat and the remains of the leather bag in which they had been contained.

"I can see," said the hunchback, joyfully, "that you haven't forgotten my old lessons. Kloum told me that Monsieur Bondonnat had continued them. Go on, my brave Pistolet, show us what you can do," While speaking, he stroked his faithful companion's curly fur tenderly.

Pistolet did not have to be asked twice. After having uttered three brief barks, he extended his paw, and, with a rapidity due to long and patient practice, he composed the word *latitude*.

Oscar was mute with surprise. Holding his breath, he followed the dog's slightest movement attentively, wondering anxiously what the choice of such a word signified.

Pistolet—who, as we know, had been admirably well-trained—only took a moment to form the entire phrase: *latitude north forty-seven.*

"What does that mean?" Oscar exclaimed, astonished. "That's not the figure we found in the bottle. There's a mystery in this." Caressing Pistolet again, he added: "Go on, old chap. The longitude now."

Imperturbably, the dog composed: *Longitude west hundred sixty-one.*

"That," exclaimed the astounded hunchback, "is amazing!"

He immediately wrote the two numbers down in his notebook, ran downstairs and hurtled into the drawing room to share the astonishing discovery that he had just made.

"I remember clearly," Kloum said, "that Monsieur Bondonnat taught Pistolet the words latitude and longitude. He tried to explain to me what they were, but seeing that I didn't understand, he didn't mention them to me again."

A minute later, everyone invaded Pistolet's attic. The latter recommenced his work in front of the numerous audience. When the same letter recurred within a word he moved it after having placed it, leaving an empty space in the original syllable. That detail excited everyone's admiration, because, in that way, the erudite animal only required a single alphabet to compose an infinite number of words.

Meanwhile, what Kloum had said had been a flash of enlightenment for Lord Burydan. "My God!" he cried. "We've been stupid cretins! Oysters! Imbeciles! Idiots!"

"Why is that, my lord?" asked the hunchback, surprised.

"We've all been complete asses, and the bandits of the Red Hand are a hundred times more intelligent than us."

"Why is that?"

"Don't you understand that the bottle supposedly found in the sea that the pirate brought to us was a trick, a false indication, designed to draw us into the ice of the South Pole? I'm convinced that Monsieur Bondonnat's letter was a forgery; I'll look at it with a magnifying-glass, and Mademoiselle Frédérique can lend me one of her father's old letters so that I can compare the handwriting."

"We can look at it right away!" exclaimed the young woman.

A rapid examination sufficed for Lord Burydan to convince himself that the document he had bought from Captain Christian Knox for two hundred dollars was the work of a skillful forger."

"But for Pistolet," the eccentric complained, "We'd have been taken for a ride."

The entire audience was plunged into the most profound amazement, but they were all obliged to recognize, after a moment's reflection, that Lord Burydan was right and that the indication given by Pistolet was the correct one.

Fred Jorgell, Harry Dorgan and the two Frenchmen, who returned from San Francisco that evening, endorsed the opinion wholeheartedly. It was in the vicinity of the Arctic Circle alone that it was necessary to search for Prosper Bondonnat, and nowhere else.

To ward off further machinations on the part of the Red Hand, however, it was decided that the secret of the discovery they had just made would be jealously kept.

The departure of the two yachts was irrevocably fixed for Friday 13 January.

10. THE PORTRAIT OF LUCRETIA BORGIA

I. Balthazar Buxton, Collector

Fritz Kramm, the wealthy art dealer, was placidly finishing lunch with his brother, Dr. Cornelius, famous in New York as the sculptor of human flesh, when a domestic handed him a telegram. He opened it, and smiled.

"Guess who's written to me," he said to the doctor.

"How should I know?"

"Balthazar Buxton."

"The maniac art-lover—the labyrinth man?"

"The same. It's been over a year since I've heard from him. I thought he'd fallen out with me.

"Why?"

"He claimed that I'd made him pay too dearly for a silver vase attributed to Benvenuto Cellini, but whose authenticity was far from proven."

"It's said that he's very rich," observed Cornelius Kramm, abruptly.

"Exceedingly rich," Fritz replied, who had read his brother's mind, "but he's a very prudent man and his money is sheltered from any sleight of hand."

"Too bad. Does he say what he wants from you?"

"No, but it's easy to guess. He doubtless wants me to procure some painting that his collection lacks. As you know, the eccentric has no other passion but works of art, especially paintings. He possesses items of great beauty that are the envy of the Louvre in Paris, the National Gallery in London and the Uffizi in Florence. He's as jealous of his canvases as an Asiatic sultan of the odalisques in his harem. Those who can boast of having visited his gallery are rare."

"But doubtless you're among that number?"

"Yes, and I admit that Mr. Buxton's collection is worthy of a prince."

The conversation went on for a little longer, and then Dr. Cornelius, remembering that two patients were waiting for him in his laboratory, hastened to take his leave. A short time afterwards, Fritz Kramm climbed into an automobile and had himself taken to the home of the aged art-lover.

Balthazar Buxton lived on William Street, one of the rare thoroughfares in New York not designated by a number, in a vast and magnificent town house surrounded by gardens. He had never wanted to break up the property in question or build a house to rent on the site, even though the land in that part of the city had acquired a value of more than two thousand dollars a square yard. The most extravagant stories were told about the dwelling, and those who had been allowed to visit it said that the truth exceeded the most chimerical suppositions.

When Fritz Kramm had got out of the automobile he went to ring the bell at a large coaching entrance that opened in the base of a high wall surmounted with sharp spikes. At the sound of her bell, a judas-hole opened, and he concierge asked the visitor in a surly voice who he was and what he wanted.

After having negotiated for a few minutes with the suspicious guardian and shown him Balthazar Buxton's telegram, Fritz Kramm was finally allowed thorough the door, which was equipped with more bolts and locks than a prison door.

"Someone will show you the way," the concierge told Fritz, "but I recommend you not to stray to the right or the left, or to take a single step without authorization, otherwise you'll be exposed to real danger."

The antique-dealer made to reply and manifested no surprise at the bizarre warning. He had visited Mr. Buxton before and he knew the precautions with which the old man surrounded himself. His house was engineered like the stage of a magical theater.

The concierge blew a strident blast on a whistle. At that signal, a silent and grave individual dressed entirely in black appeared around a bend in the circular path that made a tour of the inner surface of the enclosing wall.

"Here's your guide," said the guardian.

The newcomer bowed with a glacial politeness and gestured to the visitor to follow him. Fritz then perceived that his conductor was wearing a king of coat of mail beneath his outer garments, which gave all his gestures a kind of automatic stiffness.

After ten paces or so the path was barred by an enormous grille. The art-dealer as about to touch one of the bars mechanically but his guide stopped him with a gesture. "If your finger even brushes that grille, which is carrying a current of several thousand volts, you're dead. You'd receive a shock capable of felling an ox."

"Damn," murmured Fritz, stepping back. "It seems to me that this grille wasn't here last time I came."

"No, it was only installed three months ago. Since he was the victim of an attempted robbery, Monsieur Buxton has improved all his means of defense."

While speaking, the guide had taken a minuscule key from his pocket and introduced it into a lock fitted into the wall a certain distance away from the grille. The key turned, triggering a complicated mechanism, and the grille rose up into the air like the portcullis of a Gothic castle, sliding along two iron grooves.

Fritz and his guide hastened to go through. Instantly, the grille came down and resumed its place.

Twenty paces further on there was another grille, which was passed with the same ceremony; then the guide opened a small iron door, just wide enough to let through a single person, and the two men went into the cage of an elevator, which, a few minutes later, deposited them on the threshold of a vast room furnished in the Assyrian style. The ceiling was very high and the exposed beams, painted and gilded, were supported by stout columns with capitals in the form of winged bulls of colossal dimension.

The eyes of these animals enclosed electric bulbs that emitted a fantastic red and green light into the room, where no doors or windows were visible. Fritz could not even see what had become of the elevator.

The floor of the room was covered throughout its extent by a rich marble mosaic.

Having walked for some time through that grandiose vestibule, the man guiding Mr. Kramm came to a halt in front of one of the columns, pressed the gilded flower of one of the lotuses ornamenting the grooves, and the column immediately pivoted on its axis, uncovering the entrance to a narrow iron staircase, down which the two men went. As they descended, the column slowly and automatically resumed its position.

The staircase ended in a long corridor, at the extremity of which was another elevator. Fritz and his companion took their places in it, and after having descended for a few minutes, they found themselves in an Assyrian room so exactly similar to the one they had just left that it would have been impossible to tell them apart.

For three-quarters of an hour the two men continued to go along secret passages, climbing and descending, sometimes by means of staircases and sometimes by means of elevators, passing through a series of rooms hat were richly decorated but deserted and devoid of windows.

It would have been difficult for Fritz Kramm to say whether he was in a basement or on the tenth floor of the vast palace, whose rooms, linked by a network of corridors, stairways and tortuous galleries, formed the most complex of labyrinths.

Finally, the art-dealer and his conductor emerged into a spacious circular corridor where four men were standing guard. They were armed to the teeth with rifles over their shoulders, sabers at their sides and revolvers in their belts.

The guide knocked in an agreed fashion on a little iron judas-hole, where an emaciated and jaundiced face appeared; a moment later, a sliding door moved along its grooves and, without any further formality, Fritz Kramm was introduced into the room that the honorable Balthazar Buxton habitually occupied.

It was a vast room, round in shape, terminated by a crustal cupola that allowed a bright and vivid light attain all the objects therein. Curtains of purple velvet maintained by thick silken and golden ropes permitted the light and shade within the sumptuous room to be varied at will.

When one had reached it, the reason for all the precautions its owner had taken against intruders and malefactors became obvious. The immense room contained a accumulation of masterpieces that must have cost millions.

In the center, Michelangelo's statue of writhing *Vengeance*, which had been believed to be lost and which had been rediscovered in a castle in Moravia, extended her breasts of black bronze skywards in a dolorous fashion. On all the walls, in large ornately-sculpted gilded frames, were masterpieces of every school: a young woman by Raphael; an *Inferno* by Fra Angelico; gossiping women by Rubens; a witch by Goya; a Poussin landscape, etc. The moderns had not been forgotten; there were Rudes, Falguières, Rodins and Aristide Rousauds,[10] the cream of contemporary sculpture, and among the paintings there were Besnards, Henners, Claude Monets, Degas, Crébassas, etc.[11]

The furniture was worthy of the masterpieces that surrounded it: admirable Gothic credenzas; sixteenth century Italian dressers with curious incrustations; Spanish armchairs in ebony and Cordova leather; tables by Boulle and Riesner supporting unique items of porcelain from Saxe and Sèvres; curious items of jewelry: a whole world of rare and precious trinkets. The room, crammed with treasures of every kind, would have been worthy of a Renaissance pope.

The owner of all these marvels appeared to be at least ninety years old. He was so desiccated, withered and thin that one might almost have thought him a mummy momentarily brought back to life by some artifice of science. His skeletal visage, completely devoid of hair, was frightful to behold: the jaundiced skin was almost stuck to the bones; the smile was funereal, uncovering dentition shored up with gold plates, which invincibly suggested the disquieting impression that the singular old man might only be an artfully fabricated automaton. The nose was thin and almost diaphanous. Only the eyes, the color of gold, had an extraordinarily youthful gleam. One might have thought that all his vitality had taken refuge in his large irises, which scintillated in the dim light like those of certain cats.

The old man's meager carcass was draped in a black velvet dressing-gown, and a skull-cap, also in velvet, shelter the bald head, giving Balthazar Buxton the appearance of some Venetian doge or some physician such as one sees in paintings by Rembrandt or Gerard Dow.

That strange nonagenarian had risen to his feet in order to come to meet his visitor, extending a hand as compact and stiff as the claw of a bird of prey.

"How are you, Mr. Fritz?" he asked, in a quavering voice. "It's been some time since I've had the pleasure of seeing you."

"I'm very well, and I'm glad to see that your health is also excellent—but if you don't see me more often, you must admit that it's partly your own fault. It's more than a year since you've asked me to come."

---

[10] The lesser-known figures cited are Francois Rude (1784-1855), Alexandre Falguière (1831-1900) and Aristide Rousaud (1868-1946).

[11] The more obscure references are to Jean-Jacques Henner (1829-1905) and Paul-Édouard Crebassa (1870-1912). This list would have been considered slightly *avant garde* in its day.

"That is certainly negligence on my part, but what do you expect? When I'm shut away with my masterpieces, I forget all about the world, and time passes with surprising rapidity."

"You're not bored?"

"Never!"

Fritz Kramm suddenly uttered a cry of surprise. Thanks to the reflection in a Venetian mirror, he had just perceived a young woman of extraordinary beauty, whom he had not seen when he entered the room because his back was toward her. The young woman, her neckline plunging all the way to the brown nipples of her breasts, decked in rich pearl necklaces, was sitting in a capacious armchair with ivory arms, where she was maintaining a statuesque immobility.

When the art-dealer had partly recovered from his surprise, he could not help saying: "I understand, Mr. Buxton, that you don't have a moment's boredom in such charming company."

"Indeed, not," said the old man, with a macabre chuckle. "May I introduce Signora Lorenza, who has been kind enough to put her marvelous power at my disposal for today."

The young woman stood up, nodded her head and smiled, and then sat down again silently.

"What power?" asked Fritz, looking at Signora Lorenza and marveling.

"It's hardly permissible, Mr. Kramm," Balthazar Buxton said, "for a man like you to be unaware of the identity Signora Lorenza, the celebrated 'healer of pearls' who was recently summoned to their courts by the emperor of Russia and the queen of England in order to make use of her mysterious power."

"I confess my ignorance," Fritz murmured.

"You know," the old art-love continued, "that in order to conserve its gleam, a pearl must be worn by a living person, and, for preference, by a woman; otherwise, it loses its color and its luster. It dies, no longer anything but a fragment of opaque nacre."

"I know that. I presume, then, that Signora Lorenza has the ability to resuscitate dead pearls."

"Yes, by wearing them next to her flesh for a while."

Fritz gazed at the young woman, who remained as indifferent and impassive as if she were not the subject of the conversation.

"To what do you attribute that marvelous power?"

"It's simply that Signora Lorenza is more womanly than other women," said the old man, in his shrill and cracked voice. "Her body emits a living electricity that creates a special atmosphere around her. Her nerves are so impressionable that nothing compares to them. All the senses—taste, touch, smell—attain in her a degree of perfection that one does not encounter in any other woman."

Fritz Kramm listened in amazement, wondering privately whether old Balthazar might suddenly have gone mad. He remembered now, however, having

144

read in the papers that Lady Dudley, who owned the most beautiful collection of pearls in the world—more beautiful than those of the late Queen Victoria—had been obliged to summon the healer of pearls to resuscitate some of those she possessed and which, securely locked away, as certain jewelers recommended, in ash-root coffers, had lost their gleam.

"Signora Lorenza," said Balthazar Buxton, enthusiastically, "was born in Florence. It is only in that region that one encounters such exquisitely-organized feminine temperaments. She exercises over all creation the power of domination that Eve, the primal woman, must have possessed. Her breath is embalmed with an odor of violets and even the moisture of her skin exhales a delicate perfume of irises and fresh almond-blossom. Such powerful effluvia radiate from her being that all male animals come to brush her dress, tamed and caressant. Lions lie down at her feet and male birds come to perch on her shoulder and comb her hair with their beaks. Even vegetables are not immune to that mysterious power; mimosas deploy their nervous branches more fully in her presence and open their petals wide. Finally, pearls recover all their splendor as soon as they are in contact with her flesh."[12]

In spite of his prosaic nature and his brutal and avaricious instincts, Fritz Kramm too was beginning to feel the prestigious charm of the beautiful Lorenza. He could not take his eyes of that beautiful face, the pure oval of which was framed by thick hair as black as night—the black that has the metallic gleam of a raven's wing.

Signora Lorenza was tall and slender, and her physiognomy expressed tenderness and generosity combined with a tranquil pride. Her complexion was dazzlingly white, her lips, a perfect bow, had none of the fleshiness indicative of a penchant for gluttony or lust, and her large eyes, shaded by long lashes of an ideal tenuity, were a limpid blue that made a strange and delicious contrast with her dark hair.

There were a few moments of silence. Lorenza, discomfited by Fritz's stare, has lowered her eyes and her cheeks had colored with an imperceptible blush. As for Balthazar Buxton, he was enjoying his guest's surprise and admiration.

"Would it be indiscreet," Fritz asked, eventually, "to ask why the signora is in your house?"

"Not at all," the old man replied, nervously rubbing his desiccated hands together, which creaked as if they had been mounted on pieces of iron wire, after the fashion of certain anatomical specimens. "Signora Lorenza is here because it

---

[12] Author's note: "Such temperaments are not absolutely exceptional. The chronicles of the sixteenth century cite the case of a Genoese great lady who was followed by all the male birds in the countryside, and it is well-known that lions obey female tamers more readily than males."

pleases me to see her in the midst of my works of art. Is she not a living master-piece herself?"

"The most beautiful of all!" Fritz exclaimed.

"And then again, in her presence, I no longer feel the ice of age. It seems to me that she emits a rejuvenating force. So long as she is before my eyes, I'm happy." Balthazar was gazing at the young woman with a reckless admiration.

Lorenza could not help smiling. "Those," she said, "are very exaggerated compliments."

As she pronounced those few words, her voice had crystalline vibrations of such penetrating softness that Fritz felt his heartbeat accelerate, and understood the exactitude of such expressions as "a golden voice" and "a siren song."

"I have only come here," she continued, "To care for a few beautiful pearl necklaces that were gravely ill—for, as you know, a pearl is a living being. 'It is not a person,' as Michelet put it, 'but it is not a thing; it has a destiny.' A pearl loves, with its tony soul of precious stone the woman who wears it on her breast."

"I've always considered the mysterious vitality credited to pearls as a poetic legend," murmured Fritz, "created primarily to charm the imagination of ladies."

"Nothing is more exact or more scientific," Balthazar Buxton protested, "than the life of pearls. It is so true that the beautiful pearl necklace that Signora Lorenza is wearing at this moment was nothing more, a few days ago, than an assemblage of fragments of dull, dreary nacre devoid of any gleam."

"There's more," said the young woman. "Pearls have their preferences. Blue ones delight on the breasts of redheads and blondes, as do black ones, while orange and yellow pearls shine best around the necks of brunettes."

"This a curious and charming theory of which I was unaware," said Fritz. "I'm sure that my learned brother Cornelius would find it very interesting."

"You can explain it to him."

"Now I think of it," said the antiquary, suddenly, "I have a considerable number of pearls in my strong-boxes that are absolutely dead. Some of them come from the famous temple of Talomeco built by king Montezuma, which was said to have been constructed entirely of pearls, because long garlands of those precious stones were hanging from the vault of the edifice, all the way to the floor, or forming arabesques along the walls. The signora might be able to exert her marvelous power on them."

"I'd like nothing better," said Lorenza, "but you should know that my fees are high, for the resurrection of a necklace or bracelet sometime afflicts me with great fatigue. That's because I must yield a little of my own vital fluid to them every time."

"Fritz Kramm is in a position to recompense you appropriately," said Balthazar.

"The question of price is certainly only of secondary importance, so far as I'm concerned."

"It's agreed, then," said Lorenza. "We'll arrange a meeting for next week."

Balthazar struck a vast Chinese gong that was placed within arm's reach. A servant appeared, emerging from the shaft of an elevator set in the center of the room and so cleverly dissimulated that one would not have suspected its existence in advance.

"John," said the old man, "bring some refreshments for my guests. I have some delicious pineapple wines that the signora will appreciate particularly. I also have some antique creole liqueurs such as Kombaya, Vangassaye and Jamrosa, and the delicious Mexican pulque that is obtained by distilling yucca leaves."[13]

Lorenza and Fritz could not help smiling. "I perceive," said the young woman, "that Mr. Buxton also collects rare and precious liqueurs."

"Yes," the old man admitted, "it's one of my weaknesses, I admit. When something is little known or difficult to find, it's absolutely necessary for me to procure it."

The servant had already returned with a silver-plated tray laden with curious bottles, beautiful fruits and appetizing sweetmeats, not forgetting an ice-bucket and a compotier full of the unobtainable preserves that the Kanaks fabricate with certain berries from the virgin forests.

Lorenza and Fritz Kramm did honor to that delicate afternoon snack, and even Balthazar moistened his lips in an aventurine cup filled with Vangassaye, the best and rarest of creole liqueurs.

"Time passes quickly in your company," said the art-dealer, suddenly, "but you haven't yet told me what you want of me."

"In due course!" said the old connoisseur. "We have plenty of time, damn it!"

"Gentlemen," said Lorenza, darting a glance at a little watch inserted in the pearl bracelet she was wearing on her right wrist, "it's time for me to retire."

"I hope it's not my presence that is chasing you away?" Fritz said.

"Not at all, I assure you, but I'm expected elsewhere. In any case, you'll receive my visit, as agreed, next week."

"What day, Signora?"

"Friday, if that's agreeable to you."

The young woman placed a vast hat ornamented with a precious tuft of egret-feathers on her head, put on—with Fritz's help—a large beige silk mantle,

---

[13] Vangassaye is indeed a creole liqueur made from mandarin oranges, but jamrosa is a hybrid grass from India whose oil is normally used in perfumery and kombaya, or kumbaya, is a kind of hypothetical spiritual essence nowadays best known by virtue of its use as the title and chorus of a popular song. The Mexican pulque is made from agaves, not yucca.

and took her leave. As she reached the door of the corridor that led to the circular gallery, however, she had to wait for a moment until Balthazar had passed a copper token through the judas-hole to one of the guards, which was the passkey, the Open Sesame, without which it would have been impossible to get out of the labyrinth.

Left alone, the antiquary and the amateur looked at one another in silence for some time.

"What do you think of Lorenza?" asked Balthazar.

"She's admirable."

"Yes," the nonagenarian murmured, raising his golden eyes toward the vault, "she's bewitching. One might think that an atmosphere of joy and strength reigned around her."

"But what is the matter that led you to invite me here?" Fritz asked, again.

"There's a painting that I need to have at any price. It's Titian's portrait of Lucretia Borgia, Duchess of Ferrara."

"Impossible," said the art-dealer, bluntly.

"Why?"

"The portrait of Lucretia Borgia, as you doubtless know, is in Venice.[14] It's valued at more than two million, and is the property of the Italian government, who would not part with it at any price."

Balthazar Buxton sniggered. "Your erudition is in default in this instance, my dear master," he mocked. "The portrait in Venice is merely a copy, albeit made by Titian's own hand. The original was stolen while Venice was under the dominion of Austria and became the property of a Hungarian diplomat, Baron Czarda, who sold it himself four years ago for an enormous sum to the billionaire William Dorgan."

"I know William Dorgan. I have a considerable interest in his Trust and I can assure you that he would never consent to dispose of his Lucretia Borgia. He only has a small number of paintings, but they're first-rate and he's very fond of them."

Balthazar made an impatient gesture that made the bones of his desiccated hands creak. "I need that portrait," he murmured, in a voice trembling with emotion. I saw it once and I've never been able to forget it. It's Titian's masterpiece. Oh, if you saw that beautiful nacreous flesh fading into the russet shadow of her hair, that smile, mysterious and voluptuous at the same time, those eye full of dreams! Never has anything more beautiful been made!"

---

[14] Titian's best-known picture supposedly representing Lucretia Borgia, currently in the Borghese gallery in Rome, is an allegory rather than a portrait and does not depict her—if, indeed, it is her—in her prime. However, she commissioned several pictures from him and it is not implausible that such a portrait might exist.

"Unfortunately, it's impossible," said Fritz, in a dry and trenchant tone. "I can assure you that it will be impossible for me to obtain."

"I'm rich enough to offer a million dollars," said Balthazar Buxton, simply.

Fritz Kramm could not help shivering. "A million dollars," he stammered. "Well, I'll try. I'll attempt the impossible. I'll try to persuade William Dorgan to sell it."

"I can count on you, then?" said the old man, grimacing a smile.

"I can't promise anything. All that I can promise you is to make every effort to purchase the precious canvas on your behalf."

"Well then, that's that. I'm sure that you'll succeed. As for your commission, you can fix the figure yourself."

"Let's understand one another," said Fritz, who had recovered all his composure. "It's from me that you'll buy—in case of success, of course—the portrait of Lucretia Borgia. You won't be dealing with William Dorgan, but only with me."

"So be it. Do as you see fit. If you only pay William Dorgan half the price I'm offering you for the *Lucretia*, so much the better for you."

"That's exactly what I mean."

A quarter of an hour later, Fritz withdrew, not without having seen Balthazar pass the copper token through the judas-hole that served as an exeat to get out of the mysterious place.

II. The Check

Mr. Steffel, the chief of the New York Police, was in his office, busy reading a report that had just been deposited on his desk by Sergeant Grogmann, the man who had been charged with arresting the escapers from the Lunatic Asylum at the Grand Wigwam.

"That Grogmann really is stupid," he muttered between his teeth. "He believes everything he's told! If I only had agents like him to bring about the destruction of the Red Hand association, I dare say that it would take a very long time..."

At that moment the office boy handed Mr. Steffel a visiting card, on which the name of *Lord Astor Burydan* was supplemented by the note: *presents his respects to Mr. Steffel and would be glad to have a few words with him on the subject of the bandits of the Red Hand.*

The police chief abruptly replaced Grogmann's report, which seemed to him to be devoid of any kind of interest, in a file. "Send Lord Burydan in immediately," he said to the bewildered office boy. And he added, to himself: *But Lord Burydan is the English eccentric who caused my agents so much trouble, and with regard to whom I received orders from above to desist from all further pursuit! He ought to have interesting things to tell me.*

A minute later, Lord Burydan came into the policeman's office, accompanied by the poet Agénor Marmousier, from whom he was rarely apart, after having had the satisfaction of finding him again in the wake of so many perilous adventures.

Mr. Steffel welcomed his visitors courteously, invited them to sit down, and waited for them to make whatever communications they had come to make to him.

"I'm not unknown to you, my dear Mr. Steffel," said Lord Burydan maliciously.

"No," replied the policeman, smiling. "I have a rather voluminous file on you. You're the man who, among other jolly japes, throws stokers to feed alligators. You're the man who organizes revolutions in Lunatic Asylums to which you've been confined..."

"And the funniest thing of all," replied Lord Burydan, unemotionally, "is that in undertaking those more or less jovial demonstrations, I was absolutely within my rights."

"It's necessary to believe so, since I've received strict orders not to trouble you any further, but I confess to you that there are many points in the story that remain obscure to me."

"Then you'll be glad to know," replied the eccentric, with an imperturbable smile, "that I've come here precisely to elucidate those obscure points to which you allude."

And Lord Burydan recounted, in the greatest detail, the facts relating o the wreck of the *City of Frisco*, his imprisonment on the Island of Hanged Men, his escape therefrom, his imprisonment in the Lunatic Asylum and, finally, the audacious manner in which he had recovery possession of his wealth. He concluded his story by telling Mr. Steffel how he had been able to discover the latitude and longitude of the island that served the bandits of the Red Hand as a base."

Mr. Steffel had listened to his interlocutor without interrupting him, but with a rapid gesture he furtively noted down the exact figures of the latitude and longitude. "Thank you very much, my lord," he said. "The information you've given me is precious, and I count on extracting all possible advantage from it in the quest to arrest the leaders of the gang."

"I regarded it as a duty to communicate it to you. I'm only in New York or a few more hours, and I took advantage of the opportunity to come to see you before setting out on a expedition."

"You've been very kind, and if I can help you in any way..."

"There would only be one way, which would be to arrange for the government of the Union to put a warship at our disposal to assist in our attack on the Island of Hanged Men."

The policeman adopted a grave expression. "My lord," he replied, "I promise to do everything I can to contrive the sending of an ironclad. I'll ask for an audience with the Secretary of the Navy today, and make him party to your revelations, which change the face of things completely."

The conversation went on for more than an hour, and it was only having answered a host of questions put to him by Mr. Steffel that Lord Burydan withdrew, respectfully escorted by the other to the automobile that had brought him.

Once he was back in his office the policeman reflected momentarily, and then rang for the office boy. "Do what's necessary," he said, "to procure me, as soon as possible, the General Staff atlas compiled by the War Department."

"It's a very big atlas," the office boy replied, awkwardly. "As you know, it has a lot of pages, and takes up almost a whole bookshelf."

"That's true, but for the moment, I only need the map of the Klondike and the neighboring islands."

"Very well, sir."

Half an hour later, the office boy came back with the requested atlas. Arming himself with a pencil. Mr. Steffel carefully marked the latitude and longitude indicated to him by Lord Burydan on the map, and had no difficulty finding St. Frederick's Island, belonging to the United States. Evidently, St. Frederick's Island was the Island of Hanged Men, the secret headquarters of the bandits of the Red Hand.

A geographical dictionary furnished the policeman with a little supplementary information:

St. Frederick's Island is situated some way south of the Aleutian Islands, approximately a hundred kilometers from Sakhalin Island. It was discovered in the eighteenth century by German navigators, who named it. Since then, as it is not on any shipping route, it has been completely forgotten not only by mariners but by the majority of geographers.

At one time, it was the object of an exchange of diplomatic notes between Russia and the United States government, but the icy territory seemed so uninteresting to everyone that the question was not definitively settled until 1901. At that time it was officially allocated to America, which has since conceded it to a wealthy individual.

Mr. Steffel smiled maliciously. "Hmm!" he said. "I believe that when I know the name of the wealthy individual in question, I'll have taken an important step forward in discovering the secrets of the Red Hand."

Steffel seized the telephone receiver and asked to speak to the Colonial Secretary. Thanks to the automatic relays with which New York telephones are equipped, he obtained that connection almost immediately.

"Hello?"

"Who's speaking?"

"It's me, Mr. Steffel, the chief of the New York Police. Would you ask the head of the Office of Colonial Concessions to come to the phone."

"Here I am," said a second voice, a few moments later. "What can I do for you, Mr. Steffel?"

"Oh, a simple item of information. I'd like to know the name of the person to whom a small island named St. Frederick's Island, in the Klondike region, has been conceded."

"That's easy. St. Frederick's Island currently belongs to one of our fellow citizens, Mr. Fritz Kramm, the famous art dealer, who is making any attempt there—without much success, I gather—to farm fur-seals."

"Very good—thank you; that's all I wanted to know."

Steffel hung up the apparatus. On hearing the name of Fritz Kramm, the policeman had thought he had experienced a dazzle of enlightenment. The truth had appeared to him, confusedly, like a lightning-flash.

Thanks to the notes of his agents, Steffel was not unaware of the shady antecedents of the brothers Cornelius and Fritz Kramm. He knew that the art dealer had been suspected on many occasions of serving as a receiver of goods stolen from museums and other robberies worldwide. His conviction was formed; from now on, for him, it was only a matter of discovery material proof, which would doubtless not be difficult.

Let us say in passing that the mentality of American policemen differs greatly from that of French policemen. Mr. Steffel himself had received large

152

sums of money from the keepers of gaming-houses, or even from wealthy criminals, who had been permitted, in exchange for cash, to escape to Europe.

The police chief, after mature reflection, resolved not to rush things. Perhaps, after all, there might be a means to make an advantageous deal with the owner of St. Frederick's Island.

Prey to these preoccupations, Steffel immediately had himself taken to Fritz Kramm's house, a luxurious dwelling in the vicinity of Central Park.

The art dealer was not at home. He had, the domestic said, gone to pay a visit to his brother, Dr. Cornelius. Steffel got back into his car and had himself taken to Cornelius' house, where the Italian Leonello introduced him ceremoniously into the large Louis XIV-style drawing room.

As soon as they learned of the presence of the chief of police, Cornelius and Fritz came running, with smiles on their faces and their hands extended, but they were discomfited by Mr. Steffel's grave and almost menacing expression.

"Sirs," he said, in a curt tone, "it isn't a simple matter of politeness that brings me here, and I regret having to accomplish a painful duty in your regard."

From the corner of his eye, the policeman watched to see the effect of his words on the two brothers, but they did not flinch.

"What is it about?" Fritz asked, in a perfectly natural tone.

Mr. Steffel resolved to get straight to the point. "I won't hide from you, Mr. Fritz Kramm, that grave suspicions are weighing upon you. It is you, is it not, who are the present owner of St. Frederick's Island, better known to the bandits of the Red Hand as the Island of Hanged Men?"

Fritz had gone pale, but it was with sufficient assurance that he replied: "It's perfectly true that I'm the owner of St. Frederick's Island, but I abandoned it entirely many years ago, and I don't understand what you mean by hanged men."

"An odd story!" murmured Cornelius, softly—but while speaking he darted such a strange gaze at Mr. Steffel from behind his gold-rimmed spectacles that the policeman could not help shivering. He remembered the rumors that were going around concerning the sculptor of human flesh's subterranean laboratory.

"Take note," he thought it advisable to say, "that if I suffer the slightest violence at your hands in the course of this visit, the evidence I have against you, which is in safe hands, will be published this evening in three of the major New York papers."

"There's no question of violence," said Dr. Cornelius, still perfectly calm. "We'd simply like to have a few explanations regarding the strange accusation you've just made against my brother."

"I believe," Fritz put in, "that Mr. Steffel is making a huge blunder. Is it possible that people like my brother and myself, whose fortune is considerable and who even have a share in William Dorgan's trust, could have anything in common with the bandits of the Red Hand?"

"Futile protests!" exclaimed Steffel, getting carried away. "I know everything. You and your brother are among the Lords of the Red Hand. I have precise evidence against you."

Fritz and Cornelius exchanged a rapid glance. The situation was evidently embarrassing.

"It's you," the policeman went on, "who have abducted the French scientist Bondonnat, whom you are holding captive at this very moment. It's you who kept the honorable Lord Burydan captive for some time. But beware! The United States government is going to send an ironclad to the Island of Hanged Men, and that bandit lair will be completely annihilated." After a pause, he continued: "The best thing for you to do is to admit it frankly, to give me the names of all your accomplices, and perhaps, on that condition, I'll be able to make sure that you aren't prosecuted."

Dr. Cornelius smiled ironically. "I know that old trick," he said, "but my brother and I would find it very difficult to reveal the names of our accomplices to you, since we have none and are not guilty of any crime."

"Of course!" said Fritz. "I can guess where this denunciation has come from. It doubtless emanates from Lord Burydan, who recently escaped from a Lunatic Asylum, after having murdered an American citizen."

"The honorable Lord Burydan," said Mr. Steffel, weighing his words carefully "is still unaware that Mr. Fritz Kramm is the owner of St, Frederick's Island. I haven't yet thought it appropriate to inform him."

"You're free to do so. I'm not responsible for what happens on a deserted and glacial island that I haven't visited for years."

"Do you know what will happen if I inform Lord Burydan of the fact? He'll solicit and immediately obtain the dispatch of an ironclad. In any event, the affair will cause you considerable embarrassment, even if you don't have anything to do with the actions of the Red Hand."

Fritz and Cornelius were beginning to understand what Mr. Steffel was trying to get at.

"I can assure you," the doctor said, "that my brother has absolutely nothing for which to reproach himself, and that the investigation you will conduct with your habitual sagacity will certainly establish his innocence."

"What you say is possible," the policeman went on, hesitantly, "but how do I know that you won't try to evade the action of the law."

"Look," said Cornelius, "I'll give you proof of my good faith. I'll put in your hands a bail of fifty thousand dollars. That way, you can be sure that neither my brother nor I will try to escape."

"Evidently," said Steffel, who had led his interlocutors to the desirable point of view, "that proposition militates in your favor. It's possible, after all, that a mistake has been made in your regard. Before unleashing the kind of scandal that your arrest would cause, I want to elucidate the affair with all due impartiality."

"You'll recognize very quickly that it would be an error to denounce us. Wait here a moment; I'll sign you a check for fifty thousand dollars."

Dr. Cornelius scribbled a few lines in hieroglyphic characters in his memorandum, and then rang for Leonello and handed him the piece of paper. A minute later, Leonello returned with a check-book, one leaf of which Cornelius and Fritz countersigned, inscribing the figure of fifty thousand dollars.

Mr. Steffel took it, delighted to have conducted such a delicate negotiation so well. "Until we meet again, sirs," he said, as he withdrew. "The more I think about it, the more convinced I am that you're the victims of a slanderous denunciation. It's not men like you who are affiliated to the association of the Red Hand! The accusation is decidedly absurd, and I'll shelve the affair."

"Don't forget, Mr. Steffel," said Cornelius, in a tone laden with implication, "that if anyone accuses us in future, we're always ready to post bail."

"Understood. Farewell, my dear friends."

The three of them exchanged cordial handshakes.

As he passed through the magnificent garden that surrounded the doctor's house, Steffel told himself that it would be very stupid to settle for that first payment, and resolved to continue his investigation in the greatest secrecy, with a view to carrying out a mass arrest of all the leaders of the Red Hand as soon as he had succeeded in learning their names.

I know, of course, he thought, *that they'll never ask me to return the fifty thousand dollars and that I've tacitly promised to let the Red Hand alone, but one isn't required to deal honestly with such bandits! If Cornelius and Fritz were innocent, they wouldn't have tried to buy my silence with such a considerable sum.*

The policeman climbed back into his automobile and shouted to the chauffeur: "The Central Bank! And step on the gas, so that I arrive in time to deposit a check."

As soon as the policeman had gone, Cornelius and Fritz looked at one another anxiously. "We've had a narrow escape," murmured the art dealer.

"The danger still remains," he doctor replied. "I don't have any confidence in this Steffel, who's an unscrupulous master blackmailer. I'm sure that now he's been paid off, he'll have no more urgent mission than to betray us."

"What are we going to do?"

"I've already given Leonello orders, under the pretext of having him fetch the check-book."

"I noticed that you scribbled something, but I didn't see what it was."

"With individuals of Steffel's stripe, it's necessary to riposte promptly. At this very moment, Slug is on his way in the big automobile, and we'll be rid of the inconvenient policeman within the hour."

"Isn't that imprudent?" Fritz murmured, anxiously "What if Steffel has, as he boasted, put the denunciation concerning us in safe hands?"

"No, I know Steffel. He's too cunning to confide in anyone at all. He knows full well that the moment he reveals the name of the true owner of the Island of Hanged Men to anyone, he'll no longer be the master of the situation."

"It's a lesson, in any case," said Fritz. "It's essential that the Island of Hanged Men should no longer be in my name. I'll get busy making a fictitious sale. I'll say that I'm getting rid of the icebound island because it's absolutely impossible to extract a profit from it."

"That precaution should have been taken a long time ago. Don't forget that we need to redouble our vigilance from now on. We've never had such a run of bad luck."

"Nothing's lost yet."

"No, but it's necessary to deploy more energy. The Red Hand has suffered considerable financial losses; many of our affiliates are in prison and our prestige is diminishing. We haven't succeeded in any important affair for some time. Baruch is steering his ship so badly that William Dorgan has been reconciled with his son Harry and has made a new will dividing his wealth equally between his two sons. In consequence, it's impossible for the moment to get rid of the old billionaire and taken possession of the Trust."

"No, we need to wait. I need to put my mind at rest concerning the expedition that Fred Jorgell and his friends are undertaking against the Island of Hanged Men."

"I'm a little short myself at present," said the doctor. "I've recently spent enormous sums on experiments and I haven't obtained the results or which I'd hoped."

"I have an interesting affair in view, which might put a million dollars into our coffers."

"My God that's worth the trouble! What is it?"

Fritz brought his brother up to date with the proposition made to him by Balthazar Buxton. The two bandits put together a detailed plan to put them in possession of the famous Titian portrait of Lucretia Borgia currently in William Dorgan's gallery. They were counting on their accomplice Baruch to help them attain that goal.

From time to time, however, the two brothers darted impatient glances at the large Boulle clock, of ebony inlaid with copper and tortoiseshell, that stood at the back of the room.

"Slug's taking his time getting back," muttered Cornelius.

"Unfortunately, I can't wait," said Fritz. "I have an important meeting at home."

"Well, go then. I'll telephone you if there's anything new."

"I'd like this affair to be concluded. I'm worried that, even if we get rid of Steffel, Lord Burydan and his friends might still discover the exact location of the Red Hand's headquarters."

156

"Don't be such a coward. The news I have from San Francisco is excellent., in the sense that Fred Jorgell and his friends are still convinced that our island is in the vicinity of the South Pole. Anyway, whatever happens, all our precautions are taken. Not one of the *Revenge*'s passengers will escape the shipwreck that I'm preparing for them!"

The two brothers parted; extraordinarily, for such bandits, there had always been a perfect agreement between them; they had never had a serious dispute. The art dealer professed a veritable adulation for the scientist, and always yielded very meekly to all his decisions.

III. A Deplorable Accident

Fritz Kramm had remembered that he had agreed to meet Lorenza, the healer of pearls, and all the preoccupations conferred upon him by the sinister schemes of the Red Hand had disappeared abruptly, as if by enchantment. He no longer had anything on his mind but the sole thought of meting once again the young woman whom he had met briefly in Balthazar Buxton's sumptuous gallery.

On the way, he stimulated his chauffeur's zeal, and trembled at the mere thought of arriving late and missing a few minutes with his charming visitor.

"Has anyone arrived yet?" he asked his manservant as he hurtled like a gust of wind into a little Moorish drawing room furnished with low divans covered in tiger-skin and decorated with panoplies of oriental weapons.

"Yes," was the reply. "Monsieur Grivard is in the studio and has set to work while waiting for you."

"Good. I'll join him. If a lady asks for me, show her in immediately."

The room that Fritz had called "the studio" was a small room situated to the side of the main display-space, which served as a storeroom. It was piled high with unframed paintings, empty frames and rolled-up canvases, all heaped up randomly in a mot inartistic disorder.

Installed in front of a large easel supporting a Pinturicchio orgy scene, a young man with golden blond hair and a silky russet beard was working ardently. Under the rapid strokes of his brush, the satiny torso of a beautiful sleeping courtesan seemed gradually to be emerging from the penumbra. Her pink-tipped breasts swelled again, stretching the velvet of a corsage disarranged by amorous frolics; the blue-whit veins on the milk-white neck stood out again under the laborious effort of the artist.

The restoration was so perfect that the supplementary fragments harmonized with the rest of the composition without it being possible to sea and gaps in the continuity.

Fritz Kramm, who had entered on tiptoe, contemplated the painting silently for some time, and them, tapping the painter unexpectedly on the shoulder, he said in French: "Truly, Monsieur Grivard, you're an admirable man. You have a genius for adopting the style of masters of every epoch, and Pinturicchio himself would recognize as his own that beautiful torso of a sleeping woman, who seems to have succumbed momentarily to amorous fatigue."

"You're too kind, Monsieur Kramm," the painter replied, in a melancholy tone. "I can assure you that it isn't difficult, for a man who knows his trade to do such work."

"That's not my opinion. Thus far, I haven't found anyone else able to do it as well as you."

"That's doubtless why you keep me close at hand," said the artist, bitterly.

Fritz smiled sardonically. "Yes indeed," he said. "I'm enormously keen to keep you. What do you lack here, after all? Don't I pay you well enough?"

"Certainly."

"Don't I give you the liberty to do as you please?"

"Undoubtedly," the young man murmured, "but you retain me in New York be means of a mental violence that I can't describe, and prevent me from seeing France again, where happiness and glory await me."

"Be patient! The day will come when you'll thank me for the constraint I'm imposing on you..."

At that moment, the manservant came in and handed Fritz a dainty visiting card.

"Signora Lorenza!" exclaimed the art dealer, joyfully. "Send her in—but make sure you take her through the large galley and the two drawing rooms." Turning toward the artist, he added: "Monsieur Grivard, you're going to see a beautiful person—a young woman entirely worthy of the brushes of the old masters you admire."

Almost immediately, the door opened and Lorenza came into the room with a rustle of silk, with the harmonious and noble stride that the ancient poets attributed to goddesses, and which caused her supple and slim waist to stand out above her voluptuously swaying hips. The artist had risen to his feet, pale and bewildered by admiration. His first sentiment, instinctive and irreflective, was that he was in the presence of a princess or a queen, and be bowed to the young woman with profound respect.

Fritz hastened to offer Signora Lorenza an armchair, apologizing for not having received her in one of the rich drawing rooms through which she had passed. "This room is more intimate," he said, "and I only admit friends into it. May I introduce you to Monsieur Grivard, a painter of the highest talent...Signora Lorenza, the enchantress of pearls, who has the marvelous gift of rendering them life and splendor."

The artist remained silent, so intimidated that he could not find any compliment that appeared worthy of the young woman. He had the impression that the admirable Lorenza belonged to a race superior to mere humankind, and that she might perhaps vanish like those mysterious profiles that one thinks one perceives in moonlight shadows, which fade into darkness as soon as one moves closer.

Lorenza was emotional and confused herself. With her exquisite delicacy of sensation, she had immediately perceived the impression she had made on the artist and was profoundly touched by that mute and respectful admiration. At first sight, she felt herself attracted to the young man by a strange sympathy. That physiognomy, which respired frankness, intelligence and generosity, had charmed her.

159

The gaze of the artist, whose large blue eyes had an exceedingly soft expression, had met Lorenza's eyes, and the two young people had felt a strange commotion in their hearts. An unfamiliar disturbance invaded them. They had understood in that mysterious instant that something irrevocable had happened, as if each of them had just penetrated an unknown world.

Fritz Kramm, who had not noticed that rapid exchange of glances, fluttered around the young woman, to whom he was invincible attracted. "You know, Signora," he said, "I shall have a great deal of work to confide to you. I have considerable quantities of ancient pearls in which your marvelous power can be exercised at your ease. Would you care to look at some of them?"

"Gladly."

"Look," he said, opening a steel box that he had taken from a dresser, "here are some necklaces, bracelets, earrings and hair-slides dating from all epochs of history. These earrings were found in an Egyptian sarcophagus; their pearls are doubtless contemporary with those that Queen Cleopatra swallowed after dissolving them in vinegar. And here are some that ornamented the doublet of Charles the Bold, and later the cap of Henri III. These yellow and blue ones ornamented the hilt of the Indian rajah Tippoo Sahib's dagger..."

While continuing this learned list, Fritz Kramm placed the ancient jewels with curious gold or silver mounts on Lorenza's knees; the pearls ornamenting them deprived of their luster, had become utterly flat and dull, reminiscent of the sightless eyes of blind people.

Suddenly, a telephone bell rang in the next room.

"Excuse me," said Fritz, furious at being disturbed. "I'll be back in a moment."

His absence, in fact, only lasted a few minutes, but when he reappeared in the studio his features had taken on an expression of irritation.

"It's extremely unfortunate," he said, "but it's absolutely necessary that I go to see my brother. Fortunately, I have the car and I won't be more than a quarter of an hour. I hope that Signora Lorenza will be willing to wait for my return in the company of Monsieur Grivard."

"Certainly," the young woman replied. "In your absence, I'll examine these beautiful jewels. They're very curious."

"Yes, I have a few pieces that are quite rare. Distract yourself with these trinkets as best you can, and soon..."

Fritz Kramm leapt into his automobile and gave his brother's address to the chauffeur. A short distance from the hotel, however, his attention was attracted by a newspaper crier whose papers were being snatched by the crowd still moist from the printing press.

"Chief of the New York Police victim of a serious accident! New details!"

Fritz signaled to the hawker, showing him a dollar. The man ran over to him, delighted with the windfall, and handed the art dealer, in exchange for the silver coin, a copy of a special edition of the *New York Herald*.

Fritz's gaze immediately went to the headline of the article, composed in large capitals:

CHIEF OF NEW YORK POLICE
VICTIM OF MORTAL ACCIDENT
DRIVER'S FATAL IMPRUDENCE
UNPARDONABLE ERROR

The police chief of our city, the honorable Mr. Steffel, was on his way to the Central Bank a few hours ago—to cash a check, as he had told his chauffeur—when the automobile in which he was riding, as it was crossing Fifth Avenue, was violently rammed by a large hundred-horsepower racing vehicle driven by a lone man and traveling at vertiginous speed.

Mr. Steffel's vehicle was staved in and the chief of police, grievously wounded in the head, the arm and the torso, was thrown on to the causeway, inert. The author of the accident, doubtless fearful of the terrible responsibility that he had incurred, was not ashamed to disappear, and could not be overtaken by the vehicles of the municipal police that launched in his pursuit. Mr. Steffel's chauffeur, who was fortunate enough only to receive minor injuries, hastened to help his master and, with the aid of several witnesses of the accident, transported him to a nearby pharmacy, where the most urgent care was lavished upon him.

That zeal, alas, proved fatal to the injured man.

In the absence of the pharmacist, the honorable Mr. Wells, the latter's laboratory assistant made him drink he contents of a bottle which he supposed to be filled with ether but which, in reality, contained an etheric potion fortified with a strong dose of morphine.

The employee perceived his error almost immediately, but, in spite of the energetic case he lavished on the chief of police, the unfortunate accident victim did not take long to die without having recovered consciousness.

One singular detail: the check that Mr. Steffel was said to be carrying could not be found, no longer being in his wallet. That larceny is easily explained by the presence of a crowd of curiosity-seekers, who had invaded the pharmacy in spite of the efforts of the police.

An investigation was immediately opened into this deplorable double accident.

The good faith of the laboratory assistant, a certain Mr. Smith, a native of New York, cannot be suspected. He will, however, be prosecuted for homicide by imprudence.

Following the article was a biographical note in which the courage, intelligence, skill and other virtues of the chief of police were pompously celebrated, and the sensational arrests in which he had collaborated were listed.

After he had finished reading the exciting article, Fritz Kramm felt that he had been relieved of an enormous burden. Once again, the Red Hand had triumphed over one of its most redoubtable enemies. The crime had been committed with such lightning rapidity that Mr. Steffel had certainly not been able to take anyone else into his confidence. Everything had therefore worked out for the best.

It was with a smiling and radiant expression that Fritz Kramm went into Dr. Cornelius' house, burning to know the full details.

It was to Slug and Leonello that the success of the criminal expedition was owed. It was Slug who, with extraordinary driving skill, had deliberately rammed the chief of police, and it was Leonello who had transported the injured man to the establishment of a pharmacist affiliated to the Red Hand, and had personally supervised the poisoning of the unfortunate policeman. It was also Leonello who had filched the fifty thousand dollar check from the victim's wallet.

Fritz Kramm only remained with his brother for as long as was strictly necessary. Now that he was liberated from the anxieties that Steffel's threats had caused him, he was in a hurry to get home and see the beautiful Lorenza, with whom he was passionately smitten.

I've never loved any woman, the bandit thought, *and never felt a disturbance similar to the one I'm feeling now. Yes, I want Lorenza to be mine, even if I have to spend millions. Even if I have to marry her! Even if I have to abandon the Red Hand and split with my brother!*

Unfortunately for Fritz, it was scarcely probable that the beautiful Italian woman would ever respond to his passion. With that delicacy of sensibility that was almost a kind of divination. Lorenza had quickly detected, beneath the correct and gentlemanly appearance, the cunning, brutal, hypocritical and faithless individual that the second Lord of the Red Hand was. She experienced in his regard one of those antipathies that put weak individuals on their guard against those who might harm them. On the other hand, she had been immediately won over by the frank and timid manners of the handsome artist.

During Fritz Kramm's absence, both of them chatted quietly, while examining the jewels and works of art with which the art dealer's house was packed from the cellar to the roof. They only talked about trivial things, but there was in their opinions, even in the most insignificant matters of detail, an absolute concordance. They understood one another by means of a word or a gesture, sometimes even a simple smile.

"Mr. Kramm will come back," said Grivard, finally, "And I'll leave you to discuss the healing of his pearls with him, but I'd be very happy to see you again."

"There's no reason why not," the young woman murmured, bushing imperceptibly.

"I'd like to ask you a great favor, Signora—that of painting your portrait."

"I'd be delighted, Remember my address. I'm lodging in a small house located at 333 Broadway. I'm at home most mornings—but not a word to Mr. Kramm; he has no need to know that we've become such good friends right away."

"Don't worry, I'll be discreet. Adieu, Signora!"

Setting one knee on the ground, Louis Grivard deposited a respectful kiss on the pale and slender hand that Lorenza held out to him, and withdrew, ecstatic, his heart overflowing with a joy such as he had never known.

IV. A Drama of Poverty

The esthetic property of the pure-blooded Yankee is completely different from that of a European, even if the latter is Anglo-Saxon. The Yankee searches above all for that which is immediate and practical, and banishes all ornamentation on principle. For example, a New York billionaire makes it a rule never to have any but simple furniture, without moldings; he will have an immense arm-chair fabricated, and will spend eight or ten thousand dollars for an electricity- or water-supply, but one will never see a painting or a statue in his home. On the other hand, he will possess ultra-advanced filing cabinets and a telephone loud-speaker, and all the service at his table will be done automatically.

If one finds some master painting in his home, its presence will be primarily due to vanity. In general—for there are honorable exceptions—a billionaire possesses paintings or statues because it is fashionable to possesses them, because someone else who is as rich as he is possesses them, and it is necessary to do what other people do., because, in the final analysis, paintings and statues are an affirmation and proof of wealth, because they cost a great deal and constitute a capital capable of increasing in value. We know of one billionaire who paid ninety-two thousand francs for a superb Corot and had it placed in his drawing room, but never took the time to look at it.

In the world of the Five Hundred, one has paintings as women have jewelry. The essential thing is not to experience an esthetic sensation, which is, in any case, only accessible to a few people, but to make one's friends and acquaintances, who cannot afford such a costly item, green with envy.

Financiers who, in their inmost hearts, admire the worst lithographs or the sickening statuary of the Rue Saint-Sulpice, have a gallery of masterpieces for the same reason that certain parvenus who like mutton stew and veal with carrots dine reluctantly on truffles, caviar and American lobster because it is chic and expensive.

Fred Jorgell, in certain respects, fell into this category of vain rich men devoid of any veritable artistic sentiment, but it was not the same with his rival William Dorgan. Harry's father, English by birth, loved and understood beautiful things. The house in which he lived, and had rebuilt after the Thirtieth Avenue fire, was an exact copy of an Elizabethan castle, emphatic and mannered in its architecture. There were turrets, bell-towers and arcades overflowing with sculptures everywhere.

William Dorgan possessed a gallery composed principally of paintings of the English school of the eighteenth century and a few French moderns. He had very few old paintings. It had required a chance opportunity to permit him to purchase the portrait of Lucretia Borgia, a work incontestably more beautiful

164

than the portrait of Cesare Borgia by Raphael for which Rothschild only paid six hundred thousand francs, and which is presently in the Château de Ferrières.[15]

The portrait of Lucretia Borgia had been placed in a special room ornamented with Italian Renaissance furniture. It was there that Louis Grivard labored for several days making a copy of the masterpiece as exact as possible.

He was hard at work one morning when the door opened and he saw William Dorgan's older son, the famous Trust-administrator Joe Dorgan—or, as we know, the murderer Baruch, who has usurped his identity. As he often did, he had come to cast an eye over the artist's work and chat to him for a little while.

"What you're doing is admirable," he said to the painter. "It would certainly require a connoisseur of great skill to distinguish the original from such an exact copy."

"I do my best. At any rate, I'm taking the most scrupulous precautions to make sure that the reproduction is as exact as possible."

"What precautions do you mean?"

"The canvas I'm using, for instance, is from the correct epoch."

"You doubtless haven't been able to do the same for the colors? Although I don't know much, I know that Titian couldn't use our modern colors, which are all due to chemistry, and much less stable than the ancients' colors."

"That's where you're wrong," said Louis Grivard. "To make this painting I'm using, like Titian himself, nothing but natural compounds mixed with oil, which are absolutely unalterable. My ultramarine blue is manufactured according to the ancient method, with finely crushed lapis lazuli, and I've banished from my palette the lakes and oxides that are so liable to tarnish."

"That's very interesting! Do you know who has ordered this copy?"

A shadow passed over the artist's expressive face. "I don't know," he said. "I'm paid by Mr. Kramm; I do what he tells me and I don't know any more."

"I wouldn't be astonished if my friend Fritz Kramm, who is a distinguished art-lover himself, kept this beautiful copy for his own collection."

"As I've said, I don't have any information about that."

"In any case, I'm glad of the hazard that has permitted me to make your acquaintance, and I've given orders for you to be admitted, any time you wish, t visit the paintings my father possesses."

"I don't know whether I'll be here long enough to be able to take advantage of your kind permission. The copy of the *Lucretia Borgia* is almost finished. It only remains for me to age it slightly, and it will be done."

---

[15] The portrait to which this passage refers is a painting once attributed to Raphael but probably by an unknown student; the notion that the extant painting is a copy of a Raphael original that was surreptitiously acquired by Baron de Rothschild still persists in legend, but is surely false.

"Truly," said Baruch, stepping back in order to judge the effect more fully, "it's impossible to make a more perfect copy!" His gaze went from one portrait to the other, in mute admiration.

The beautiful courtesan princess who was the mistress of her father, Pope Alexander VI and his son Cesare, had been represented by Titian sitting in a large and rigid Venetian armchair. Her beautiful blonde hair, separated over the forehead into two bangs, was secured by a fine gold chain which contained, directed above the eyebrows, a large emerald. A green velvet robe accentuated the suppleness of her figure and left her white arms and throat exposed, the neckline cut to the small, high-set breasts. What was most fascinating about it was the innocent smile on that beautiful face with pure and limpid eyes and a child-like mouth. At the time when the portrait had been painted, however, Lucretia, already thrice widowed and a mother, had frightened her contemporaries with her crimes and orgies.

The two men chatted for a few more minutes about the enigmatic Lucretia, with whom Lord Byron had been in love centuries after her death, and for a lock of whose hair, extracted from her tomb at Ferrara and which he kept about his person for a long time, he had paid an immense sum.[16]

It was not out of idleness or mere curiosity that Baruch was given proof of so much interest in Louis Grivard's work. He had monitored the latter's work at close range for reasons that had nothing to do with artistic preoccupations. Fritz and Cornelius had informed him of the proposition made by Balthazar Buxton, and, as all three of them knew very well that William Dorgan would never consent to dispose of his painting, it had been decided between them that the portrait of Lucretia Borgia would be stolen, in such conditions that the larceny could never be discovered.

In order to succeed in that, Fritz had thought of employing the talent of Louis Grivard. It had been agreed that the artist would make a faithful copy of the painting, and that, at the last moment, the copy would be substituted for the original, which would be delivered to Balthazar Buxton.

The plan had every chance of success, William Dorgan being absent at present on a tour of inspection of the immense estates owned by the cotton and corn Trust of which he was the director.

Fritz Kramm had good reason to believe that was entirely at his discretion and, in spite of the latter's indignant protests, had given him an order to effect the substitution. Louis Grivard had pretended to accept, while intending to find some stratagem at the last moment that would avoid making him the accomplice of that dishonorable action.

Baruch did not want to appear to have anything to do with the affair, but he was the one who had introduced the artist into the paternal palace and made the

---

[16] In fact, Byron claimed to have stolen the lock of hair that he carried, alleging, fancifully, that it had once belonged to Lucretia Borgia

theft of the painting possible. After having resisted the suggestions of his two accomplices for some time, he had begun to believe that the larceny would be a complete success. The exactitude of the copy rendered it entirely plausible.

For his part, Fritz Kramm believed that the artist would carry out his instructions with the most blind docility.

When he left Louis Grivard, Baruch went to see Fritz to tell him that everything was proceeding to plan and that the Red Hand would doubtless not be long delayed in taking possession of the promised million dollars. Fritz was not at home; he had gone to pay a visit to the healer of pearls, with whom he was increasingly infatuated. Baruch was therefore obliged to head for Cornelius' house, in order to bring him up to date.

Left alone in the magnificent Italian drawing room with the gilded leather furniture and the ceiling ornamented with a crystal chandelier the color of Murano fabric, Louis Grivard worked ardently for a further two hours, increasingly enthused by his work the further it progressed.

Suddenly, he threw down his brushes with an exclamation of great satisfaction.

"I shan't touch it again," he exclaimed. "I've never achieved such a perfect imitation. I believe, at the risk of blasphemy, that Titian himself, if he returned to earth, wouldn't be able to distinguish his painting from mine!"

The artist remained plunged in a profound reverie for some time. Then, distractedly, he stated riffling through an album filled with sketches, and stopped at a page where there was a profile of Baruch, traced energetically with a few strokes of charcoal.

"A singular physiognomy, that of Joe Dorgan," he murmured. "I've never seen one like it. So many muscles are out of place. One might think that the face had been molded, reworked by hand. That Joe is decidedly troubling. He has two or three facial expressions that are totally different from one another; under the influence of some passion, his ordinary features disappear to give way to others, as if he had two distinct individualities within him. There's definitely a strange mystery there."

While following his train of thought Louis Grivard had folded up his easel and packed up his box of paints; then he took off his smock and rapidly made his exit from the billionaire's house. He knew that Lorenza was expecting him, as she did almost every day, and that he only had time to have a rapid meal in order to be at the beautiful Florentine's house at the agreed time.

A Yankee who spends his day in the offices of immense thirty-story buildings generally retires in the evening to a little cottage of his own, surrounded by a garden and situated in a tranquil street. By night, the monstrous skyscrapers are almost uninhabited; the suburbs and some of the outlying districts of New York are entirely populated by these small houses, all constructed on an identical model, with a courtyard protected by a grille, a bed of geraniums, three white stone steps and a door on which the resident's name is resplendent on a large copper or nickel plate.

It was a habitation of that sort that Lorenza had chosen; it was there that Louis Grivard went every day to spend all the free time he had outside of his work.

There had sprung up between the two young people one of those sudden amities that would be inexplicable if they were not almost always the commencement of an ardent and durable love. It already seemed to Louis and Lorenza that they had known one another for years. They were only happy when they were together, and their mutual confidence was so great that they had no secrets from one another.

An old woman with a friendly face furrowed by thousands of wrinkles, whose eyes were still lively beneath the brightly-colored headscarf surrounding her white hair, opened the door to Louis Grivard and introduced him into the small drawing room in which Lorenza spent most of her time. It was a bright and cheerful room, with unbleached wallpaper with golden florets, filled with flowers and charming trinkets. Near the window, turtle-doves were cooing in a large silver filigree cage, and beside it there was a mimosa plant in a blue faience pot.

The furniture, ornamented with nacre arabesques, was in the Italian bad taste that is sometimes exquisite. It was, in any case, evident that the beautiful Lorenza had a true passion for nacre. It was everywhere: nacre paper-knives, nacre shelves and, on the mantelpiece, a collection of beautiful seashells with iridescent gleams.

Lorenza was wearing a superb pearl necklace herself, only slightly more dazzling than the white bosom over which it was displayed.

At the sight of the artist, the young woman got up and ran to meet him, smiling. "How are you, my dear Louis?" she said. "I'm glad to see you. Can you imagine that I dreamed last night that you were ill."

"I can assure you, my beautiful friend, that I'm perfectly well."

"But how worried you seem!"

"No!" protested the young man, feebly.

"You can't lie. Something must be wrong. I'm very superstitious; I believe in dreams. There must be a grain of truth in the one that I had last night."

Louis could not help smiling. "You're a true enchantress," he said. "Well, I confess that I'm slightly preoccupied at present. One can't hide anything from you, my dear Lorenza."

"You must tell me about it. Come on, sit down here, beside me, and if I'm satisfied with your frankness, I'll allow you to kiss me."

"All right—but I want to be paid in advance."

With a simplicity and a lack of coquetry that proved the candor and the purity of her intentions, Lorenza lowered her eyes, and, with a gracious gesture, offered her cheek to the young man, who deposited a long kiss thereon.

They were sitting side by side, and Louis had taken Lorenza's hands in his; she did not think of pulling them away.

"Now," she murmured, "I'm listening."

The artist's expression had darkened. "What I have to tell you is serious," he said, "and I wouldn't make such a confidence to anyone but you."

Briefly, he recounted the difficulty that he was in now that the portrait of Lucretia Borgia was finished.

"It's impossible for me to make myself the accomplice of a theft," he concluded. "I'll never reconcile myself to that. On the other hand, if I don't obey that wretch Fritz Kramm, I'll expose myself to terrible reprisals."

"How is it, then," the young woman asked, full of concern, "that the man has such power over you? If you owe him money, I'll lend you what you need to pay him. Am I not your friend?"

"It's not just a matter of money," murmured Louis, somberly. Then, as if coming to an abrupt decision, he continued: "I'll tell you everything; it's best that you know the truth. My father was a French manufacturer. He owned a factory making automobiles and airplanes near Paris. Until last year, the business was going admirably, but then a banker to whom my father had confided all his capital fled the country, leaving a deficit behind of more than three million. We were ruined.

"In order to honor his debts, my father had to sell everything he possessed, including his factory, but our creditors were paid in full, to the last sou. It was then that I began to exhibit my work, and my name gradually became known to dealers and collectors. My father and I had resolved to struggle courageously against adversity, but as they say, misfortunes never come singly. My mother and my sister died; my father, in despair, prematurely aged by grief but not defeated, assembled a few thousand francs with my help and embarked for New York, where, thanks to his competence as an engineer and manufacturer, he hoped to rebuild his fortune."

"I presume that he did not succeed," Lorenza put in, squeezing her friend's hands affectionately.

"Alas, no. After three months I received a telegram informing me that my father had committed suicide after having exhausted his last resources. I sold everything I possessed and left for New York. A major Parisian dealer had furnished me with the means of organizing an exhibition here, the profits of which would serve to reimburse the money I had borrowed to pay for my passage and for my father's funeral..."

"That's a sad story!" the young woman murmured, her eyes moist with tears.

"But I have to go on to the end of the story. In spite of the heavy customs duties that were imposed on the paintings on entering America, my exhibition was a success, and left the organizer and myself with a tidy sum. It was then that I made the acquaintance of Fritz Kramm. He had acquired two or three of my canvases, without haggling, and had loudly manifested his admiration for the particular skill with which I was endowed for copying old masters, so I wasn't astonished when I received a note from him asking me to call at his house on a matter that would brook no delay."

"He must have caused you to fall into some trap?"

"Judge for yourself. After taking me into his study, he suddenly took a letter out of his wallet, which he handed to me. I went pale on recognizing my father's handwriting, and it was with a heart constricted by anguish that I read these terrible words: 'Ruined, old and ill, there is nothing left for me to do but die. It is freely and voluntarily that I give myself to death. I have stolen fifty thousand francs from Mr. Fritz Kramm and cannot survive my dishonor. Jérôme Grivard.'

"I was astounded. The characters of the fatal letter danced before my eyes. 'What are you going to do, Monsieur?' Fritz Kramm demanded, without giving me time to think. 'You're under no obligation, as you know, to assume responsibility for your father's debt.'

"Extremely emotional, I replied: 'You'll be reimbursed in full, Monsieur, but I'll need time, alas. I have almost nothing left from the proceeds of my sale.'

"'I'm delighted to find you so well disposed,' he said, with satisfaction. 'That sentiment of noble probity does you great honor; I'll tell you how you can acquit yourself of your debt to me. I can appreciate your talent, which is great. A restorer of paintings with your skill would be very useful to me. Enter into my employment at a reasonable salary, therefore, which will be set off—in part, at least, for you'll need to live—against the total of your father's debt. In a few years, you'll have settled your obligation to me.'"

"But how much was this salary?" asked the young woman, emotionally.

The artist made an angry gesture. "Three thousand dollars a month. And even by exercising the strictest economy, I'm obliged to spend at least a thousand for my nourishment and accommodation."

"With the result that it will take you five years to liberate yourself entirely."

"If I really owed him that sum," said the young man, with increasing irritation. "But I'm convinced that my father, who was honor and probity personified, never stole fifty thousand francs from that wretch."

"It seems very implausible to me too."

"The day after I had signed an obligation of fifty thousand francs to Fritz Kramm and a legal contract binding me to him for five years, I received a letter from Paris that had crossed with me during my journey and had been sent on to me in New York, where it had originated. It was a letter from my father! In four pages of compact handwriting, which still bore the traces of tears, the unfortunate man explained to me that, having exhausted his strength and resources, he had decided to die—and he insisted that he would die without owing a sou to anyone and that his son would have the right to respect his memory as that of an honest man!"

In a voice moist with tears, Louis Grivard added: "I'll let you read that letter some day, my dear friend. My father laid bare therein his most poignant dolors, and told me about the supreme disappointments that had led to his fatal resolution—but at the same time, he gave me the most noble advice. He told me that it was better to remain permanently poor and unknown than to obtain success and fortune by dishonest means!"

"So your father hadn't stolen from Fritz Kramm. What is the significance of the letter, then? A forgery, no doubt?"

"No, not entirely. By virtue of reflection and investigation, I believe that I've discovered the truth. The first lines were written by my father, but Fritz Kramm must have taken advantage of that fact that there was a blank space between the text and the signature to add a further sentence, skillfully imitating his handwriting."

"That's abominable."

"Fritz Kramm thus found the means to procure himself a slave cheaply. I estimate at more than ten thousand dollars the sum that my work must have brought him in the space of a year."

"There's still one obscure point," said Lorenza, pensively. "How did the note written by your father come into the art dealer's hands? That doesn't seem easy to explain."

"I ended up discovering how it came about. The physician summoned to certify the death of my unfortunate father was none other than Dr. Cornelius, the sculptor of human flesh. He must have taken possession of the note at hazard, of which his brother made use a short time later, when my exhibition permitted him to observe that I was exactly the man he needed."

"You've never told Mr. Kramm about these discoveries?"

"Yes. We had a violent argument on the subject, but he maintained with a glacial self-composure that the letter that had come into his hands was not a forgery, and demonstrated to me with a cruel irony that no one would give any credence to my claim, since I had implicitly recognized the authenticity of my father's handwriting by signing the obligation of fifty thousand francs. Finally, he added that any attempt on my part to avid payment would expose me to a lawsuit and the publication of the letter in the French newspapers. I understood that even if I won the case, my poor father's memory would be dishonored nonetheless, and I gave in."

"This Kramm is decidedly a great villain!"

"You don't know everything yet. Some time ago, he repeated his threat to publish the letter and ordered me to make a copy of the portrait of Lucretia Borgia and substitute it for the original. Such is the scoundrel we're dealing with!"

Lorenza's beautiful face had become pink with indignation. Her nostrils were flared by anger, and her dark furrowed eyebrows gave her physiognomy the majestic expression of an irritated goddess.

"Now," said Louis, "what do you advise me to do?"

"It's necessary to recover possession of your contract and the obligation of fifty thousand francs. Unfortunately, I can't see, as yet, any means of doing that."

"But what about the painting?"

"Content yourself with bringing Kramm the copy you've made and telling him that it's the original. Do you think that he can be deceived?"

"I'm sure of it. My copy is very good. Furthermore, I've just applied a layer of varnish that I'll leave in the sun to scale, and the painting will give every appearance of appropriate age." The anguished artist added: "But I don't want Mr. Buxton to be robbed either. The situation is inextricable, you see!"

"Don't lose heart—I'll think about all this. Just take your copy to Kramm tomorrow; that will gain us a little time; between now and then, I'll have found a plan!"

In spite of his charming friend's promises, Louis Grivard remained somber and silent. Lorenza made every effort to cheer him up and console him.

"I can see," she said, with her soothing smile, "that we won't be doing any work on my portrait today." And she pointed at an easel covered by a sheet of cloth at the back of the room.

"I'll get to work, if you want me to," he artist said, without enthusiasm.

"No, you're out of sorts today. You'd only do poor work. Then against, see how ungallant you are—you haven't even thought of claiming the kiss I promised you."

Louis could not help smiling. "There's still time!" he exclaimed, throwing his arms around Lorenza's wait. She drew away coquettishly, but eventually consented to offer him her forehead. By virtue of some false movement, however, it was on Lorenza's mouth that Louis' burning lips were posed in a long and voluptuous kiss.

V. A Fire of Joy

In the wake of Louis Grivard's confidences, Lorenza had spent a sleepless night. A thousand plans presented themselves to her mind, but she had rejected them all, one after another, as impracticable.

The first rays of dawn were already penetrating through the gap in the lilac velvet curtains lined with orange silk that protected the young woman's sleep, and she had not yet closed her eyes. Her face was pale, her eyes slightly ringed by fatigue, but she seemed satisfied.

She rang for her maid, old Graziella, who brought in her morning chocolate and inquired maternally about her health.

"I slept badly," the young woman replied, "but it doesn't matter. Bring the little lemonwood desk over to the bed; I wasn't to write a telegram."

The old woman did as she was asked. Leaning over in a fashion that was uncomfortable, but would have delighted a sculptor, Lorenza traced a few lines in a feverish hand and put them in an envelope addressed to Mr. Fritz Kramm, the art dealer.

"Take that to the Post Office right away," she said to Graziella, "but draw the curtains first, so I won't be inconvenienced by the sun; I need to sleep until midday."

The old woman hastened to obey and, leaving the room plunged in darkness, went out on tiptoe, not returning until midday.

Lorenza had slept well, and those few hours of rest had restored her strength completely. The necklace of large pearls that she never took off, even while she was sleep, was radiating a soft gleam. She stroked them distractedly with her hand, talking to them as if they were animate beings.

"I can see by the beauty of your luster, my little darlings," she said, "that my sleep has done me good. I have all my wits about me, and am ready for battle."

Lorenza got up, dressed after taking a bath and had a very light lunch. She had arranged to meet Fritz Kramm at three o'clock in the afternoon. She waited for him with a slight nervous impatience, busying herself by copying into a dainty notebook with a nacre cover the departure times of trains and liners that she found in a voluminous timetable.

She interrupted that work to summon Graziella.

"What does the Signora desire?" asked the old woman.

"Light the fire in that hearth for me."

"Very good, Signora."

"Then throw a few pastilles of scent into the perfume-burner and put two bottles of the Moscato spumante that I received from Florence last month into an ice-bucket to chill. After that, pack our trunks." As Graziella failed to suppress a start of surprise, the young woman added: "Yes, we need to leave this evening on a long trip…oh, I forgot! Get rid of that easel and the painting on it. Take them up to my bedroom."

Graziella hastened to do as she was told, and these various preparations were soon concluded.

Lorenza was lying on the Venetian leather divan with broad golden arabesques, in an adorably feline pose. Her bare arms emerged from the sleeves of a large red silk peignoir embroidered with Japanese chimeras, and a profoundly pensive gleam appeared from time to time in her blue eyes, beneath the dark helmet of her thick hair.

Three o'clock had just chimed when Fritz Kramm, with typical Yankee punctuality, presented himself at the door of the cottage. Graziella introduced him immediately.

On the threshold of the little drawing room the art dealer delightedly breathed in the subtle and penetrating atmosphere therein; the cassolettes were exhaling fumes of aloe-wood and incense; the large bouquets of flowers in the vases were swooning in the warm air and languid heady effluvia were rising from Lorenza herself, as if her entire body were nothing but a great flower of delicately embalmed flesh.

Fritz had the sensation of entering the enchanted cavern of some Circe; his heart was beating at the gallop; his hands were trembling and he understood obscurely that he would not be able to refuse anything that the woman asked of him.

Lorenza immediately put him at his ease with a gaiety and vivacity of repartee that he had never seen in her before.

"You wrote to me," he stammered, in a voice trembling with emotion. "Is that because you've decided to be a little less cruel?"

Lorenza emitted a burst of frank laughter. "Not so fast, Signor Kramm," she murmured. "Your imagination is carrying you away."

"Why did you ask me to come, then?"

"Do I know myself?" Lorenza said, laughing more loudly. "Let's say, if you wish, that it's because I had nothing to do this afternoon, or because I wanted you to taste my excellent Muscat."

"Whatever the reason," Fritz replied, deeply disturbed, "I'm profoundly grateful for your gracious invitation."

The young Florentine had risen to her feet; she went to the sideboard where there was a tray bearing pink and gilded cups, which were soon brimming with the blonde and sparkling foam of the precious wine.

"How do you like my Muscat?"

"It's exquisite, signora."

"Entirely at your service. Although not as well-supplied as those of Fred Jorgell and William Dorgan, my cellar is entirely at your disposal."

The conversation continued for some time in this trivial tone. Fritz was stimulated by the badinage, and he never took his gleaming eyes off the beautiful young woman, whose slightest movements seemed to have the elasticity of a panther.

"Listen, Signora," he said, standing up abruptly. "Enough of these pleasantries. Stop playing with me as a cat plays with a mouse. You know that I love you...that I'm mad about you..."

"Unfortunately," said the young woman, showing her dazzling teeth in a burst of laughter, "it's a passion that I don't share."

Fritz's face was red; his eyes were shining. "I'm not asking you to love me overnight," he said, pleadingly, "but just show a little generosity toward me, a little affection, and I'll make you the happiest of women." He threw himself at the Italian's knees.

She continued to gaze at him with a mocking smile. "Get up," she said. "Now you're making me formal declarations. That's an abuse of my hospitality. Look, sit down and drink another glass of Muscat. It's said in Italy that it's a wine that has the taste of kisses."

"But after all," exclaimed Fritz Kramm, "what do you want? I'll give it to you. Do you want me to marry you?"

With her head and her maliciously-raised index finger, Lorenza made a negative gesture.

"Do you want some jewelry, some adornment? Tell me! Express any wish whatsoever, and it will be granted." Fritz was breathless. All his composure had abandoned him; he was burning with fever. Mechanically, he drank two cups of the volcanic wine in quick succession, which ran through his veins like fire. "Lorenza!" he stammered, in an imploring tone. "Be mine, and I'll set piles of gold and banknotes at your feet!"

"That's promising a great deal," the young woman replied, in a bantering tone. "I'm sure that if I only asked you for the banknotes you have in that wallet that I can seen bulging in the inside pocket of your jacket, you'd think twice about it."

Fritz uttered a cry of triumph. Did not those words indicate that the Italian woman was as venal as all the rest, that she had only been so difficult in order to put a higher price on her favors, and that she would be his, provided that he met that price?

With an enthusiastic gesture, he took the wallet from his pocket and held it out to Lorenza. "Here," he said. "Take it. There are several thousand dollars in it; they're yours. Go on, keep it all—and I promise you even more."

Without ceasing to smile, Lorenza had nonchalantly taken the wallet and opened it. While putting on a show of counting the banknotes that she was riffling between her fingers, she examined with an inquisitive eye the other papers that it contained.

As long as the letter is here! she thought. *If the wretch has locked it way in some sage, all is lost!*

But her searching eye had discerned a piece of paper covered with a few lines written in violet ink. With a glance she verified the signature: Jérôme Grivard. It was undoubtedly the fatal letter of which the artist had spoken. With a rapid gesture she seized it and slipped it into her corsage. In the same way, she took possession of the obligation that Louis had mentioned.

Fritz was so convinced that Lorenza only wanted his banknotes that he smiled stupidly, sipping Muscat from a cup.

Meanwhile, Lorenza had taken two banknotes. She screwed them up and, having thrown them into the fireplace, watched them burn.

On seeing that, the bandit started. "What are you doing?" he said. "That's stupid! You're burning banknotes now?"

Lorenza shrugged her shoulders. Her only response was to throw another two banknotes into the fire. There was a strange expression in the young woman's bright eyes, simultaneously hateful and mocking, which rendered Fritz Kramm vaguely anxious.

"After all," he stammered, "you can burn them if you want to. I gave them to you."

"I hope you aren't regretting it," she jeered, throwing five or six more banknotes into the flames.

"No, no," he said. "They're yours; I promise you others. But give me back the papers that were with them. They're letters I want to keep."

"Letters from women, no doubt!" she exclaimed, with a feverish joy. "I'm jealous! Into the fire with the love-letters! Into the fire with all the papers!"

Continuing to laugh, nervously and stridently—crazy laughter—she emptied the entire contents of the wallet into the flames.

Fritz had gone white. He launched himself forward to snatch some of the papers from the blaze, but Lorenza, still pretending that she was teasing, held him at bay with a kind of torch made of flaming banknotes, which she shoved in his face.

It was already too late; the papers and banknotes were no longer anything but a large pile of black ashes, through the midst of which ran little sparks like fiery insects.

The art dealer was flabbergasted. He did not understand that bizarre conduct. He was a hundred leagues from any suspicion that Lorenza, during her night of insomnia, had coolly and minutely premeditated her slightest gestures.

At the moment when she had thrown the papers in the fire, he had wanted to strangle her, but at the same time, he found her adorable.

"You're terrible!" he cried, with an ill humor that he attempted to dissimulate. "You'll see"—he was still addressing her as "*vous*," not daring to adopt the intimate firm of address—"that I can tolerate without too much annoyance the loss of my banknotes and my papers."

"You weren't so gracious just now. If you love me as much as you say, it's necessary to be absolutely and entirely submissive to my wishes."

"I'll try," he said, piteously, and added, humbly: "But haven't you promised to be a little less cruel? I've done what you asked, after all."

"You've done it in too sullen a fashion. Don't go to work so quickly. In any case, I haven't promised you anything. I'm not yet sure enough of your affection." While speaking, she had become calm and smiling again.

Again, he felt powerless before her bewitching smile.

"Listen," she said. "I confess that I've been a little irresponsible. You must forgive me that childishness; I'm very nervous. Come back tomorrow, and I'll reward you as you deserve, you can be sure of it—and above all, don't forget to bring me some banknotes!" That sentence had been calculated very carefully to give the bandit hope.

"Why don't you want me to come back this evening?" he begged, persistently.

"No, not this evening; I have to go out. Besides which, I need to think. I'm not entirely decided."

Twisted by all kinds of captious assertions, Fritz Kramm ended up retiring, but promising himself an explosive revenge for the following day.

As soon as Lorenza, watching from the window, had seen the automobile carrying Fritz Kramm disappear in the distance, her physiognomy relaxed and expressed a profound and blissful satisfaction. Her face was radiant with tenderness and bounty. "Poor Louis!" she murmured. "How happy he'll be." Then she shouted: "Graziella, leave the trunks. Finish them later. Go and fetch me a taxi right away."

While the devoted Italian carried out this mission, Lorenza hurried threw a mantle over her shoulders and put on a hat.

A few minutes later she climbed into a cab, and gave the driver Balthazar Buxton's address.

VI. The Hand

Fritz Kramm went home in a hurry. He had suddenly remembered that he had to meet Louis Grivard, who was to deliver the painting stolen from William Dorgan, and that he was late for the meeting.

"Has Monsieur Grivard come?" he asked his domestic.

"Yes, but he's just left. He left a large box for you; I had it placed in the great hall."

"I know what it is. Open it carefully. It contains a painting that I want to see before I deliver it myself."

Fritz watched the flat box containing the portrait of Lucretia Borgia being opened, and could not help marveling at the splendor of the masterpiece dazzling with youth beneath the dark varnish, cracked by age, with which it was covered. He did not imagine for an instant that it was the copy and not the original that he had before his eyes.

"Good," he murmured. "The Frenchman kept his word. He's a little naïve. As long as he believes that I still possess the famous letter that Lorenza has just reduced to ashes, I hold him under my thumb. It's only five o'clock; old Balthazar is expecting me at six. I'll arrive in time in spite of the delay caused by my visit to the lovely Italian witch."

Evidently, Fritz had taken the adventure of the burned letters in his stride. He climbed into a taxi after having had the box containing the portrait set on the seat next to him.

A short distance from the art lover's house, his cab cross the path of another, in which there was a woman who moved sharply backwards on seeing him. He did not recognize Signora Lorenza, who had emerged from Balthazar Buxton's house a few minutes earlier.

He got down outside the mysterious palace and went through the labyrinth, following the usual ceremony, passing under portcullises and traversing bizarrely decorated windowless rooms. Finally, he reached the circular gallery in which the sliding door was set that gave access to the old art-lover's gallery, where armed men mounted guard.

His visit was announced and he was immediately introduced. The skeletal old man, warmly wrapped up in his black velvet dressing-gown, received him with his habitual politeness. The maniac's golden eyes seemed to be sparkling with covetousness as they examined the box that contained the painting. However, Fritz thought that he seemed more preoccupied and less cordial than usual.

"Come on," he said, impatiently. "Let's see the admirable Lucretia, that masterpiece of her sex, who was loved by so many princes, celebrated by so many poets and immortalized by so many men of genius."

178

"You'll be satisfied," said Fritz, who, with the aid of a chisel he had brought, rapidly removed the light planks of poplar that constituted the painting's wrapping.

"Your checks are all ready, you know," said Balthazar Buxton, sniggering. "I have five of them, each fir two hundred thousand dollars, payable at the Central Bank."

"Oh, it's well-known that you're solid," said Fritz, obsequiously. "You're the only billionaire rich enough not even to take the trouble to augment his fortune."

"That's because I'm so old," murmured Balthazar, bracing his emaciated torso with a macabre coquetry that belied his words.

Fritz had taken the painting out of its case. He balanced it on a dresser, in such a way that the light fell directly on to the canvas.

Balthazar had become grave. He set himself three paces away from the canvas and considered it carefully with his sharp eyes. A long minute went by.

Without knowing why, Fritz Kramm felt very uncomfortable. He was still smiling—an obsequious smile that might have been called "commercial"—but a vague dread was beginning to overtake him.

Without saying a word, Balthazar Buxton threw his check-book into an open drawer, and then sat down in his leather armchair, no longer looking at the Lucretia.

Fritz dared not be the first to break the silence pregnant with menace.

"Mr. Kramm," said the old man, finally, in a severe tone, "you're either a thief or an imbecile—which is it?"

"Me!" stammered the dealer, who had become livid.

"Yes. If you've brought me this copy—which is very good—instead of the original knowingly, you're a thief. If, on the other hand you've bought this painting believing it to be a Titian, you don't know your trade and you're an imbecile."

Signora Lorenza, after Fritz Kramm had left, had gone to warn the old collector about the substitution of which he was about to be the victim, but the latter, with the vanity of a connoisseur, had dissimulated until the last moment, wanting to attribute the sole credit for the discovery of the forgery to himself.

"Mr. Kramm," he added, assailing the other with a scornful gaze, "You'll do me the pleasure of taking away this canvas immediately, and never setting foot in my house again."

Fritz felt fury gripping him. So the superb windfall that he had patiently prepared as about to escape him! He would not get his hands on the million dollars that would have kept the Red Hand afloat! It was too much. He resolved to repay that audacity.

"Mr. Buxton," he said, with an affected calmness, "That's not how business is done. You might be a great connoisseur, but you're capable of making a mistake, like everyone else in the world. I only know one thing: you commissioned me to but a painting for you belonging to William Dorgan. I've bought it and paid for it."

"Not very dearly, I assume?" the old man put in, sarcastically.

"That's not your concern. You promised me a million dollars; that's what you owe me. I want them and I'll have them. I'm sure, myself, that the painting really is a Titian."

"Or by a dauber in your pay."

"I refuse to take back my painting. The courts will decide its value."

The most piquant thing was that Fritz believed what he was saying. He was convinced that it really was the original *Lucretia* that Louis Grivard had delivered to him. Obviously, he had no intention of going to court, for he would be obliged to call William Dorgan as a witness, which would have embarrassed him greatly, but he hoped to be able to intimidate Balthazar.

A very lively argument broke out between them, and the little old man, who, on the orders of his physician, ought to have avoided all violent emotion, did not take long to find the importunity of the dishonest merchant excessive.

"Mr. Kramm," he said, "I'm not as young as you and I can't shout as loudly, but you're wearying me. Get out! You can address yourself to the court if you wish. Take away your copy or don't; it's all the same to me."

Those words brought Fritz's fury to a peak. He wanted to reply, but Balthazar extended his finger toward an electric bell-push in order to summon his men and have the intruder thrown out.

Fritz grabbed the old man's hand as it was about to touch the button and pulled it back brutally, saying into his ear in a low and menacing voice: "No one throws me out like that. I want my money! Give me the five checks, right away!"

"No," murmured the old man, obstinately. "You're a wretch. Let me go or I'll call for help."

"Don't do that, or I'll strangle you." Fritz saw red. Matching word and action, his hands, with their enormous thumbs, seized Balthazar by the throat. He felt that his hand, at that moment, were acting independently of him, as if they had a will of their own.

An atrocious fear was reflected in Balthazar Buxton's golden eyes. He uttered a shrill and faint scream, like the wail of an infant.

It was his last cry.

Prey to the demon of murder, Fritz squeezed, ever more forcefully. The neck, as slender as a bird's, flattened beneath the murderer's enormous thumbs; the golden eyes capsized and were extinguished in the depths of their sockets. There was a crack of splintering bone.

Balthazar was dead.

Abruptly, Fritz hurled away the cadaver with upturned eyes, the horror-stricken face already flecked with blood at the corners of the lips. Then he opened the drawer, took out the check-book, stuffed it into his pocket, and, with the instinctive movement of a hunted beast, ran to the door.

He had not taken three steps before he stopped dead, his face invaded by a mortal pallor. He had just remembered that, in order to permit his visitors to leave, Balthazar Buxton passed a special token through the judas-hole, which served as a safe conduct to get out of the inextricable labyrinth.

The murderer had not thought of that. He was caught in a trap, stupidly. He would be found locked in with the cadaver. There was certainly no hope of escaping from the house, in which, without a guide, one could wander for an entire month before discovering an exit.

The bandit had a fit of cold rage. His teeth clenched, his eyes injected with blood, he circled around the luxurious rotunda like a wolf caught in a trap. With an impulsive gesture, he pulverized a fragile alabaster statue with a blow of his fist. Further on, he smashed a painting with a kick.

How could he get out? It was, however, necessary to get out. He had to find a good idea right away, because someone would become anxious about the length of the meeting and would come in.

He took his head in his hands. He tried to think, strove to reason.

Impossible! He found nothing.

The monotonous *tick-tock* of a large ebony clock clawed at his brain. He had a material sensation of the precipitate, galloping, hectic flight of the hours, minute and seconds.

Suddenly, his eyes went to the cadaver, which, head tilted backwards, seemed to be contemplating him with a vengeful snigger. Again, a formidable anger took hold of him. "No!" he exclaimed. "It won't be you who triumphs, old skeleton! I'm not afraid of you! I'll be the stronger!"

Feverishly, he stated rummaging in the pocket of the velvet dressing-gown, and soon uttered a cry of joy on discovering the token that permitted someone to exit from the labyrinth.

It was, however, Balthazar Buxton himself who had the habit of passing it through the judas-hole and Balthazar Buxton's hand was recognizable in a thousand, as much by its bony emaciation as its brown color and the enormous emerald worn on the ring-finger. The difficult remained.

Fritz tried to detach the ring, but it seemed to be an integral part of the dead man's finger. Besides which, it was so narrow that even if he had managed to get it off, he would not have been able to put it on one of his own stout fingers.

The problem seemed insoluble, and the inflexible hand of the clock was still advancing around the dial. It was time for Balthazar Buxton's meal. Someone might come at any moment.

In the overexcitement of peril or anguish, the murderer had a desperate and macabre inspiration.

He felt the cadaver. It was still warm, perhaps a trifle lukewarm but not yet possessed by the glacial cold of death.

Well, yes, it would be Balthazar Buxton himself who would hold out the liberating token through the judas-hole. That was the only means; there was no other. And it was necessary to hurry.

He picked up the cadaver, as light as a feather, approached it to the judas-hole, gave the hand, still flexible, the shape that was required, wedging the token—just—between two fingers, in such a way that it would come out easily, and, prey to an atrocious anguish, he hid behind the cadaver, which he supported beneath the armpits with one hand. With the other hand, he took hold of the dead man's wrist, ready to give it an abrupt jerk, rapid enough for the token to fall out.

Fritz rapped on the judas-hole, doing his best to imitate Balthazar Buxton, whose mannerisms and procedure in such circumstances he had observed many a time.

By the most inconceivable luck, the stratagem, which was closely akin to the sick imagination of madness, was a complete success. With a distracted gaze, the guard saw the skeletal hand throw out the token and retire precipitately. He did not even think of looking through the judas-hole, which closed again immediately.

The guards in the circular corridor had seen that same mechanical gesture so many times before that they no longer paid any attention to it.

A moment later, the door to the corridor opened and Fritz Kramm, guided by one of the men, arrived without a hitch at the automobile that was waiting for him.

He had taken care not to forget the five checks, each of two hundred thousand dollars, payable at the Central Bank.

VII. Disappointment

Fritz Kramm's first thought was to get out of New York as quickly as possible. It seems to him that he could already see his house surrounded by policemen. On reflection, however, he told himself that, after all, Balthazar Buxton's servants did not know his name, and there was a good chance that it would not be discovered. Could he not claim, in any case, to be innocent? Balthazar had given the necessary exeat with his own hand; the guards in the corridor could testify to that.

Slightly reassured, he went to see Cornelius, and told him what had happened, without omitting the slightest detail. The sculptor of living flesh also thought that the danger was not urgent, and, even more audacious than his brother, he went so far as to envisage the possibility of cashing the checks.

After a long conversation, they resolved not to do anything until the following day. Their decision would depend on the turn that events took.

Fritz had just woken up, after an exceedingly agitated night, when Cornelius came into his bedroom, holding a morning newspaper.

"Everything has sorted itself out," he declared, with satisfaction. "A fire broke out in Balthazar's house; his body was found, carbonized. The painting and other *objects d'art* were reduced to ashes and most of the servants were asphyxiated trying to get out of the labyrinth."

"How can that be explained?" murmured Fritz, in amazement. "One might truly think that a diabolical Providence were protecting us."

"Nothing is simpler. In order to be better served and not to give his employees any reason to want him dead, Balthazar—as he told me himself—paid them high wages, which he increased further every year, but would not leave them anything in his will. That way, they had an interest in him living as long as possible."

"I can see that they must have been furious when they found his body."

"Not only that, but they must have been afraid of coming under suspicion, so they took a big risk in order to obtain a big profit. It's evident to me that they only started the fire after having surreptitiously removed all the most valuable items."

"But what about those who were asphyxiated?"

"They were the ones not in on the conspiracy. The others have removed their booty to a place of safety; there's not a shadow of a doubt about it."

"What about the portrait of Lucretia Borgia?"

"Burned, annihilated."

"All's well, then!" cried Fritz, cheerfully. "We can cash the checks."

"All the more easily as Balthazar must have notified his bank of the important withdrawal he was about to make."

The two bandits separated, delighted by the unexpected turn that events had taken.

Fritz Kramm ate a hearty breakfast; liberated from all preoccupations, he was no longer thinking about anything but going to see the lovely Lorenza, who would doubtless not be so reckless this time.

A disappointment awaited him on Broadway, however; the cottage rented by the healer of pearls was deserted, the shutters tightly closed and a placard saying HOUSE TO LET was swinging over the gate. The neighbors, when questioned, said that the Italian and her maid had departed with abundant luggage the previous evening for an unknown destination.

Furious and distressed by what he considered to be a betrayal, Fritz got back into his car and gave the driver Louis Grivard's address. He intended to take his anger out on the artist, who would be obliged to give him an explanation regarding the fake Titian. Was it not, after all, the wretched dauber who was the cause of Balthazar's death?

But at Louis Grivard's lodgings, as at Lorenza's, Fritz Kramm found the door closed and everything boarded up.

"An admirably beautiful dark-haired young lady came to collect him in an automobile at dusk yesterday," the concierge explained.

"You don't know where they've gone?"

"Mr. Louis, it seemed, gave the driver the address of the transatlantic liner station."

Fritz got back into his car without saying a word. He understood that he had been tricked, but he possessed astonishing self-control. His anger had dissipated now. It was in a perfectly calm tone that he gave his chauffeur Cornelius' address.

Setting aside all other preoccupations, the two bandits were due to depart for Sa Francisco the next day, in order to supervise in person the execution of the plan that would lead to the loss of the yacht *Revenge* with all her passengers.

11. A GYPSY'S HEART

I. Wireless Telegraphy

Ten o'clock in the evening had just sounded, not very distinctly, in the thick fog that covered the docks, buildings and ships in Vancouver harbor like a shroud of gray cotton wool.

The city was already asleep and the deserted quays were plunged in silence. Through the solitude of the streets, where it was scarcely possible to see one's way through the thick mist, a dozen people were hurrying, stopping from time to time to decipher the inscriptions placed at each street corner, difficult to read in the blue-tinted halo of electric lights.

The strange pedestrians in question were uniformly dressed coarse reefer jackets and each one was carrying a valise in his hand. They were obviously travelers, but if any curious individual had taken it into his head to watch them, he would have been very surprised to see that they turned their back on the main station of the Canadian Pacific Railroad and went along the quays at which ships were moored ready to depart for the Klondike, Japan and the Indies.

Soon, they left behind the last houses of the city, the lights of which were no more than a pale patch in the humid darkness and went along the low and sandy coast, where a glacial wind was blowing and the Pacific waves were breaking.

Thus far they had been walking without saying a word, but when they arrived at a clump of elder-trees and dwarf willows that seemed to serve them as a reference-point, they halted and gathered in a circle to confer.

"I'm wondering exactly where we're being taken," murmured a man of colossal stature, a veritable giant, to a thin individual on whose shoulder he was leaning in familiar fashion.

"I don't know anything, my dear Goliath," the other replied, "but all this does indeed seem rather mysterious to me."

"What can we do," said a third, "since we've been paid in advance?"

"Besides which," put in a young woman with a shrill and piercing voice, "it's our friend Oscar Tournesol, the likeable hunchback, who got us into this affair, and he's incapable of doing us a bad turn."

"Possibly," muttered the giant Goliath, "but it's damnably cold, and with this mist, I'm damned if we'll be able to see the signal."

"*Heu heu!*" coughed a plaintive voice. "I'd gladly drink a glass of gin to warm me up. You ought to have bought a traveling flask, my dear Regina."

"You'll have a drink soon, Mr. Sleary. Be patient."

"The signal!" cried Goliath, suddenly—and, with his enormous hand, he pointed at a luminous patch in the livid darkness, which seemed to be increasing in size and getting closer.

Immediately, Mr. Sleary took an electric torch from his pocket, and turned its switch. A bright light lit up the deserted strand and the gray, foaming waves.

Two minutes went by; then, the signal doubtless having been perceived, the distant lantern abruptly disappeared. Immediately, Mr. Sleary switched off his own torch.

Ten minutes later, the rhythmic plash of oars was heard and a yawl manned by four oarsmen came to run aground gently on the sand. A puny individual with a slight hump on his back was seated at the tiller; immediately, he leapt ashore and put a finger to his lips.

"No noise!" he said. "Everybody get aboard as quietly as possible. It's very important that no one sees you, and that no policeman or customs officer takes it on himself to ask you where you're going."

Everyone seemed to understand the merit of this advice, and it was without pronouncing a word that the little troupe piled on to the benches of the yawl. Regina sat down next to the hunchback and huddled against him, shivering.

When everyone was aboard, the oarsmen bent over their oars and the light vessel, so heavily laden that the water was almost lapping its rim, set off between the waves.

Searching the darkness with his sharp eyes, the little hunchback corrected the heading from time to time with a tug on the tiller, guided through the fog by the strident blasts of a steam-siren.

As they drew further away from the shore the waves became higher, breaking over the yawl from time to time and covering its passengers with clouds of spray. The hunchback saw Regina shivering beside him. Finally, the somber mass of a ship and its rigging stood out against the darkness; they yawl came alongside it to starboard, a rope-ladder was thrown down and the passengers climbed up on to the deck one by one.

An individual luxuriously dressed in a fox-fur cloak and wearing a hat made of the same fur welcomed the newcomers and took them into a comfortable ward-room furnished with a circular divan and a vast rocking table on which the elements of a cold meal were set out.

"Take your places, gentlemen," he said. "Permit me to introduce to you the yacht *Ariel*, which will take us to our destination. While you have a hot toddy—which is not an unnecessary precaution in this terrible fog, I'll explain the purpose of a voyage that must seem to you all to be somewhat mysterious."

"*Heu heu!* I believe, milord," said Mr. Sleary "that a hot toddy is indeed an indispensable precaution…*heu heu!*…but we're all ears!"

The man in the fur hat took off his cloak, selected a dry Havana from a cigar box, which he lit tranquilly, and then, in the midst of a tranquil silence he started speaking.

"My name, as you know, is Lord Astor Burydan, and my principal occupation is spending, in the most interesting fashion possible, the immense fortune that I possess. I have never recoiled before any eccentricity, provided that it's amusing, and that's doubtless what has earned me, in America as well as in old Europe, the popular nickname of Milord Bamboche."

And Lord Burydan, with great clarity of expression and a great luxury of details, related how he had been cast away on an unknown island that served as a lair of criminals who called it, among themselves, the Island of Hanged Men. There he had been held captive for months, along with an aged French scientist, the celebrated Prosper Bondonnat, and a brave Indian named Kloum. The eccentric aristocrat and Kloum had succeeded in escaping in an airship constructed according to Monsieur Bondonnat's plans, but the old scientist had remained a prisoner of the bandits.

"You must understand," Lord Burydan concluded, after a long account of his adventures, that henceforth, I had only one goal: to rescue Monsieur Bondonnat, and exterminate the inhabitants of the Island of Hanged Men. It's to attain that end that I've had this yacht, the *Ariel*, constructed in the greatest secrecy. It's manned by twenty-four crewmen and is formidably armed.

The audience had followed the noble lord's story with a keen interest, and were beginning to glimpse the truth.

"My friends," he continued, "When I told you in San Francisco that I had a caprice to be an impresario, I deceived you. The truth is that I had the idea of utilizing your acrobatic talents to lay siege to the headquarters of the Red Hand. It's up to you now to tell me whether that enterprise suits you. Those who don't want to accompany me have only to say so. They'll be immediately taken back to Vancouver, after having, of course—as is only just—received the agreed indemnity. Those who want to remain in America please raise your hands."

No one budged.

"Milord," said the giant Goliath, speaking on behalf of the company, "no one wants to leave you; you've been our benefactor, and we're ready to follow you wherever it pleases you to take us. If there are dangers to run, so much the better. We're artistes, and we love noble and adventurous enterprises!"

A smile of satisfaction spread over the eccentric's features. He was about to respond, but the little hunchback did not give him time.

"My dear comrades," he said, "I expected no less of your courage. You are sustaining the ancient renown of the Gorilla Club, of which we're all proud to be a part. With your precious collaboration, we're certain to triumph!"

Addressing each of the artistes in turn, Oscar went on: "The garrison of the Island of Hanged Men will have to be exceedingly strong to resist an army that includes in its ranks Goliath, the strongest man in the world, who can break steel chains at a stroke as if they were threads of oakum, whose biceps are a meter around, who, suspended from a trapeze, can lift up a horse and its rider with his teeth; Fulguras the salamander, the human torch, as comfortable in flames as if they were his natural elements; Bob Horwett, the expert swimmer, nicknamed the modern triton; Romulus the human cannonball, who, fired from a canon, seizes a trapeze while flying through the air; our comrades Macoco and Cambo, as robust and agile as the gorillas and orangutans whose costumes they borrow...!"

The hunchback was interrupted several times by frantic applause and toasts proposed in honor of Milord Bamboche, but, like the heroes of old Homer, he intended to make a full list of the paladins of the Gorilla Club.

"How," he continued, "can the Red Hand resist the dexterity of our friend Matalobos, the famous prestidigitator, whom could, if he wanted to, put up his sleeve a horse and its rider, a locomotive or a flock of sheep? The Chinaman Yan-kai, the sharpshooter with the infallible eye? The clown Robertson with the hamstrings of steel and muscles of rubber, capable of leaping moats and drawbridges in a single bound?"

In the same eulogistic fashion, Oscar Tournesol introduced the clown Bombridge, the professor of acrobatics, the master and example of the whole company of artistes, and Mr. Sleary, the founder of the Gorilla Club and director of the troupe.

At that moment, the acrobats perceived that the yacht was pitching and rolling violently, and that the trepidation of the engines had augmented.

Lord Burydan was smiling. "Yes, my friends," he said, "the *Ariel* is already *en route* for the Island of Hanged Men. While you were listening to Oscar I gave the order to the engineer via the acoustic tube. To gain time, the moorings have been cut, and in three quarters of an hour we'll be out of sight of the American coast.

"I have my reasons for wanting our departure to take place in the greatest secrecy. I've informed the newspapers that I've returned to England; I've even bought a ticket in my name on a liner from New York. No one has laid eyes on me for a week. I think, thanks to those precautions, that we've escaped the spies of the Red Hand. It was of the utmost importance that they remain unaware of our departure. Now, I'm sure of having given them the slip."

"In any case," said Oscar, "we're not alone in attempting this expedition. Tomorrow, the thirteenth of January, a yacht more powerful and better armed than this one, the *Revenge*, will set off from San Francisco. It has been fitted out by the billionaire Fred Jorgell and will remain, thanks to wireless telegraphy, in constant communication with us. You'll see that, in these conditions, the risks are considerably diminished and success is certain."

"You understand now," Lord Burydan went on, "the reasons that prevented me from bringing the ladies of the Gorilla Club with us—Miss Winny, the tightrope-walker, the beautiful Nudita and the charming bareback riders Olga and Isabelle..."

Lord Burydan interrupted himself and his expression expressed a certain discontent. He had just perceived the blonde Regina Bombridge, who, until then, had been hidden behind the vast bulk of the giant Goliath. "I see," the eccentric said, "that one of the ladies has thought it a good idea to do otherwise and embark by deceit!"

Miss Bombidge had risen to her feet, utterly confused. "Milord," she murmured, in an emotional voice, "I hope that you'll forgive me for that trickery, but I didn't want to be separated from my father. Besides, I'm a skillful rider and might, I hope, be useful to you. Finally, if I'm no use for that, I can fulfill the functions of nurse. I'll be the Red Cross and care for the wounded."

"Let's hope there won't be any," said Lord Burydan, who had ended up being reconciled to the young woman's presence on board.

"Anyway," said the hunchback, swiftly, "it would be very difficult to send Mademoiselle Bombridge back now that the *Ariel* is under way."

Lord Burydan acquiesced with a good grace. By the glances exchanged between the hunchback and the little circus rider he had understood that Oscar was no stranger to the trick that had permitted the young woman to slip in among the members of the expedition.

At that moment, a large black barbet with curly hair threw himself impetuously on to Oscar's knees and covered him with caresses.

"Down Pistolet!" said Lord Burydan, stroking the faithful animal. "Go and fetch Kloum for me."

"Yes," said Oscar, looking at the dog in a particular fashion. "Go find Kloum and tell him to come."

Pistolet launched forth, as rapid as an arrow, and soon came back followed by the Indian, who was as grave and impassive as ever.

"Kloum," said Lord Burydan, "As it's nearly midnight, I think these gentlemen will be glad to go to bed. Will you show them to their cabins, please?"

This proposal was welcomed enthusiastically, for they were all somewhat tired. One after another the acrobats took their leave of the eccentric lord.

Soon, everyone aboard the *Ariel* was asleep, and nothing could be heard on the deck of the yacht but the monotonous tread of the men on watch and the trepidation of the engines, mingled with the whistling of the wind and he melancholy grinding of the rigging on its pulleys.

The night passed without incident.

The next day, on going up to the deck, Lord Burydan found all his passengers already up and about, amusing themselves watching the frolicking of a school of porpoises that were following the ship. The fog was not as dense as the day before, and the *Ariel* was moving over a gray sea beneath a pale sky, which seemed to presage a snowfall. The cold was not excessive, however. In sum, it was excellent weather for untroubled navigation.

Lord Burydan presided over a meal taken communally in the ship's dining room; he took advantage of it to set out various plans of attack that he had formulated, and to show his allies a map of the Island of Hanged Men, drawn from memory, which must have been fairly accurate.

The acrobats and clowns manifested a healthy appetite and adapted themselves patiently to Lord Burydan's regimen. No one had yet complained of seasickness—not even the delicate Miss Bombridge.

The young woman scarcely left Oscar Tournesol's side; he took pleasure in explaining the use of all the objects aboard the ship to her. An instinctive sympathy had been established between the hunchback and the rider, of the kind that is often the prelude to a more serious affection. Very sentimental by temperament, the blonde rider had been profoundly touched by the hunchback's attentions, and felt a great pity or the being disgraced by nature, or whom the other women of the Gorilla Club had thus far only had scornful smiles.

In the afternoon, both of them went into the wireless telegraph post installed near the poop deck, and Oscar did his best to demonstrate the functioning of the apparatus. Then the conversation took a different turn.

"Alas," the hunchback sighed, "I'll doubtless never know the love of a beloved woman. I'll never know the tenderness and affection of a wife. What young woman would want to unite her destiny with that of a miserable hunchback?"

"Don't talk like that," murmured Regina, profoundly moved. "You're making me feel bad."

"I'm ugly, puny and deformed. Everyone makes fun of me and no one loves me."

"That's not true, of course," the young woman replied, hotly. "Do you think I don't love you, for example?"

"Yes, I know," Oscar sighed. "You love me as a friend, as a sister, but not the way I'd like."

"I can assure you, my dear Oscar, that I think very highly of your qualities and that I have a real affection for you." As she pronounced that somewhat ambiguous phrase, Regina had blushed cherry-red.

"You don't understand, Regina," the young man murmured, bitterly. "You have a good deal of amity for me, but you'd never consent to marry me."

"Who knows?" said the young rider, in an almost imperceptible voice.

They both looked at one another in silence. Oscar had taken hold of Regina's little hand tenderly, and the young woman did not have the courage to take it away.

At that moment, however, the bell of the wireless telegraphy apparatus started ringing. Oscar and Regina stood up precipitately, like two schoolchildren caught doing something naughty, and hastened out of the cabin to inform Lord Burydan.

The eccentric went to the apparatus immediately; he was fully competent in its operation.

A few minutes later, he came back with a reassuring dispatch that Fred Jorgell and Harry Dorgan had just sent him from San Francisco. The *Revenge* had put to sea in excellent conditions, the engineers manning her having carefully checked her engines, hull and rigging before departure. The crew, well disciplined, seemed full of good intentions. In accordance with a plan made in advance, the rumor had been put about that the yacht was heading southwards; that way, there was a serious chance of avoiding the conspiracies of the Red Hand.

Lord Burydan hastened to reply to the marconigram, giving his friends a report on the situation of the *Ariel*. He reminded them that it had been agreed far in advance that he would enter into communication with the wireless station installed aboard the *Revenge*, and that once that communication was established hey would exchange information on an hourly basis, until they were able to meet up, which ought to take place at a precisely determined point in the Pacific, some ten leagues from the Island of Hanged Men.

"Why aren't we telegraphing our friends aboard the *Revenge* today?" Oscar asked.

"I have an excellent reason for that. By waiting until the *Revenge* is considerably closer to the *Ariel*, I'll reduce the risk of our messages being intercepted by one of the posts installed on the coat and then transmitted to the Red Hand. It's agreed, for the same reason, that I'll only communicate with San Francisco again in case of absolute necessity."

"In that case, it would have been more prudent not to communicate today."

"That's true, but we'd have to be very unlucky for our first message, which might be the only one, to fall into the hands of the leaders of the Red Hand."

Oscar and Lord Burydan were still discussing this question, while strolling at a leisurely pace along the main deck, when the bell of the receiver rang once again in the cabin.

Lord Burydan ran to it, vaguely anxious about the further call. He remained shut in the cabin for half an hour. When he emerged he was very pale.

"What's happened?" asked Oscar, anxiously.

"Something terrible. The Red hand is already aware of our plans."

"But that's impossible! How could they know?"

"I've just intercepted a message, or rather a fragment of a message, addressed to one of the stations in the direction of the Island of Hanged Men. You know that when the waves emitted from a transmitter encounter *en route* an apparatus other than the one to which they're addressed, it's very easy for the operator stationed at the intermediate apparatus to take possession of it, without the correspondents placed at either end of the line being able to perceive it. That's what I've done."

"Well?"

"This is the fragment—the only fragment, unfortunately, that I was able to overhear: 'Put all the forts on the defense. Double the sentinels. Make frequent patrols. Check the torpedoes. The Island of Hanged Men might be attacked.'"

"What do you conclude from that?" Oscar asked.

"It's unfortunately all too obvious. The Red Hand's spies are aware of our intentions. Instead of taking the garrison on the Island of Hanged Men by surprise, we'll find them on the alert."

"It's impossible for them to be so well-informed."

"The facts speak for themselves. I can even explain how they guessed the secret."

"I can't see how."

"I can. I'm all the more furious because it's my fault. Was I not stupid enough, during my last trip to New York, to go to warn Steffel, the chief of police, and give him the exact latitude and longitude of the island."

"He wouldn't have betrayed us—and in any case, he was the victim of an accident on the very day of your visit."

Lord Burydan reflected. "Who knows," he said, "whether it might not have been precisely because he knew too much that he was made to disappear. To me, it's evident that it's Steffel who's betrayed us. Everyone in New York knows that the highly placed functionaries in the administration are far from incorruptible."

"Wouldn't it be advisable," said the hunchback, "to warn Fred Jorgell and Harry Dorgan right away?"

"No, it's not a good idea. My message would certainly be intercepted, and the one I've already sent might well have been. Oh, I'm furious with myself for having been so naïve as to go to that policeman."

At that moment, the dinner bell rang.

"Above all," said Lord Burydan, heading for the dining room with Oscar, "not a word about this to our brave acrobats. It would discourage them needlessly."

"Don't worry, my lord—I'll be discreet."

Everyone took their places around the table, served with as much luxury as abundance, but the acrobats noticed that Lord Burydan seemed less cheerful than usual. The meal was affected by his preoccupation, and the party broke up earlier than the day before.

Lord Burydan spent a very agitated night. One of the first to get up, he immediately went to the telegraphy cabin in order to make contact with his friends on the *Revenge*. To his great surprise, however, he could not obtain any response.

After two hours of futile efforts, he was obliged to give up. In spite of the beauty of the weather and the power of the emitted waves, the *Revenge* gave no sign of life.

II. The Mail

A large automobile stopped abruptly at the corner of California Street and Montgomery Street in San Francisco. Three men, dressed in the greatest elegance, got out and went into the imposing edifice that stood at the corner of the two streets, which bore, in gigantic golden letters, the inscription: *California Safe Deposit and Trust Company.*

The building in question, whose walls were five meters thick and were built with large blocks of stone linked with iron anchors, only had a few windows, fitted with enormous steel bars.

The three men went into the great hall, decorated with statues of Croesus and Plutus, along with those of two Californian billionaires, Stanford and Fload. They followed a corridor with a vault and walls of steel, at the end of which was an office protected by a solid grille.

The first man approached the grille and handed the employee stationed behind it a visiting card, saying: "Dr. Cornelius Kramm of New York."

"Yes sir," the man replied, passing a nickel token between the bars, perforated with three numbers disposed in a triangle.

The second man advanced. "Mr. Fritz Kramm of New York," he said. Like the first, he received a nickel token.

Then it was the turn of the third, who declared that his name was Joe Dorgan, of New York.

All three went into a broad corridor, the floor, ceiling and walls of which were similarly lined with steel, which was interrupted by three grilles, at to each of which an employee as stationed, who carefully checked each of the here numbers on the nickel disk. After these formalities, which reminded Fritz Kramm, albeit in a less original fashion, of the labyrinthine palace of Balthazar Buxton, the three men were allowed to go down a gigantic staircase that led to the cellars of the bank, and two employees armed with bunches of keys were placed at their disposal.

The monumental cellars were entirely constructed in iron and steel, but they were decorated with statues of Medieval knights with gilded suits of armor, helmets on their heads and shields on their arms.

Beside these bronze warriors, twenty athletic policemen armed to the teeth mounted guard night and day in the external corridor, in one-hour shifts.

The three men stopped in front of their respective strong-boxes, which were set side by side.

After having opened the locks, the employees withdrew, leaving Dr. Cornelius and his two companions free to fill or empty their strong-boxes.

"How much do we have in the coffers?" asked Cornelius.

"Three hundred thousand dollars each," Fritz replied. "But that doesn't, of course, include the sums produced by the Balthazar Buxton affair. It's prudent not to put all our capital in the same bank. One never knows what might happen."

"Very true," said the third person, impatiently, "But you know that we're in a hurry today. How much do we need?"

"I believe, my dear Baruch—or, rather, my dear Joe," the doctor replied, with a snigger, "that thirty thousand should be sufficient, so let's take ten thousand each."

The three associates each counted out a wad of banknotes, which they slipped into their wallets. Ten minutes later, they climbed back into the automobile and were taken to the Palace Hotel, where they had a rapid meal in a private dining-room reserved in advance.

It was almost nightfall when they went back to their car, but this time it was to undertake a veritable voyage. For two hours they traveled at top speed through the suburbs of San Francisco.

Finally, the chauffeur stopped in an utterly deserted spot. It was a wild heath a few miles from the sea shore, bristling with brushwood and dotted with stagnant pools covered with reeds.

All three of them seemed perfectly familiar with the desolate location. Leaving their driver with the automobile, they went along a narrow path that snaked between the pools and bushes. The chauffeur, the Italian Leonello, followed them for a while with his gaze, but they were soon lost in the darkness.

Doubtless having no anxiety in their regard, Leonello climbed back into the vehicle, philosophically, to take shelter from the fine drizzle that had begun to fall.

The three men continued on their way, but, some distance away from the auto, each of them put a rubber mask over his face and checked his Browning.

The path they were following led them to a profound excavation, which looked like an abandoned quarry. They were about to go down into it when a man loomed up before them and barred their way. Cornelius only had to pronounce one word, however, and the man stood aside respectfully.

They passed a second, third and fourth sentinel in the same manner without any difficulty. Then they found themselves at the very bottom of a vast hole, doubtless once hollowed out by miners in the heyday of the gold rush. There, backed up against the rock, there was a cottage made of shapeless blocks of stone covered with a roof of reeds, which had no other entrance than a low door. They lifted the latch and went in.

The interior of the cabin offered more comfort than one would have expected in such a place. A good fire was burning in the clay fireplace and there were two candles in brass candlesticks on a table.

Two men of grim appearance were sitting on stools to either side of the fire. They got to their feet respectfully when they saw the visitors, for whose benefit these preparations had doubtless been made, and then they withdrew.

Cornelius, Fritz and Baruch sat down at the table. No sooner had they done so than four raps, regularly spaced, sounded on the exterior door.

"Come in!" shouted Cornelius.

A kind of cowboy with muddy boots and a red flannel short came forward, his broad-brimmed hat in his hand.

"Here it is, Milords," he said, in a tone that was respectful but not obsequious. He placed a piece of paper on the table on which a few hieroglyphic signs were traced. At the bottom was a hand crudely drawn in red ink, and in the left-hand corner a similar but smaller hand.

Cornelius and Fritz examined the paper carefully. The man waited.

"That's three hundred dollars," said Cornelius.

"Three hundred dollars," Fritz repeated.

Baruch took three hundred-dollar banknotes from his wallet and handed them to the man, who took them, bowed and withdrew, without saying a word.

The scene was repeated many times over, exactly similar, with hardly any variation.

Finally, Cornelius declared that all those to whom the Red Hand owed money had been paid.

"Can we go now?" Fritz asked.

"Not yet," said Baruch. "We're awaiting important news."

A quarter of an hour passed. Nothing was audible but the howling of the wind, which was becoming tempestuous over the sea. The fire was beginning to die out. Suddenly, there was another knock on the door. The man who entered in response to Cornelius' invitation was covered in mud from head to toe. He had large Mexican spurs on his boots. It was easy to see that he had made a long journey on horseback; his face was streaming with rain and sweat.

"Here are the letters, Milords," he said, removing his hat. He deposited a large cloth envelope on the table, sealed with red wax.

Fritz broke the seal and took a stack of papers of various sizes out of the envelope. Some were covered in fine and compact handwriting, others only bore a few words awkwardly raced in pencil. Among the heap of papers there were several unopened letters and telegrams.

Silently, the three Lords of the Red Hand set about sorting out the mass of documents. They were the reports of all the Association's spies in the region; they had been gathered in the hands of a few reliable men whose sent them on directly to the supreme leaders.

Throwing insignificant items on to the fire, they carefully set aside the interesting messages, and when they found one that was more important than the rest they communicated it to one another immediately.

They had almost concluded that work when Baruch put his hand on a note written in an awkward feminine hand, the only signature on which was a capital D.

"Damn," he said, handing the note to Cornelius. "This is serious! It appears that Paganot and Ravenel know the exact location of the Island of Hanged Men. They didn't add any credence to the message in the bottle, and if they've allowed us to believe that they're heading southwards, it's simply to put us off the track."

"Where does that information come from?" asked Fritz. "We'll have to modify our plan."

"It comes from a gypsy named Dorypha, a dancer who's the mistress of Edward Edmond, one of Fred Jorgell's trusted servants. She's very devoted to us. Following Slug's instructions, she's entered into the service of the two Frenchwomen for the duration of the voyage, in the capacity of chambermaid."

"So we can trust her affirmation?" asked Baruch.

"I believe so." With speaking, Cornelius had unsealed two of the telegrams. Suddenly, he murmured a discontented exclamation.

"That tops it off!" he growled. "The famous Lord Burydan, who hasn't shown any signs of life, and who was thought to have returned to England, has also fitted out a yacht, whose intended destination in the Island of Hanged Men. He's taken the Redskin Kloum with him, and that damned hunchback who's got in our way several times. The information comes from Vancouver. Our agents were alerted too late; Lord Burydan set sail yesterday evening. We can't stop him, and the most serious thing of all is that his crew, recruited in great secrecy, doesn't include a single member of the Association."

"That's serious," Baruch murmured.

The three bandits looked at one another momentarily with a kind of consternation.

It was Cornelius who recovered his presence of mind first. "Calm down," he said. "Let's not get carried away. Nothing's lost yet. It's a matter of examining the situation coolly."

"We need to take measures," said Fritz.

"They are, indeed, indicated. I'll send orders to alert the garrison tonight. Lord Burydan has been very cunning, but in order to land in our possessions he'll still have to get through the ring of torpedoes surrounding the island. On the other hand, whether the *Revenge* is heading south or north, it remains the case that almost all of her crew is devoted to us, body and soul. You can see, on due consideration, that the peril isn't as grave at it appeared at first glance."

"We could send the Red Hand's yacht in pursuit of Burydan," Fritz suggested.

"I don't think so," Cornelius retorted. "Our own ship isn't fitted with the oil-fired engines invented by Harry Dorgan, and it would arrive too late. In any case, I don't think it's prudent at the moment to draw attention to our yacht."

"What decision are we going to take with respect to Fred Jorgell and his company?" asked Baruch.

"Let's leave Fred Jorgell alone for the moment. Neither he, nor his daughter Isidora, nor his future son-in-law Harry Dorgan is part of the expedition directed against us. We can take care of them later, when we've got rid of the French party."

"In sum," remarked Fritz, "aboard the *Revenge* there's only Paganot, Ravenel, their fiancées, Andrée de Maubreuil and Frédérique Bondonnat, and the other Frenchman who helped Burydan escape from the lunatic asylum, Agénor Marmousier."

"It seems to me," Cornelius replied, "that with regard to those five individuals, there's no question of hesitation. They've got in our way long enough. It's necessary to be rid of them once and for all."

Baruch stood up, prey to a singular emotion. "Permit me to offer my personal opinion on that subject," he said. "I'm utterly determined that Andrée de Maubreuil should be saved."

"You're definitely in love, my dear fellow," said Fritz, sniggering. "You haven't been able to overcome that weakness, then?"

"You're a fine one to talk," Baruch riposted, "when it's scarcely a week since you imperiled the Association and compromised its interests by becoming infatuated with an Italian adventuress who made a complete fool of you. It wouldn't have taken much for Lorenza, the beautiful healer of pearls, to send you to the electric chair and us along with you!"

"Let's leave that stupid episode aside," murmured the art dealer, discontentedly. "Just take note that I got out of the predicament with remarkable self-composure."

"It's absolutely necessary," Baruch said, "that Andrée de Maubreuil is excepted from the massacre, and not only because I've sworn that she'll be mine, but because my marriage to her is the basis of a project that I want to put to you. Let's suppose that, once the other Frenchies are dead, I save Mademoiselle de Marbreuil, am reconciled with my brother Harry, and liberate old Bondonnat myself—who will then be forced to show his gratitude in my regard."

"I don't see where this is leading," said Cornelius.

"Patience! Bondonnat has no other family than Andrée, who's his ward and will be his heir—and we too, without violence and in a perfectly natural fashion, will be the possessors of all the old scientist's discoveries! It's a great plan! It will only remain thereafter to get rid of Isidora and Harry, and then, later, Fred Jorgell and William Dorgan, to concentrate two or three Trusts and as many billions in our hands."

"It's certainly an admirable plan," said Cornelius, "but it's audacious. For my part, I don't have any great objection to make to it."

"Permit me to make one," said Fritz. "Isn't it to be feared that Bondonnat might recognize Baruch, whom he glimpsed in his new guise as Joe Dorgan during the abduction by airplane?"

Baruch shrugged his shoulders. "The argument doesn't stand up," he said. "Bondonnat scarcely caught a glimpse of me at a moment when he was far too emotional to pay attention to my physiognomy. Besides which, I've changed a lot since then. A slight modification will suffice—letting my moustache grow, for instance—to put the old man off the scent. Then again, it's quite impossible that he'll recognize the son of the billionaire William Dorgan, and the man who will have saved him from the bandits of the Red Hand, as the same person who had him taken to the Island of Hanged Men."

Cornelius approved of that summation of the situation, and Fritz ended up yielding to the argument. The new plan elaborated by Baruch was as ingenious as it was bold. The three bandits agreed therefore, that it would be followed point by point.

"Except," concluded Cornelius, getting to his feet after having thrown the rest of the papers on to the fire, "that we need to hurry. The *Revenge* is due to set sail shortly after midnight. I have a meeting with Slug at half past ten at the Old Grille bodega; that's when he'll receive his final instructions."

The three bandits hastened to leave. A quarter of an hour later they climbed back into their automobile, which set off in fourth gear in the direction of San Francisco.

III. An Indiscreet Soubrette

The *Revenge* was a magnificent vessel with a tonnage almost double that of the *Ariel*. Constructed according to the plans of the engineer Harry Dorgan, further improved by Roger Ravenel and Antoine Paganot, it was equipped with an ultra-light nickel hull and gasoline engines that permitted it to attain a prodigious speed.

In essence, she was constructed on the same theory as the Lightning Steamships of the company founded by Fred Jorgell, which made the crossing from New York to Le Havre in four days. She was armed with sixty-millimeter cannons with hydropneumatic shock-absorbers of the latest model and also possessed a torpedo-launching tube. The crew consisted of a hundred and fifty men, armed with Winchester repeating rifles.

Fred Jorgell had insisted that the sailors on the Revenge should have served as soldiers or as marines, and he had ordered Edward Edmond, who was responsible for hiring them, to recruit in preference men who already had experience of warfare—as in the expedition to the Philippine Islands, for example.

Unfortunately, Edward Edmond had had no difficulty in reconciling the billionaire's instructions with the orders of the Red Hand. The majority of the men he had engaged, and who could show evidence of military service, belonged to the redoubtable organization.

As for the captain, he was none other than the ex-tramp Slug, Cornelius' trusted man, the former governor of the Island of Hanged Men. The audacious bandit, who had sailed aboard a pirate ship in his youth, had sufficient nautical knowledge to direct a ship. Besides which, he had taken on as first mate an experienced sea-dog and fine sailor in the person of Captain Christian Knox. The former pirate had eventually decided to accept the brilliant proposition that had been made to him and, by modifying the shape of his beard and donning spectacles, he had camouflaged himself sufficiently not to be recognized by the young women, who had seen him at Golden Cottage when he brought the famous bottle found on the sea-bed.

In order to achieve that result, Slug had presented Fred Jorgell with first-rate certificates, and Edward Edmond had completed the picture by saying that he knew him personally.

In any case, Slug had also modified his physical appearance. He had got rid of his long beard, only retaining a tuft of hair beneath his chin in the Yankee fashion. His face, with coarse and angular features, the skin tanned by the sun and fresh air, gave him the exact appearance of a naval captain, a trifle brusque but honest. His imposing bearing stood out in a superb blue uniform with gilded epaulettes, and he really did look the part.

It is obvious how terrible the consequences of Edward Edmonds treason had been. Of the hundred and fifty crewmen, a hundred and twenty belonged to the Red Hand. As Slug had said to Cornelius a few hours before the departure, he only had to lift a finger to become the compete master of the yacht. The *Revenge* belonged to the Red Hand, from the captain to the stoker, including the cook, the head waiter and the employee specifically taken on to operate the wireless telegraphy apparatus.

Edward Edmond had been imprudent enough to hire the gypsy Dorypha, his mistress, as a chambermaid in the service of Andrée de Maubreuil. A young Scotswoman named Ketty, a distant cousin of Mrs. MacBarlott, served the same function with regard to Frédérique. To begin with, the Irishman had had a great deal of trouble persuading the dancer to take on such a position, but in the end, the unexpectedness of the adventure had triumphed over her hesitations. Dorypha had remembered that she had once been in service with the wife of a *corregidor* in Grenada, at the prospect of playing the role again had seemed amusing.

On Edward Edmond's recommendation the dancer had immediately been accepted, all the more easily because all the maidservants that had been approached had flatly refused to involve themselves in such a mysterious expedition, which did not appear to be devoid of danger.

Dorypha was an admirable actress. Leaving behind the riotous costumes, the audacious necklines and the brazen make-up, she had donned a costume tailored in black cloth, severely cut, and her beautiful blonde hair was hidden under a frilly bonnet, which gave her a most engaging hypocritical and puritanical appearance. Thinking the name Dorypha too indiscreet, the gypsy had introduced herself under that of Mercedes. Andrée had accepted her trustingly, although remarking that she seemed rather bold.

"That Mercedes doesn't seem to have a sober gaze," she had said.

"In fact," the naturalist Ravenel had added, "she has eyes that shine like infernal embers beneath her black velvet lashes."

However, the gypsy, supple, seductive and obliging, full of attention for her mistress, whom she befriended, had not taken long to have that first impression forgotten; she performed her service with an exemplary skill, and her pert cheerfulness had endeared her to everyone. There was, in any case, nothing for which to reproach her in her costume or her conduct.

In that company of intellectuals of refined urbanity, that daughter of the gutter, elegant by instinct and race, found the means of not putting a foot wrong. Once again, Dorypha was an admirable actress. No one would have suspected that the soubrette with the mischievous smile, who brought the demoiselles their chocolate or their mail on a silver tray, was the same brazen hussy who had been seen performing high kicks in sailors' dives and swinging her rump like a filly on a Cordovan stud-farm.

The passenger cabins aboard the *Revenge* were luxurious and comfortable. From the very first day, Andrée and Frédérique thought that the voyage would be most agreeable. Thanks to the yacht's formidable armament and the collaboration of Lord Burydan, they regarded the deliverance of Monsieur Bondonnat as a certainty. It seemed impossible to them that the garrison of the Island of Hanged Men could put up serious resistance, and for them, the expedition had the appearance of a veritable pleasure trip.

Paganot, Ravenel and Agénor were not far from sharing that point of view. How could there be anything to fear on that beautiful ship, so formidably armed, which, under a blue sky, in magnificent sunlight, was flying at top speed over the calm surface of the Pacific Ocean? Simply seeing the suntanned faces of the crewmen, who in their new uniforms, looking like worthy men, honest battle-hardened heroes, made them feel reassured.

"They're solid fellows," Paganot repeated.

"Very solid," Agénor agreed.

"I think we can have confidence in them from every point of view," concluded Ravenel.

The three Frenchmen were making a grave mistake, but how could they suspect that they had been the victims of such a machination? Their confidence was such that they put themselves entirely in the hands of honest Captain Slug, who, admitted to their table, delighted everyone with his picturesque anecdotes as well as his hearty appetite. It occasionally happened that the captain let slip some crapulous expression, but that was put down to the "rough frankness" typical of old sea-dogs.

One thing that should have alerted the suspicions of the two engineers was the sudden taciturnity of the captain as soon as the conversation turned to any technical matter. Slug knew well enough how to run a ship by routine, in the fashion of pirates or the copra merchants of the Coral Sea, but he would have been immediately thrown into confusion is he had been interrogated on the subject of latitude, and he was absolutely incapable of taking a reading that would allow him to calculate the exact location of the vessel. It was Captain Knox who took charge of that concern and gave him exact figures relating to latitude and longitude every day, taken from the pages of his notebook.

At any rate, Slug had not manifested any surprise—and for good reason—when, once they had left San Francisco harbor, Fred Jorgell's official delegate, Antoine Paganot, had given the order to steer northwards.

On the first day of the journey, the engineer ordered the telegraphist to enter into communication with the station at San Francisco to inform Fred Jorgell and Harry Dorgan that everything was going well; after a sort interval the employee brought the billionaire's reply, which offered his best wishes for his friends' success. That same day, however, sailors lowering a boom too rapidly did so with such clumsiness that an enormous piece of wood struck the glazed cabin in which the apparatus was contained at an oblique angle, and put them completely out of action.

The Frenchmen did not attach very great importance to the accident, especially given that the telegraphist promised to repair the damage, which should not require more than two days work, as soon as he could.

Everyone, therefore, was completely confident, and no one had any suspicion of the storm gathering over their heads.

Andrée had noticed that Edward Edmond, who was on board in the capacity of senior steward, who was eating at a separate table with the service staff, appeared to be in a very bad mood, but the young woman attributed it to the discontentment of the disruption caused to him by the voyage. She had not noticed the strange glances, simultaneously ardent and irritated, that the Irishman darted at the pretty Spanish chambermaid every time that she appeared on the poop deck.

Edward Edmond was, in fact, furious at having to undertake the voyage, and almost as furious at having to bring Dorypha with him. The Spaniard never quit her mistress by day or night, because she occupied a cabin adjacent to Andrée's, so the Irishman could only have occasional furtive meetings with his mistress.

Dorypha, who, in reality, was not at all smitten with him, was amused by that situation, and took pleasure in teasing him in various ways. When she passed within a few feet of him on the deck she had an ironic fashion of smiling that drove Edward Edmond into a fury. Sometimes she came to the cabin he occupied, advancing stealthily and looking around cautiously, and then, when he thought he was finally about to satisfy his reckless desires, she escaped, laughing, as light and nimble as a bird. She excited him in a thousand ways. Sometimes she offered him her lips in some dark corner, then abruptly pulled away from the kiss and ran away, exclaiming: "Mademoiselle...Mademoiselle is looking for me!"

By contrast, the gypsy showed all possible amiability to the naturalist Roger Ravenel. Very experienced in matters of passion, she thought the naturalist a very handsome man; his intelligent and Don Quixotesque physiognomy, his enormous nose, his keen brown eyes and his bellicose moustache went straight to the gypsy's heart.

He has the look of a true man! she sometimes said to herself. *I believe that I could love him truly, at least for a week.*

From that particular viewpoint she was less appreciative of Antoine Paganot. With his pink and clean-shaven face, the engineer seemed to her to be too similar to all those Yankees whom she could not stand. For her, a man without a moustache did not exist; that was an absolute principle.

Among the crewmen, however, there were several who had had the opportunity to admire Dorypha in her provocative dances at the Old Grille bodega or other dives of a similar kind. It had not taken long for her to be recognized. Her name had flown from mouth to mouth and now, when the gypsy appeared on the bridge, the sailors formed little groups to get a better view of her, some sniggering stupidly and the eyes of others igniting with lust.

As vicious as a true daughter of the Devil, Dorypha, when she believed herself to be unobserved, favored the mariners with mocking winks, or sometimes walked slowly across the death, winging her rump and hips imperceptibly, as if she were on the point of launching into one of those habaneras or tangos that caused an entire audience to leap and howl madly.

When he was able to trap her between two doors, Edward Edmond reproached her bitterly for that kind of behavior, but she only laughed at his sermons and his anger.

"They can hang out their tongues," she replied, "but they can't have me. I'm all yours, *querido mio, alma de mi corazon.*"

She boxed the Irishman's ears playfully, and escaped.

As soon as the second day, Slug had not failed to notice the demoralizing influence that the gypsy's presence was having, and he was obliged on several occasions to break up the groups that the ecstatic mariners formed when the Spaniard appeared. He too tried to reprimand Dorypha, but the hussy had always stood up to him, and his threats and promises had no effect on her.

That was not Slug's most serious cause for concern. Habituated for many years to commanding tramps, and being intimately familiar with the particular psychology of men of that stripe, he suddenly perceived that his crew, whom he had believed to be completely under control, were already showing signs of indiscipline. Some of the bandits stayed in their bunks, smoking and drinking, or playing cards, and nothing could change their attitude. Others were holding mysterious meetings in corners.

On the very first day, as soon as they had lost sight of the American coast, Slug had been obliged to set an example. In the crew's quarters a sailor named Wallis, too drunk to stand up, had insulted him coarsely, calling him a "bloody rogue," a "damned pirate" and other similar epithets. In any other circumstances, Slug would have blown in the insolent fellow's brain out on the spot, but as he did not want to awaken the suspicions of the Frenchmen for any reason, the captain had contented himself with felling the man who had insulted him with a blow of his fist. There was a sound of breaking bones, and the man had fallen to the ground, his skull fractured, his eyes vitreous and his tongue hanging out. Death had been instantaneous.

"Hide that carrion in some corner," Slug ordered, "and throw it in the sea after dark. There's no lack of sharks in these parts!"

A deathly silence greeted his words. Two men hastened to carry the drunkard's cadaver away, but Slug had understood that in taking command of the *Revenge*, he has assumed a heavy responsibility.

On due reflection, he soon found the cause of the propensity to revolt that he had detected among his men. The only person who could be responsible for it was Captain Christian Knox, who, now that his nautical talents rendered him indispensable, was putting on ironic airs, showing Slug an exaggerated and mocking deference, calling him by the title of "Captain" a hundred times a day on the most trivial pretexts.

Slug then repented bitterly having taken on the old pirate, capable of any treason, who must certainly have made sure in advance that he had numerous partisans among the crew. He resolved to watch the old rogue as closely as possible, and to blow his brains out at the first opportunity.

Knox, however, did not appear to pay the slightest heed to the very visible ill humor of the captain-in-name. He whistled cheerfully while strolling on the foredeck, his hands in his pockets and a cigar in his mouth, like a man who feels at home and considers himself to be the master of the situation.

Knox was one of those who, when Dorypha appeared, winked at her or waxed ecstatic over her bearing. Slug remarked to him, very calmly, that he ought not to set the men a bad example, and Knox appeared to accept the criticism with a good grace—but the pirate had his plan. An imperious desire drove him toward the dancer, for whom he was experiencing one of those bouts of fever, one of those hot-blooded ardors, that are irresistible to temperaments as impulsive and alcohol-fueled as his.

One evening, Andrée de Maubreuil, who was increasingly satisfied with the care of her new chambermaid, made her the gift of a pretty ring ornamented with an opal, which she had bought during her trip to New Orleans. Andrée had suddenly remembered the hatred her father had had for precious stones and, repenting of her purchase, had given the ring to her faithful Mercedes.

The latter, who had coveted the gem for some time, had thanked her mistress with all the exaggerations of Spanish bombast, kissing her hands and swearing eternal devotion to her. Andrée de Maubreuil was most amused by the scene. A short while afterwards, feeling tired, the young woman had gone back to her cabin and, after having said goodnight to Frédérique, her immediate neighbor, she had Dorypha help her to undress, and went to bed.

When the gypsy was sure that her mistress was asleep and that no lights were showing in the other passenger cabins, she took the risk, as she often did, of going up on to the deck.

Wearing nothing on her feet but dainty slippers, she emerged from the corridor where the cabins were without anyone seeing her. She reached the deck, sat down on a bench and, with her head tilted back and her hips arched, almost naked in her thin peignoir, she let herself go in a voluptuous relaxation or her entire being, offering all her quivering flesh to the fresh caress of the nocturnal breeze.

Suddenly, she uttered a stifled exclamation.

A man, hidden until then behind a pile of coiled up rope, had just leapt upon her and, seizing her neck with one hand, foraged brutally with the other for the splendors of her half-exposed bosom.

Ten meters away, the men on watch, evidently accomplices, had their backs turned and were whistling, pretending not to have seen anything.

"If you scream I'll strangle you!" murmured the hoarse voice of Captain Knox in the gypsy's ear. When she did not try to get away, he went on: "Come to my cabin and I'll give you ten dollars."

Dorypha made no reply.

"Do you want twenty? You'll have them. I want you, and you'll be mine."

He had relaxed his grip slightly, but the gypsy abruptly straightened up, like a bow whose string has broken, and Captain Knox felt a sharp pain in his arm.

During the few seconds when he had thought she was unmoving, perhaps consenting, Dorypha had slyly sought the stiletto that was always attached to her leg, and now, mocking and sniggering, not even taking the trouble to call for help, she stood up to him, pricking him with brief thrusts of the pointed tip of her weapon.

The captain was foaming with rage.

"Little slut!" he croaked. "I've a good mind to gut you!"

While beating a retreat before the gypsy he groped for his knife, but, just as he had finally found it was and getting ready to open it, he felt himself rudely grabbed by the collar, and Dorypha immediately took advantage of the unexpected opportunity to disarm him and take possession of the knife, not without having made her own stiletto disappear into her corsage.

Exasperated to the point of fury, Knox attacked his new adversary, in whom, by the light of the moon, he recognized Roger Ravenel. He was dealing with a strong man, however; the naturalist, a keen sportsman, was a first-rate boxer. Before being able to take account of what was happening to him, Knox received a punch on the jaw that almost caused him to bite through his tongue and knocked out two of his teeth. He fell to the deck, spitting blood and swearing like a man possessed.

The men on watch came forward, but almost at the same time, Slug, distressed by the scene, the consequences of which he feared, demanded to know what had happened. Roger Ravenel told him, in a few words.

Slug expressed the most vehement indignation, and, with a courtesy that would have been perfectly grotesque in any other circumstances, said: "If I weren't afraid of waking the ladies at such an hour, I'd shoot this rogue on the spot—but don't worry, Monsieur Ravenel; he'll be put in irons. Sprinter! Kolbak! Come here! Take this fellow, disarm him and take him down into the hold, to the disciplinary facility."

Sprinter and Kolbak, two former residents of the Island of Hanged Men, were devoted men on whom Slug could rely completely. In the blink of an eye, Christian Knox, in spite of his howling and kicking, was securely tied up and carried away.

Slug took his leave of the naturalist, asking him to keep silent about the little drama in order not to cause any scandal, and assuring him in a dignified manner that he would make sure that no such regrettable incident would occur again.

Dorypha had watched that entire scene in an indolent pose, not at all afraid, but rather amused by the succession of events. When she found herself alone with Roger Ravenel, however, her features took on a fearful and dolorous expression.

"You haven't been hurt, Mademoiselle?" asked the naturalist, solicitously.

"No," the gypsy murmured in a very soft voice, putting her hand to her heart, as if to calm its beating. "I was very frightened! Oh, *Madre de Dios*, it seemed to me that I was about to come to harm." She held out her hands, tottering, and collapsed into Roger Ravenel's arms as her stepped forward to sustain her.

At the same time, as if, in her distress, she did not know what she was doing, she had put her arms round the naturalist's neck, and her cheek to his cheek, and the young man felt that beautiful warm and tremulous body, almost naked save for the light fabric, pressing against his.

Roger Ravenel lost his head. A strange emotion invaded him, and in order to retain the gypsy, still ready to fall, he was obliged to take hold of her around the waist. She took advantage of that to wind her arms more tightly around his neck. Their lips met, and the young man felt the delicious burn of a kiss.

The naturalist, fighting violently against the mad desire by which he was consumed, took his lips away from the siren's, and then set her down on the bench, gently relaxing the grip of the beautiful cool arms that were wound round him.

The gypsy had already opened her eyes, and smiled, with a sigh that had nothing dolorous about it. "A thousand apologies, Monsieur Ravenel," she said, with a delightful smile, "but I believe I've just fainted. It's nothing. I feel better already."

"You have no further need of my care?" he asked, politely.

"Thanks you," she said. "Another time. I'm very well. Goodnight Monsieur Ravenel."

The naturalist went back to his cabin, simultaneously disconcerted and charmed by the adventure—but neither he nor Dorypha had perceived the hateful face of Edward Edmond, who, while lurking in the shadow of the corridor, had witnessed the entire scene. He had waited for nightfall and lain in wait, watching for the gypsy, who often came up on to the deck, when her masters were in bed and her service was concluded, to breathe in the fresh air.

IV. Jealousy

Frédérique had just finished dressing. Her hair, an ardent blonde that was almost red, was gathered under an elegant hat made of Panama fiber, which gave her cheerful physiognomy a casual air, and her agreeable figure was outlined by a light trouser suit with green and blue stripes.

The young woman's face did not offer the classical beauty suggestive of severe mediation. She was pretty rather than beautiful and more gracious than pretty. Her nose was slightly turned up, her mouth a trifle wide, but her delicate pink complexion had the admirable freshness that one usually only encounters in certain Scandinavian countries. Her eyes were an exceedingly soft gray, and her entire physiognomy radiated generosity, tenderness and *joie de vivre*. A nicely rounded bosom added to these charms.

At first glance one divined in her a predisposition to take all the happiness from the elements life offers to us that they can provide. Happy herself, Frédérique liked to render those around her happy. An observer might, however, have remarked—a slight fault in the context of so much perfection—that her upper lip, a trifle forceful and curled, indicated a certain predisposition to jealousy. But what woman is not a little jealous of the man she loves?

The young woman was about to go down to the dining room, to which her friends had doubtless preceded her. She had finished tidying away the toilette items of which she had just made use and was looking at the deep azure of the sea, as flat as a lake, sparkling in the sunlight. It was beginning to get hot, and Frédérique could not help noticing the fact.

That's odd, she thought. *I might be mistaken but one might think that the further north we go, the warmer it becomes. I need to ask Roger about it.*

At that moment, someone knocked gently on her cabin door.

"Come in!" the young woman called.

Frédérique expected to see her friend Andrée or her chambermaid Ketty. She experienced some surprise on recognizing the early morning visitor as the Irishman Edward Edmond, one of Fred Jorgell's trusted servants. He came in and bowed respectfully, but Frédérique noticed immediately that his manner seemed hesitant and awkward.

"Excuse me for disturbing you, Mademoiselle," he said, "but I need to have a few words with you in private."

"Speak, Mr. Edmond," she said, her curiosity keenly excited.

"You know that Mr. Jorgell holds me in a certain esteem," the Irishman said, "and that he has given me specific instructions to make use that everything aboard is in good order and that the members of staff are well-behaved."

"I don't understand what you're implying. I hope you don't have any complaint to make about anyone. The conduct of all the service staff seems to me to be perfectly correct."

"Permit me to tell you, Mademoiselle, that I don't entirely agree with that opinion. To speak frankly, the conduct of Mercedes, Mademoiselle de Maubreuil's chambermaid, is scandalous."

"She seems a trifle lively, it's true, but she's a good girl! I don't believe she's capable of any misconduct. In any case, it's none of my concern. It seems to me that you ought to be addressing yourself to my friend Andrée."

"You will see that it is you, above all, that the matter concerns."

"How can that be?" demanded the young woman, becoming impatient with these oratory precautions. "Tell me frankly what crime poor Mercedes has committed."

"She is continually winking at the sailors, but that's trivial. Yesterday evening, she had, I assume, arranged to meet one of the men. An argument broke out between them. The sailor drew his knife and, but for the intervention of Monsieur Ravenel, who reckoned with the drunkard, the amorous rendezvous might perhaps have finished in a bloody fashion."

Frédérique felt a constriction in her heart. "Monsieur Ravenel intervened?" she said, faintly.

"Yes, Mademoiselle. He disarmed the brute and helped Mercedes, who had fainted in his arms. She had put her arms round his neck, and whether she did not know what she was doing—which is possible—or because she wanted to demonstrate her gratitude to him in her own fashion, she kissed him. Monsieur Ravenel had great difficulty disengaging himself from her grip."

Frédérique's face had become pink with indignation and anger; a sob rose into her throat, and her gray eyes, usually so soft, became fiery. "That's a lie!" she exclaimed. "I'm certain that Monsieur Ravenel did not kiss that girl."

The Irishman was nonplussed by the young woman's fury. "Notice, Mademoiselle," he replied, "that I did not say that Monsieur Ravenel kissed Mercedes. It was the other way around. She was distressed by fear, and he was unable to prevent her from doing it."

Frédérique made a heroic effort to hold back the tears that were rising to her eyes. "That's all right, Mr. Edmond," she stammered, in a halting voice. "I'll speak to Monsieur Ravenel. I'm certain that in the circumstances, he only did what he had to do."

"Don't you think, Mademoiselle," the Irishman said, "that a young woman of that sort ought not to remain in Mademoiselle de Maubreuil's service, and that it would be prudent to relegate her to the staff cabins, where I can more easily keep watch on her actions?" After a momentary pause, he added: "I won't permit myself to give you advice, Mademoiselle, but don't you think that it might be preferable, as I've said, to send Mercedes away on some pretext or other, and not to say anything to Monsieur Ravenel?"

Frédérique's anger was only waiting for a pretext to overflow. "What are you insinuating?" she exclaimed, her face red with indignation. "Do you fear, then, that Monsieur Ravenel might defend the girl?"

"Mademoiselle..."

"I don't want to hear any further mention of this matter. Besides which, was it not you, Mr. Edmond, who hired this Mercedes, and wasn't it you who guaranteed her morality?"

The Irishman bowed his head piteously. "I was gravely deceived," he stammered, beating a retreat. "Mercedes had excellent references."

"Go away, Monsieur. I've told you that I don't want to hear any more."

Exasperated, the young woman slammed the door in Edward Edmond's face. He went away, greatly discomfited. Fundamentally, however, he was de-lighted with his ruse. He had no doubt that, in the wake of such a denunciation, Dorypha would be sent to the service quarters and would be allocated one of the cabins near his own, where he would have her at his disposal and prevent her from committing any infidelities.

Left alone, free to abandon herself to her chagrin, Frédérique began to weep copiously. "Roger doesn't love me!" she stammered, between sobs. "He's paying court to that girl. That rascally Irishman didn't tell me everything, but I know enough. It's shameful. If Roger has done that, it would serve him right if I broke off our engagement. I will break it off! My God, how unhappy I am!"

After shedding a torrent of tears, Frédérique ended up calming down somewhat, but remained mortally sad. The Irishman's revelations had struck her full in the heart.

She washed her reddened eyes in order that no one would see that she had been weeping, and finally went down to the dining room.

"You seem upset," Andrée de Maubreuil said to her. "Your expression is vexed."

"I slept very badly last night," Frédérique replied, to avoid any explana-tion.

"One would think that you'd been crying—your eyes are red," said Roger Ravenel in his turn.

"Why would you think I'd been crying?" he replied, in a glacial tone that he did not understand.

In the midst of the general animation, however, Frédérique's preoccupation attracted little attention and the breakfast continued cheerfully, as usual. After-wards, the guests separated, the majority going up on deck to get some fresh air.

Roger Ravenel was about to follow his friends Agénor and Antoine Paganot when Frédérique stopped him with a gesture.

"Roger," she said to him, in a grave tone to which he was not accustomed, "I'd like a few words with you."

"At your orders, Mademoiselle," the naturalist replied, stepping aside to let he young woman pass as she preceded him into a small drawing-room-cum-library, which was empty for the moment.

At first Frédérique tried to conserve the ceremonious tone that she had adopted "Monsieur Ravenel," she began, "serious facts have been brought to my attention..." She could not sustain the role for long however; her natural vivacity took over. "Roger," she exclaimed, already on the brink of tears again, "what you've done is very bad! You're breaking my heart! What, you're deceiving me with a chambermaid!"

"I can assure you, Frédérique..." The naturalist protested, blushing.

"You kissed her! I know it. You held her in your arms! Go on, say that it isn't true, if you dare!"

Roger Ravenel loved Frédérique with all his heart. Before such an accusation, which was capable of reducing his dearest hopes to nothing, he was overwhelmed, as if stunned.

Frédérique was no less emotional. "Well, defend yourself, then!" she cried. "You're not even protesting! So it's true! Roger, you've stabbed me in the heart!"

Those few seconds had given the young man time to get a grip on himself. "Frédérique!" he cried, holding out his arm to hr in a tender gesture. "I swear to you that you have nothing for which to reproach me—nothing, you hear? But there must be nothing between us resembling a lie. You shall know the exact truth."

Very honestly, Roger Ravenel recounted, in every detail, the scenes of which the deck of the *Revenge* had been the theater the previous evening. During the story, Frédérique blushed and went pale by turns, but she did not interrupt the narrator once. When he fell silent, her physiognomy was completely serene, and a happy smile was shining once again in the young woman's features.

"Roger," she said, "I was very upset. I was convinced that you were Mercedes' lover. I wept with shame. That girl is odious to me. Whether or not she kissed you voluntarily, I don't want to see her again. It's necessary that she leave her cabin today to take up accommodation in the servant's quarters."

"Would you like me to give her immediate orders to that effect?"

"Certainly not. I don't want you to speak to her. The girl might be in love with you—who knows?"

"You're jealous!"

"One is only jealous of those one loves."

"So you do love me a little."

"Do you doubt it, wretch?" And Frédérique, with an adorable and modest gesture, offered her forehead to Roger, who brushed it with a chaste kiss.

At that moment, Andrée de Maubreuil suddenly came into the small room.

"Ah!" she said, laughing, "I've caught you, the lovebirds!"

210

Frédérique drew away, utterly confused. "We were in the process of being reconciled," she murmured.

"Don't let my presence prevent the completion of the reconciliation!" Andrée exclaimed, making as if to go.

"On the contrary, my dear friend, stay," said Frédérique. "I need to talk to you."

"Then I'll leave you, Mademoiselles," said Roger, who was not sorry to escape a second rendition of his adventure with Mercedes.

Andrée listened patiently to the confidences detailed by her friend.

"You'll understand," the latter said, in conclusion, "that after what's happened, Mercedes can't remain in your service."

"You're right," Andrée replied. "I'll go now to tell her that she's dismissed. It's a pity, though, for she's very devoted to me. Would you like to come with me?"

"No—I might not be able to control myself. I might insult her—a girl who's permitted herself to kiss my Roger!"

"Well, so be it. I'll take charge of the chore myself."

Andrée de Maubreuil returned to her cabin and rang for her soubrette, who came immediately.

Very calmly, Mademoiselle de Maubreuil explained to her hat although, on her own account she was very satisfied with her zeal, she found herself forced, because of the previous evening's scene, to deprive herself of her services.

On hearing this verdict, the dancer went pale. She was both humiliated and desolate, for she was sincerely attacked to Mademoiselle de Maubreuil, who, while commanding her without rudeness, and giving her little presents from time to time, had won her amity.

"But I have so much affection for Mademoiselle," Dorypha murmured. "Truly, I have a heavy heart in quitting Mademoiselle in this fashion. Do you think that if I made my apologies to Monsieur Roger that I might be permitted to remain with you?"

"Impossible, my poor Mercedes. Mr. Edward Edmond has personally requested that you should reside henceforth in the part of the yacht reserved for the staff."

At the name of Edward Edmond the gypsy had started. Her dark eyes flashed. "What! It was him?" she exclaimed hoarsely, her fist on her hip in a pose that recalled one of her favorite stances on the boards of the music halls. "Well, since that's the way it is, I'll tell you something. Edward Edmond is my lover, and has been for a long time—and it's in order not to be separated from me that he made me enter your service." Bracing her torso in an attitude that was more than proud, she added: "Do I look like a chambermaid? I'm a dancer, a gypsy, a good-time girl—anything you like—but I'm not a servant."

Her voice took on crapulous and strident intonations that were unfamiliar to Mademoiselle de Maubreuil. The young woman was amazed by the sudden transformation.

"Yes," the gypsy continued, becoming increasingly irritated, "if Edward Edmond wants to move me to the staff quarters, it's to have me near his own cabin and to slip into my bed at night when everyone's asleep!"

"Be quiet!" Andrée exclaimed, blushing at that crudity of expression.

It would have been as impossible to make Dorypha be quiet, however, as to stop an unleashed torrent in its course. She spoke with an incredible volubility, heaping insults upon the Irishman in all the languages she had collected in all the low dives in the world.

Andrée was astounded by that deluge of slang, whose meaning, for the most part, fortunately escaped her. It was as if the dancer were being shaken from head to toe by a terrible fury. She paused for a few seconds to catch her breath, then launched once more into a further hymn of invective. In the end, however, Andrée succeeded in quietening her down, and assured her that she would always retain a pleasant memory of her. She gave her the agreed sum for her wages and also made her a gift of a little feminine watch in silver, which the gypsy had envied for a long time.

That munificence touched the dancer profoundly.

"I'm not worthy of your generosity, Mademoiselle," she murmured. "I've deceived you, but you've been very good to me, and I'll never forget it. Before leaving you, I'll give you some advice and tell you a secret. Don't trust Edward Edmond and the others. There are men of the Red Hand aboard the yacht who intend to do you harm. Be on your guard—that's all I can tell you."

Before the astonished Andrée de Maubreuil could think of asking further questions, Dorypha spun on her heels and left the cabin.

For a few minutes, Andrée remained plunged in the silence of consternation; she was convinced that the dancer had not lied and now, a host of petty facts to which she had paid no attention at first, appeared to her in their true light.

"I have to warn Messieurs Ravenel, Paganot and Agénor about all this!" he murmured.

Without losing another moment, she headed for the reading room where the three Frenchmen were sitting.

V. The Punch

When Andrée de Maubreuil came into the little reading room, Antoine Paganot signaled to her to be quiet for a moment, because he and his two companions were engrossed in complicated calculations.

After three minutes, they communicated the results of their work to one another, and Roger, who was a first-rate mathematician, announced he figures obtained by a final operation. Consternation and anxiety were written all over his face.

"Do you know," he said, "what the present position of the ship is? At the moment, the *Revenge* is at forty degrees north latitude and a hundred and seventy east longitude."

"Which is to say," said Paganot, "that we're more than two hundred leagues from where we ought to be. We've continue to travel westwards when we should have been heading northwards."

"I noticed first," said Agénor, "that the heat was excessive. Mademoiselle Frédérique noticed the same thing."

Agénor rang. The young Scottish chambermaid appeared. "Ketty," said the engineer, "will you ask Mr. Edward Edmond to come to see me; I have something to ask him."

The soubrette went away, and came back five minutes later, her expression distressed. "Mr. Edward Edmond," she said, "said that he doesn't have time to come, that he's very busy. He virtually threw me out."

"That's all right, Ketty, thank you," said Roger. "You can go." He added: "This insolence on the Irishman's part justifies our suspicions only too fully. It's absolutely necessary to get out of such a dangerous situation. With the Red Hand, one can expect anything. We might have our throats cut without even having had time to adopt a defensive stance. We might be thrown on to some Pacific reef. Oh, why was Fred Jorgell so imprudent as to entrust that Irish traitor with the recruitment of the sailors?"

"Fortunately," said the engineer, "we had the idea of calculating our position today. If we hadn't, we might have been taken to God knows what unknown shore."

"There's no point dwelling on the past," Roger declared, firmly. "It's now a matter of making energetic resolutions and getting out of the situation as best we can. This is what I propose. The *Revenge*, as you know, is divided into compartments sealed by nickel plates. The first thing to do, it seemed to me, is to isolate the rest of the ship from the part we occupy by tightly closing the internal metal partitions. That we, at least we'll be sure that the bandits can't get to us. Monsieur Agénor will take immediate charge of that operation.

"In the meantime, Paganot and I will go to find Slug and demand categorical explanations from him, informing him of what we've just learned. We'll be able to see immediately whether he's honest. If he is, we'll take the necessary measures in concert with him—for instance, putting all the suspect sailors in irons without the slightest delay. There must be a considerable number aboard."

"What shall I do?" asked Andrée. "How can I be useful?"

"First of all, bring Frédérique up to date with the situation, but avoid frightening her. During our absence, both of you make sure that no one gets into the cabin quarters, under pretext whatsoever."

These resolutions were approved by everyone, and they set about putting them into effect without any delay.

Andrée went to rejoin Frédérique, Agénor ran to close the internal nickel barriers, and the engineer and the naturalist, having carefully checked their Brownings, went in search of Captain Slug.

Night was falling. The sun was setting behind an accumulation of clouds the color of blood, and against that tragic backcloth, the silhouettes of the sailors, grouped on the deck and arguing animatedly, took on a sinister appearance. The two Frenchmen noticed immediately that none of the crewmen was doing any work. They all had pipes or cigars in their mouths, and the unruly crowd bore no resemblance whatsoever to a disciplined crew.

"I believed, Roger Ravenel murmured, "that the situation is even more serious than we thought. All these men look like bandits. I've never been able to take such clear account of it."

"Ssh!" said Paganot. "I can see Slug holding forth in the middle of one group."

The two young men moved forward. At the sight of them, the man surrounding Slug dispersed. The captain came forward with his habitual amiable smile.

"What can I do for you?" he asked. "What magnificent weather! Not a breath of wind! One might think that the ladies were favored. I've rarely had such a calm crossing."

"That doesn't matter," Roger replied, curtly. "We need to talk to you, Captain. Things are happening that you ought not to tolerate."

"What?" said Slug, surprised.

"Why is it," the young man continued, having great difficulty controlling himself, "that the *Revenge* is heading westwards instead of northwards, as we instructed?"

"Hmm!" Slug replied, nonplussed. "I can explain that. There are areas of more favorable wind that we've been obliged to follow and that have caused us to veer slightly westwards. Then again, it's necessary to avoid floating icebergs."

Slug launched into a confused and very tangled explanation, from which only one thing emerged clearly: that he was very embarrassed by the question that had been put to him.

"Let's pass on," Roger continued. "We'll come back to that subject shortly, but I have another question to ask. It concerns the wireless telegraphy apparatus. Why is it that it has been unusable since the beginning of the voyage?"

"The repair work is in hand, I assure you..." the captain protested, with the indignant tone of a man unjustly suspected.

During this conversation the sailors had imperceptibly drawn nearer to the group formed by Captain Slug and the two Frenchmen, and their attitude was nothing less than aggressive. They were listening to what was being said with a tranquil impudence.

As Slug was saying that the repair work on the telegraphy apparatus was in hand, a threatening murmur drowned out his voice.

"Slut up, Slug!" shouted the mariners. "It's not worth the trouble of giving so many explanations to these people. You only have to tell them that they're prisoners of the Red Hand—that's all they need to know."

"Shut up, all of you!" shouted Slug, in a thunderous voice.

"Shut up yourself," retorted several voices.

"Yes, shut up."

"Not so much parleying with the Frenchies. One might think you were on their side!"

"Long live the Red Hand!" bellowed another, whose acclamation was repeated by fifty voices.

The tumult was at its peak. Roger Ravenel and Paganot could see that they were about to be surrounded by the ever-increasing crowd of bandits. No one was even listening to Slug any longer; a furious group was jostling him, to cries of: "Down with Slug! Up with Captain Knox! We want Captain Knox!"

Slug's partisans, who rallied to the cry of "Long live the Red Hand!" raced to his aid. A brawl broke out, in which punches and revolver shots followed one another without respite. The two Frenchmen took advantage of it to beat a retreat toward the cabins, but not without several bullets whistling past their ears.

They might not have got out of it so easily had not Dorypha, who had thrown away her maidservant's apron and frilly cap, suddenly appeared on deck. She was wearing a red ribbon in her hair and her plunging neckline allowed the sight of an opulent cleavage. By virtue of an abrupt metamorphosis, she had once again become the acclaimed dancer of the music halls and taverns. Her arrival produced profound sensation and provided a diversion from the pursuit of the two Frenchmen. As some of the sailors tried to get past her she shoved them back violently.

"Don't concern yourselves with the passengers!" she cried. "Do they care about you? Anyone who tries to annoy them will have to reckon with me! For a start, I won't dance again unless you leave the Frenchies alone!"

215

There was a general acclamation.

"Long live Dorypha!"

"She has to dance!"

"Damn the Frenchies!"

"We're the masters," said an athletic sailor with tattooed arms. "Let's have a party!"

This proposition rallied all opinions. One might have thought that Dorypha's presence had inflamed all the men. In the midst of the racket, Slug could not make himself heard, and Knox's partisans, who had been demanding his liberation so ardently a few moments earlier, were no longer giving him a thought.

In a matter of minutes, the orgy was organized.

Two men brought an enameled iron tub on to the deck that had been found in a cabin. A barrel of rum was opened; sugar was procured from the kitchen and the tub as soon transformed into a gigantic punch bowl. A large livid blue flame rose into the tranquil evening atmosphere. Armed with tinplate tankards, the sailors dipped into the burning liquid simultaneously, and whenever the tub threatened to become empty it was filled up again.

Soon, the drunkenness attained its paroxysm. A considerable number were howling drinking songs; others, knocked out by the alcohol, were snoring, sound asleep sprawled on the deck; the great majority, however, had formed a gigantic circle and were dancing around the punch with a vertiginous rapidity.

Dorypha had taken her place in the center, close to the flame, which, illuminating her with its fantastic reflections, made her appear alternately blue and green, and gave her beauty a spectral quality. She then seemed akin to the sacrilegious dead women of whom legend speaks, who emerge from time to time from the sleep of the tomb to reappear in the theaters of their ancient debauchery.

She danced with an indefatigable ardor, deploying in turn all the riches of her repertoire of stimulating frolics and lascivious poses. One might have thought that she had fire in her veins. And the hectic circle-dance continued to rotate around her, with contortions and demonic laughter, in a hurricane of vertigo.

From time to time she paused, out of breath, and rested briefly, panting, her forehead moist, her silk bodice soaked in the sweat from her armpits; then the circle-dance stopped too and everyone drank in long draughts.

Then the dance resumed, more furiously than before, to cries a thousand times repeated of: "Long live Dorypha!"

It was in one of these brief interludes that Edward Edmond, who was only half-delighted by the orgy, approached the dancer with his heart in his mouth and tried to kiss her—but a mighty slap recalled him to a sentiment of propriety and send him sprawling on the ground, to the great joy of the audience.

216

The sight of the Irishman had reanimated all the gypsy's anger against him. "Get away!" she shouted at him. "I never want to see you again! I detest you! You're a traitor! A blackguard! You're ugly! You're stupid! Get away!"

That scene amused the sailors infinitely, and they lavished all kinds of noisy encouragement on Dorypha.

The Hercules with the tattooed arms, who had first had the idea of making the punch, approached the dancer with a gaze replete with desire, but humble and imploring. "Señora," stammered, emboldened by the enormous quantity of punch he had ingurgitated, "I love you! If I asked it of you, would you refuse me a kiss?"

Dorypha looked the solicitor up and down with a single glance. His athletic build and youthful cheeks pleased her, and the furious expression of the Irishman in his corner made up her mind. "Well, all right," she stammered, lowering her eyes with a smile of false modesty.

She extended her lips, which the sailor crushed with a kiss, as brutal and gluttonous as a bite.

Dorypha put her hand on her heart. "You hurt me," she murmured, "but that's all right. Would you like me to kiss you again?" Her eyes half-closed, she let herself fall backwards in the arms of the man, who was kissing her frenziedly.

But that scene had awakened the dormant passions of the multitude. One cry, and then a thousand cries, rose up.

"And me, Dorypha! Won't you kiss me?"

The tattooed Hercules, a Fleming named Pierre Gilkin, did not mean that to happen; Dorypha had let him understand that she loved him, and no one other than him was to touch the dancer. He was firmly decided on that point. Fists clenched, he placed himself in front of her, and the first ones who tried to get closer were sent flying, their jaws somewhat damaged.

"No one move!" shouted Gilkin. "Or I'll gut them!" To support his claim he drew a Bowie knife out of his pocket, as long and shiny as a sword.

The Fleming's friends—and he had a number of them on board—arranged themselves around him. There was certainly about to be murder done.

Dorypha, her fist on her hip, contemplated the spectacle with a smile, as the beautiful Helen might have done on seeing the Greeks and Trojans killing one another for the possession of her beauty.

It was then that an old mariner, full of prudence, advanced toward the punch-bowl and, in a voice that rose above the tumult of cries and oaths, said: "Calm down, comrades! Dorypha is free. She has the right to do what she wants with her body. If she loves Gilkin, well, so much the worse for you and so much the better for him!"

This speech, full of wisdom, obtained the approval of the greater part of the audience, and numerous cries went up of "Silence!" and "Listen to him!" which encouraged the orator to continue.

"We're dancing, we're drinking," he said, "We're having a good time. Why not carry on? There are enough opportunities in life to fight."

The marine philosopher had won his case; a minute later, the songs and the dances, the laugher and the stamping of feet had resumed as if nothing had happened.

The party went on long into the night. By two o'clock in the morning, the scene on the deck of the *Revenge* resembled a battlefield. By the last glimmers of the dying punch, the sailors, sprawled in the posture in which drunkenness had taken hold of them, were almost all deeply asleep.

Dorypha, exhausted, wiped her sweat-soaked brow. Pierre Gilkin was brooding over her with this gaze, like a miser over his treasure. Then, suddenly, he seized the gypsy in his arms, lifted her off the deck as if she were no heavier than an infant, and carried her off to his cabin.

It must be admitted that Dorypha did not put up the slightest resistance.

VI. The Shipboard Revolt

When they had got back to the aft cabins, Antoine Paganot and Roger Ravenel immediately set about barricading the two corridors that led to the deck, in order that they would not be the victims of a surprise attack.

They were well-armed and they had abundant ammunition. What worried them most, for the moment, was the question of food supplies. The kitchens and storage lockers were outside the compartment sealed by the watertight partition and there was no possibility of crossing the deck. That would be certain death. Fortunately, they managed to find tinned food, boxes of biscuits and a few bottles of wine and mineral water in the cupboards of the dining room.

All of them faced up to misfortune with stout hearts, and ate with more cheerfulness and appetite than might have been expected.

They took tea and went to bed at the usual time, but as a measure of prudence the three Frenchmen took turns to mount guard, and watched from a distance the vile orgy of which the deck of the *Revenge* was the theater.

In the morning, the scene aboard the yacht was lamentable. The deck was covered with filth of every sort and still strewn with drunks who had spent the night in the open. One might have thought that it was a pirate ship.

The three Frenchmen decided among themselves that, by virtue of that disorder, it might perhaps be easy for them to get to the storage lockers and bring back enough food to last for several days. In consequence, they risked a sortie, sidling along the bulwarks and hiding in all the propitious corners, but they had scarcely passed the foot of the mizzen mast than they were spotted. They only just had time to get back to the stern in a hail of bullets.

That morning, they shared out the last biscuit-crumbs and the dregs of the bottles. The situation became manifest in all its horror. The morning meal was bleak and silent. When it was over—which did not take long—Andrée and Frédérique retired to their cabins, while Agénor, Paganot and Avenel held council. Such a situation could not go on for long. Any means of getting out of it, however perilous, or even desperate, would be welcome.

While the three Frenchmen considered a hundred plans one by one, each more impracticable than the last, the deck of the *Revenge* was the theater of further scenes of disorder. The revolver shots had woken the majority of the drunks. Quickly pulling themselves together, being men who were used to that kind of excess, they had not taken long to form groups, some around Slug and some around Captain Knox, who had been set free by an unknown hand during the night.

The previous day's dispute resumed, rendered more bitter and more ardent by the presence of the old pirate. It was the latter who assembled the greater number of partisans, because he was endowed with a persuasive eloquence, and the promises he made were considerably more extravagant than Slug's.

"Comrades," Knox cried, "if you follow my advice you won't let a unique opportunity pass by—an opportunity that will never present itself again. We have beneath our feet a magnificent ship, well-equipped and well-provisioned, in which we can navigate for three months without making a landfall.

"Personally, I ask for no more to make all of us a fortune. I know Oceania like the back of my hand, thank God, down to the smallest islet. I know where to find pearl fisheries, storehouses of copra and tortoiseshell. I know all the German and English trading posts from Malacca to New Zealand. Where else would you find a captain who knows his trade as well as mine?

"Slug is using you. It's all the same to him whether or not you remain vagabonds all your life or whether you risk your necks in the service of the Red Hand. He gets well-paid regardless! He's one of the leaders of the gang and, compared to him, you don't exist. You're just poor imbeciles, good, at the most, for cannon-fodder."

There was so much plausibility in these allegations that the number of Captain Kox's partisans, who devoted themselves to an indefatigable propaganda, was increasing by the hour. However, Slug had his disciples; he promised them that the Red Hand would reward them royally, whereas terrible punishments would be reserved for the mutineers.

"What future awaits you with Knox?" he asked. "That of being hanged high and short from the yard-arm of a cruiser. Does the captain think that things can go on like this for thirty years? I can tell you in advance what will happen. You'll pillage a few merchant ships, a few copra depots, and then the news will spread that there are pirates in these parts; the telegraph will spread it, two or three warships will be sent in your pursuit, you'll be captured. You know the law: hanged without delay."

The two rival bands did not restrict themselves to words. Shots were exchanged, but every time, Slug and Knox intervened personally in order that single combats did not turn into a general skirmish. Each of the two leaders thought that it was in his interest to conserve the status quo. Knox thought that the longer he waited, the more the number of his partisans would increase; Slug, for his part, thought that by gaining time he would find some stratagem that would render him master of the situation.

Neither of the two parties, however, wanted to be disarmed or deprived of food and alcohol, so Knox and Slug placed sentinels at the doors of the holds where the food-supplies and munitions were kept.

Discussion regarding the fate of the French party had been equally agitated in both camps. Slug, in conformity with the orders he had received, wanted them to be killed, with the exception of Andrée de Maubreuil. In a spirit of contradiction, as soon as he knew his rival's intentions, Knox declared that the lives of the French men and women were sacred. They represented a fortune in themselves. Were they not friends of the billionaire Fred Jorgell? It would be sufficient to hold them prisoner on some desert island, only setting them free in exchange for an enormous ransom.

The old pirate attached such importance to the capture of the French party that he tried to effect the capture that afternoon by means of a direct attack on the cabins. Slug let him do it, thinking that if one of the scientists were killed, that would be as much work done on behalf of the Red Hand.

However, Captain Knox had a reception that was far from the one he expected. The first of his men who tried to approach the aft cabins fell to the ground, his skull fractured by a bullet. A second, and then a third met the same fate.

Knox was furious, understanding that the death of his partisans might have a serious effect on his popularity. On the other hand, because of the ransom, he wanted to take the French party alive.

The latter did not seem at all disposed to let him do that. They directed a well-nourished fire against their enemies, for Agénor and the two scientists were all excellent shots, and Frédérique and Andrée, aided by the Scottish chambermaid, cleaned and reloaded the weapons as they were fired with heroic coolness.

Knox and his partisans ended up retreating to the bow in order to confer, and, in spite of the laughter and booing directed at them by Slug's supporters, they were organizing a second attack, better planned than the first, when an unexpected intervention occurred

The Fleming Pierre Gilkin, surrounded by a dozen friends, suddenly advanced toward Knox and put an enormous fist on his shoulder. "If you don't leave those people alone," he said, "I'll crack your skull like a walnut."

Knox uttered an oath, but he beat a retreat. He understood that if he made enemies of the Fleming and his gang, it would be the end of his power. Thus, he took Pierre Gilkin to one side to explain to him that it was Slug who wanted to kill the French party, and that he, Knox, only wanted to hold them to ransom.

After a long discussion, Knox promised to leave the passengers in the aft cabins alone until the following day, on condition that Gilkin's band did not take Slug's side.

It was to Dorypha's influence that this unexpected protection was due. Having become Pierre Gilkin's official mistress, she could do with him as she wished. She had had no difficulty persuading him that he had everything to gain by taking the side of the billionaire Fred Jorgell.

"Only listen to me, *querido mio*," she had said to him, "and you'll come out of it well. It's easier for Fred Jorgell to hand over a wad of banknotes than for you to earn a dollar."

These remonstrances, punctuated with kisses and maddening caresses, had had the result for which she hoped. There were now three quite distinct parties on the *Revenge*, and each one guarded its positions while waiting for the decisive battle to be engaged.

The rest of the afternoon passed without incident. The sailors resumed drinking, gambling and smoking insouciantly; at dusk they went down to have their meal, which the kitchen staff had prepared at the usual time.

Slug had taken advantage of this truce. He had gathered around him fifteen of the oldest and most faithful affiliates of the Red Hand, an elite on whom he could count absolutely, for almost all of them had spent time on the Island of Hanged Men. He had explained his plan to them.

It was simply a matter of escaping in the large launch after having set fire to the ship. To achieve that, it would be sufficient to pour out the contents of two or three cans of gasoline near the aft cabins, the woodwork and paint of which would offer easy fuel to the flames. While Knox tried to put out the first fire, a second, started in the vicinity of the powder store, would complete the work of destruction.

The launch was large and solid. It would be provided with the necessary food supplies, and there were numerous islands known to be less than two days distant.

Slug ended up persuading all his men, to whom he promised exceptional rewards, on behalf of the Red Hand.

That audacious project had only one fault, in Slug's estimation, which was that it implied the death of Andrée de Maubreuil, whom the Lords had instructed him to spare, but he told himself that, after all, the main objective would be achieved and that he would find a means of making his excuses.

After the evening meal, he announced his intention of having a good night's sleep and retired to his cabin. His men did the same, and Knox, deceived by the comedy, went to get some rest in his turn; the presence of the sentinels placed on the stores of food and armaments reassured him fully as to the fashion in which the night would pass.

Soon, the most profound silence reigned aboard the *Revenge*. The lights were out and everyone was asleep, or pretending to be asleep.

At about ten o'clock in the evening, Slug's fifteen men emerged silently from their hammocks and, carrying crates of food and barrels of rum that they had taken care to secrete during the day, headed to the large launch, suspended on its davits.

They filled the boat with the objects necessary for a long voyage. They took care not to forget a compass, munitions and spare clothing.

Slug supervised these preparations personally. It was only when he was certain that nothing essential had been forgotten that he drew away in order to take personal charge of setting the fires, which would be lit by means of long fuses prepared in advance.

VII. The Heroic Gypsy

In the French camp, the day had ended miserably. Andrée and Frédérique had only eaten a bar of chocolate that Agénor had discovered in his cabin, which the two young women had shared; the men had only had a few mouthfuls of mineral water; even that resource was on the point of running out.

That afternoon, the heat had been overwhelming. It was obvious that the bandits who had taken over the ship were heading south-westwards, doubtless to land on one of the small islands in the north of Polynesia; that observation caused the engineer and his friends great anxiety.

After a melancholy evening, everyone except Agénor, who was on watch, thought about retiring to their cabins. They wished one another goodnight and Andrée and Frédérique kissed their fiancés more tenderly than usual. They needed all their courage to hold back the tears that rose to their eyes, and before they separated, once they were in Andrée's cabin, they threw themselves into one another's arms, weeping.

"Dear Andrée!

"Dear Frédérique!"

"I sense that I won't close an eye tonight. I tremble that some misfortune might happen to Roger."

"Oh, I'm also sure that I won't sleep. If you stay with me in my cabin, I might be less frightened."

"Well, yes, that would be better..."

"Shh! I think I heard something..."

The two young women listened attentively.

Andrée was not mistaken. Soon, a voice—Dorypha's voice—became audible in the silence, cautiously calling: "Mademoiselle de Maubreuil! Mademoiselle de Maubreuil!"

"Is that you, Mercedes?"

"Yes, Mademoiselle."

"Where are you?"

"In the cabin next to yours. Go to the window—but speak quietly."

"What is it?"

"Do as I say. Reach out your hand...good! Now, take the package I'm holding out to you. Be careful—it's quite heavy."

"Indeed—but what is it?"

"Don't say anything. It's a ham. I know you're hungry. But listen, that's not all! Here's a box of tins. Have you got it?"

"Yes. I don't know how to thank you."

"Just take it—you can thank me later. Here's some bread and chocolate now. Now it's the turn of the bottles, for one can't eat without drinking, can one, Señora?"

And the gypsy, still insouciant, laughed merrily.

At that moment, Andrée and Frédérique heard the noise of a struggle, and then the porthole of Dorypha's cabin closed with a dry click, and they distinguished the accents of a brutal masculine voice on the other side of the partition.

"My God!" said Frédérique, "the poor girl has fallen victim to her devotion. She's just been caught by one of those wretches. They won't forgive her for having tried to help us."

Trembling with anguish, the two young women tried to listen to argument that was taking place in the next cabin, and which was continuing in loud voices, but they could only catch snatches of phrases and odd words.

At the moment when the gypsy had been about to pass the bottles of wine she had mentioned to Andrée, she had been abruptly grabbed by the shoulders. She had turned round and had found herself face to face with the Irishman, who, furious at being abandoned, had not ceased spying on her since the previous evening.

"I've got you!" the wretch sniggered. "It's you who's supplying the people in the cabins with food. I'm going to tell everyone about your treason."

The gypsy fought like a hyena to escape the Irishman's grip. When he would not let go quickly enough she planted her ten fingernails in his cheeks and blood flowed. Edward, furious, lost control and started shouting at the top of his voice: "Help, Slug! Help me, men of the Red Hand! You're betrayed! Help! Come quickly!"

"Shut up, you vile toad!" growled the gypsy, searching for her dagger with an impatient and feverish hand.

The struggle between Dorypha and her former lover continued, implacably and grimly, in the darkness of the cabin. But the Irishman's cries had been heard. At the words "Red Hand" and "treason" people were on their feet in the blink of an eye. The electric lights were switched on, and the men of Captain Knox's party arrived on deck at the very moment when Slug's men were beginning to operate the lifting-tackle that retained the launch on its davits.

There was an explosion of rage on both sides.

"No one shall touch that launch!" declared Christian Knox. "It belongs to the ship and I, as captain, have the sole right to dispose of it."

"The only captain here is me!" shouted Slug, departing for once from his habitual phlegm. "A little nerve, the rest of you," he added, to his men. "Don't listen to him, and haul away on those pulleys!"

"I forbid anyone to touch that launch!" cried Knox, cocking a large revolver.

"We'll touch whatever we want!" replied Slug, exhibiting an enormous Browning in his turn.

"We'll see about that!"

"It's already seen!" With a rapid gesture, Slug had pressed the trigger of his weapon before Knox had had time to take aim.

The old pirate collapsed like an inert mass, with a hole in his chest. The bullet had struck him in the heart, killing him outright.

"That's how I treat the enemies of the Red Hand!" Slug roared, with a terrible expression. "Whose turn is it now?"

No one moved, and it was in the midst of a profound silence that Slug ordered: "The rest of you, leave this boat alone. It's not worth the trouble. Now that scoundrel has bitten the dust, I hope that every man here will behave..."

He did not have time to finish his sentence. A jet of flame had just sprung from the aft cabins, illuminating the entire ship with a bloody light.

"My God!" the bandit swore. "I forgot about the fire! I must have miscalculated the length of the fuse! Quickly! Someone go put out the other fire, near the powder store."

"The powder store!"

Those terrible words gave wings to the lamest legs; in the blink of an eye, a dozen sailors armed with buckets of water rushed toward the forecastle, arriving just in time to extinguish the fuse of the second fire. The others, with Slug in the lead, ran toward the aft cabins, the resinous wood of which, covered with a thick layer of paint, was burning with sinister crepitations.

In the midst of the flames women's screams could be heard.

Slug, whose composure had not abandoned him for a moment, ordered the pumps to be manned, and torrents of water were soon being directed into the heart of the fire.

The fire, however, which found fuel in a host of eminently combustible materials, did not appear to be diminishing in intensity. The heart-rending cries of the Frenchmen and women, who were being roasted alive in their cabins, could be heard.

Even Slug, by virtue of a contradiction that would require explanation by a psychologist, was sincerely moved, and gave orders to save the passengers. He had been prepared to murder the young people, who had never none him any harm, but he did not want them to be roasted alive; that was not in his orders.

It must be said that the crew, armed with buckets, axes and iron bars, worked ardently. An immense cheer went up from all throats when a man who clothing had been reduced to ashes and his beard burned away, appeared on the threshold of one of the cabins. It was the poet Agénor, who had just snatched the little Scottish chambermaid from the flames.

Almost at the same moment, Roger Ravenel, holding Frédérique in his arms, fell unconscious into the arms of one of the sailors, who had run to his aid. Shortly thereafter, Pierre Gilkin himself pulled the inanimate body of Paganot from the flames. All kinds of care were lavished upon him, but as soon as he opened his eyes he uttered heart-rending cries.

"Andrée! Where's Andrée? I must save her!" But the unfortunate man, his hands and body atrociously burned, was incapable of any movement.

"Andrée!" he repeated. "Save Andrée!"

At that moment, the gypsy Dorypha cleaved through the crowd of sailors. After a long battle she had finally succeeded in felling Edward Edmond by slipping her stiletto between his ribs. She was glad, smiling. "I'll save Mademoiselle de Maubreuil!" she shouted, and, grabbing a sailor's reefer-jacket, she soaked it in a bucket of water and threw it over her shoulders. Then, without hesitation, she launched herself into the midst of the flames.

For ten seconds there was a deathly silence. Nothing could be heard but the crackle of the conflagration and the hiss of water immediately volatilized by contact with the ardent embers. Dorypha had disappeared behind a curtain of red-brown smoke spangled with sparks.

"She won't come back!" cried a voice in the silence of the breathless crowd.

"Who said that?" cried Pierre Gilkin. "I'll go fetch her myself!"

Shoving away all those who tried to hold him back, the Hercules advanced toward the fire, but just as he was about to penetrate it, Dorypha repaired, carrying an inert body over her shoulder, wrapped in the wet garment with which she had equipped herself.

There was a mighty cheer.

"Long live Dorypha!"

Every one hurried toward her to relieve her of her burden, and at that moment, she could have done what she wanted with all of those men.

Andrée de Maubreuil was set down on a bunk in one of the service cabins. Antoine Paganot lavished his most devoted cares on her, although he was suffering himself from cruel burns. He had hastily swallowed a mouthful of whisky, and a kind of fever prevented him from paying any heed to the terrible pain he was experiencing.

Andrée, whose cabin had been adjacent to the wall sealing the compartment, had hardly been burned at all, but when the dancer had seized her she was already half-dead of asphyxia.

The engineer, to whose cares those of Agénor and the naturalist were added, the latter now being confident of Frédérique's wellbeing, applied the energetic treatments usual in such cases, including rhythmic tractions of the tongue and artificial respiration. Dorypha, whose blonde hair had only been slightly reddened, gave proof of an indefatigable devotion to her former mistress. It was only after two hours of care, however, that Andrée could be considered to be out of danger.

By that time, the sailors had mastered the fire, with which water alone could not have reckoned, but had ended up yielding to extinguishing smoke-bombs, of which Paganot had fortunately laid in a supply.

The luxurious aft cabins, the dining room and ward-rooms had been completely destroyed. Nothing remained of them but charred and blackened beams. It was only a matter of luck that the fire had not reached the supplies of oil for the engines, which were not far away.

The drama had unfolded so rapidly that that it was only when the Frenchmen had recovered somewhat that they began to take account of the frightful danger they had been in. Dorypha brought them up to date, not forgetting to make a fervent eulogy to her new lover, Pierre Gilkin.

"It's absolutely necessary," the engineer said, "that I talk to Slug. Now that he's recovered his authority, I hope that things have changed."

"I'll go with you," said Agénor.

They both went along the corridor that separated the cabins, but they ran into two sailors who were standing guard, rifles over their shoulders with bayonets fitted to the barrels.

"No one goes though!" said one of them to the Frenchmen.

"But I needed to see the captain," said Agénor.

"No one goes through. Go back, or I'll shoot.."

Dorypha had witnessed this scene from the threshold of her cabin. "Caramba!" she cried. "We'll see whether I can't go through!" She walked boldly to the sailor and placed herself boldly in front of him. "Is it true that you want to stop me going through?" she said.

"My orders don't apply to you," the man replied.

"That's just as well! But I'll be back shortly."

Her absence did not last long. When she reappeared at the entrance to the corridor, she was accompanied by Pierre Gilkin and half a dozen of his most robust companions. Slug was following them, some way behind, with a surly expression. The Red Hand's sentinels yielded their places without any argument.

"From now on," said the dancer to the Frenchmen, "it's my friends who'll take responsibility for your safety. Install yourselves as comfortably as you can in the empty cabins, and I swear to you, on the word of a gypsy, that you won't be deprived of anything. Captain Slug has understood that if he tries any nasty tricks, Pierre Gilkin's friends, allied with the former partisans of Captain Knox, won't let him alone for long. It's been agreed that Slug will let us disembark at the first port we put into. After that, he and his men can go to the Devil, if they want, with the *Revenge*. That was the only way I could find to sort things out."

"We couldn't ask for any more," replied Paganot, speaking on behalf of his friends. "As long as we're safe, with the young women that have been confided to us."

"That way," said Slug, with his amiable smile, by which no one was any longer taken in, "everybody will be happy." The bandit could hardly conceal his ironic satisfaction.

An hour later, thanks to the collaboration of the older sailors aboard the vessel, he had calculated the exact position of the *Revenge* and ordered the helmsman to set a course northwards.

In two or three days, he thought, *we'll reach the Island of Hanged Men. My mission will be accomplished. I'll put the Frenchies and their little friends ashore, and the Lords of the Red Hand can do what they want with them. I wash my hands of them! I believe that I haven't steered my boat badly, in difficult circumstances.*

The members of the French party were in no position to see through the ruse. The fire had deprived them of all the instruments necessary determine the yacht's position, and they were completed absorbed by the cares necessitated by Frédérique's condition, and Andrée's even more so. Finally, they had confidence in the protection of Dorypha, who had been their good genie.

After so much incident, the journey seemed to them to be completed in the most placid conditions.

12. THE GORILLA CLUB CRUISER

I. Dynamite

A small, heavily-formed ship with a black-painted hull, at the stern of which floated the tricolor flag of the kingdom of Holland, was moored in the port of Vladivostok, at a respectable distance from the other ships.

Thanks to an adjustable gangplank, the deck of the Dutch ship was almost level with the quay, and it was over this gangplank, which had been fitted with rollers, that a dozen Chinese coolies, overseen by a squadron of Cossacks, was embarking with extreme slowness and infinite precaution square crates of medium dimension but great weight.

On the deck of the ship, the captain, a jovial individual with a long blond beard, was personally supervising the loading of these precious crates.

All the care that was being taken was explicable on reading an inscription in large black letters of the sides of the crates, surmounted by the Russia, coat-of-arms:

RUSSIAN IMPERIAL FACTORY
DYNAMITE CARTRIDGES FOR USE IN MINING
FRAGILE: BEWARE OF SHOCKS AND HEAT

The redoubtable explosive, which Cossacks had brought in a special wagon, was destined for the gold prospectors of the Klondike, who consumed a great deal of it in the course of their work, and the crates containing it were reinforced with lead and secured by the imperial seal.

For several months that captain of the steamship the *Lovely Dorothea* had been making the journey between Vladivostok and the Klondike, and, as one might suppose, he demanded a very high fee for transporting such dangerous merchandise. Thus, even though he had only ever taken on relatively light cargoes, he had been able to make considerable profits without ever suffering any accident.

Very phlegmatic in temperament, like the good Dutchman he was, Captain Willem Van Blook slept well alongside a mass of dynamite capable of blowing up a dozen villages, and did not even refrain from smoking his pipe in the vicinity of the redoubtable crates stacked in the foremost hold, as far away as possible from the engines and the kitchens.

When he was congratulated on never having had an accident, he replied facetiously: "If I had an accident, you can be sure, it wouldn't be a small one. The

229

Lovely Dorothea would explode like an onion skin; there wouldn't be a single fragment of her left as big as my pipe." He laughed wholeheartedly, delighted with that joke, which he repeated at least two or three times a day.

In spite of this apparent nonchalance, however, Willem Van Blook was very prudent, not permitting anyone other than himself to smoke and making sure that two men, who were replaced every two hours, remained on watch night and day beside the precious crates.

When the coolies had completed their task, and each man had collected the silver rouble he had been promised, they went away hastily, delighted to have finished the dangerous maneuver.

Willem took the Cossack sergeant down to his cabin, signed a formal receipt in which the registration numbers of each case were carefully listed; then the Russian and the Dutchman each drank a glass of Hollands gin to the health of their respective sovereigns, and parted.

It was then shortly after midday. The ten men comprising the crew had eaten. Willem went to his first mate, Karl, who he treated more as a friend than a subordinate, and in whom he had complete confidence.

"Karl, old man," he said, "we need to get ready to sail right away. Finish taking aboard the supplies we need while I go to the harbormaster's office to complete the formalities."

"I thought," said Karl, surprised, "that we weren't leaving until tomorrow morning."

"Yes," said Willem, winking, "but I've changed my mind. We need to be out of the port in an hour—an hour and a half at the most."

"Very well, Captain," Karl replied. "Understood!"

"Above all," said Willem, as he was about to go over the gangplank that had served to embark the dynamite, "be careful with the crates."

"Understood!"

Willem drew away at his phlegmatic pace in the direction of the harbormaster's office, while the ten crewmen under Karl's orders hurriedly made the final preparations for the departure.

When the captain returned, the engines were under pressure, the gangplank had disappeared and the anchors were being raised.

Willem Van Blook took the helm himself; he never left it to anyone else to steer in and out of Vladivostok harbor, in which it is difficult for a vessel to maneuver in the midst of fleets of English, American, Japanese and German steamers and sailing ships.

As usual, he carried out his task admirably, and the *Lovely Dorothea* was soon putting on full steam, and, favored by a good wind, heading out to sea. The sun had not yet set when the Russian coast was nothing more than a long strip of mist on the western horizon.

"The time has come!" Willem murmured to Karl. "I believe I've already done a good day's work."

"How's that, Captain?"

"You'll see. Bring a hammer and chisel and come with me."

Somewhat intrigued, Karl followed his superior to the other extremity of the deck, where fourteen crates of dynamite had been left, doubtless with some secret intention, the captain having forbidden them to be securely stowed in the hold with the others.

Karl noticed that all the crates in question had a cross in one corner crudely traced in red paint, and observed, with surprise, that the slats of the crates were ill-fitting, which had never happened in previous consignments, whose packaging had always been very careful.

Willem had taken the hammer and chisel and began to strike with all his might.

"What are you doing?" exclaimed Karl, stepping back fearfully.

"Don't worry," the captain replied, with a broad smile. "There's no danger."

Already, without any respect for the imperial seal, one of the slats had come away.

Karl uttered a cry of terror. In the gap left by the slat he had just perceived a human foot—a naked foot with long toenails, as horny and curved as talons.

Karl was more convinced than anyone of the mildness and honesty of his captain, but his first thought was that he had rendered himself accomplice to some crime. His hair stood n end in fear, and he stammered, as his teeth chattered: "You knew, then, Captain, that there as a cadaver in that crate?"

The captain burst out laughing, like a man who had been told an excellent joke, and gravely continued to detach the other slats.

The pretended cadaver moved and pronounced words in an incomprehensible language.

"Come out, then, *tarteifle!*" exclaimed the captain. And he helped the inhabitant of the crate to crawl out on all fours through the narrow cap.

A bizarre individual appeared; he had long gray hair and a beard, solid brass-rimmed spectacles on his nose and a doctoral manner. He wore no other garments than a pair of long underpants and an old sheepskin overcoat that was doubtless substituting for a shirt, trousers and waistcoat. His torso was visible, covered with thick gray hair, like that of an aged orangutan.

At first, the captain and his mate laughed wholeheartedly at the sight of this phenomenon. Then, Willem Van Blook—because business is business—took a notebook from his pocket in which a list of names was inscribed, and he said in Russian, a language he had eventually learned to speak fairly fluently: "You, no doubt, are the honorable Dr. Stepan Rominoff, whom I've been commissioned to transport to America?"

"The very same!"

"I'm Captain Van Blook."

"Well, Captain, you'd be the most obliging of men if you'd care to give me something to eat. I've been in that crate for thirty-six hours, and not only am I atrociously cramped, but I'm dying of hunger, because all I had with me were two little loaves of rye-bread and a flask of cold tea."

The captain found his new passenger very amusing. "Karl, old man," he said to the mate, "take the worthy doctor to the galley and have him served a nice dish of red beans and a sausage. There must be some leftovers from the crew's meal—and when he's had his fill, look in my wardrobe to see if there's a pair of trousers and a shirt that will fit him. It's cold, and even though he's got a belly furrier than the lid of an old trunk he might catch a cold."

"Aye aye, Captain!"

The doctor had regained his feet, however, and, with a gravity that his strange costume rendered exceedingly comical, he said: "Captain, I'll gladly accept the red beans and bread, and will only refuse the sausage, but I have no need of trousers or a shirt."

"You need have no fear of being indiscreet," said the Dutchman, "but you can't remain dressed like that."

"Know, Captain, that I am the patriarch of the new sect of the Mystic Vitalists; we reduce the necessities of life to a minimum. As nature indicates to us, we go abroad as nakedly as possible and our health is very good. For preference, we eat fruits and roots, everything that does not cost an animal its life..."

"You can explain all that later," replied the astonished captain. "Go and eat instead of making long speeches."

The patriarch of the Mystic Vitalists disappeared in the direction of the galley and Willem, given an appetite of curiosity by this commencement, began to break up the second crate.

A lady with a considerable embonpoint emerged, who declared that her name was Ivanovna Rominoff, the apostle's legitimate spouse. She was dressed as raggedly and summarily as her lord and master, whose principles she shared.

"What is all this?" wondered the captain, attacking the third crate. "It's going to be very strange on board if they're all like that! But after all, what do I care? I've been well paid by the terrorist committee in Lausanne to transport these strange bipeds to the land of free America; it's a cargo like any other."

While engaged in this monologue Willem Van Blook had proceeded with the opening of the third crate. This time, it contained a tall, slender and emaciated individual who was still wearing the gray uniform of a labor camp; his features presented the most emphatic Cossack type. His nose was thick, his cheekbones jutting and his little oblique eye were like a Chinaman's. His physiognomy radiated candor and naivety.

"Well," said the captain, after having looked him up and down from head to toe, "are you also a member of the sect of trouserless vegetarians?"

"No," replied the Cossack, making a military salute. "I like meat very much, and would like nothing better than to put on a costume other that this one."

"Good," said the captain, "but why were you in the prison camp?"

"A peccadillo. One day, when I'd drunk too much vodka, I threw one of my officers into the latrine. I was almost shot, but our little father the Tsar had mercy on me and sent me to the verdigris factories."

"You seen like a good fellow. What's your name?"

"Ivan Rapopoff."

"Good—run along to the galley," said the Dutchman, ticking off the name in his notebook, as he had done for the previous two.

At that moment, a cannon-shot resounded in the distanced, and then a second. The Cossack looked at the captain with a certain anxiety.

"What's that?" asked the latter.

Rapopoff did not reply immediately. He counted the canon shots on his fingers.

"Thirteen," he said, finally. "That's the signal they make when there's been an escape from the camp."

"Bah!" said Willem, insouciantly. "No one will take it into his head to suspect me. I have an honorable reputation in Vladivostok. Besides which, it's too late to pursue me, and night's falling. We'll be far away tomorrow."

The Cossack manifested his joy by thumbing his nose irreverently at the "little father" the Tsar and the principal dignitaries of the Empire; then, in his turn, he went down to the galley.

Willem, who was beginning to get bored with his task, called upon the aid of his sailors to open the other eleven crates, each of which, like the first, contained a prisoner.

Women were in the majority; including Madame Rominoff, there were ten in all, and all ten, being affiliates of the vitalist prophet's sect, were in the same state of negligence and semi-nudity. Their bodies had been hardened against the cold by long habitude. In spite of the rigor of the temperature, they took an icy bath every day without even catching a simple cold. The majority of them were robust matrons whose ugliness was a serious guarantee of virtue, but a few were young and pretty. Before converting to the vitalist doctrines that had led to their imprisonment, Wanda, Fedorewna, Maslowa, Katinka and Staniska had been incarcerated in a "home" for immortal young women and had escaped, From their former existence they conserved a liberty of behavior and language that made a pleasant contrast with the pedantic attitude and doctoral speeches of the prophet Stepan Rominoff.

In addition to the prophet and the Cossack there were only two men. One of them, a little old man with an amiable and smiling face and exceedingly polite manners, had no peer for the fabrication of panclastite bombs equipped with a clockwork mechanism that triggered the explosion at a predetermined time.

Outside of that mania, which had earned him many whippings and prison terms, Serge Danicheff was a mild-mannered and inoffensive fellow and it was a veritable pleasure to hear him talk of the happiness of future humankind, regenerated by progress.

His companion, Galitzine, also belonged to the terrorist sect, but he was somber and silent, hardly pronouncing four words a day. He had been condemned to twenty years in the prison camp for having attempted to bow up a train in which the tsar was traveling, and if he had not been hanged or subjected to the knout it was only because the prosecution had not been able to establish the facts in a sufficient manner.

Captain Willem Van Blook installed the prophet and his disciples in a large cabin between the decks and gave them no further thought, but he allowed the Cossack and the two terrorists, who seemed to him to be more sociable, to dine at his table.

In granting them the honors of his table, the Dutchman did not fail to ask them a host of questions regarding their escape. He knew almost nothing about it himself; an unknown man had come to see him in private, saying that he had been sent by the terrorist committee in Lausanne, and had explained to him that on his next voyage, fourteen of the crates of dynamite of which he would take delivery would contain escaped prisoners. The sum offered had been considerable and Willem had had no hesitation in accepting; on the contrary, he justly considered it a meritorious action to snatch a few unfortunates from the torture of the Siberian labor camps. What surprised him, however, was the choice of prisoners set free; he had expected to take aboard sinister and mysterious conspirators, but it was an old maniac and a gaggle of more-or-less addle-pated women that had been extracted from captivity at great expense.

Serge Danicheff, the bomb-maker, could not help smiling. "I'll explain the anomaly," he said, filling his glass of gin to the brim. "An escape like ours is very costly..."

"Well," the captain put in, "that's because it involves risks; everyone values his life and liberty, and only risks such precious wealth in exchange for a benefit that makes it worthwhile."

"I know that, of course, but if I tell you that escapes are very expensive, it's to explain why they're so rare. In Russia, with money, you can have anything you want; if the terrorists had more considerable capital at their disposal, they wouldn't remain locked up for long."

"So you're a rich capitalist?" asked the captain.

"Not at all; the person who paid the expenses of our escape is the old Countess Alexandra Basileff, a cousin of the tsar, worth several million roubles. The old crackpot, whom the police lave alone because of her illustrious relative, is a fanatical disciple of the prophet Stepan Rominoff; she didn't spare any expense in saving him and his women."

"What about the rest of you?"

"We got out cheaply, because a few strong men were required to empty the crates of dynamites and get over the walls of the penitentiary. That's why we got involved in the plot. Those weaklings and sluts, and their apostle—who's as idle and slovenly as they are, in spite of his sex—wouldn't have had the courage to do what we did. Once we were over the wall and had found the road to the railway station in the pitch darkness, we had to break into the hangar where the wagon was, open the crates at the risk of our lives and throw the dynamite cartridges into the river. I can assure you that the prophet Rominoff wasn't so proud at that moment!"

"I understand that," said the captain, "but once you were all in your crates, how did you reestablish the imperial seals?"

"We'd taken our precautions. Among the employees at the station there's a terrorist who had made an imprint of the seals in wax beforehand. In less than an hour, it was all over; we had arrived just in time. The wax was still warm when they hitched our wagon to your express train."

"They wouldn't have discovered that we were gone until the morning," said the Cossack Raponoff in his turn, "and I'm certain that no one had any idea that we'd been able to take the train. They must have wasted a lot of time beating the steppe and the forest looking for us."

"All's well, then!" said the captain, cheerfully. "It's worked out better than I would have dared to hope. I know how to arrange things on my own account once I get to the Klondike. I'll say that a fire stated on board forced me to throw some of the crates overboard; that's a circumstance foreseen in my contract with the mine owner. To your health, sirs!"

They drank a long draught, and then each of them returned to his cabin. The Russians were in great need of rest. Their long sojourn in the crates had put a strain on all their limbs. They were also in pain because they had al received blows with the knout, or at least beatings with sticks.

The next day and the days that followed, the *Lovely Dorothea* was favored by superb weather; leaving behind the Empire of the Rising Sun, she headed north-eastwards. Captain Van Blook, for whom the voyage represented a considerable benefit, was in an excellent mood, and he was full of attention for his bizarre passengers.

The Russians were no less satisfied. The vitalist prophet and his female adepts were rejoicing in advance in the happy life that they were going to lead in Switzerland, in a beautiful park belonging to Countess Basileff, where they would be able to live in a state of nature without anyone thinking of disturbing them. The Cossack and the two terrorists intended to go to Paris, where their revolutionary comrades were in large quantity, and find some employment with them.

All of them, in sum, were recompensed for the poor nourishment and hard labor of the prison camp by eating four meals a day and sleeping twelve hours in every twenty-four.

The brave Cossack Rapopoff gave the sailors joy by virtue of the enormous appetite he had for alcohol and fatty substances, in whatever form they were offered to him. On several occasions he was persuaded to absorb engine-oil, on the pretext that it was as sovereign tonic for the chest, and not a day went by when he did not drink a few small glasses of burning alcohol, which he declared excellent and enjoyed as a connoisseur.

Begun in such a favorable fashion, the crossing promised to be one of the most pleasant and rapid that Captain Van Blook had made for a long time. Six days went by in that manner without the slightest noteworthy incident.

One evening, at about ten o'clock, the captain was tranquilly smoking his pipe at the stern when the sailor on watch shouted: "Land on the port bow!"

The captain gave such a start of surprise that his pipe, a superb kummer pipe perfectly seasoned, escaped from his lips and fell on to the deck, where it broke in two.

"Land?" he repeated. "There isn't any land hereabouts! I examined the map only an hour ago. The man's mad, or had drunk too much gin."

The captain took from his pocket one of the powerful marine telescopes knows as night-glasses and explored the horizon.

After a minute, he was forced to admit that the man on watch was neither drunk nor demented. Two or three miles away, in a north-north-westerly direction, he could see land, with steep promontories. He thought at first that what he had before him was a vast iceberg, but as he continued to examine it more attentively, he made out lights and even, it seemed to him, buildings.

The captain could hardly believe his eyes. He went back down to his cabin, where he found the chart on which he mapped the ship's position every day. Although it was very recent, the chart bore no trace of the island or of any land whatsoever.

"That's unexpected," he said, very intrigued. "I haven't made any error with regard to the route, though. The weather's been so beautiful. I don't understand it at all."

Prudently, he gave the engineer an order to slow down and told the helmsman to skirt the island at a modest distance. The *Lovely Dorothea* therefore changed course, heading closer to the island, but not so close as to run into reefs or the sea-bed.

In spite of those precautions, however, the steamship did not take long to run into a rock beneath the surface, and scraped against the reef several times with a dull noise.

The engine was thrown into reverse. Given the slow speed of the vessel and the calmness of the sea, the collision had not had any serious consequence, but the captain was not reassured. He knew that, for some unknown reason, he had found himself in a region unrecognized by hydrographic engineers and inexactly marked on charts. It was therefore necessary to act with the greatest circumspection.

He therefore had a launch lowered into the water. He put two sailors aboard; they were to check the steamer's course, with a sound in hand, making sure that there was enough depth for a vessel of her tonnage.

In those conditions, they proceeded for about half a mile.

Suddenly, however, there was a violent detonation; the launch and the steamer were lifted upwards, elevated on the summit of a mountain of water.

Clinging to a rope, Captain Willem had had time to see the launch blasted into a thousand pieces by the explosion.

"Only a torpedo could do that," he murmured, shivering with fear at the thought of the crates of dynamite in his hold.

In that rapid second, a terrible shock made the iron hull of the *Lovely Dorothea* resonate throughout her framework. The mountain of water raised up by the explosion had launched the steamer with uncommon brutality on to a group of reefs, where she now remained immobile, listing slightly to one side.

Willem Van Blook wiped away the sweat that was streaming down his forehead. "We've had a narrow escape," he murmured. "It's a real miracle that my ship didn't go up like a rocket."

Meanwhile, the Russians and he sailors were running around the deck in confusion. The women and the patriarch were uttering screams of terror.

"There's a leak near the keel," declared Karl. "We're sinking. There's already two feet of water in the hold."

"No," said the Ditch captain. "The danger's not as great as you think. The steamer's held between the rocks like a piece of wood between the jaws of a vice; we're not going to sink. In a few hours, when it's daylight, we'll be able to reach the land, which isn't far away. No one's in any danger—but my ship is doomed."

"Look captain!" shouted one of the sailors, all of a sudden. "One would think that someone were coming to rescue us."

His arm extended in the direction of the land, he was pointing to lights that were moving back and forth along the shore. Suddenly, an electric searchlight was switched on, and the triangle of blinding light oscillated over the sea for some time, until it reached the spot where the steamer had run aground.

By that unexpected light, houses could be clearly distinguished, and then a crowd of men running along the shore and gesticulating.

"I believe," the captain said, "that we won't even have to wait until tomorrow. Those people seem to be making preparations to come to our rescue. But that's no reason to let the sea invade the hold. Karl, take two or three men with you and do your best to plug the leaks by nailing tarred and tallowed sail-canvas over them, or with sheets of metal, if there's any means of doing that.

While this order was being carried out in feverish haste, Willem Van Blook, standing pensively on the deck, sought in vain to figure out what the name of that island might be, which could not be found on the map. While reflecting, he did not lose sight of the shore, now brightly lit. He could see men clad in large hats putting a yawl into the water, which maneuvered in such a way as to head toward the stricken steamer.

Six oarsmen caused the light boat to fly over the tranquil waves, and as it drew closer, the people aboard the steamship noticed the peculiar costume of the oarsmen, who were wearing some kind of uniform: broad-brimmed hats turned up at the rim, decorated with red insignia and sturdy vestments of black leather—except for the man at the tiller, who was dressed entirely in red.

"They look like Boers," said the Dutch captain.

"No," said Karl, "it's more likely the uniform of some Canadian militia."

"In any case, they don't seem to have evil intentions."

"We'll soon see!"

In the meantime, the yawl had come alongside the steamer. The red-clad steersman came up on deck on his own. He had a long beard and his somewhat coarse features expressed energy and self-confidence. As soon as he as aboard he asked for the captain and, after having greeted him, enquired about the circumstances in which the shipwreck had occurred.

Willem Van Blook hastened to give the necessary explanation, stressing the dangerous presence on board of crates of dynamite, but without saying a word about the escaped Russians. He concluded by asking what the name of the island was on whose coast they had just run ground, astonished that it was not featured on official charts.

The man in red smiled imperceptibly.

"This island is called St. Frederick's Island, Captain," he said. "It is marked on some charts, but there is so little traffic in the region that it has, it's true, escaped the attention of many geographers. At any rate, the island is a tiny independent state under the protectorate of the United States of America. In case of war with Japan, it would be a very useful naval base; it has been fortified by American engineers and, as you discovered to your cost, it's protected by a ring of submarine mines and dormant torpedoes."

"In that case," the captain said, ill-humoredly, "it's the administration of your island that is at fault. International maritime regulations state that where there are submarine mines of that kind, their presence must be signaled to navigators by conspicuous beacons or buoys."

"Possibly, but as St. Frederick's Island is not on any shipping route, we didn't think it necessary to take such a precaution."

"That's an offense, and I'm within my rights to bring a lawsuit against you."

"I would advise you not to do that," replied the man in red, with a hint of irony. "Your suit would be lost in advance. But I propose that we help you re-float your ship, and I offer you the most generous and cordial hospitality among us."

"I can see that we can't reach agreement. I'll take advantage of your offer immediately."

"It would indeed be very imprudent to spend even a single night on a ship loaded with explosive materials, which might be set off by a violent wave."

This conversation had take place in English and the Russians had hardly understood a word of it. They had only deduced that they would be taken ashore, and were delighted by that."

The transportation of the shipwreck victims began immediately. It required no less than five trips to be all the *Lovely Dorothea*'s passengers and crew ashore.

Captain Willem was about to be the last to descend into the yawl when he suddenly remembered that he had not seen the Cossack Rapopoff. He assumed that the unfortunate fellow had been thrown overboard by the enormous wave lifted up by the torpedo and had drowned, but it was necessary to make sure.

A search was mounted, and they finally found the poor devil in his cabin. At the moment of the explosion he had been hurled out of his bunk and had broken a leg. He was carried to the yawl with the utmost precaution.

"It's nothing," said the man in red, having retaken his place at the tiller. "We have a first-rate scientist on the island, Monsieur Bondonnat, who will take a veritable pleasure in caring for him and healing him."

Captain Willem was already congratulating himself for having saved his crew and his papers when, on raising his eyes, he perceived by the light of the electric bulbs a signal-mast planted on top of a hill.

At the top of the mast was a large flag which bore, on a black background, a hand the color of blood. That flag, so similar to those of pirates and sea-raiders, caused him to frown. He turned to the man in red, who was watching him with a mocking expression.

"What is the name off the independent state installed in this island?" he asked.

"Captain, the island that German geographers call St. Frederick's Island, we call the Island of Hanged Men, and it's the property of the Lords of the Red Hand, in whose name I'm taking you prisoner."

Captain Van Blook looked around. He was surrounded by armed men. Any resistance would be futile. He had often heard mention in the Klondike of the association of the Red Hand, which terrified all of America. He wondered, in anguish, what would become of him and his companions—but Willem was courageous, and did not let his impressions show.

"Very well," he said, coldly. Then, addressing the man in red directly, he said: "May I know exactly what your position is in this new State?"

"On behalf of the Lords, I exercise the functions of governor of the island and commandant of the garrison. My name is Job Fancy."

A few moments later, the castaways, arranged in pairs, were marched into the interior of the island under a strong escort.

II. Grave Events on the Island of Hanged Men

Because of his injury, the Cossack Rapopoff had been separated from the rest of the castaways. He spent the night in a small hut situated near the shore, where he was set down on a mattress of wrack. In the morning, two men placed him on a stretcher and carried him to a wooden house protected by a double rampart of palisades, some distance away from the landing-point.

Sentinels dressed in the strange uniform that made them resemble Boers were mounting guard around the dwelling.

They went through a courtyard and a large room surrounded by glass-fronted cupboards containing bottles and metal objects, whose function the Cossack could not determine. Finally, the injured man was deposited in a small room whose only furniture was an iron-framed bed, a table and a chair. It was illuminated by a window fitted with thick bars, from which the Cossack immediately inferred that he had only escaped one prison to enter into another.

He was left alone for a few moments, and then Commandant Job Fancy came in, followed by an old man with a physiognomy full of kindness. His exceptionally high forehead was shaded by snow-white hair, and, although his face expressed a profound melancholy, he had a radiant charm in his bright eyes and his features, framed by vast side-whiskers as white as his hair, respired intelligence, serenity and benevolence.

Just as the red-clad man, whose face only expressed a brutal energy, was instinctively antipathetic to Rapopoff, so he felt confidence in the old man who advanced toward his bed, clad in a long laboratory smock and carrying a surgeon's instrument-case under his arm.

"This is the injured man I mentioned," said the commandant. "I'm certain, Monsieur Bondonnat, that with your immense knowledge it will be the easiest thing in the world for you to get him back on his feet."

"We'll see about that," the old man replied, and set about examining the injured leg. "Hmm," he said, after a few minutes. It's a simple fracture of the fibula, not very serious. We can try to reset it, but I'll need splints, modeling plaster and everything necessary to set up a traction apparatus."

"You'll be given all that, my dear Master," said the commandant, respectfully. "I'll leave thus brave muzjik in your care, then. He'll occupy this room, which was previously inhabited by that rascally Redskin who got away at the same time as Lord Burydan."

Monsieur Bondonnat asked the Cossack, first in English, and then in French, what his name was, but Rapopoff shook his head energetically at each question to signify that he did not understand.

"How stupid I am!" the scientist exclaimed. "Since he's a Cossack, he must speak Russian, damn it."

Monsieur Bondonnat was a remarkable polyglot; he read or spoke seven or eight languages fluently. He repeated his question in Russian, and this time had the satisfaction of seeing the face of is patient light up with a smile. They immediately struck up a conversation.

Rapopoff related in minute detail all the circumstances of his escape and the wreck of the *Lovely Dorothea*.

"Listen, my brave fellow," said Monsieur Bondonnat, when he had finished his story. "It's very important that no one here knows that I can speak Russian. Whenever there's another person here, you must pretend not to understand what I say to you."

"Why?" asked the Cossack, opening his eyes wide.

"Because you're in a lair of bandits here. The Island of Hanged Men is inhabited by murderers and thieves, and like you, I'm their prisoner. They snatched me from my family and friends in order to steal my discoveries, and thus far, all my attempts to escape have failed.

Monsieur Bondonnat recounted his strange adventures to the Cossack, toward whom he felt drawn by a natural sympathy.

After a week, the physician and the patient were the best of friends. Rapopoff, whose broken leg was well on the way to healing, was able to get out of bed and was already rendering the old scientist useful service as a laboratory assistant.

To Monsieur Bondonnat's great surprise, Commandant Job had not come back. It was the subaltern bandits who brought the two prisoners their food every day. The Commandant had never gone such a long time without coming to the laboratory; the old scientist inferred that grave events must be occurring on the island. The Cossack seemed to have been completely forgotten.

At any rate, Rapopoff, with the sort of oriental fatalism that is fundamental to the Russian soul, seemed very glad to be living in the company of the scientist, and was not overly preoccupied with the future. Laborious, scrupulous and docile, he went to a great deal of trouble to make himself useful in the laboratory—except that Monsieur Bondonnat thought that certain materials seemed to be disappearing.

One morning, the mystery was clarified. He found Rapopoff in the process of consuming a black bread tart smeared with something yellow and shiny. Beside him was a flask of burning alcohol.

"What are you eating?" asked Bondonnat, bewildered.

Rapopoff pointed at a bottle bearing the label *Boric Vaseline* and added, passing his hand over his stomach with a satisfied smile: "It's good for breakfast, this Vaseline."

Monsieur Bondonnat could not keep his face straight in the face of that barbaric appetite. "But my poor Rapopoff," he said, "You'll contract an inflammation of the gut. To eat Vaseline tarts and drink lamp-alcohol, you must have a stomach like an ostrich, my friend."

"Then it's bad, what I'm doing?" asked the Cossack, anxiously.

"No, it's all the same to me—except that if you carry on eating unfamiliar substances, you'll end up poisoning yourself."

Rapopoff swore solemnly by Our Lady of Kazan and the apostles Peter and Paul not to touch alcohol again and not to eat Vaseline.

The Cossack kept his word, but he substituted castor oil, which caused Monsieur Bondonnat considerable anxiety, for Rapopoff, carried away by his greed, purged himself in such an energetic fashion that the scientist thought momentarily that he had been afflicted by cholera. A further sermon and a new prohibition followed.

Apart from that slight fault—common to all his compatriots, who, since time immemorial, have had weakness for candles and strong liquor—Rapopoff was the most faithful of servants.

One morning, Monsieur Bondonnat, who had come down to the courtyard of the laboratory early, observed to his profound surprise that the sentinels who usually mounted guard outside the palisades were not there. It was the first time that the old scientist's jailers had relaxed their vigilance in that manner. Something extraordinary had to be happening.

"My brave Rapopoff," said Bondonnat to the Cossack, "you're going to go outside and go to the houses you can see over there."

"Yes, Little Father."

"You're going to try to find out something about what's happening on the island. Try to find one of our companions and, if you can do it without attracting the attention of the Red Hand, bring the captain here. At any rate, tell him my name and tell him who I am. Perhaps I'll finds a means, thanks to him, of getting a letter to my children and my friends in France."

"Understood, Little Father."

"Go, and come back quickly. I'm relying on your intelligence."

Rapopoff went through the palisades and, without trying to hide, headed tranquilly toward the houses, behind which Bondonnat lost sight of him.

Less than half an hour had gone by when the Cossack came back, his expression consternated.

"Little Father," he said, "a great misfortune has occurred. The boat has gone."

"You mean the ship that bought you here?"

"Yes."

"But I thought it was half-demolished."

"The men of the Red Hand have repaired it. Many of them have left the island with the Dutch captain, and they've left the poor Cossack here." Rapopoff had tears in his eyes.

"Don't be upset," said Bondonnat. "Is it so bad to have to stay here with me?"

"That's not what I meant, Little Father."

"Soon, I hope, we'll be able to escape. I promise that I'll take you with me to France."

That promise dried up the Cossack's tears. He rendered a faithful account of the mission he had been given. He had found the habitations situated by the bay almost completely abandoned. No one remained there but an octogenarian tramp who had told him about the Dutchman's departure.

"What's his name?" asked Bondonnat.

"I don't know. As he doesn't speak Russian, it was by sign-language that he showed me the place where the ship had run aground and made me understand that they had all gone."

"That's all right. I'll go to see the old man myself. If he's the man I believe him to be, he'll give me all the information he can."

The scientist put on his fur coat and his fur hat, and, for the first time since he had been living on the Island of Hanged Men, he ventured outside the palisade. Rapopoff followed him.

A prisoner for many months, Bondonnat studied the landscape surrounding him with a keen curiosity. In front of him was a small harbor where a few canoes were anchored, and wooden houses of shabby appearance from which a stony path extended that plunged into the interior, turning around a hill covered in birch trees, sorb-trees and stinted willows.

At the door of one of the houses an old man with white hair was sitting on a stool placidly smoking his pipe. He ran forward joyfully to meet Monsieur Bondonnat, who had cured him of an attack of the gout not long before

The old man was the veteran of the bandits of the Red Hand. He was ninety-two years old and since his early childhood he had been engaged in an incessant war with society. He had been hanged and lynched so many times that he no longer remembered the exact number.

In spite of so many fatigues and adventures, he was still in excellent health, eating with a hearty appetite and, as he was proud of repeating, still finding whisky an excellent thing.

He greeted Monsieur Bondonnat respectfully, who asked after his health.

"Still as solid as a post, thanks for asking. Thanks to the generosity of the Lords, I'm enjoying a happy and tranquil old age. He was about to launch into one of the long stories that he liked to tell, but Bondonnat, impatient for news, interrupted him and got straight to the point.

"Is it true, Father Marlyn, that the Dutch ship has gone?"

"Yes, sir," said the old man, uttering a sigh. "Oh, funny things have been happening here. I don't know what the Lords of the Red Hand will say when they next come, but I fear that all of this is going to be spoiled."

"What's happened?" asked the scientist, his curiosity vividly stimulated by this preamble.

"Well, the major part of the garrison has taken flight with the Dutchman, with Captain Job Fancy in the lead."

"Impossible!"

"It's exactly as I have the honor of telling you," said the old bandit, shaking his head. "That Job was decidedly not a man as serious as his predecessors, Mr. Slug and Sam Porter, whom the Lords have promoted. He only thought about drinking and organizing all manner of plots."

Bondonnat was listening attentively. He understood that he was about to learn things of the greatest importance.

"Yes," old Marlyn went on, "they're all alike. You know that there's a factory of forged banknotes here; each of them has taken an abundant supply, and I believe they've gone to Alaska, where they think they'll be able to pass their merchandise to the miners and adventurers from all lands who are working the gold-fields."

"You didn't want to go with them?"

"Lord, no. I'll end my days here. At my age, one doesn't like change. Besides, would it not have been showing the blackest ingratitude to the Lords, who have treated me so generously?"

These revelations filled Bondonnat's heart with joy. He understood that from now on he would no longer be watched so closely, and that an escape might become possible. He continued to question the old tramp.

"Yes," the other went on, "the conduct of Job and his men is shameful. Not only have they filled their pockets with fake dollars and banknotes, but they pillaged the island before leaving. They've taken away a considerable quantity of seal-skins, blue fox furs and eider plumes. Furthermore, they've emptied the cellars and the arsenal and stolen everything of value that was in the Lords' private lodgings."

"That's not very honest," said Bondonnat, trying to keep the conversation going.

"It's ignoble! But they won't get away with it. The Red Hand will be able to winkle them out wherever they hide, and then, woe betide them! The Lords' vengeance will be terrible!"

"In sum, approximately how many men are still on the island?"

"Sixty—not counting the Eskimos, of course, and the Russian women."

"The Russian women haven't gone, then?"

"No. They've set up home with their prophet in a valley in the interior and they've taken lovers among our men."

"One more question," said Bondonnat. "Why didn't all your comrades leave with the Dutchman?"

"Some of them were afraid of disobeying the Lords. Others are veterans like me, who don't ask for anything more than to spend their last days here in tranquility. Then there are some who hope that the Red Hand will reward them handsomely for their fidelity."

Bondonnat took his leave of the old bandit and, still followed by his faithful Cossack, set off along the path that led to the interior.

He had not taken a hundred paces when a strange individual appeared in the distance. He was a middle-aged man whose gray hair fell untidily over his shoulders; his beard came down to the middle of his chest and, except for a light loincloth, he was completely naked. His snub nose was surmounted by solid brass-rimmed spectacles and he seemed humble and timid.

Bondonnat rubbed his eyes, to see whether he might be the victim of a hallucination, but the Cossack was already making signs to the newcomer, who responded to him with an amicable smile. "It's Rominoff," he explained. "You know—the prophet I told you about."

"Ah! Very good! I'm delighted to make his acquaintance. Doubtless he can tell us some interesting things."

The prophet had come forward. Rapopoff made the introductions and a conversation was immediately struck up in Russian. Bondonnat explained his situation and recounted his adventures, and then invited his interlocutor to do likewise.

"Oh, sir," said the vitalist apostle, sadly, "What has happened to me is unimaginable. I've been truly unfortunate, and I'm glad to encounter a man like you, to whom I can confide my troubles. These bandits of the Red Hand are infamous rogues."

"I'm astonished that you've remained among them instead of continuing your journey."

"That wasn't possible. The wretches have taken possession of the young women I had converted to my doctrine and appropriated them! I must admit, though, that they didn't take much persuading to become the companions of these bandits."

"In your place, I wouldn't concern myself with them any longer."

"That's what I would have done—but the swine have captured my respectable spouse, Madame Rominoff and, as with her companions, have used her to slake their brutal passions. I couldn't abandon my wife in such circumstances, so I stayed."

"I'm sincerely sorry for you," said Bondonnat—who, in spite of the gravity of the circumstance, had difficulty preventing himself from laughing.

"You don't know the full extent of my misfortune. These wretches, twenty-nine in number, each take turns, every ten days, to serve as the spouse of one of my pupils. The only favor they've granted me, in an egalitarian spirit, is to count me as the thirtieth, so that I can only spend ten days a month with my unfortunate wife."

After having received the just tribute of condolences that Monsieur Bondonnat accorded to his lamentable situation, the Russian told him how the bandits had forced Captain Willem, with a gun to his head, to take them away in his ship.

After that, he could not resist the desire to expose the basic elements of his vitalist theory to an eminent scientist like Bondonnat.

"What renders human life so short," he explained, "and what makes humans so unhappy and perverse, are the unhealthy refinements that have been introduced into their way of life. Personally, I preach a return to simplicity: no unnecessary and unhealthy garments, no spicy and indigestible aliments; no fire; no houses—that's the secret of true happiness! Look at me: I'm as fit as a fiddle!"

"It seems to me," Bondonnat objected, timidly, "that there's some exaggeration in your way of seeing."

"None at all," the prophet retorted, sharply. "The naked human being acquires an admirable strength and beauty, and nature, as it has done for other animals, does not take long to cover the human body with a soft natural pelt that defends it against the rigor of the seasons. Look—the transformation has already commenced for me."

The prophet Rominoff proudly showed off his hairy chest, which Captain Willem Van Blook had compared to the lid of a trunk.

"Furthermore," he continued, vehemently, "I always sleep out in the open. Houses and beds are merely a bad habit. In Siberia, I've seen Kalmuks sleeping in the snow at ten degrees below zero , and they didn't come to any harm—quite the contrary! I never light a fire and never eat cooked food. My diet consists of fruits and roots, and, in case of necessity, raw meat and fish."

"And thus far," the doctor queried, "none of your adepts have died of pleurisy, influenza or fluxions of the breast?"

"None. They're all marvelously well, although they don't yet possess—but it won't be long delayed—the thick fur with which nature endows all animals in cold climates. It's true that the climate of this island is much more temperate than one might have imagined, given its latitude. That must be due to the existence of a warm marine current originating in the equatorial regions. I'll take you to see the valley where my ten pupils and their twenty-nine spouses live; you'll see that, from the viewpoint of vegetation, as well as in other respects, it's a true terrestrial paradise."

"Yes, I'll come to see that—but not today. Look, I have a idea—come with me to my laboratory."

"Why?"

"I want to give you something. You were complaining just now about the insufficiency of the pilose system among your adepts. I'll give you an elixir of my own invention, thanks to which, in a matter of days—I guarantee it—your charming pupils will be provided with a natural vestment as warm and soft as the one possessed by Tibetan yaks, or even polar bears."

The prophet Stepan Rominoff accepted this offer with an enthusiastic gratitude, and left the laboratory carrying a round flask filled with the precious capilogenic elixir discovered by Monsieur Bondonnat.

Left alone with his Cossack, the old scientist declared that he was going to take advantage of the relaxation of surveillance, and to begin that very day to make preparations for an escape that would have every possible chance of success.

From then on, a new life began for Monsieur Bondonnat. He did not see any tramps on sentry duty at the door of his laboratory. They had given up watching him; he was neglected to the point that they forgot to bring him food on several occasions. The old scientist was obliged to have old Marlyn take him to the new Commandant, a certain Montgomery whom Bondonnat had once had occasion to cure of an access of *delirium tremens*.

Montgomery was an insouciant and idle individual as well as a drunkard. His philosophy of life could be summed up in a formula that answered to any circumstance, and which he repeated a hundred times a day: *Don't complicate things*.

"Do you know, Monsieur Bondonnat," he said to the scientist, "that it's a great inconvenience to have to bring you food twice a day?"

"I can't die of hunger, though. If I'm an inconvenience to you, set me free."

"That's a different matter. Let's not complicate things. The Cossack can come twice a day to collect your food from the canteen." And Montgomery added, to Bondonnat's great satisfaction: "There are comrades who'd have liked me to confine you more narrowly, but what's the point? It's all the same to me if you get to know the island, since you'll probably be ending your days here, and I'm not as stupid as my predecessor Sam Porter, who left an airplane at your disposal. It's necessary not to complicate things. I'm sure, myself, that you'll never escape from here."

Bondonnat left the new commandant, who tried very hard to persuade him to drink a glass of whisky, in terms that were almost cordial. The scientist was delighted to have obtained a relative liberty, and he made use of it that day and on the ones that followed by undertaking, in the company of his faithful Rapopoff, interminable exploratory excursions into the interior of the island.

He was surprised to find that the territory, which he had believed to be sterile, was abundant in richest of all kinds, and that it was perfectly equipped, fortified and organized.

In the northern region, which comprised a vast bay strewn with rocky islets, there was a colony of fur-seals, supervised by a hundred Eskimos, who also occupied themselves with fishing and the preparation of skins. Their grass huts formed a picturesque village in the depths of the bay. Bondonnat had treated a few of the poor savages, who greeted him enthusiastically.

Later, he visited, in the center of the island, a veritable village in which the tramps' barracks were located, now almost empty. Along with the arsenal and the warehouses of clothing, food and munitions, he also saw, a short distance from his laboratory, the luxurious cottage reserved for the Lords of the Red

Hand when they visited the island. It was only into the southern part of the island that he was unable to venture, because it was there that the workshop of the forgers of documents and banknotes was located. Finally, he visited the batteries of cannons of the latest model installed on the heights, which enabled the island to withstand a long siege.

What charmed him the most, however, were the admirably cultivated region punctuated here and there by woods of birch trees, sorb-trees and willows, the species most resistant to cold. Game was abundant, including reindeer, beavers, Arctic foxes and aquatic birds. Steams of fresh water, which ran through the meadows, were full of salmon and trout. Thanks to the beneficent current of warm water, the island, which one would have assumed to be desolate, could have passed for a veritable Eden.

In his excursions, Bondonnat was careful not to forget the prophet Rominoff and his adepts, camped in the open air in a clearing sheltered from the wind. There he received the felicitations of all the ladies, who thanked him for his capilogenic elixir, whose beneficial effects they were beginning to feel.

It was on quitting the vitalist prophet that Bondonnat and Rapopoff reached an uncultivated and desolate region situated at the western extremity of the island. The tormented soil was bristling with blocks of granite and only covered in some areas by sparse grass. There were stagnant pools in places bordered by dwarf willows, in which a whole society of aquatic birds frolicked, including wild mallards, teals, pintails and plovers. Bondonnat even noticed a few swans and wild geese, which flapped their wings heavily as they took off. It was evident that the region had only been visited rarely by the island's inhabitants, and he understood the reason for that when he perceived a hand crudely traced on a rock in red paint.

"This must be an area forbidden to the bandits," he said, "which the Lords have reserved to themselves."

"Perhaps in order to hunt here, Little Father?"

"I don't think so. The prohibition must have a more serious reason; we'll try to find out what it is."

They went past the rock on which the red hand was painted, and descended into a valley with deep ravines, bordered rocky cliffs where eiders and sea-eagles had built their nests.

At the bottom of the valley there was a well-traced path on which footprints and ruts made by wheels were visible. They followed it for some distance. They soon perceived that the valley was narrowing, becoming a kind of defile or ravine, enclosed by sheer rocks, leaving only a narrow passage. They kept going, but their disappointment as great when they found the way bared by a block of granite that fifty men would have had difficulty shifting.

"That's singular," said Bondonnat. "This path certainly seemed to be leading somewhere."

"Perhaps the block fell as a result of a landslide?" suggested the Cossack.

"It can't have. You can see by the gray color of the moss that it's been here for a long time, perhaps years, occupying the same place."

"And yet, Little Father," said the Cossack, "look!" He pointed at footprints cleanly cut off by the granite, as if someone had walked across the place where the enormous block now stood. "Perhaps there's a secret passage hidden in the stone," said the Cossack.

"I don't think so."

Rapopoff had approached the block, as if he wanted to displace it, but he might as well have tried to move a mountain.

"I think," said Bondonnat, "that it would be best to turn back..."

As he pronounced that phrase, however, a last effort on the Cossack's part caused the gigantic mass to swivel. The scientist uttered an exclamation of surprise. It seemed to him to be materially impossible that Rapopoff could have obtained such an effect solely by means of his own strength.

The anomaly soon became explicable. Like the rocking stones that are seen in Wales and Brittany, the block of granite was delicately balanced. When it was touched in a certain place, a child's finger was sufficient to displace it; it was that spot that the Cossack had finally found.

As it rotated, the block had uncovered a tenebrous opening.

"Let's go in!" declared Bondonnat boldly.

"Yes, Little Father, let's go in..." repeated the faithful Cossack. And while speaking, he slid a few flat pebbles into the gap under the rock in order to prevent the block swinging back into its former position of its own accord.

Fortunately, the two explorers were equipped with a pocket electric torch. They switched it on and advanced into the black hole, which resembled the ventilation-shaft of a cellar.

They had only taken a dozen steps along the narrow corridor, whose walls were scintillating with saltpeter, when they emerged into a round subterranean chamber entirely filled with glass-fronted cabinets arranged concentrically.

At first, they could not see very clearly what the cabinets contained, but when they got closer they recoiled with a frisson of disgust and horror. The subterranean room, whose secret had been revealed to them by chance, was a veritable anatomical museum. There were hundreds or organs and entire bodies there, seemingly conserved in all their freshness by unknown procedures.

Immersed in vast bottles, doubtless in accordance with the methods of Dr. Carrel, further perfected, hearts were beating in baths of colorless liquid; lungs were inflating and deflating with a the sound of breathing; masses of blue and green intestines were twisting, still agitated by the reptilian movements that accompany digestion in living beings.

There were also living fetuses in large crystal test-tubes, the umbilical cords of which were prolonged by rubber tubes that terminated in strange crystal pumps full of warm blood.

When the first fit of stupor had passed, Bondonnat became exceedingly interesting in that frightful assembly. He had never seen such admirable anatomical specimens. He was observing discoveries here that were still completely unknown to official science, and he wondered, pensively, who the great scientist might be who, while capable of doing such prodigious work, was also a leader of bandits. He could understand now why he, a scientist, had been abducted, with the sole aim of appropriating his discoveries.

"It was, after all, necessary for the bandits to be perfectly familiar with my work. But what a pity that such a man is presiding over a rabble of murderers instead of acting frankly, working in the open!"

Plunged in his reflections, Bondonnat continued to examine the anatomical specimens. He had arrived in a part of the room where admirably embalmed bodies were standing upright in crystal coffins. The skin had conserved its coloring, and the limbs their exact dimensions; the faces, with red lips, were neither tarnished nor decomposed. One might have thought that all those human beings were still living a mysterious life, only waiting for an order from their master to quit their pensive immobility.

Throughout this examination, Rapopoff was giving signs of the most acute terror; his teeth were chattering and he was looking at Bondonnat with an imploring expression, as if begging him to get out of that diabolical lair as quickly as possible.

Suddenly, he leapt backwards with a veritable howl.

"Little Father! Little Father! Look at this!"

He pointed his finger at a glass case in which Bondonnat, amazed and frightened in his turn, perceived his exact resemblance, his double; another Bondonnat of flesh and bone, admirably embalmed, seemed to be contemplating him with a tranquil smile.

"Now that," exclaimed the old scientist, "is too much! I wonder how a subject could be doctored in such a fashion as to obtain so frightful a similitude!"

Bondonnat and the Cossack stood there for a full five minutes in profound silence, literally struck dumb by amazement. Suddenly, however, the old man slapped his forehead with a cry of triumph.

"That's it!" he exclaimed. "A certain means of escape, remarkable and practical."

"What do you mean, Little Father?"

"You'll see. But it'll be dark in an hour; we won't leave here until the darkness is complete."

"I'd rather go now," Rapopoff protested, energetically.

"No, you don't understand. When we leave, we'll take the other Bondonnat—the one you see there in the glass case—with us."

It was not without difficulty that the Cossack allowed himself to be persuaded, but in the end, by dint of arguments and demonstrations, he gave in.

When they both left the subterranean anatomical museum, whose door of rock they were careful to close again, Rapopoff was carrying a heavy burden over his shoulder, enveloped in gray cloth.

Two days later, the doyen of the tramps, old Marlyn, came to the laboratory, as he sometimes did, to obtain news of Monsieur Bondonnat.

Finding all the doors wide open, he went through the experimental room and the library and thus arrived at the scientist's bedroom—but he stopped on the threshold, amazed and consternated.

Monsieur Bondonnat was dead, and his cadaver, lying sideways across the unmade bed, was hanging there limply, head down.

"Rapopoff!" shouted Old Marlyn. "Help!"

When Rapopoff did not come, the old tramp set about searching for him, but in vain. The Cossack had disappeared.

Deeply affected by what he had just seen, and even sincerely afflicted—for the old man, like all the people of the island, adored Bondonnat—Old Marlyn hastened to inform Commandant Montgomery.

The latter emerged from his habitual apathy and went to the laboratory in haste in order to conduct a personal investigation. The initial result of that investigation was to discover a deep wound on the cadaver's temple.

He was still occupied in his macabre investigation when an Eskimo, who had been looking for him for an hour, came to tell him that two of the best fishermen in the bay had disappeared during the night, taking the largest of the boats with them. No one had seen them leave, but there was no doubt that they had gone without any intention of returning, because they had taken their sealskin smocks ornamented with glass beads, their necklaces of walrus teeth and all the precious items from their hut.

This revelation was a flash of enlightenment for Commandant Montgomery. With a perspicacity that even astonished him, he had reconstructed the entire drama.

"I can see what happened as if I had witnessed it," he declared to the tramps surrounding him. "It's the Cossack who killed the poor old man, doubtless to rob him. He must have persuaded the two Eskimos to accompany him in his flight."

"It's a pity," said Old Marlyn, "that we can't wring the neck of that vagabond Rapopoff."

"Bah!" said Montgomery. "What's the point? He must be far away by now. We don't know what direction he's taken, anyway, and I don't want to risk one of our boats in such a pursuit."

Montgomery's hypothesis was supported by a further circumstance. It was observed that a small chest of drawers in which Bondonnat had put a wad of banknotes given to him—against his wishes—by the Lords of the Red Hand

252

during one of their previous visits had been broken open, and the banknotes had disappeared.

Montgomery was somewhat embarrassed. It was a disagreeable start to his tenure as governor, but he could not let such an incident pass without notifying the Lords of the Red Hand.

By means of the wireless telegraphy apparatus installed in the center of the island, he immediately send a coded dispatch, and an hour later he received the reply, thus conceived:

The Lords of the Red Hand are extremely displeased by your negligence, in the matter of which they intend to mount an investigation. The guilty parties will be severely punished. In the meantime, increase vigilance and be on the alert. The island might be attacked at any moment.

Montgomery grimaced on reading this message. The old scientist's murder had placed him in a singularly awkward situation. In fact, it had been agreed when Job Fancy had left that the Lords of the Red Hand would only be notified of that desertion when the fugitives had had time to reach safety. Montgomery had kept his word faithfully, but he perceived a trifle belatedly that, for want of having told the truth, he was the one who would be held responsible not only for the death of the old scientist but also for Commandant Job's escape.

He went back to his lodgings furiously, wondering how he was going to get out of the mess. In his preoccupation, he forgot to give the order for the old scientist to be buried.

IV. Phantasms

The dispatch from the Lords of the Red Hand had thrown Montgomery into great anxiety and had extracted him from his habitual apathy. The day after the discovery of the crime, and the day after that, he deployed a veritable activity.

The tramps, who had for some time been allowing themselves to live as veritable men of leisure, and had abandoned all discipline, were obliged once again to mount guard in the various parts of the island where a surprise attack was to be feared. Montgomery placed sentinels in all the threatened locations and got up during the night to make rounds and make sure that everyone was actually at his post. The cannons set on the heights were checked and loaded. Finally, they made sure that the torpedoes were in place and that none of them had been carried away by the current.

On the night of the third day, Commandant Montgomery had a dream. He saw himself surrounded by a howling mob and, as had already happened to him once or twice in the course of his existence, he was tied up and dragged to a tree, from the branches of which a rope was swinging, ornamented with a sinister noose. He was menaced with fists and jostled, and finally, a few zealous individuals put the noose around his neck, while others hauled with all their strength on the other end of the rope, to hoist their victim into the air.

The Commandant woke up with a start, very frightened, and put his hand to his neck precipitately, where he could feel the constriction caused by the rope.

He smiled at his terrors, realizing that the painful sensation that was affecting him was caused by his cravat, which he had knotted too tightly. He realized at the same time that, doubtless in consequence of a slightly excessive absorption of whisky, he had laid down on his bed fully dressed.

It took him some time to get over that alarm, and, observing that he was no longer sleepy, he thought that the best things to do was to get up and to make a tour of inspection along the coast of the island.

In the blink of an eye he was on his feet, and accompanied by a tramp named Moller, who normally served as his bodyguard, he set out, not without having checked the two revolvers from which he was never separated.

The night was dark. Large black clouds were fleeing across a starless and moonless sky, and in the great silence, nothing could be heard but the monotonous sound of the breakers on the shore.

The two bandits arrived a short distance from the laboratory that Monsieur Bondonnat had occupied, when Montgomery stopped dead.

"Tell me, Moller," he said to his companion. "Did you just see something?"

"No," the other replied.

"I don't know whether it was an illusion, but I thought I saw a bright flash of light out to sea just now."

"Perhaps it was a flash of lightning."

"No, the weather isn't stormy."

They both stood still for a few moments, anxiously, trying to piece the opacity of the darkness. Suddenly, however, an exclamation escaped their throats, and they were nailed to the spot, stunned with amazement by an extraordinary vision.

A hand of fire, a gigantic Red Hand, had just appeared on the horizon against the dark backcloth of clouds, and that hand bore a chain at its writs, whose last links seemed to be lost in the sea.

"What's that?" stammered Moller, more dead than alive.

"I don't know," Montgomery replied, in the same tone.

"Let's get away from here. I've got the shakes. I don't want to stay here a minute longer."

"No," Montgomery murmured. "Let's stay. We need to see." Involuntarily, his eyes remained invincibly fixed on that gigantic and bloody hand, which stood out against the background of the sky. He was wondering anxiously what the terrifying meteorological phenomenon was when the noise of a loud explosion rent the air.

"I know what that is, at least!" growled Moller. "That's one of our torpedoes going off!"

Montgomery was unable to reply. A second, a third and a fourth detonation burst forth almost simultaneously, making a deafening racket. One might have thought that it was a salvo of cannon fire. Then the explosions multiplied further, resounding from second to second in a thunderous rumble majestically reverberated by al the echoes.

It was the double row of dormant torpedoes that protected the vicinity of the shore, which the Red Hand's mysterious enemies were in the process of destroying. Tall columns of foaming water sprang up toward the sky, as if the island were surrounded by a ring of geysers.

"I don't know what all this means," said Montgomery, in a low and tremulous voice, "but we're cooked!"

When the last torpedo had been detonated and silence feel again, the hand of fire, whose bloody reflection lit up the whole sky, descended into the sea and disappeared.

Meanwhile, the island's inhabitants, plunged momentarily into consternation and stupor in the presence of these supernatural phenomena, set about organizing resistance against the as-yet-invisible enemy. Gunshots bursts forth from all directions, alarm bells rang and electric searchlights were abruptly illuminated. Squads of tramps ran out at the double, rifles over their shoulders and revolvers in their belts.

But the disappearance of the symbolic red hand into the waves had been the signal for another kind of phantasm.

The sky was now populate by hundreds and thousands of hideous diabolical faces which seemed to be swinging on the clouds and sniggering: hanged men and heedless men performing infernal round-dances in the company of monsters with blazing eyes and animal faces. All those phantoms were frolicking in a phosphorescent atmosphere like liquid fire, lighting up the entire horizon like an immense conflagration.

It was only then that Montgomery perceived, scarcely a cable from the shore, a ship that was advancing at full steam, and which also seemed to be surrounded by a dazzling aureole of light. Its hull, its rigging and its masts were outlined in streaks of flame, and in the shrouds, monsters were playing similar to those visible in the sky. The strange beings were sliding along the ropes and leaping from yardarm to yardarm as if the laws of gravity did not apply to them.

Moller, who, as an Irishman, was superstitious, felt his hair standing on end. His teeth were chattering, and he could already see himself gripped by the claws of all the nightmare creatures that seemed to be about to fall upon the island.

"We're doomed!" he cried. "I knew that it would all end badly! The Lords of the Red Hand have made a pact with the Devil! Now, the moment has come when we'll all be carried off, and the island with us, to the utmost depths of Hell!"

"Imbecile!" Montgomery shouted, to whom the very excess of his terror had rendered courage. "I don't care whether it's the Devil himself; I'll defend the island while there's still a drop of blood in my veins. I don't believe in devilry, me! Go on, get moving! This isn't a time to stand there whimpering."

"What shall I do?"

"Run to the battery overlooking the bay. Take the necessary number of men with you and open fire on that diabolical ship! We'll see what they have to say when the shrapnel starts raining down on them!"

Moller left as fast as his legs could carry him.

Commandant Montgomery, now surrounded by twenty tramps, hastened to send more men to the battery on the cliff; then he gathered two squadrons of his best sharpshooters, and sent them to lie in ambush behind a group of rocks overlooking the entrance to the bay.

"Comrades," he said to his men, "I hope that you'll do your duty. We have arms and ammunition in abundance; the enemy can't win a fight against us. Let everyone fight courageously! You know that the Lords of the Red Hand aren't niggardly when it comes to rewarding the brave!"

That little speech, delivered without much conviction, did not have the effect that Montgomery hoped. The tramps were demoralized in advance, convinced that they were fighting against supernatural beings.

There was no time for longer reflection; the battle had already begun. The batteries on the cliff and in the bay gave the signal by opening fire almost simultaneously, with full volleys. Montgomery observed despairingly, however, that the diabolical enemy ship was now too close to the shore to be reached by the Red Hand's cannon, whose projectiles were lost out to sea. All that he could do was order the troop lying in ambush at the entrance to the bay to maintain a sustained fusillade.

"Is that a naval vessel?" he wondered, anxiously, while still giving orders furiously. "No, it can't be. If it were, the passengers wouldn't be indulging in such devilries."

At that moment, the flanks of the enemy ship were clowned by a triple flash of lightning. A tramp standing two feet away from Montgomery had his head blown away by shrapnel; a shell had burst in the very midst of the troop lying in ambush behind the rocks. There was a general stampede.

At the same time, the monstrous faces in the clouds, immeasurably magnified, extended their clawed feet as if they were about to devour the island and its inhabitants.

The frightful phantasmagoria only increased the panic of the fleeing men. It was every man for himself. The cannons of the fantastic ship continued firing without respite. An incendiary shell fell on the roof of the tramps' barracks and the building, constructed in resinous wood, caught fire. It was burning with a vast livid flame that shot straight up into the calm sky.

Montgomery, bewildered but not discouraged, rallied his men in a little wood overlooking the bay, but at that moment, two large launches that the smoke had hidden reached the shore, and some sixty men disembarked armed with repeating rifles whose sharp bayonets glinted in the light of electric lamps.

The leader of that troop, wearing a silver helmet, had no other weapon than his sword. A light blue mantle embroidered with gold floated over his shoulders. By his side, an enormous dog whose body was protected by a coat of mail, wearing an iron collar with sharp spikes, was howling furiously, as if impatient to launch itself into bodily combat.

Close by, a hunchback with a martial attitude was holding a bugle, only waiting for his leader's signal to sound the charge.

From the little wood where he had concentrated his men, Montgomery saw the disembarked company line up in battle order, ready to assail the heights. He observed with a certain emotion that all the old tramps, the veterans of the Red Hand, had gathered around him; not one of them had failed to respond to the appeal. Old Marlyn, the octogenarian, the doyen of the bandits; old Jackson, agitated by a nervous tremor since he had been electrocuted; the superstitious Moller who neck had been permanently titled since he had been hanged in Canada; Berway, whose arm had been amputated after being roasted in gasoline by a lynch-mob—they were all there, impassive, ready to give their lives, without hesitation, for the Red Hand, which was their sole family and fatherland.

257

They had formed up into a square, not hoping for victory but determined to sell their lives dearly. The other, younger tramps, electrified by their noble example, were full of enthusiasm.

"Nothing's lost yet," declared Montgomery, in a vibrant voice. "We have the advantage of position. Everyone lie flat in the bushes and get ready to fire on my command."

Terrible cries rose up then in the dense wood. It was the Eskimo fishermen, who, having almost been driven mad by the sight of the apparitions, were fleeing, screaming, seeking some cavern in which to hide.

"I know the enemy leader," said Old Marlyn rapidly in Montgomery's ear. "It's that Lord Burydan who escaped in the company of the Redskin—who is also, I can now see, among our enemies..."

"So much the better. It proves two things that ought to reassure us. Firstly, we're not dealing with a navy ship, and secondly, that all those phantamagorias have nothing supernatural about..."

He did not finish his sentence. His voice was drowned out by the din of clarions and drums; then, in the midst of a profound silence, Lord Burydan's voice commanded: "Fix bayonets! Fire at will!"

The crepitation of the fusillade then drowned out all other sounds, including the voice of the canons aboard the ship, which continued to launch incendiary shells and shrapnel bombs at the more distant points of the island. A whirlwind of bullets scythed through the branches of the little wood where the tramps were lying in ambush. As they were lying flat on the ground, however, not one of them was hit, and not one of them budged.

Now the bugle was sounding the charge, and Lord Burydan's soldiers were hurtling up the steep slope of the hill.

They had covered almost half the distance when Montgomery gave the command to open fire in his turn. An avalanche of bullets swept the path, cutting down Lord Burydan's soldiers, who beat the retreat in disorder.

"Hold hard!" shouted Montgomery. "Victory is ours! We'll exterminate them to the last man! Let them try a second attack!"

In fact, Lord Burydan did not take long to rally his men. "This time," he told them, "we won't let ourselves be stopped by enemy fire. No matter what the cost, he have to reach the top of the hill and flush out the enemy."

Twice the attack was renewed without success. Lord Burydan was wounded in the shoulder. The little hunchback continued to blow his bugle, which had been dented by rifle shots. Finally, during the third attack, a dozen strange combatants which Montgomery took to be monkeys, decided the victory. Simply armed with hatchets, they leapt several meters in a single bound, seemingly passing invulnerably through the rain of bullets. Having reached the heights first, they fell upon the veterans of the Red Hand furiously, and wrought frightful carnage.

Oscar Tournesol, the hunchbacked bugler, who had followed his friends closely on to the battlefield also acquitted himself heroically, communicating the bravery that animated him to everyone else.

"Bravo, Romulus!" he cried. "Bravo, Robertson! Strike hard, my dear Macoco! One more for Goliath!"

The Goliath in question was a kind of giant who, disdaining to make use of any other weapon, smashed the tramps with his fist. They went down under his blows like oxen in an abattoir, their skulls fractured and blood jetting from their nostrils.

Silently and rapidly, the Indian Kloum, armed with a sharp saber, sent enemy heads flying all around him with a surprising vigor and dexterity.

Soon, Lord Burydan's victory was complete. Only Montgomery, surrounded by a dozen veterans, was still fighting like a lion, refusing to give in. By his side, Old Marlyn was methodically firing his revolver, while uttering shrill cries of "Long live the Red Hand! Long live the Lords!" from time to time.

Astor Burydan was touched by such bravery.

"Surrender!" he shouted to Montgomery.

"Never!" The latter replied. At the same moment, however, he fell, struck down by the formidable fist of the giant Goliath. Completely surrounded, the veterans were disarmed, tied up and confided to the guard of the clowns Macoco and Cambo.

Lord Burydan's victory was definitive, and glorious. He wanted to haul down the Red Hand's standard, which was fluttering at the top of a mast at the culminating point of the Island of Hanged Men, with his own hands.

V. A Night Patrol

The electric lights on the island and the searchlights on the yacht *Ariel*, still anchored in the bay, illuminated the battlefield covered with the dead and wounded. Lord Astor Burydan was sitting on a grassy bank, resting for a moment. At his sides sat the Indian Kloum and the little hunchback Oscar Tournesol. All three were covered in blood and dirt, breathless and sweating. One of the mariners of the crew brought them a flask full of cold coffee, from which they drank a few mouthfuls with pleasure.

Lord Burydan was radiant in spite of his fatigue.

"That," he said, "is what I call a real battle. If I'd had more days like that one, I believe that the spleen—or, in more modern terms, the neurasthenia—that torments me would have vanished soon enough."

Lord Burydan was interrupted by furious barking. It was the dog Pistolet, which, after having fought valiantly on his own account, arrived at top speed, still clad in his suit of armor and collar with iron spikes.

Oscar stroked the animal, but Pistolet continued barking furiously.

"Perhaps he wants us to take off his war harness," said Lord Burydan.

"No," said Kloum, sententiously.

"No!" exclaimed the little hunchback in his turn. "Pistolet's showing us our duty. He's telling us, in his own way, that we don't have the right to even a minute's rest until we've freed Monsieur Bondonnat."

"That's true!" said Lord Burydan, getting up impetuously. "Let's run to the laboratory, quickly. "In the disarray caused by our arrival, the sentinels that usually guard him have probably fled."

"We need to be ready for anything," said the hunchback. Let's take four solid and well-armed men with us." With a gesture he summoned to the strong man Goliath, the human cannonball Romulus and the Robertson brothers to accompany him.

The laboratory was no more than a quarter of an hour's march from the small wood, and the little troop soon reached it. As Lord Burydan had anticipated, there were no sentinels on the circular path and the exterior doors were wide open.

"Perhaps Monsieur Bondonnat's taken advantage of the battle to make his escape," said Oscar.

"We'll see," said Lord Burydan, who had found the electric light switch immediately.

A vivid light blazed. The laboratory seemed to be in total disorder; the floor had not been swept and bore numerous footprints. The bottles and the display cases were covered in dust.

"One might think," said Lord Burydan, anxiously, "that the laboratory had been abandoned some time ago. If Monsieur Bondonnat were still here, he would already have come to meet us."

"Let's search," said Kloum.

Perfectly familiar with the building, the Indian opened the adjacent doors that had served as the scientist's living space, and where he had been lodged himself during his captivity.

When he reached the door of Monsieur Bondonnat's bedroom, however, he stopped dead, and with a gesture of alarm and desolation, he pointed to the cadaver lying sideways across he bed.

"They've killed him!" he murmured, with profound sadness. "We've arrived too late."

Lord Burydan and Oscar exchanged heart-broken glances. So, all the courage, all the ingenuity and all the science deployed in the course of the expedition had been for nothing. The bandits of the Red Hand had murdered the old man in a cowardly fashion, after having stolen his discoveries! They stood there in silent dejection.

"Do you think," said Lord Burydan, "That it's a long time since the bandits murdered Monsieur Bondonnat?"

Oscar, who was busy readjusting the position of the corpse on the bed, uttered an exclamation. "Yes!" he exclaimed. "It's a long time since they killed him!"

"What makes you say that?"

"Monsieur Bondonnat has been embalmed."

"That's incredible!"

Lord Burydan was obliged to yield to the evidence. The body of the venerable scientist was emitting a powerful balsamic perfume; there was no doubt that it had been subjected to an extremely sophisticated process of conservation, since the flesh retained all its suppleness and the face all its color and expression.

All three of them knelt down beside their friend's body and contemplated it silently.

Pistolet barked woefully, but, singularly enough, far from licking his deceased master's hand, as many dogs would have done in such circumstances, he prowled around the laboratory and the other rooms, growling in a muffle and menacing fashion. Then, he suddenly launched himself outside and disappeared.

"Grief has driven the poor dog mad," said Oscar. "He's no longer in his right mind, so to speak."

"Never mind about him!" said Lord Burydan. "We must, after so much effort, do honor to the mortal remains of the great scientist that Monsieur Bondonnat was, and put them beyond the reach of any profanation. Four men must stand guard over the body night and day until the ship's carpenter has made an oak coffin, for I believe that Mademoiselle Frédérique will want her father's remains to be laid to rest in the soil of France."

On the Lord's orders, Goliath and his three companions remained in the laboratory.

Lord Burydan withdrew with Oscar and Kloum to make the arrangements required by the situation. All three were profoundly distressed. By pronouncing Frédérique's name, the eccentric had reawakened their anxieties.

"It's singular, though," said Oscar, "that the *Revenge* wasn't at the arranged rendezvous, and that our friends haven't replied to the numerous marconigrams we've sent."

"I don't understand at all," replied Lord Burydan, whose expression had darkened. "It's true, though, that the delay might have a perfectly natural explanation. It would have sufficed, for example for their engines to have had a minor breakdown, or—who can tell?—that the presence of a Red Hand yacht might have forced them southwards."

"But we haven't seen any such yacht."

"That's true."

"And none of that would have prevented them from replying to our messages."

"I'm just as anxious as you are. So, the *Ariel* will take to sea again tomorrow and will cruise in the vicinity of the island. In addition—which we might have been remiss not to do already—we'll send a message to Fred Jorgell in Chicago to bring him up to date with the situation."

"Ours is a funereal and futile victory!" sighed the little hunchback.

All three continued walking silently back to the battlefield.

During their absence the *Ariel*'s crew had not been idle. A tent had been set up in a clearing and furnished with straw pallets, on which the dead and wounded were laid. The uninjured tramps, solidly tied up, were taken to one of the buildings situated close to the bay.

In the middle of that scene of desolation, the genteel bareback rider Regina Bombridge, dressed in a simple nurse's smock, was running hither and yon to help the wounded, dividing her cares without distinction between the tramps and the crewmen.

All of Oscar's sadness vanished at the sight of the young woman. Mademoiselle," he said to her, shaking her hand effusively, "you're admirable!"

"I have to make myself useful for something," she murmured, blushing.

"Would you like me to help you?"

"Yes indeed—but what a frightful thing war is!"

"Thanks to his immense fortune," Oscar said, "Lord Burydan will be able to attenuate the disasters caused by the battle to some extent. He's promised large pensions to the widows and mothers of the mariners who've been killed, as well as to the wounded. No one will have any complaint to make to him in that regard."

At that moment, Lord Burydan came over himself. "All my compliments Mademoiselle," he said, courteously, "but do you need Oscar?"

"Yes," said the young woman. "I know that he understands how to dress wounds."

"In that case, I won't deprive you of him," said the nobleman, smiling.

"Where did you want to take me?" Oscar asked.

"Oh, simply to mount a patrol with twenty men, to inspect the interior of the island and get our hands on any bandits who were able to run away."

"If you think that it will be useful for me to go with you..."

"Not at all—you'll do very well with Miss Regina; stay here. I'll take the two clowns Macoco and Cambo, the prestidigitator Matalobos, the Chinese juggler and a few sailors."

A short time later, the little troop, about twenty strong, went on patrol armed with electric lanterns, with the aid of which the remotest corners were carefully explored. The precaution was by no means unnecessary, as they did not take long to discover; thanks to the electric searchlights they were able to capture a further dozen tramps, who, some of them being wounded and others having panicked, had sought refuge in the woods and fields.

The little troop had arrived in the heart of the island, in a clearing sheltered against the wind from the sea, which enclosed some beautiful trees, when Macoco and Cambo, the two clowns who constituted an advance guard, thought that they perceived suspect shadows moving in the branches. They immediately fell back to the center of the column and the searchlights were pointed in the direction indicated by the two clowns.

To the general amazement, they then perceived a dozen hairy individuals somewhat reminiscent of orangutans perched in the branches, who were uttering cries of fright, jabbering in an incomprehensible language and making extravagant supplicant gestures.

"Have we come across a subsidiary branch of the Gorilla Club?" said Cambo, laughing.

"That would be amusing, but they aren't monkeys. These bizarre beings have long hair hanging down over their shoulders. One might think that they were furry women."

"Perhaps," Lord Burydan declared, "We're in the presence of a scientific discovery of the highest importance. We must capture one of these hairy animals alive, at all costs."

"I'm a good shot," said Cambo. "I'll try to wound one of the monsters with my rifle."

He was about to put this plan into execution, and was already taking aim at the most beautiful of the pretended monkeys when a being hairier and more heavily bearded than all the rest—doubtless the patriarch of the band—ran toward Lord Burydan waving a white handkerchief as a sign of peace.

Lord Burydan, who thought he was dealing with a savage of a new species, made him understand by signs that he had nothing to fear, and the other hairy animals, equally reassured by his pacific pantomime, came down from their aerial perches.

Lord Burydan and his friends soon had the explanation of the mystery.

"I am Stepan Rominoff, the prophet of Mystic Vitalism," declared the patriarch with the long beard. As almost all the Russians had a certain education, they spoke French quite well, and he had suddenly had the idea of expressing himself in that language, which Lord Burydan, who had spent a great deal of time in Paris, understood perfectly.

Hurriedly, the prophet recounted his adventures and those of the ten women he had converted to his doctrine, and explained that it was Monsieur Bondonnat who had made him a gift of a capilogenic elixir of such force that all the women who had made use of it had soon been covered with veritable fleeces, in the midst of which the mouth and eyes remained scarcely visible.

The prophet applauded that result, which he proposed to try out on a large scale on thousands of people as soon as he returned to a civilized country. He could already foresee, in the near future, a more vigorous humankind, forever rid of tailors, shirt-makers and milliners.

After having diverted himself for a while with the singular maniac, Lord Burydan assured him that he had nothing to fear and that, on the contrary, the tramps having been reduced to impotence, he would happy to repatriate him and his companions.

He took his leave of the Russians thereafter, but he had obtained some interesting information from them. Rominoff had told him about the exodus of a party of tramps on the Dutch ship, on which the two nihilists had also embarked. He also knew all the details of the murder of Monsieur Bondonnat by the Cossack Rapopoff, which disposed Lord Burydan to show more forbearance toward the tramps, on whom he had initially decided to exact an exemplary vengeance.

The night came to an end, and a pale dawn seemed to be disengaging itself with difficulty from the mist when they reached the Eskimo village. There, the Indian Kloum found the dog Pistolet, who was still barking lamentably and wandering along the shore like a soul in torment. Caresses and kind words eventually succeeded in calming him down.

With the aid of a tramp who spoke a little of their language, Lord Burydan told the poor Eskimos, most of whom had come back after wandering all over the island, that they had nothing to fear from him and that he would take them under his protection.

Once that last corner of the Island of Hanged Men had been visited, Lord Burydan thought that the fatigues of the night were over. "I'm going to get a few hours' rest," he said to the members of the Gorilla Club who had accompanied him. "I think that you and I have earned it. We haven't searched the northern part of the island in its entirety, but we'll do that this afternoon. There's nothing to fear from the few enemies who might still remain at liberty."

They headed back toward the yacht. Suddenly, however, Lord Burydan saw Oscar Tournesol running toward him, seemingly in a state of extraordinary agitation.

"What's happened now?" asked the nobleman, impatiently.

"Grave news!" he said. "We know where the *Revenge* is. I've just received a message via the wireless telegraphy apparatus installed on the island."

"That's one anxiety less, then!" cried the eccentric. "Now we can be reassured as to the fate of our friends."

"Don't rush to celebrate," murmured the young man, sadly. "The *Revenge* has fallen into the hands of the bandits of the Red Hand."

Lord Burydan went pale. "But," he stammered, "Do you know whether Mademoiselles Andrée and Frédérique are safe, as well as their fiancés and my brave Agénor?"

"They're all prisoners, and the yacht is sailing toward the island at this moment. When you've read this, you'll know as much as I do."

He handed the nobleman a piece of paper, on which he had scribbled the following sentences in pencil:

Am master of the yacht Revenge *in spite of on-board revolt. Will be there in a few hours with French prisoners. Have fifty armed men ready to assist me when we disembark.*

Captain Slug

"What should I reply?" asked the hunchback when Burydan had finished reading.

"Just this," said the other, after a moment's reflection. "*Come. Everything ready to receive you.*"

The hunchback departed at a run in the direction of the wireless telegraphy station, while Lord Burydan went back aboard the *Ariel* and ordered the anchor to be raised immediately. It was vital that the bandits who had taken possession of the Revenge did not see that there was another vessel in the vicinity of the island. The yacht would take up a position behind the eastern cliff, where it would be impossible to see it while coming in the direction of the bay.

At the same time, he ordered that the flag of the Red Hand should be hoisted once again on the mast overlooking the island.

Further dispositions were then made. All the uninjured men, acrobats and mariners, dressed in costumes taken from the tramps and put on broad-brimmed hats ornamented with red hands. Thus disguised, they were unrecognizable.

All traces of the battle were then made to disappear, so that the signatory of the dispatch would not see anything suspect when he arrived in sight of the island.

When all these precautions had been taken and the men had taken up the positions assigned to them by Lord Burydan, they waited.

It was nearly midday when the lookout set on the highest point of the island signaled a ship of heavy tonnage in an easterly direction. A black flag ornamented with a red hand was flying majestically from its mizzen mast.

When the ship was within sight of the bay, it fired a salvo of thirteen shots, to which the island's batteries replied in kind.

VI. *The* Revenge

Mademoiselle Andrée de Maubreuil, her friend Frédérique, their fiancés Antoine Paganot and Roger Ravenel and the poet Agénor Marmousier, taken prisoner by Slug in the wake of the fire he had started, were not allowed out of the cabins that had been assigned to them.

But for the intervention of the gypsy dancer Dorypha, there was doubt at all that they would all have been massacred, but she had courageously undertaken their defense, powerfully seconded in that by her lover, the Belgian Pierre Gilkin, and the latter's partisans.

The French party, gathered in the same cabin, were confiding to one another the anxiety to which they were prey. They had heard the cannon shots fired on Slug's orders. They could see in the distance the coast that was becoming more clearly visible with every passing minute, and were wondering fearfully what they fate would be.

Would Slug, as he had vaguely promised the Fleming Gilkin, deposit the prisoners on land and leave them at liberty to go wherever they wanted? They had thought so momentarily—but when they had seen Slug proudly hoist the black flag with the bloody hand, and they had seen the inhabitants reply to the *Revenge*'s salvo with an identical one, they had become mortally anxious.

It was at that moment that Dorypha irrupted into the cabin, her hair in disorder and her face distraught.

"We're doomed!" she cried. "That swine Slug has brought us to the Island of Hanged Men. I've just seen the flag of the Red Hand floating above that accursed land!"

A silence of consternation greeted these words.

"It only remains to us," said the engineer, exchanging a despairing glance with Roger Ravenel, "to sell our lives as dearly as possible."

"I beg you, my dear Roger," said Frédérique, "to kill me rather than let me fall into the hands of those bandits alive."

"Yes, kill us," murmured Andrée de Maubreuil, sadly.

The gypsy took a marine telescope that she had stolen from Slug's cabin out of her corsage and held it out to Agénor. "Look," she said. "See for yourself."

The poet out the instrument to his eye and aimed it—but he had scarcely had time to dart a glance at the coast than he uttered an exclamation of joy and triumph. "We're saved!" he stammered, astonished. "Do you know who I've just seen, admirably disguised as a tramp? You'll never guess."

"Don't leave us in suspense!" Frédérique exclaimed.

"My excellent friend Lord Burydan, in person."

"What does that mean?" asked the gypsy, astonished by the abrupt change of mood.

"That the Island of Hanged Men is now in the power of our friends. But don't say a word about what I've just told you. If Slug suspects any such thing, he's capable of killing us all."

"I've every possible reason for being discreet, but I hope you won't forget what my brave friend Pierre Gilkin has done for you."

"Don't worry—but don't say anything to anyone, even to Pierre Gilkin. Just make sure that he and his friends, in their own interest, stay as close to us as possible."

A few minutes later, Slug came into the French party's cabin himself. His expression was both triumphant and menacing.

"Now," he said, brutally, "the joke has gone on long enough. You'll obey my orders, without making the slightest objection. Now, Messieurs et Mesdames, you're in the domain of the Red Hand, and here your protectors will be no use to you. So hurry up on deck, all of you." With a mocking laugh, he added: "You wanted to be put ashore; well, so be it. I'll put you ashore. I'm a man of my word, me!"

To the bandit's great surprise, none of the prisoners made the slightest objection. They all went up on deck, and from there, descended into the large launch, manned by seven or eight tramps.

Dorypha had taken her place beside them. Pierre Gilkin and the most devoted of his partisans joined them. Slug made no attempt to stop them. He told himself that once they were ashore, they would all be completely at his mercy. Dorypha had time to whisper a few words in the Belgian's ear; he awaited events, silently.

Slug, who was the last to embark, took the tiller and he too remained silent—but his face expressed an insolent triumph.

The launch came alongside the quay, and the people aboard disembarked in an orderly fashion, led by a group consisting of Slug's partisans; then came the prisoners, and finally Dorypha, Gilkin and his friends. Slug brought up the rear.

Lord Burydan's men, lined up to the left and the right, formed a hedge, rifles on their shoulders and revolvers in their belts. Slug looked at them with a piercing gaze, and the cunning bandit, not recognizing the long beards that were, so to speak, part of the uniform of the tramps, suddenly became vaguely suspicious. Under the pretext of mooring the launch to a ring, he remained some way behind the group.

It was a wise move. His companions had scarcely taken a few steps when they found themselves surrounded, hemmed in and disarmed.

Pierre Gilkin's partisans would have be subjected to the same fate had Paganot not intervened. The bandits, solidly tied up, were thrown to the ground at the feet of the two young women, who were so startled by the *coup de théâtre* that they were speechless.

Slug had seen enough. He judged the situation at a glance. All of a sudden, he dived into the sea, and set about swimming underwater.

"Fire!" ordered the engineer. "That's one of the leaders of the Red Hand. It's necessary to take him, dead or alive!"

Slug, an excellent swimmer, had dived again, reappearing ten meters further on. A few bullets whistled past his ears, but they ended up losing sight of him.

With his habitual rapidity of decision, he had understood that it would be imprudent for him to return to the *Revenge*, which, anchored under the cannons of the island, could not possible get back to the open sea.

After having swum for a quarter of an hour between the reefs, he came ashore In an isolated bay and, hiding in the bushes like a hare pursued by hunters, he plunged into the interior of the island, which he knew admirably, and soon reached the subterranean museum that contained the strange collection of anatomical specimens previously visited by Monsieur Bondonnat.

After making sure that no one had followed him, he moved the stone at the entrance and introduced himself into the cave.

Two men, the only ones apart from him who knew the secret of the cave, were waiting for him there. They were Julian and Johnnie, the two engravers of false documents, one of whom as we know, resembled Dr. Cornelius, feature for feature, while the other offered the exact physiognomy of Fritz Kramm.

Once the stone was back in place they secured it internally with a heavy iron bolt. They were sure from then on that no one would search for them in that hiding place.

In the meantime, Lord Burydan and Oscar had thrown themselves into their friends' arms. The eccentric began by informing Paganot discreetly of Monsieur Bondonnat's death, and the young man and his friend Ravenel took the two young women o one side in order to break the terrible news to them gently.

At the same time, Lord Burydan told Agénor the story of the taking of the island. He explained to him how, by means of a method employed by American advertising agencies, he had projected cinematographically, using the clouds as a screen, the apparitions that had frightened the tramps so much. The acrobatics of the clowns in the rigging and the phosphorescent paint in which the yacht had been coated had completed the effect of the phantasmagoric stage-setting. Finally, it was the troupe's swimmer who, at the risk of his life, had caused the torpedoes to explode.

An hour later, the bandits occupying the *Revenge*, demoralized by the loss of their leader, surrendered voluntarily.

The Red Hand was vanquished, beaten, so to speak, at its own game. The Frenchmen were thus able to inflict a severe punishment on the bandits; to recompense Dorypha and her friends, as they deserved; and finally, to accord a just tribute of tears to the memory of the unfortunate scientist murdered by the bandits.

TO BE CONCLUDED IN VOLUME 3:
THE ROCHESTER BRIDGE CATASTROPHE

APPENDIXES

Cover gallery of the first edition (18 magazines)

thanks to Jean-Luc Boutel.

The Mysterious Doctor Cornelius on French TV and Radio

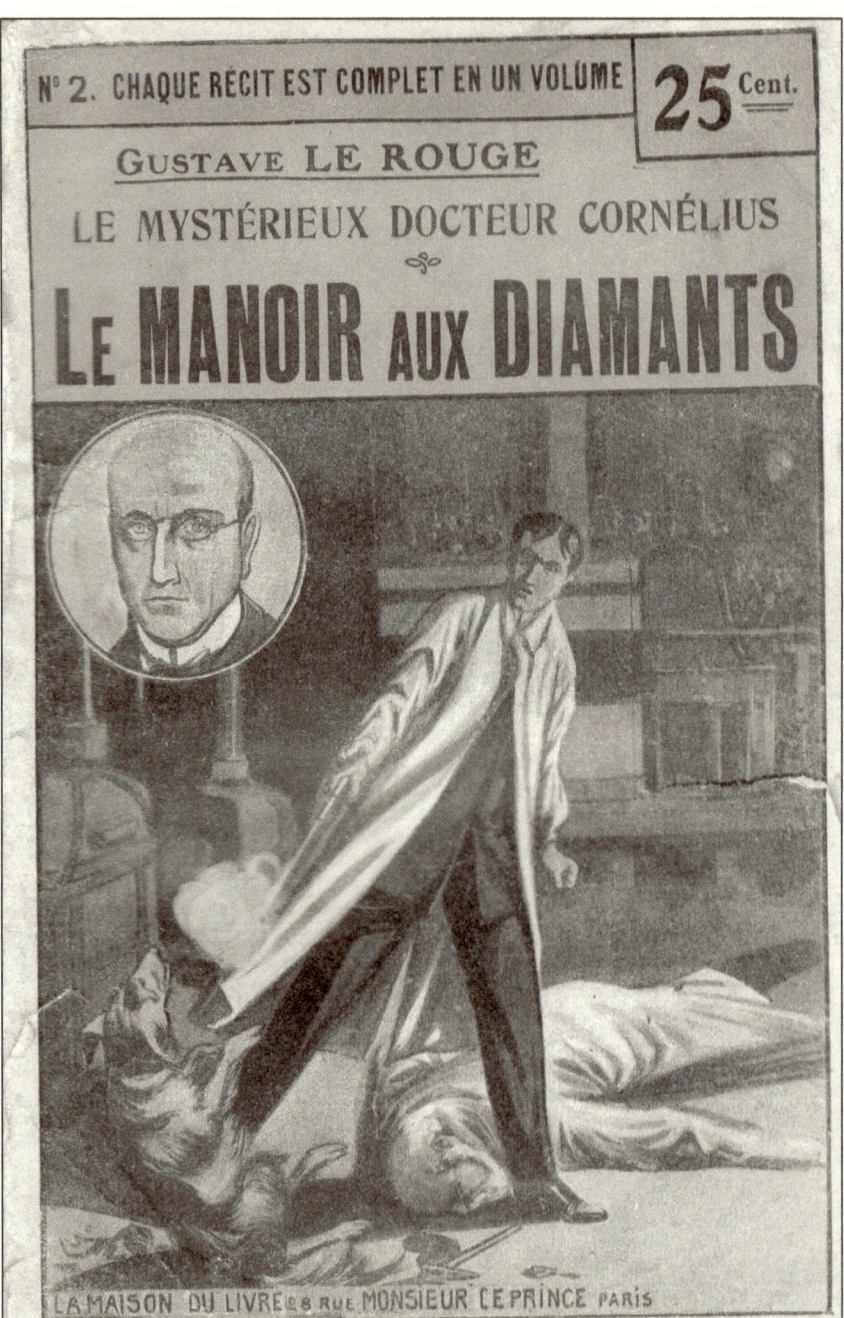

Nº 2. CHAQUE RÉCIT EST COMPLET EN UN VOLUME — **25** Cent.

GUSTAVE LE ROUGE

LE MYSTÉRIEUX DOCTEUR CORNÉLIUS

LE MANOIR AUX DIAMANTS

LA MAISON DU LIVRE 28 RUE MONSIEUR LE PRINCE PARIS

N° 3. CHAQUE RÉCIT EST COMPLET EN UN VOLUME — 25 Cent.

GUSTAVE LE ROUGE

LE MYSTÉRIEUX DOCTEUR CORNÉLIUS

LE Sculpteur de Chair Humaine

LA MAISON DU LIVRE 28 R. MONSIEUR LE PRINCE PARIS.

Nº 4. CHAQUE RÉCIT EST COMPLET EN UN VOLUME

25 Cent.

GUSTAVE LE ROUGE

LE MYSTÉRIEUX DOCTEUR CORNÉLIUS

LES LORDS DE LA MAIN ROUGE

LA MAISON DU LIVRE 28 RUE MONSIEUR LE PRINCE PARIS

LA MAISON DU LIVRE 28 RUE MONSIEUR LE PRINCE PARIS

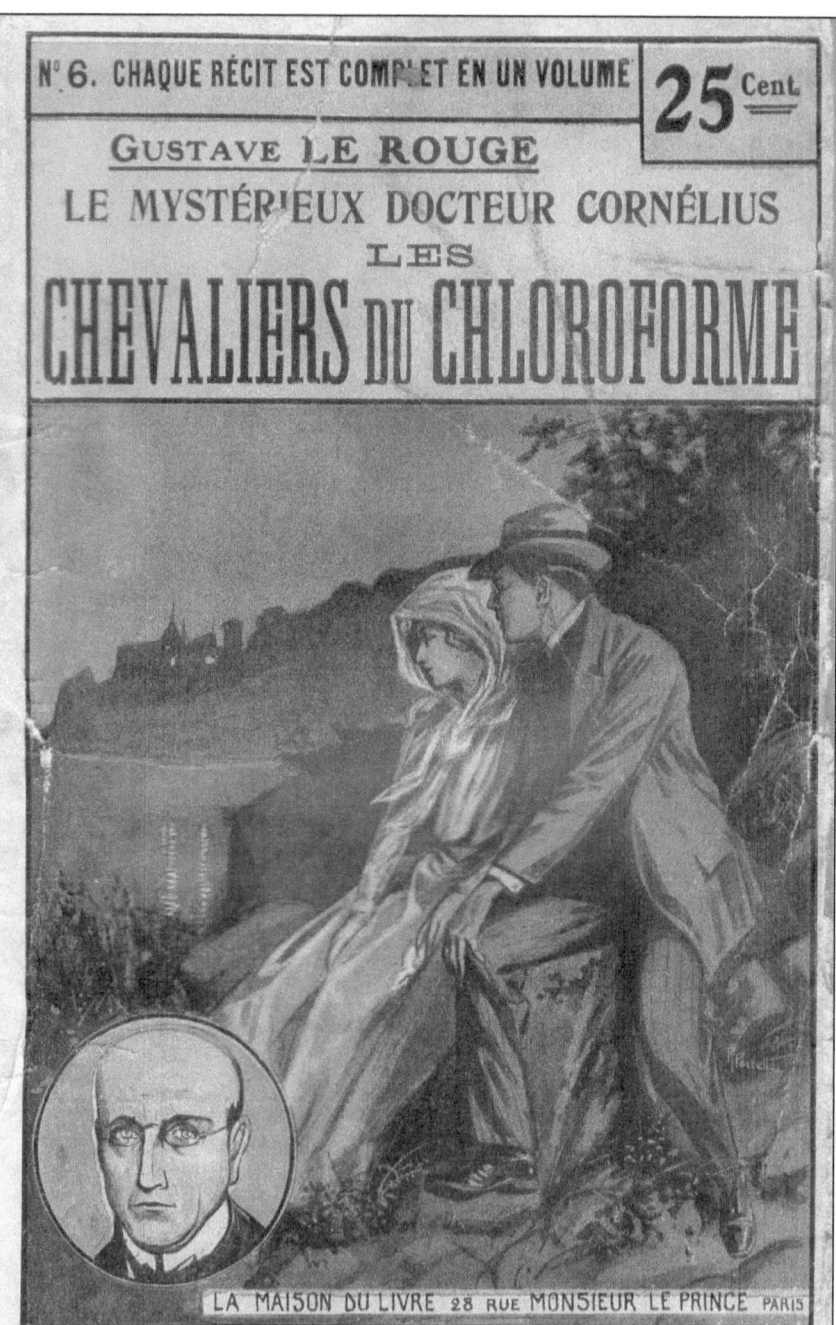

N° 6. CHAQUE RÉCIT EST COMPLET EN UN VOLUME

25 Cent.

GUSTAVE LE ROUGE

LE MYSTÉRIEUX DOCTEUR CORNÉLIUS

LES

CHEVALIERS DU CHLOROFORME

LA MAISON DU LIVRE 28 RUE MONSIEUR LE PRINCE PARIS

N° 7. CHAQUE RÉCIT EST COMPLET EN UN VOLUME — 25 Cent.

Gustave LE ROUGE

LE MYSTÉRIEUX DOCTEUR CORNÉLIUS

UN

DRAME AU LUNATIC ASYLUM

LA MAISON DU LIVRE 28 RUE MONSIEUR LE PRINCE · PARIS.

N° 8. CHAQUE RÉCIT EST COMPLET EN UN VOLUME

25 Cent.

GUSTAVE LE ROUGE

LE MYSTÉRIEUX DOCTEUR CORNÉLIUS

L'AUTOMOBILE FANTOME

LA MAISON DU LIVRE 28 RUE MONSIEUR LE PRINCE PARIS.

Nº 9. CHAQUE RÉCIT EST COMPLET EN UN VOLUME — 25 Cent.

GUSTAVE LE ROUGE

LE MYSTÉRIEUX DOCTEUR CORNÉLIUS

LE COTTAGE HANTÉ

LA MAISON DU LIVRE, 28 RUE MONSIEUR LE PRINCE, PARIS.

Nº 10. CHAQUE RÉCIT EST COMPLET EN UN VOLUME — 25 Cent.

GUSTAVE LE ROUGE

LE MYSTÉRIEUX DOCTEUR CORNÉLIUS

LE
PORTRAIT DE LUCRÈCE BORGIA

LA MAISON DU LIVRE   28 Rue MONSIEUR LE PRINCE   PARIS

N° 11. CHAQUE RÉCIT EST COMPLET EN UN VOLUME — **25** Cent.

GUSTAVE LE ROUGE

LE MYSTÉRIEUX DOCTEUR CORNÉLIUS

CŒUR DE GITANE

LA MAISON DU LIVRE 28 R. MONSIEUR LE PRINCE PARIS.

N° 12. CHAQUE RÉCIT EST COMPLET EN UN VOLUME — 25 Cent.

GUSTAVE LE ROUGE

LE MYSTÉRIEUX DOCTEUR CORNÉLIUS

LA CROISIÈRE DU GORILL-CLUB

LA MAISON DU LIVRE 28 RUE MONSIEUR.LE.PRINCE PARIS

13. CHAQUE RÉCIT EST COMPLET EN UN VOLUME — **25** Cent.

GUSTAVE LE ROUGE

LE MYSTÉRIEUX DOCTEUR CORNÉLIUS

LA FLEUR DU SOMMEIL

LA MAISON DU LIVRE MODERNE, 28, Rue Monsieur-le-Prince PARIS,

No 14. CHAQUE RÉCIT EST COMPLET EN UN VOLUME — 25 Cent.

GUSTAVE LE ROUGE

LE MYSTÉRIEUX DOCTEUR CORNÉLIUS

LE

BUSTE AUX YEUX D'ÉMERAUDE

LA MAISON DU LIVRE MODERNE, 28, Rue Monsieur-le-Prince, Paris

Nº 15. CHAQUE RÉCIT EST COMPLET EN UN VOLUME

25 Cent.

GUSTAVE LE ROUGE

LE MYSTÉRIEUX DOCTEUR CORNÉLIUS

LA DAME AUX SCABIEUSES

LA MAISON DU LIVRE MODERNE, 28, Rue Monsieur-le-Prince, PARIS

N° 16. CHAQUE RÉCIT EST COMPLET EN UN VOLUME

25 Cent.

GUSTAVE LE ROUGE

LE MYSTÉRIEUX DOCTEUR CORNÉLIUS

LA TOUR FIÉVREUSE

LA MAISON DU LIVRE MODERNE, 28, Rue Monsieur-le-Prince, PARIS

N° 17. CHAQUE RÉCIT EST COMPLET EN UN VOLUME

25 Cent.

GUSTAVE LE ROUGE

LE MYSTÉRIEUX DOCTEUR CORNÉLIUS

LE DÉMENT DE LA MAISON BLEUE

LA MAISON DU LIVRE MODERNE, 28, Rue Monsieur-le-Prince, Paris

N° 18. CHAQUE RÉCIT EST COMPLET EN UN VOLUME — 25 Cent.

GUSTAVE LE ROUGE

LE MYSTÉRIEUX DOCTEUR CORNÉLIUS

BAS LES MASQUES

LA MAISON DU LIVRE MODERNE 28 RUE MONSIEUR LE PRINCE PARIS

Jean Bouise (Fritz Kramm) and Gérard Desarthe (Cornelius Kramm)

THE MYSTERIOUS DOCTOR CORNELIUS
on French Television and Radio

Le Mystérieux Docteur Cornelius

A2, color, six 60 mins. episodes, 16 September - 21 October 1984.

Director: Maurice Frydland; *Writers*: Jean-Pierre Petrolacci, Jean-Daniel Simon, Pierre Nivollet, based on the novel by Gustave Le Rouge.

Cast: Gérard Desarthe (Cornelius Kramm), Jean Bouise (Fritz Kramm), François Eric Gendron (Harry Dorgan), Hugues Quester (Barruch Jorgel), Renzo Palmer (William Dorgan), Robert Rimbaud (Bondonnat), Caroline Sihol (Isadora Jorgel), Georges Geret (Fred Jorgel), Maurice Vaudaux (Joe Dorgan), Maria Blanco (Frédéricque Bondonnat), Anne Fontaine (Andrée de Maubreuil), Enzo Robutti (M. de Maubreuil), Jacques François (Lord Burydan).

Le Mystérieux Dr. Cornelius

France-Culture, 35 30 mins. episodes, 1978.

Director: Alain Barroux; *Writer*: Édith Loria, based on the novels by Gustave Le Rouge.

Cast: Jean Topart (Fritz Kramm), Michel Bouquet (Cornelius Kramm), Denis Manuel (Harry Dorgan), Guy Tréjean (M. de Maubreuil), Jean Wiener (Bondonnat), Pierre Vaneck (Lord Burydan), Catherine Hubeau (Isidora Jorgell), Naïa Simon (Andrée de Maubreuil), Catherine Laborde (Frédérique Bondonnat).

SF & FANTASY

Adolphe Alhaiza. *Cybele*
Alphonse Allais. *The Adventures of Captain Cap*
Henri Allorge. *The Great Cataclysm*
Guy d'Armen. *Doc Ardan: The City of Gold and Lepers*
G.-J. Arnaud. *The Ice Company*
Charles Asselineau. *The Double Life*
Cyprien Bérard. *The Vampire Lord Ruthwen*
S. Henry Berthoud. *Martyrs of Science*
Aloysius Bertrand. *Gaspard de la Nuit*
Richard Bessière. *The Gardens of the Apocalypse*
Albert Bleunard. *Ever Smaller*
Félix Bodin. *The Novel of the Future*
Louis Boussenard. *Monsieur Synthesis*
Alphonse Brown. *City of Glass; The Conquest of the Air*
Emile Calvet. *In a Thousand Years*
André Caroff. *The Terror of Madame Atomos; Miss Atomos; The Return of Madame Atomos; The Mistake of Madame Atomos; The Monsters of Madame Atomos; The Revenge of Madame Atomos; The Resurrection of Madame Atomos; The Mark of Madame Atomos*
Félicien Champsaur. *The Human Arrow; Ouha, King of the Apes; Pharaoh's Wife*
Didier de Chousy. *Ignis*
Jules Clarétie. *Obsession*
Michel Corday. *The Eternal Flame*
Captain Danrit. *Undersea Odyssey*
C. I. Defontenay. *Star (Psi Cassiopeia)*
Charles Derennes. *The People of the Pole*
Georges Dodds (anthologist). *The Missing Link*
Harry Dickson. *The Heir of Dracula*
Jules Dornay. *Lord Ruthven Begins*
Alfred Driou. *The Adventures of a Parisian Aeronaut*
Sâr Dubnotal *vs. Jack the Ripper*
Alexandre Dumas. *The Return of Lord Ruthven*
Renée Dunan. *Baal*
J.-C. Dunyach. *The Night Orchid; The Thieves of Silence*
Henri Duvernois. *The Man Who Found Himself*
Achille Eyraud. *Voyage to Venus*
Henri Falk. *The Age of Lead*
Paul Féval. *Anne of the Isles; Knightshade; Revenants; Vampire City; The Vampire Countess; The Wandering Jew's Daughter*
Paul Féval, *fils. Felifax, the Tiger-Man*
Charles de Fieux. *Lamékis*
Louis Forest. *Someone is Stealing Children in Paris*
Arnould Galopin. *Doctor Omega; Doctor Omega and the Shadowmen* (anthology)
Judith Gautier. *Isoline and the Serpent-Flower*
Léon Gozlan. *The Vampire of the Val-de-Grâce*

G.L. Gick. *Harry Dickson and the Werewolf of Rutherford Grange*
Edmond Haraucourt. *Illusions of Immortality*
Nathalie Henneberg. *The Green Gods*
V. Hugo, P. Foucher & P. Meurice. *The Hunchback of Notre-Dame*
Romain d'Huissier. *Hexagon: Dark Matter*
Jules Janin. *The Magnetized Corpse*
Michel Jeury. *Chronolysis*
Gustave Kahn. *The Tale of Gold and Silence*
Gérard Klein. *The Mote in Time's Eye*
Fernand Kolney. *Love in 5000 Years*
Paul Lacroix. *Danse Macabre*
Louis-Guillaume de La Follie. *The Unpretentious Philosopher*
Jean de La Hire. *Enter the Nyctalope; The Nyctalope on Mars; The Nyctalope vs. Lucifer; The Nyctalope Steps In; Night of the Nyctalope; Return of the Nyctalope; The Fiery Wheel*
Etienne-Léon de Lamothe-Langon. *The Virgin Vampire*
André Laurie. *Spiridon*
Gabriel de Lautrec. *The Vengeance of the Oval Portrait*
Alain le Drimeur. *The Future City*
Georges Le Faure & Henri de Graffigny. *The Extraordinary Adventures of a Russian Scientist Across the Solar System* (2 vols.)
Gustave Le Rouge. *The Mysterious Doctor Cornelius* (3 vols.); *The Vampires of Mars; The Dominion of the World* (w/Gustave Guitton) (4 vols.)
Jules Lermina. *Mysteryville; Panic in Paris; To-Ho and the Gold Destroyers; The Secret of Zippelius*
André Lichtenberger. *The Centaurs; The Children of the Crab*
Jean-Marc & Randy Lofficier. *Edgar Allan Poe on Mars; The Katrina Protocol; Pacifica; Robonocchio; Return of the Nyctalope;* (anthologists) *Tales of the Shadowmen 1-10*
Xavier Mauméjean. *The League of Heroes*
Joseph Méry. *The Tower of Destiny*
Hippolyte Mettais. *The Year 5865*
Louise Michel. *The Human Microbes; The New World*
Tony Moilin. *Paris in the Year 2000*
José Moselli. *Illa's End*
John-Antoine Nau. *Enemy Force*
Marie Nizet. *Captain Vampire*
C. Nodier, A. Beraud & Toussaint-Merle. *Frankenstein*
Henri de Parville. *An Inhabitant of the Planet Mars*
Gaston de Pawlowski. *Journey to the Land of the 4th Dimension*
Georges Pellerin. *The World in 2000 Years*
Ernest Pérochon. *The Frenetic People*
Pierre Pelot. *The Child Who Walked on the Sky*
J. Polidori, C. Nodier, E. Scribe. *Lord Ruthven the Vampire*
P.-A. Ponson du Terrail. *The Vampire and the Devil's Son; The Immortal Woman*
Edgar Quinet. *Ahasuerus*
Henri de Régnier. *A Surfeit of Mirrors*
Maurice Renard. *The Blue Peril; Doctor Lerne; The Doctored Man; A Man Among the Microbes; The Master of Light*

Jean Richepin. *The Wing; The Crazy Corner*
Albert Robida. *The Adventures of Saturnin Farandoul; The Clock of the Centuries; Chalet in the Sky; The Electric Life*
J.-H. Rosny Aîné. *Helgvor of the Blue River; The Givreuse Enigma; The Mysterious Force; The Navigators of Space; Vamireh; The World of the Variants; The Young Vampire*
Marcel Rouff. *Journey to the Inverted World*
Han Ryner. *The Superhumans*
Brian Stableford. *The New Faust at the Tragicomique;The Empire of the Necromancers (The Shadow of Frankenstein; Frankenstein and the Vampire Countess; Frankenstein in London); Sherlock Holmes & The Vampires of Eternity; The Stones of Camelot; The Wayward Muse.* (anthologist) *News from the Moon; The Germans on Venus; The Supreme Progress; The World Above the World; Nemoville; Investigations of the Future; The Conqueror of Death*
Jacques Spitz. *The Eye of Purgatory*
Kurt Steiner. *Ortog*
Eugène Thébault. *Radio-Terror*
C.-F. Tiphaigne de La Roche. *Amilec*
Louis Ulbach. *Prince Bonifacio*
Théo Varlet. *The Golden Rock. The Xenobiotic Invasion; The Castaways of Eros; Timeslip Troopers* (w/André Blandin); *The Martian Epic* (w/Octave Joncquel)
Paul Vibert. *The Mysterious Fluid*
Villiers de l'Isle-Adam. *The Scaffold; The Vampire Soul*
Philippe Ward. *Artahe*
Philippe Ward & Sylvie Miller. *The Song of Montségur*

MYSTERIES & THRILLERS

M. Allain & P. Souvestre. *The Daughter of Fantômas*
A. Anicet-Bourgeois, Lucien Dabril. *Rocambole*
A. Bernède. *Belphegor; Judex* (w/Louis Feuillade); *The Return of Judex* (w/Louis Feuillade); *The Shadow of Judex*
A. Bisson & G. Livet. *Nick Carter vs. Fantômas*
V. Darlay & H. de Gorsse. *Arsène Lupin vs. Sherlock Holmes: The Stage Play*
Séamas Duffy. *Sherlock Holmes in Paris*
Paul Féval. *Gentlemen of the Night; John Devil; The Black Coats ('Salem Street; The Invisible Weapon; The Parisian Jungle; The Companions of the Treasure; Heart of Steel; The Cadet Gang; The Sword-Swallower)*
Emile Gaboriau. *Monsieur Lecoq*
Goron & Emile Gautier. *Spawn of the Penitentiary*
Rick Lai. *Shadows of the Opera: Retribution in Blood; Sisters of the Shadows: The Curse of Cagliostro*
Steve Leadley. *Sherlock Holmes: The Circle of Blood*
Maurice Leblanc. *Arsène Lupin vs. Countess Cagliostro; Arsène Lupin vs. Sherlock Holmes (The Blonde Phantom; The Hollow Needle); The Many Faces of Arsène Lupin*
Gaston Leroux. *Chéri-Bibi; The Phantom of the Opera; Rouletabille & the Mystery of the Yellow Room; Rouletabille at Krupp's*
Richard Marsh. *The Complete Adventures of Judith Lee*

William Patrick Maynard. *The Terror of Fu Manchu; The Destiny of Fu Manchu*
Frank J. Morlock. *Sherlock Holmes: The Grand Horizontals; Sherlock Holmes vs Jack the Ripper*
Jean Petithuguenin. *The Adventures of Ethel King*
Antonin Reschal. *The Adventures of Miss Boston*
P. de Wattyne & Y. Walter. *Sherlock Holmes vs. Fantômas*
David White. *Fantômas in America*
Pierre Yrondy. *The Adventures of Thérèse Arnaud*

SCREENPLAYS

Mike Baron. *The Iron Triangle*
Emma Bull & Will Shetterly. *Nightspeeder; War for the Oaks*
Gerry Conway & Roy Thomas. *Doc Dynamo*
Steve Englehart. *Majorca*
James Hudnall. *The Devastator*
Jean-Marc & Randy Lofficier. *Royal Flush*
J.-M. & R. Lofficier & Marc Agapit. *Despair*
J.-M. & R. Lofficier & Joël Houssin. *City*
Andrew Paquette. *Peripheral Vision*
Robert L. Robinson, Jr. *Judex*
R. Thomas, J. Hendler & L. Sprague de Camp. *Rivers of Time*

NON-FICTION

Stephen R. Bissette. *Blur 1-5. Green Mountain Cinema 1; Teen Angels*
Win Scott Eckert. *Crossovers* (2 vols.)
Jean-Marc & Randy Lofficier. *Shadowmen* (2 vols.)
Randy Lofficier. *Over Here*

ART BOOKS

Jean-Pierre Normand. *Science Fiction Illustrations*
Raven Okeefe. *Raven's L'il Critters; Rave's Faves*
Randy Lofficier & Raven Okeefe. *If Your Possum Go Daylight...*
Daniele Serra. *Illusions*

HEXAGON COMICS

Franco Frescura & Luciano Bernasconi. *Wampus*
Franco Frescura & Giorgio Trevisan. *CLASH*
L. Bernasconi, J.-M. Lofficier & Juan Roncagliolo Berger. *Phenix*
Claude Legrand, J.-M. Lofficier & L. Bernasconi. *Kabur*
Franco Oneta. *Zembla*
L. Buffolente, Lofficier & J.-J. Dzialowski. *Strangers: Homicron*
Danilo Grossi. *Strangers: Jaydee*
Claude Legrand & Luciano Bernasconi. *Strangers: Starlock*

www.ingramcontent.com/pod-product-compliance
Lightning Source LLC
Chambersburg PA
CBHW030348020726
47493CB00003B/735